P9-AFW-431

A WALK IN THE CITY

DANIEL SMITH

IN THE CITY

The World Publishing Company | New York and Cleveland

Published by The World Publishing Company
Published simultaneously in Canada
by Nelson, Foster & Scott Ltd.
First printing—1971

Library of Congress catalog card number: 70–133477
Printed in the United States of America

WORLD PUBLISHING
TIMES MIRROR

For my wife and children.

A WALK IN THE CITY

BOOK

ONE

GARNER was cold. He had fought his way further into bed as best he could, but his brothers wouldn't give ground. He was eight years old and not heavy enough to move the two bigger boys. Luther had pulled most of the blanket over to the other side of the bed. This left Garner's back and buttocks exposed to the wind which squeezed into the unheated room between the cardboard and broken glass in the window. Luther was the oldest, a hard, muscular boy of fourteen. He slept fitfully, maintaining control of the blanket with one large hand. Terry, eleven, was sleeping in the middle.

Clutching a corner of the blanket with both hands, Garner turned onto his right side and jerked and burrowed, trying to make Terry roll over. Had he been able, he would have wrenched the blanket out of Luther's hand. Instead, he began to dig with his feet, wedging them under Terry's legs. Then he bumped away until his brother moaned and rolled onto his side, throwing his arm around Luther. Garner could now get his body under the blanket, but his feet were another matter. Finally he was numbed by the cold and fell asleep.

He woke before Luther and Terry. Daylight was filtering through the gray, broken window. Garner watched it, as he had done many times before, observing, but not seeing, the disorder that the light revealed. Strewn across the floor were sticks, tin cans, bottles, and the remnants of real toys found, exchanged, or stolen. There were clothes, too, scattered throughout the room, on the door knob, the chair, the dresser, amongst the toys. Actually, they were no longer real clothes, but wrappings pressed into service for want of something better. He heard the sounds of his mother moving around the kitchen. Struggling to hold his place in the bed, he moved his knees in again and tightened his hold on the blanket. As he shifted he heard a rat in the corner on the other side of the room.

He hated rats. A rat had bitten Terry once. Garner shuddered, remembering his screams. Unconsciously, he began to hold his breath so that he could hear the rat, listening, trying to gauge the distance between the rat and the bed. He thought of waking his brothers, but knew it would be difficult to corner and kill a rat in this dim light.

Garner wanted to get up and go into the kitchen, but that would involve a long trek across the cold bedroom and on through the living room. He dreaded the first shock of cold. But he knew his mother would call them any minute. He lay still, body rigid, waiting.

"Garna?"

He sat bolt upright.

"Garna, ya heah me, boy?"

"Yes'm. Ah'm comin'."

"Ya brothas up yit?"

"They sleepin'," Garner answered without looking at them.

"Well, hurry up now, gotta go tha sto'."

Garner grabbed some clothes and looked for his shoes. Finding one shoe on the dresser, he jerked his head around, seeking the other. He kicked some toys aside and dropped to his knees to look under the bed. There were shoes there but none matched the one he had. Now he was cold and angry, too. He dropped a T-shirt and snatched it up again, then spotted the shoe near the door, scooped it up, and ran for the kitchen.

The warmth of the kitchen always buoyed his spirits. It calmed him, relaxed him, and even drove the rat from his thoughts.

"Come on, boy, git'cha se'f dressed. Charlie ain' come home agin'. Don' stan' on tha flo', boy! Stan' on that paper. Ain'cha got no sense?

"Ya hear what ah say, boy? Hurry up theah, fa' gawdsake."

"Yes'm."

"Ah wan'cha ta git ovah ta Sy's an' git three them packages corn flakes fa' y'all ta eat. Git a qwodda milk too. An' bring me some cig'rettes. If Sy start holl'rin' 'bout money ya tell'im ah be ovah ta see'im ta-day."

"Yes'm," Garner muttered, looking down at his feet. "Ma?"

"What'cha want?"

"Sy say he don' wanna—"

"Don' *care,* don' care what he say! Tell'im what ah tol' ya. Tell'im ma kids hongry. Gotta right ta eat same's his—Jes' tell'im ah'm comin' ovah lay-da. Now you hurry."

"But, Ma," Garner whined, "Sy say he ain' gonna gimme no mo' stuff."

"Don' *care,* ah tol' ya! Don' care," she shot back angrily. "Ah don' care what he say! Don'choo sass me, boy."

"Wuzn't sassin'."

Her hand flew out and slammed against his face, snapping his head back. Tears welled up in his eyes. He held his face and stared at the floor, silent now, no longer protesting.

"Go 'long now—go 'long—. It's afta seven. No 'count man. He know it's Friday. Ain't nothin' ta eat heah. Hurry, boy. G'wan, git ta Sy's."

Garner threw on his dark, red coat and opened the door. The cold wind hit him as soon as he stepped into the hallway. He shuddered as it cut into him, whipping through the holes in his coat. The coat had only one button in front and flopped open from the chest down. The neck was open too.

He slipped and stumbled on the run down the front steps, regained his footing, and skipped nimbly over and around some overturned ash cans which lay frozen in the ice and snow at the foot of the stairs.

The streets he crossed were deep-rutted with unplowed snow, now frozen to ice. Overturned trash barrels lay frozen, their contents spilled, partly or completely buried under new trash and rubbish. A thin layer of new, white snow covered everything, making for treacherous footing. Garner ran on toward Sy's store, past Johnny's Liquor Mart, past the barroom and the alleys.

He turned the corner onto Washington Street and bumped into an old, black wino who stood freezing in the middle of the sidewalk. The man's eyes were closed. He muttered incoherently when Garner bounced off him, but his eyes only flickered momentarily, and he stood his ground. He was waiting for the liquor store to open up at eight. Garner dodged nimbly, glancing quickly at the other winos who stood against the building, or in the doorway under the sign—STARK'S LIQUORS. They were quiet, eyes closed, shivering. Some wore coats, some did not. They were dirty, unshaven, and ragged, waiting patiently to spend the bit of change hustled up for their common cause.

Garner went into the store—Sy's Spa, a small crowded place. Meat—Skinless Pure Beef Franks 99¢—Lean Bacon 99¢—Chicken Wings—Fresh Liver—Garner could only read a few of the posters. His eyes wandered: fruit—Grapefruit—which he had never eaten—Apples—Oranges—these he knew by taste, having stolen them from street peddlers, fruit stands, and from Sy—Have A Coke—. His eyes lingered at the candy counter. He was hungry now. His stomach muscles contracted spasmodically. He wished the boy ahead of him would hurry.

Out of the corner of his eye he saw someone move. Jerry the Cop stood in the doorway to the back room. He had come in to keep warm and to get some free coffee. His cold, blue eyes lingered on Garner momentarily, then he turned and moved back into the room out of sight.

Jerry the Cop—Garner was afraid of him. He had, on two occasions, beaten Luther severely; once when he caught him marking up windows on Halloween and once when he caught him climbing on a fruit truck. Garner wished he could leave.

Sy Rosenthal's voice was impatient, "C'mon, Alvin. What else do you want?"

"Qwodda milk," the thin yellow-skinned boy answered.

Sy waddled over to the big cooler, shaking his balding head. "What else?" he sighed in resignation.

"Jes' tha numba, an' thass all."

Sy took a slip of paper from the boy. "Your mother's still playing three two two? Okay, ten cents."

Alvin left.

"What can I do for you, Garner?" Sy droned indifferently, his fat, pink face impassive.

"Momma send me ta git some corn flakes."

Sy looked down at the counter, placing his hands there and leaning forward, his fat neck bulging and pink over the collar of his blue shirt. "Did Momma send some money along to buy it with?"

Garner shifted around uncomfortably. "An' a qwodda milk."

"And a quart of milk—*crap,*" Sy hissed. "Where's the money, goddammit?" He held up his hand, rubbing his thumb and middle finger together as though fingering dollar bills. "What's with the *money?*" His voice rose in anger.

Garner looked down at his feet. His stomach felt queasy. Jerry came back and stood in the doorway, sipping his steaming coffee. Garner looked up at him, then quickly he looked away. He looked at the door—no place to go, no place to hide, trapped. "Uh—an' some cig'-rettes, too," he stammered, unrelenting.

Sy looked up at Jerry and shook his head. "Isn't this something? *Isn't this something?* And he wants *cigarettes,* too! He just goes right on telling me what he wants! I tell you, this is murder."

The policeman's heavy stomach shook convulsively as he started to laugh. Sy was laughing now, too.

Jerry gave Garner a serious look and said, "You're one of the Hawkins kids, ain't ya?"

Garner looked up at him, frightened.

"I know your brother, don't I?"

Garner shook his head slowly in denial.

"Yeah. Name's Luther—ain't that right?"

"Naw," Garner answered finally, continuing to shake his head.

"Yeah. Luther Hawkins. I got my eye on him, boy. He's gonna get inta real trouble one of these days."

Sy cut in, "You tell your mother there's not going to be any more free food. Christ, she doesn't look *that* good—what do you people think this is?"

Garner hesitated, eyes riveted to the floor. "Momma say she comin' ovah."

"Over *here?*" Sy glared at him. "You tell her to stay home! You tell her I'll be over later on."

Garner shifted his feet, jammed his hands in his pockets, and fidgeted nervously. He stole a glance at Jerry the Cop, who moved back out of sight again. "Ah'm hongry, Sy—Momma say—"

"Boy, your mother's a fine-looking woman, and I like her, but she's either damn stupid, or crazy. How old are you, boy?"

"Uh—ah'm eight, Sy—Momma—"

"Jesus," Sy cut in angrily. *"Horseshit,* Momma say! I don't *care* what your mother says!" He ground his cigarette out. "Okay, okay, Garner. What the hell do you want?"

"Three them boxes corn flakes, qwodda milk, an' Pall Mall," he blurted.

Sy broke open a family pack of breakfast-size boxes of cereal and placed three of them on the counter, then waddled over to get the milk. "Tell your mother I'll be over this afternoon," he muttered. "And tell her *not* to come over here." He put the food in a brown bag and dropped in a pack of cigarettes.

Garner nodded, snatching up the bag of food. And as Sy turned toward the back room, his hand snaked out and scooped two bars of chocolate from the counter. He slipped them into his pocket.

He ran by the winos, thinking of the candy in his pocket. Around the corner he ducked into the hallway of an abandoned house, dug out his candy, and devoured it quickly. He threw the wrapper away, and stepped out of the building. He was cold again. He ran along toward home.

Ella Hawkins took three bowls out of the sink and filled them with corn flakes.

"What Sy say?"

"Say he comin' ovah," Garner answered.

"Well, ah guess ah know what he want. Git tha sugar, Lutha."

Garner fixed a covetous eye on the bottle of milk. "Kin ah have glass milk, Ma?"

"No."

"Ah'm thirsty, Ma."

"Don' care. Ya git nuff milk wit'cha corn flakes. Drink wawdda."

Garner put his elbow on the table and rested his face on his palm. Luther and Terry wanted some milk, too, but they were old enough to know better than to ask.

"Ya git any candy?" Terry asked him.

"Yeah."

"Wheah ya got it?"

"Ate it, fool, what'cha think?"

"Don' call me no fool, nigga. Whyn'cha git me some?"

"Whyn'choo go tha sto'?"

"Ya coulda got me some," Terry whined, his bright, orange face taking on a pained expression.

"Man," Luther giggled, "that nigga ain' thinkin' 'bout nothin' but his own belly."

"Sho' ain'," Terry growled.

"Don' call me no nigga, neither!"

Luther laughed. "Heah that, Terry? This nigga ain' a nigga! Ain'choo a nigga, nigga?"

"You nigga, too," Garner yelled back. "An' so you," he spat at Terry.

"Sheet, ah ain' black as you, nigga."

Luther's head jerked up quickly. "Who you callin' black?" he demanded menacingly through a mouthful of food.

"Aw, man, ah'm talkin' ta Garna."

Luther was extremely sensitive about his color. He was very dark, the color of ebony—like Garner—and he was always ready to fight anyone who teased him about it.

Their mother interceded, "Y'all stop alla that nigga an' black talk! Ya heah? Stop alla that damn fool talk! Ya soun' jes' like a bunch a' dumb niggas, settin' theah arguin' 'bout who black an' who ain'."

"Yes'm," Luther mumbled peevishly.

Garner and Terry stared at their food.

"Y'all hurry up an' eat," their mother continued. "Gonna be late fa school."

They fell silent and ate the rest of their cereal.

The sun was bright and warm as the boys walked to school. The new snow had softened a bit. Luther made a snowball and threw it at a passing truck. Garner made one and threw it into the street at nothing in particular. Terry trudged along, watching the elevated trains overhead and looking at billboards: a pretty blond girl offered him a bottle of soda saying, REFRESH YOURSELF . . . another blond offered him a cold beer, BREWED THE WAY YOU LIKE IT . . . still another blond who looked like a young girl offered him a loaf of white bread as her little blond children ate a breakfast of bacon, eggs, toast, butter, orange juice, milk, and cereal—BUILDS STRONG BODIES EIGHT WAYS.

A police cruiser went by on the other side of the street. The driver, a white man, glanced idly at the boys who watched the cruiser intently, turning in order to keep it in sight.

Luther scowled. "Tha fuzz, man," he muttered slowly.

"Fuck'em," Terry hissed.

"Yeah," Garner whispered.

Luther shook his head "Yeah, mutha-fuck them bastids. Hey,

theah's Leroy. Hey, Leroy," he yelled, breaking into a run. "See you cats, man. Hey, wait up, Leroy."

Leroy was fifteen, almost as tall as Luther, very fair, with a pink flush to his face and thick, light brown, wavy hair. He stood waiting for Luther, calmly puffing a cigarette. Luther caught up to him, grinning broadly.

"Gimme drag, man."

Leroy handed him the cigarette and they started walking again. There were a lot of people on the streets now, many of them on their way to work. Cars moved slowly; some got stuck, their wheels spinning uselessly on snow-covered ice. It was still cold but the sunlight was taking the bitter chill out of the air. The liquor stores were open now, too. Winos huddled in alleys and doorways passing around bottles in brown paper bags, or stood on the corners shivering. Children were everywhere, and of every shade of black, brown, yellow, and orange—and white, like Leroy.

A stocky black boy ran up to join them with a big grin.

"What's happ'nin', Buzz?" Leroy greeted him.

"Nothin' shakin', baby." He broke out a package of cigarettes.

"What say, Lutha'?"

"What say, man?"

"Wanna cig'rette?"

"Yeah."

"You want one, Leroy?" Buzz asked, offering the pack to both boys as he fished around in his leather jacket for some matches.

"Yeah, baby. Me an' Lutha jes' killed my last one."

"Picked up some change last night," Buzz said proudly.

Luther's ebony face took on an expression of acute interest. "How much, man?"

"A hunnerd an' sevenny-five bucks."

Leroy let out a long, low whistle.

"Sheet," Luther said with admiration. "Wheah ya pick up that kinda bread, man?"

"Caught me a fish," Buzz laughed.

"Wheah at?"

"Ovah by Slade's. Ah wuz comin' home frum a party, an' ah met this white cat. He wuz real high, man. Ah mean his head wuz *all* tore up, just sailin' 'long on good booze. So ah stopped an' cooled it. Ya know? Started checkin' this cat out. Too many people 'roun' ta start fuckin' up. Ya know what ah mean?"

Leroy and Luther nodded wisely.

"Well," Buzz continued, "ah cools it neah tha resta-rant—by Slade's, like ah said—an' pretty soon ah seen this cat go 'roun' tha corna ta this pretty red car an' git out this bottle a' likka, an' ah cooled it awhile, watchin'im. He wuz jes' settin' theah, drinkin' in his car. Ah mean, feelin' no pain. Ya know? So ah cooled it til ah could git'im 'lone. Alla time ah'm tryin' ta figga how ah'm gonna fuck this cat outta his bread. Ya know? Then ah gotta idea. Ah mean, like ah wuz all dressed up, ya know? Ah mean, ah wuz *clean,* man. So ah cools it on up ta this cat an' ah asks'im if he wanna gal. Ya know? So tha cat look at me an' say, 'Yeah, boy, ah wanna gal. Ya got one?' Then he start laffin'. So ah say, 'Ah got *lotta* gals.' An' ah ask tha fish what kinda gal he want, dark, light, or white. Ya know? Ah mean ah wuz *really* layin' tha shit on this cat. So tha fish figgas ah ain' bullshittin'. Ya know? An' he say he like his women *hot,* man. *Real* hot. An' he say he wanna real *black* gal. Somethin' real fine. So ah say, 'Ah got one like that right 'roun' tha corna, jesta little ways frum heah.' An' he say, 'Les' go.' Then ah say, 'Wait a minnit, man. Ya got any money?' An' he wanna know how much it gonna cost. So ah tell'im ten dollas. An' he say, 'Sheet, boy, les go.' So ah tell'im agin', 'Look, man, ah cain' be wastin' ma time.' An' ah hadda be sho' he had tha bread. Well, then he gits evil, man. Ah mean, *real* salty. 'Ten dollas,' he say. 'Ah gotta nuff money ta buy alla black cunt they is!' So ah play it cool then. 'Don' git mad,' ah say, 'ah'm a bid'nessman, an' ah gotta see some money befo' ah kin make a deal.' Well, man, ah mean ta tell ya this cat got evil as a *mutha-fucka* an' pulls out this big-ass wallet an' hol's it out that winda fa' me ta see alla bread in it. Ya know?"

Luther and Leroy howled, laughing hysterically.

"Well," Buzz went on, "ya know what happined."

"Man," Luther gloated, "you sho' a lucky som'bitch, Buzz."

"Yeah," Leroy joined in. "Imagine anybuddy that dumb? Nobuddy but a gray boy be that fuckin' dumb, man. Did he chase ya, Buzz?"

"Sheet, man, wuzn't no *needa* him chasin' *me!* Ah wuz gone ta tha races! Sheet, ah don' think he could even git outta tha car. Anyway, ah wuz haulin' ma ass, ah didn't have *no* time ta see what he doin'. He wuz mad as a bitch though, ah could *heah* tha som'bitch screamin'."

Luther laughed, wiping the tears from his eyes. "Sheet, Buzz, ah bet'choo wuz haulin' yo' ass fa' real."

"You fuckin' right. Sheet, ah woulda even beat'choo last night, Lutha."

"You musta really been haulin'," Leroy said.

"You betta believe it, man. Ah wuz gone."

Luther grinned. "Say, Buzz, that mean we don' hafta go ta school ta-day. Ya got any a' that bread wit'cha, man?"

"Only brought a dolla, man. Ya know ah hadda hide that shit. If ma ol' lady see me wit' alla that change, she gonna know ah been fuckin' 'roun' an' kick ma ass."

"Sheet. She gotta ket'cha first, man. You holdin' any bread, Leroy?"

"Naw, baby, ain' holdin' nothin'."

"Well," Buzz said, "ah wouldn't hook no school ta-day, anyways. Thass how ya git fucked, baby."

"Thass right, Lutha. Buzz tellin' ya wheah it's at, man. Afta hit like that he *gotta* cool it. Gotta do eva'thin' same's always."

Buzz nodded quickly. "Playin' it cool, baby. No fuckin' 'roun'."

The three boys walked along, smoking. Luther was still thinking about hooking school. But he was ashamed, still, of having revealed his ignorance about how to behave after a big score.

"Hey, Lutha," Buzz began. "What ol' man Tracy have ya down tha office fa', yestidday?"

"Lotta bullshit, man. Collins sent me down fa' fightin'. Caught me in tha shithouse an'—"

Buzz was astonished. "Who you fightin' wit', Lutha? Ya already whip evah som'bitch in—"

"Ah punched Reardon in his fuckin' mouth."

"*Reardon?* Man—shit, he ain' nothin'. He git ta thinkin' he bad a' somethin'." Buzz started to laugh then. *"Reardon,* man. Ain' thatta bitch?"

"He called Tobey a nigga, man," Leroy said.

"Huh? Sheet! Man, what Tobey do?"

"Man, thass why ah hadda kick Reardon's ass. Fuckin' Tobey, man—that nigga ain' done a fuckin' thing! He wuz gonna let tha white mutha-fucka git away wit'it!"

"Gawddamn! What'choo do, Lutha?"

"Sheet—ah hit'im in his fuckin' mouth. Thass what ah did."

"Man," Leroy said, "Lutha fucked that paddy boy's face *all* up."

They started across the street in front of the school. "Sheet, Lutha, you shoulda beat tha shit out that som'bitch. *Man!* Shoulda fuckin' kilt that mutha-fucka."

"Aw, man—Collins caught me. Him an' Burke, too."

"Burke's a mean som'bitch, baby—*hates* niggas."

Leroy flipped his cigarette away, scowling. "Fuck'im. Fuck all them white som'bitches."

"Fuckin' right, baby. Man—somebuddy gotta talk ta Tobey. He gotta know us niggas run this mutha-fuckin' school. Sheet, what'choo tell'im, Lutha?"

"Ah tol'im ah shoulda hit'im in *his* mouth first an' *then* kicked Reardon's ass! Fuckin' nigga ain' shit, man. Jesta gawd-damn sissy."

"Shit," Leroy said. "He jes' like Harold, 'fraid his ol' lady gonna beat his ass. Sheet—alla fuckin' time kissin' teachers' ass."

"Sheet, Leroy, you fuckin' neah's bad. Yo' aunt done kicked yo' ass a whole lotta times fa' sneakin' out tha house."

"Fuck you, Lutha, man! What'choo talkin' 'bout? Ah ain' skeered."

Buzz cut in, "Man, Harold an' Tobey *both* silly mutha-fuckas. Ah don' think them niggas *wanna* do nothin'."

Luther shook his head angrily. "They gotta quit fuckin' up in school, man. Ah don' give a fuck *what* they doin' outside, but they gotta stop this heah shit in tha school."

Buzz and Leroy nodded in agreement and followed Luther into the schoolyard.

* * *

Garner was asleep and did not hear Miss Wagner calling his name. The other boys in the class were staring at him, grinning expectantly. Miss Wagner, a tall, blond woman, wearing a smart gray flannel suit, walked briskly down the aisle and shook him roughly. "Wake up, Garner! Garner Hawkins, *do you hear me?* Wake up!" She shook him again.

He sat up quickly, a surprised look on his face. "Yes'm. Ah heah ya. Ah'm 'wake."

"Well, you certainly don't act like it. Honestly, Garner!"

Garner stared down at his desk.

"Don't you sleep at home?"

"Yes'm."

"Then why do you sleep in here all day?"

"Ah dunno."

"Well, *I,* for one, would certainly like to find out. Garner, what's *wrong* with you?"

"Nothin'."

"If you can't stay awake, I'm going to keep you after school again. Do you understand me?"

"Yes'm."

"The rest of you stop your foolishness," she snapped at the class.

She turned and strode quickly to the front of the room, brushing her blond hair with the side of her hand.

"Please pick up your book, Garner, and follow along with the rest of us."

"Yes'm."

Garner opened his book.

"William, would you stand up and read, beginning with 'See, Sally,' please?"

A small, dark boy stood up, holding his book nervously in front of him.

" 'See, Sally,' " he read haltingly, " 'there's Tom's new pony. . . . His name is Hoppy. . . .' Sally said, 'Tom's new pony is . . . gray. . . .' Dick said, 'Tom let me ride him yesterday. . . .' "

Garner glanced around furtively at the desks of his classmates, trying to find his place in the book.

"Very good, William, thank you. Peter?"

"Sally said, 'Hello, Tom. I like your new pony,' " a short black boy was reading. Sally was blond—like Miss Wagner. But Sally was tiny and only a picture, not real. Miss Wagner was old.

"Dick said, 'May I ride Hoppy again, Tom?' " the boy read on. Dick was Sally's brother; he had red hair with blue eyes and freckles.

Garner only understood vaguely that the children depicted in the book were representations of real people. They were like television or movie people—white.

The only blond child Garner had ever met was a little girl who used to live across the street from him. But her brother, unlike Dick, was slightly copper-colored—like his own brother, Terry. Garner did not, however, connect Sally's image with the girl he knew. This Sally was associated with cows, chickens, ponies, hills, and green mountains. Except for coloring, he didn't associate Miss Wagner with Sally either. He knew that in some far-off time, Miss Wagner had been a child. Children were small people. They were young. He was small, and young. *But he was black*. He wasn't blond and his eyes were not blue. And Miss Wagner was big too—old. He did not conceive, at all, the notion that Sally could have been some kind of representation of Miss Wagner's childhood, or anyone else's. And even if she had been black, whatever connections he might have made between her and himself would have been vague. He didn't understand it all. The connection between real people like his mother, and Miss Wagner, his brothers and his playmates, and tiny, brightly colored, clean little book people like Sally and Dick, escaped him. The conception of birth, growth, and maturity remained confused in his mind.

People like Miss Wagner were teachers. Garner never considered the idea that she had a life, some other human functions and interests, apart from her association with him at school. Miss Wagner was strange, blond, and pink, all in a swirl of bright, clean, and dazzling colors. She smelled funny too. It was an odd smell that Garner only found at school—from Miss Wagner. It was pleasant, agreeable, sweet and heady. And she wore pretty clothes everyday. That's how Garner knew she was rich. She didn't talk like other people, either. She talked like a teacher and often he didn't understand what she was saying. Garner was awed by Miss Wagner. She pleased him, bewildered and frightened him. When she wasn't angry with him, or when he wasn't asleep, he would watch her carefully, wondering at her. He searched his memory for someone who looked like Miss Wagner, someone who was pretty. *Was Momma pretty?* She wasn't *white;* she didn't look like Miss Wagner. He continued to grope for a connection with pretty. Weren't mommas pretty, too? He thought back to the time when Miss Wagner had taken them, along with the other children in the school, to the junior high school where Luther went, to see a movie: *Snow White and the Seven Dwarfs*. He remembered Snow White. She was pretty; she was the prettiest girl in the whole world. She was so pretty that her skin was white as snow—. She was very fair and very white. Yet, she wasn't as white as Miss Wagner, was she? Her hair was dark, and Miss Wagner's hair was almost white. *She was white all over;* anyone who was that white was even fairer, even whiter than Snow White —even *prettier* than Snow White. Momma was black. *Miss Wagner was white*. She was pretty. Momma was his momma. *She wasn't pretty*. Momma was black—*like he was*.

"Thank you, Matthew. Garner?"

He stood up, holding his book with both hands. He had found his place by turning the pages until he saw the right pictures.

"Sally ask—Tom," Garner began in a halting, incoherent monotone, "if—she—ride—pony—too." He looked up, hesitating, unsure.

Miss Wagner crossed her arms, her pretty face wearing a frown. "Garner Hawkins, you're simply going to have to stay awake in this class and pay attention. You're not following along with the rest of us. And you're not reading. You're poking at this word and that one and—I don't know what. I don't think you're trying, Garner." She hesitated as his eyes plunged down to the floor, leveling her tone. "You cannot sleep the day away and expect to learn anything," she pleaded, trying to control her temper. "How can you hope to keep up with the rest of the class if you're always asleep?"

"Yes'm."

"What?"

"Yes'm. Yes'm, Miz Wagna."

He kept his eyes down, away from hers.

"Yes'm."

"Garner, are you *listening* to me?" she begged.

"Yes'm."

She stared at him then, seeing his discomfort. Her voice softened. "Would you rather sit down for a while and try it again later, Garner?"

"Yes'm. Yes'm, Miz Wagna, ah wanna sit down."

"Very well, then, we'll try it again later."

But she knew that she wouldn't have the heart to call on him again that day.

Garner sat down, and a fat coffee-colored boy stood up. He saw Miss Wagner watching him and quickly lowered his eyes.

Barbara Wagner frowned. *He's terrified!* Well—maybe she was wasting her time. *God, he's a beautiful child.* She almost smiled then as her thoughts slipped away—*They were going to the junior high school to see a movie. It was snowing. The boys were buzzing around her, chattering excitedly—except Garner. He and another black boy kept trying to run off by themselves, throwing snowballs at the children up ahead of them. She yelled at them then. "Stop that, Johnny—Garner." Tom Ryan, a short dark-haired man who taught math, caught Johnny by the ear and shoved him back in line. Garner jumped quickly in place beside his buddy before Mr. Ryan could get to him. Barbara smiled. As soon as Mr. Ryan moved away, they started again. "Garner," she yelled. Both boys fell quickly back into line. She watched them, trying not to laugh. Garner was sulking. He kicked at some loose snow and gave her a positively malevolent look. Barbara frowned then and looked away. When she looked again, he and Johnny had moved to the front of their line. Garner threw a snowball toward the class ahead of them. It hit a tall yellow boy on the back of the head. He spun around angrily, but when he saw Garner grinning at him, he quickly averted his eyes. Barbara sloshed angrily through the snow until she caught up with Garner. "Garner Hawkins, you see me right after school. Do you hear?" "Yes'm, ah heah ya." He trudged along then, not looking at her, eyes down. Johnny whispered something to him and Garner shook his head angrily. After the movie, Garner shoved his way into line beside her while they were walking back to their school. She noticed him peeking at her guardedly. His face, flat and black, the eyes oddly slanted, looked cute. The snow topped his nappy hair with a wet, white cap. She saw him looking at her again and laughed softly as he quickly ducked his head. She tried to catch him at it then. He started to giggle, trying to catch her not catching him—a little devil, she mused. If only she could*—"Thank you, Marcus—Paul, would you go on, please?" Barbara tried to focus her attention on the boy who was reading.

When the bell rang, she watched Garner hurry out without looking at her. She suddenly felt very tired.

Ed Collins stood in the cloakroom, tapping the switch in his hand, watching Luther carefully. He was a medium-sized man, with brown, thinning hair. He wore an old, wine-colored corduroy jacket, with black leather patches sewed on the elbows.

The light fixture overhead barely gave off enough of its yellow light to make out the shadowy outline of coats hanging on the walls, or the boots and rubbers on the floor.

It was impossible to see Luther clearly, which struck Mr. Collins as funny; for a moment, an abortive smile tugged at the corners of his mouth. Luther's black skin almost blended into the dark brown of the shirt tucked into his black chinos. His features blurred in the weak light. He's so black, Mr. Collins thought, *it's a wonder you can see him at all! Should be able to see the whites of his eyes, though. Yes, or at least his teeth. Black as unmined coal.*

Mr. Collins glared at the boy. Luther was bigger than he was, and heavier, a tall boy, wide through the shoulders, with a flat, narrow waist and slim hips. Mr. Collins envied him his youth and that build.

He thought of his wife then—small, pretty, with red hair—*"Don't, Eddie—Father Ryan—"* he gripped the switch tightly with both hands—*"Not now, please don't—"*

"Did you throw that spitball, Luther?"

"Naw."

"Well, who did?"

Mr. Collins watched the boy stare back at him. Yes, he thought, *the nigger bastard hates me, but there's nothing he can do about it, and he has no place to hide.* He scowled in the dim light, "You're a liar! *You* threw it, didn't you?"

"Naw!"

"Who did then, dammit?"

"Don' know."

"You did, Luther!"

"Naw!"

"What were you doing with the rubber bands and wads of paper?"

"Nothin'!"

"You're a liar," Mr. Collins declared in a low, bitter voice as he raised his switch.

He was furious now. He hadn't actually seen who threw the spitball. After the gooey missile splattered against the blackboard, landing just inches from his head, he had turned to see Luther. It wasn't often that he caught a troublemaker red-handed as he thought he had this time. But when he did, he made the culprit pay dearly.

"Luther, if I don't get the truth out of you, I'm going to beat you until your hands are bloody! Do you understand me?"

They stood, glaring at each other. The students were quiet in the other room, waiting to hear the beating.

The switch that Mr. Collins was holding was a rattan, a thin, cylindrical, yellow rod, about three feet long. Luther had been rattanned many times. It was painful. Of course, he wouldn't cry; he never cried about anything anymore, and he certainly wasn't going to cry for Mr. Collins. He hated the man. Mr. Collins had beaten him on two previous occasions. Luther would have killed him had he known how to do it without paying the consequences. He glowered angrily at him, wishing Mr. Collins were a boy, *like Mike Reardon.* A feeling of satisfaction surged within him as he thought of Reardon. Luther liked to fight; it made him feel good, especially when he fought white boys.

Fighting boys of his own race was something he did for the sheer joy of proving himself in combat. *He was hard.* White boys were different; fighting them was a crusade. He wanted to hurt them; he enjoyed seeing them bleed. He thought of Tobey then, backing down, cowering in fear after Mike Reardon called him a nigger. Luther's thick lips quivered in anger.

"Stick out your right hand, Luther!"

Luther was still for a moment; he thought of refusing. Why should he take a whipping? He glared at his teacher. He even thought of fighting with him, debating in his young mind the possibility of getting away with it. He was nearly beside himself with fury now. His eyes began to water. He knew that the beating he was about to receive was his punishment for bullying white boys. Well, he thought, *you haven't seen anything yet, white folks.*

"I said, stick our your hand, *goddammit!* Did you hear me?"

Luther remained still. He continued to watch Mr. Collins with sullen, bitter fury.

Mr. Collins struggled to control himself. *"Goddamn you,* you—you *black—ape!* I'm going to give you six on each hand!"

Luther remained unresponsive. He was glad that the man was upset. He wanted him to know that he wasn't afraid. He wanted desperately to win some small victory.

"I know what you're thinking, nigger, but there's no place to run."

"Y'ain' s'posed ta call me no names," Luther blurted.

"I *ain't,* huh? Okay, *nigger,* after I strip some of that black hide off you, you can go to the office and tell Mr. Tracy. Yes, and when you're all done, I'll tell him *my* story and we'll see who he believes." Collins hesitated, grinning. "Maybe I'll have to give you another licking for lying."

Luther knew that he was right: he would get no help from Tracy. He had once called him a nigger himself. Luther was certain that he detested blacks as much as Collins did.

"Stick out your hand! C'mon, *stick it out there!* None of you niggers is big enough to take his beating like a man. You're yellow, Luther. You're a bully who knows how to dish it out, but you turn yellow when it's your turn to take what's coming to you. Stick out your god-damn hand."

Luther had one last thought of flying at the man, maybe getting a thumb in his eye, or at least hitting him with one good punch—maybe on the nose. It would almost have been worth the trip to Disciplinary School—to see blood spurting from the teacher's nose while he held his face, writhing in pain.

Luther offered his hand, palm up, fingers straight, as he had done many times before. He watched the rattan being raised—he had heard that teachers administering this form of punishment were not supposed to raise their arms above their heads, but they always did.

He took six strokes on each hand, three across the fingertips and three across each palm and thumb. The whipping was done in this manner in order to induce more pain. Mr. Collins was good at it. But Luther did not cry out; none of the "tough" kids, black or white, ever yelled or cried during a beating. To do so was to invite the most perverse ridicule and disgrace. Luther upheld the tradition, defying Mr. Collins with his watery eyes as the switch came whistling through the dark stillness of the room again and again and again and again. It bent slightly as it came down, then it snapped wickedly across his fingers and palms. Mr. Collins struck three blows at one hand, then three on the other, then he went back to the first, finishing on the second. This prevented numbness.

When it was over, Mr. Collins was red-faced and short of breath. A thin film of sweat covered his brow. He took a handkerchief from the pocket of his old jacket and wiped his face.

Luther continued to glower at him, but he could feel the tears trying to force their way out. He fought them, laboring mightily to hold them back. His hands swelled with terrible pain as if he were holding fiery, red coals. He couldn't move his fingers.

He wished as hard as he could that Mr. Collins would die, that the man's mother would die, that his whole family would die. He saw it happening in his mind—*He was shooting them, punching, kicking, and cutting them. They moaned, blood gurgling in their mouths and spewing out all over them. Then they were alive again, mothers, brothers, sisters, wives, and children, and he was killing them all over again. All at once white people were dying all around him as he struck out in all directions with varied and sundry devices for inflicting wounds: knives, guns, swords, stones, and fists. Their noses were bleeding, and they begged, but he kept killing them. He stomped on their faces. Then he jumped up and down on their faces with both feet. They were all bloody. They kept screaming and begging for mercy even though they were dead. He threw cold blood on them to revive them.*—Luther looked at Mr. Collins, wishing he were bloody-dead.

Mr. Collins was still angry. He had been able to vent some of his rage during the beating. But he knew that it hadn't made any difference to Luther. It didn't matter; he could hit the boy twelve times or twenty times, and the response would be the same. Nothing. Silently, he cursed the boy; the nigger was mean, that's all. He had, at least, hoped to make him cry this time. None of the teachers had been able to make him cry. Mr. Collins watched him, holding the switch down at his side. He wanted to beat the boy again, break him down, bring him to heel. Luther's cocky, persistent defiance constantly peeved him. He had refused Mr. Tracy's repeated offer to recommend the boy for Disciplinary School. He didn't want to admit defeat. God, no! Not defeat by a fourteen-year-old nigger! Yes, he thought, you'll get into trouble again, black boy, and when you do, I'll be waiting. *I'll be waiting!* God, yes. He couldn't whip him again now; he had already gone far enough, and he was tired. He looked at the boy. "Okay, Sambo," he rasped, "next time it'll be ten on each hand. Back to your seat." He pushed the boy roughly toward the door.

The other students in the class had been waiting expectantly and turned to look at Luther as he walked to his desk. He maintained his normal, easy, loping style, pretending nonchalance. His hands were held rigidly at his sides, the only evidence of pain.

He sat down carefully, using the edge of his palms to brace himself as he eased into his seat. His eyes were still watery, but he held back the tears. He held his hands in his lap, staring straight ahead. He gingerly tried to move his fingers to ease the pain but had to give it up; it seemed to make it worse. His hands were swelling now and the pain was becoming more intense. He knew that the pain would peak soon, then it would begin to numb, and finally subside.

His classmates stole furtive glances at him, trying to see how well he was bearing up. Some of his enemies were smiling. But they were careful about it, lest he see them and take his revenge at their expense. Luther wanted revenge. Again he conjured his vivid scenes where he was fighting his teachers—*One by one, he tore into them, smashing teeth, cutting eyes, splitting lips open. They begged and cowered in fear and pain. He smashed their faces again and again. They were all familiar: Mr. Collins—who was singled out for special treatment—Mr. Burke, Tracy, and others.* Then he began to imagine that he was crippling them instead of killing them so that their agony was not interrupted by death—*School had to be discontinued now because so many teachers were injured, or afraid to come to work. All the teachers in the world were afraid of him then, and even the cops stayed out of his way.*—He could almost feel the flesh and bone of his enemies, tearing and splintering beneath his fists which he imagined had grown to incredible size and had become capable of smashing and breaking anyone.

A grim smile worked around his thick mouth. The pain in his hands began to diminish. He looked around the room. The other boys quickly averted their eyes. He saw Leroy and smiled at him. Leroy nodded and grinned as if to say, "Ah know tha white som'bitch cain' git ta ya, man."

Luther and Leroy loved each other. They were "boys," "ace buddies." And they were a lot alike: mean, tough, and angry. They both hated white people; if anything, Leroy's hatred of whites was even more intense than Luther's.

The differences between the two boys, however, were many. Luther was more direct than Leroy. He was inclined to lash out at anything and anyone. It was only in the face of overwhelming, immediate, and dangerous opposition that he held back. Leroy would wait, figuring and planning, nursing his hurts until the opportunity to get his revenge presented itself. He, unlike Luther, seldom got into trouble at school. He was more dangerous than Luther because he was quiet, brooding, and bitter. He didn't enjoy fighting, either. He understood, perhaps better than Luther, what fighting was all about. When he had to fight, he fought to defend his person or his honor, for defense rather than for pleasure. Therefore, he fought desperately and viciously, not to demonstrate any physical prowess or superiority, but to avoid a beating—to survive. His objective in any fight was the elimination of any possible danger to himself. He was mean and vicious because he wanted his opponent to fear him so much that he wouldn't dare challenge him again. He did not believe in the "fair fight" either.

Luther took a sadistic kind of pleasure in beating a boy with his fists while Leroy preferred to use a rock or a stick or anything else he could find. If an opponent fell or tripped, he would stomp him frantically. Luther, on the other hand, would wait for the boy to get up to enjoy the fun of knocking him down again to further display his superiority. To be hurt in any way put Leroy in a rage. He would wait then, and when he saw his chance, he would get even.

Once, during the fall just past, a white boy, Billy Mitchell, having learned that Leroy was actually black, walked up to him and declared, "You're a fuckin' nigger, for crissakes!"

Leroy had been waiting for Luther who was in the drugstore and Luther heard the remark as he came out. He stared at Mitchell in furious, outraged disbelief. "Man, ya gonna take that shit, Leroy? Man, what's wrong wit'choo?"

Leroy stared at the white boy, his blue eyes flashing angrily. "Who tha fuck you callin' a nigga? Ah'll kick ya fuckin' ass fa' that, ya som'bitch!"

Mitchell grinned. He was a big, redheaded boy, squat and strongly made. "Try it," he snarled, "and I'll kick ya teeth in."

"Sheet," Luther bawled, "if he cain', *ah* beat'cha ass, mutha-fucka!"

"Christ, Luther, I didn't say nothin' to *you!* Why can't he do his own fightin'? You weren't even here, for crissakes!"

"Ah heard ya, ya som'bitch. You know me'n Leroy's boys."

"I didn't know he was colored, Luther!"

"Ah'm gonna beat tha shit out'choo, Billy!"

"Leave'im go, man," Leroy whispered.

"Naw, man, ah'm gonna—"

"We's boys, ain' we?"

"Yeah, man, thass why—"

"So leave'im—Go 'head, Billy."

Mitchell looked at Leroy gratefully. He fidgeted, shifting his sneakers around nervously on the sidewalk. Then, carefully he said, "Shit, Leroy, I didn't mean nothin'. I didn't know you're colored. I mean—"

"Fa'git it, man," Leroy offered in the same quiet whisper. "No sweat."

"Jesus, you're okay, Leroy. I didn't mean nothin', see. All I—"

"Fa'git it, Billy."

Luther stared at his friend incredulously. His black face scowled and he shook his head. "Man, ya cain' let'im git away wit'it, Leroy, ya *cain'!* This shit gonna be all ovah tha fuckin' school, fa' crissake!"

"Don' worry 'bout it, baby," Leroy muttered, reaching in his jacket to dig some cigarettes out of his pocket. He watched Mitchell go across the street. The white boy stopped in front of the schoolyard and looked back, then he walked on down the hill. Leroy smiled cruelly. "Wanna cig'rette?" he offered calmly, eyes still fastened on Billy Mitchell.

"Naw."

It took two weeks. Leroy discovered that Billy Mitchell liked to go up to the top floor of the school during the long recess which followed lunch. He went up there, usually with some friends, to sneak a smoke. One day, he went up by himself; Leroy was waiting at the top of the stairs. Billy looked up at him, surprised, hesitating with one foot on the top step.

"How ya doin', Billy?"

"Gee, hi, Leroy. What are you doin' here? Come up for a butt?"

"Yeah. Got one?"

"Sure." Billy nervously averted his eyes as he reached in his pocket.

Leroy pushed him backwards.

Billy landed on the back of his neck at the foot of the staircase.

He had two cracked vertebrae and a broken leg. Leroy stood smiling. Then he unbuttoned his gray shirt and tore the collar and ran down the stairs. He ran by Billy Mitchell down the next flight, and the next, until he bumped into Mr. Burke coming out of the teachers' room. Burke grabbed the boy and threw him against the wall. "Boy, how many times do we have to tell you kids?" he yelled. "You don't run in this school!"

"Billy fell, Mr. Burke," Leroy screamed excitedly. "Billy fell and he's hurt bad!"

"What? What're you talking about? Where?"

"Upstairs, Mr. Burke! We wuz wrasslin' an'—"

"Show me," Burke cut in, alarmed.

They hurried along the dark corridor and ran up the stairs to Billy.

"Oh, God," the teacher exclaimed, examining the unconscious boy. "Get down the office—*double time*—and tell Mr. Tracy! We need a doctor up here, for God's sake! And see if you can find Mr. Murphy," he shouted after him.

Later, Leroy stood in front of Mr. Tracy, the old, white-haired principal, answering questions. Mr. Tracy sat back in his chair and stared at the quiet boy in front of him and said, "Leroy, when Billy regained consciousness at the hospital, he told his mother that *you* pushed him down the stairs."

"Naw, we wuz wrasslin'!"

Mr. Tracy fingered the lapel of his gray suitcoat. "I—see. You say you *didn't* push him, huh?"

"Nawsuh!"

"But he claims you did, Leroy."

"Nawsuh. Ah ain'—"

"What were you kids doing up there?"

"We wuz gonna play cards."

"You know cards aren't allowed in the school."

"Yassuh. But it wuz recess time—"

"Then what happened?"

"Well, we wuz foolin' 'roun' an' wrasslin', an' Billy fell, an' ah wuz skeered. Thass why ah wuz runnin'."

"But why would Billy say you pushed him?"

"Ah dunno, Mr. Tracy."

"Leroy, as far as I know, you've never been in any trouble before and I think you're telling the truth. But—this is very serious. We won't discipline you this time, Leroy, but I *do* hope you've learned something from all this. I really do."

"Yassuh."

After school that day, Luther and Buzz met Leroy outside the drugstore and congratulated him enthusiastically. "Man," Luther said, "that wuz cool! You *bad,* Leroy. Ah thought'cha wuz gonna let'im git away wit'it."

"Yeah, so did he."

Buzz gloated. "Leroy hard, man. Thass all. The nigga is *hard!*"

Billy Mitchell never returned to that school.

Luther remembered his father only vaguely. Sometimes his strong, black face would flash into his mind. Then it would fall away, fleeting, out of reach, never really there. As a very small boy, he had often questioned his mother—*"Ma?" She sat on her bed, holding the baby, Terry. "What, boy?" "Ma, is ah got a daddy?" "Yeah, boy, natcherly ya got a daddy." "Wheah, Ma?" "Well—Lutha, he gone ta git work—yeah, thass all. He gone ta git work. You go 'head out now. Ah gotta feed ya brotha," she said, unbuttoning her blouse. "Go 'head—go 'head, now." "Terry got one, too?" "What, boy—what'cha—" "Is Terry got a daddy, too?" Luther persevered. "Huh? Now, look, boy—yeah—yeah. Now, you go 'head out an' play. Go 'head, now, ya heah?"*

Leroy was illegitimate. He had never met either of his parents. He lived with an aunt and her husband. They were quiet, proud people who made him a decent home. He had learned to hate the color of his skin, his "whiteness," when he had overheard his uncle, and his aunt, discussing his mother and father. He was too young, at first, to understand what was being said, but he *wanted* to understand and he made a habit of sitting on the steps which led up to his room while they talked in the parlor evenings. In time, he learned that his mother was a prostitute and that he was an unplanned and unwanted consequence of one of her professional ventures. His father was a white man. His uncle, unaware that he was listening, had often expressed the opinion that his father "bought a black whore" because "he couldn't get a woman any other way."

Leroy learned what a whore was and what they were for. This happened when he was thirteen. It was before he met Luther, when his family lived in a different house. His mind frequently wandered back to that old building and the woman who lived upstairs. She was a prostitute, a pretty, respectable-looking young woman who went to church every Sunday. He used to run errands for her and she sometimes brought him into the apartment and fed him cake and ice cream.

Her name was Velma. He remembered her vividly—*"Leroy, you gonna be a beautiful man when ya git big, ya know that?" He blushed deep red, peeking timidly at the back of her pretty legs and thighs as she bent over to rearrange the soft yellow pillows on the sofa. She sat down and crossed her legs and smiled at him. He dropped his eyes, wondering at her doll-like face and the dark honey of her skin. Her body enchanted him; it glowed under her negligee. The nipples of her soft, brown breasts were caught in the filmy material, poking out like dark buds. He peeked again; he wanted to touch her breasts but he didn't know why. She spoke to him in a gentle voice, "Why don'cha sit ovah heah beside Velma, Leroy?" He got up slowly, pretending reluctance and walked over to her and sat down. He enjoyed sitting with her like that. Sometimes she kissed him on the cheek, or the neck; that embarrassed him. One day, she hugged him and nestled his head against her breasts. He felt funny then. She stroked his chest and stomach and he thought he was going to be sick. She whispered soft, gentle sounds to him, "You such a pretty boy, Leroy. Ya got pretty hair an' them pretty eyes. Ah could jes' love ya ta death, ya know that? Ah could jes' love ma pretty little Leroy ta death." Then she giggled. "Ah sho' wish ya wuz a man, boy. Ah be no good wit'choo 'roun', no good fa' nothin'." Leroy thought he was going to have to pee. "Ah gotta go ta tha bathroom," he whined, standing up.*

When he came back, he sat down on the floor in front of her. She frowned and curled her legs up on the sofa. The negligee was short and he could see her knees and thighs. Then he felt funny again and wondered about going back to the bathroom. He tried not to stare. He stole quick glances at her. She grinned then and brushed her black hair back over her shoulder. He was fascinated, wanting to touch her again but afraid. She shifted her weight in the sofa and the negligee fell open. She didn't have anything on underneath. He saw something between those smooth, dark thighs—hair; it was hair. He couldn't take his eyes off it. It looked soft, black, and downy. He had never felt like this before. Now he wanted her to call him and hug him and whisper to him again. Why? He didn't know. His eyes bulged; he strained to see more. She was smiling, and her face, flushed darkly, looked warm. Tiny beads of sweat rose up on her forehead. "Wuz it col' out, honey?" Leroy nodded jerkily, unable to speak, his stomach swimming with near nausea. He gaped at her, pretending to himself that somehow she couldn't see him staring. His stomach felt awful—but good. Oh, he thought, if only she couldn't see him looking. But he couldn't help himself now. He thought of the magazines that he often looked at in the drugstore, and the naked women he saw in them. He felt funny then, too. But that was nothing like this. He had never seen the hair before, and Velma was real-life, full-bodied—and that look on her face. He thought of the light, soft hair which had begun to grow thicker between his own legs. That was where his stomach hurt the most. He still didn't really know what he wanted. Briefly, he thought of throwing himself in her arms, but instead, he pretended to be sleepy, lying down, leaning on his elbow. Now he could see everything, the whole V of soft, black curls between her thighs. He wanted very badly to touch her now. His own thighs felt as if they were burning, and he wanted to go to the bathroom. He began to shiver. "Ya got a col' a' somethin,' honey?" Her voice was unsteady, wavering, and warm. He shook his head very slowly and stared. He didn't care any more if she saw him or not. Suddenly he wanted her to see him stare. Then she moved onto her back saying, "Don'cha feel good, huh, baby?" She raised one gleaming, brown leg up, resting the knee against the back of the sofa, putting her other leg on the floor. Her negligee had fallen completely open. Leroy thought he was going to die, or pee all over himself. He didn't move; his mouth hung open as his eyes gulped in her ample, dark breasts which quivered slightly above her flat stomach—and that hair between her thighs. He felt something wet on his leg and thought he needed to go to the bathroom again. A wonderful, warm, and glowing pain attacked his loins. "C'mere, baby," she sighed huskily. "C'mere and sit wit' Velma, huh? C'mon." He wanted to go on staring, but the urge to be near her was overpowering.

When she hugged him to her breasts, her skin felt hot. Exquisite pain throbbed in his guts. He poked his lips timidly against her breasts. She groaned gently. He was surprised, happy to please her. He did it again. She eased her hand under his sweater and slid it up his chest. Then she sighed and began to knead one of his nipples. He had to pee very badly. He touched one of her nipples with his tongue. "Go 'head," she moaned. "Go 'head an' do that agin. You learnin'. Nat'rul little man, thass all." Then she told him to stand up. He was reluctant, but she urged him gently, and he complied. She began to undress him. She worked slowly, carefully, kissing his cheeks, his nipples, and his mouth. He knew he was going to pee on her, but he couldn't speak. His mouth was open, and there were tears in his eyes. Then she reached down and grasped his straining erection as she slid the other arm behind him and gently, urgently, guided him down to her. When he entered her body, he whined in surprised, ecstatic delight. He knew he wasn't going to have to pee after all.

They made love often after that. Leroy secretly wished that Velma might somehow become his mother, that he could stay with her always. After his family moved, he went back, one day, to visit her.

A tall, white man answered the door. "You're a little young, ain'cha kid." Leroy stared at him. The man had thick, black hair; he was wearing a T-shirt, gray pants, and he was barefooted. His heavy stomach pushed out over his belt. "Ah wanna see Velma," Leroy stammered angrily. "Christ, kid, where would you get that kinda money?" "Who is it?" Velma inquired as she walked up behind the man. She was wearing a sky-blue negligee similar to the one Leroy remembered. "Leroy," she exclaimed. The boy didn't answer; he stood in the hallway, his blue eyes fierce and cold. Velma looked nervously at the man and then back at Leroy. "Baby—Leroy, this is—this is Sergeant—" "Mr. Benson, for crissakes, Velma," the man cut in. He scowled and went back inside the apartment. "C'mon, Velma, get rid of the kid. It's almost six. I gotta go on duty, goddammit." "Yeah, yeah, honey." She looked helplessly at Leroy's face, then slowly started to shut the door. Leroy took a step forward. There were tears in his eyes. "Baby—Leroy, baby, ah cain' talk ta ya right now, see. Uh—ah gotta—be wit'ma company heah. Okay baby?" She closed the door. He never tried to see her again.

Despite his shame and his hatred of whores, Leroy often wondered about his mother. He tried to tell himself that he didn't care about her, but that wasn't true. He longed to know her. But he was ashamed to be white. He was ashamed of the fact that his mother had sold her body to white men—like Velma did. And his white skin was a constant, painful reminder of the bastard circumstances of his birth. He sometimes dreamed that he saw his mother—looking strangely like Velma—*She and a white man were lying in bed naked. He was between her legs and she was holding some money in her hand. He couldn't make out her face and blinked his eyes, trying to see more clearly. When her face came into focus, it looked like Velma's face. She looked black now. Then without knowing why, or being able to prevent it, the scene changed: suddenly, he was in the room with them, and he was spitting on the white man. But he went on making love to his mother. She wrapped her legs around him and told Leroy to stop it. Then Leroy was urinating all over them, only now, his mother was white. Then abruptly, Leroy himself was black and he was between his mother's legs, beating his body savagely, feverishly, against hers. Her skin began to change from white to black to white to black to white.*—Then he was awake and he was crying.

* * *

"Ah wish ah wuz black," Leroy told Luther one night as they left a movie theater.

"Sheet," Luther scoffed, zipping up his jacket against the sharp cold.

"Ah ain' kiddin', man."

"Man, stop bullshittin', fa' crissake, Leroy."

"Ah ain' bullshittin'."

"Man, les' go git us a car."

"It's too cold," Leroy muttered, turning to watch a short, black boy usher a pretty, coffee-colored girl into a taxi. "Sheet, anyways, man, Buzz ain' heah."

"Sheet. Ain' that cold, man. We kin drive tha fuckin' thing. Ah kin—"

"Too icy. Les' git a gal—git some pussy, man."

"Wanna go up Marilyn's?"

"Bitch is fat, man, an' her sister sells pussy."

"You kin fuck Marilyn."

"Sheet—okay."

"Say, Leroy? Why ya say—why ya wanna be—dark, man?"

They stopped to light their cigarettes, standing close together to shield the burning match from the cold wind. Luther lit up and watched the flame flash in Leroy's white face. Three young white girls walked by. They saw Luther looking at them and one of them giggled.

"Why ya say that, Leroy?"

"Huh?"

"Why ya say ya wanna be mo' cullid?"

"Cuz."

"Cuz why, man?"

"Then ah would *look* cullid."

"Sheet!"

Up ahead of them, they saw a white policeman, standing outside a bar. He looked at them idly, then took out a large, red handkerchief and blew his nose. They stopped talking, watching him out of the corner of their eyes as they walked by.

"Leroy, why ya wanna *look* cullid, man? What niggas evah done?"

"Sheet, niggas done evah'thin' anybuddy done, man."

"*Huh?* What? What they done?"
"Lotsa shit."
"*What?*"
"Ah dunno. Theah wuz kingdoms an' lotsa shit, cowboys too."
"Sheet," Luther guffawed loudly, ignoring the people who turned to look back at him. "*You crazy!* Wheah ya heah that shit at?"
"Uncle Richard. He say niggas did all kinda shit, man. Say niggas even fought Indians an'—"
"He fulla shit."
"Why ya say that, Luther? How you know?"
"He fulla shit, Leroy."
"Ah dunno, Lutha. Ah mean, he say niggas wuz in tha army fa' tha North an' that—"
"Huh?"
"Tha Civil War—an' afta, some a' them fought tha Indians."
"Man, now you know thass bullshit. Niggas wuz *slaves,* Leroy! They wuz—couldn't read a' nothin', fa' crissake."
"They run away. Join tha army."
"When, nigga? If they wuz gonna fight, why they let white folks make'em inta slaves?"
"Uncle Richard say evah'buddy wuz a slave."
"Man, yo' uncle's a silly mutha-fucka."
"Fuck you, Lutha, shit."
"Ya evah read 'bout soldiers and slaves?"
"Naw."
"Well, *gawddammit* then, nigga, what'cha mean?"
"Aw, man, ah dunno."
"Ya didn't see no niggas fuckin' wit'tha Indians ta-nite, did ya?"
"Naw."
"When ya evah see niggas fuckin' wit'Indians in tha movies?"
"Ah dunno."
"Well, shit then, Leroy, what'cha talkin' 'bout?"
"Ah dunno, man."
"Sheet."
Luther flipped his cigarette out into the street, his face scowling as

he watched the red glow trail through the dark and die on the ice. "It's cold," he growled.

Leroy didn't answer.

"Seem like it gettin' colder, too. Hey, man—Leroy?"

"Yeah?"

"Les' git us a taxi, man."

"Yeah."

When Luther looked in a mirror, what he saw shamed him. Though he was an extremely handsome boy, even beautiful, in the masculine sense of the term, he knew that he was a nigger, *black-and-ugly*. He tried to deny his shame. Even when he caught himself wishing, in some roundabout way, to be white, or at least, lighter in color, he attempted to persuade himself that he was only wondering what it would be like. One of the reasons why he liked Leroy so much was because of his white skin. Leroy was white, yet black like he was.

Garner had to stay after school. He had expected a scolding, but it hadn't come. Instead, Miss Wagner was asking him questions.

"Why do you sleep in class, Garner?"

"Ah dunno."

"Do you stay up late at night?"

He hesitated, looking down at his desk. Miss Wagner leaned forward in her chair watching him. He looked small in the empty, old room.

"Garner?"

"Yes'm?"

"Come up here, would you please?"

"Yes'm," he answered, climbing reluctantly out of his seat.

He walked slowly to the front of the room and stepped up onto the small platform where her desk was and stood beside her chair. She turned to face him.

"Do you go to bed late?"

"Naw, goes ta bed early."

"Can't you look at me?"

He tried to look at her face but turned away, embarrassed. She smiled gently and reached out to take his hand. He stared down at her soft, white hand holding his and held his arm stiff, afraid to offend her.

"I hope you're not *afraid* of me."

"Naw."

"Maybe you just don't like me," she suggested, pretending to be hurt.

"Naw—ah mean, you okay."

"Maybe you want another teacher," she said mischievously.

"Naw," Garner protested vigorously, "naw, you okay."

He began to shift his feet around nervously, looking at the floor. His eyes fixed on her shiny, black, high-heel shoes. He peeked at her legs then; they looked smooth and pink.

"Well, I'm glad of that, Garner. Do you believe me when I say that I like *you?"* she asked, smiling affectionately.

"Ah guess so. Sometimes."

"Oh, Garner. Only *sometimes?"*

"Naw. Ah mean—sometimes ah don' do good."

"Do you want to do well—better?"

"Yes'm."

"Do you believe me when I say that I want you to do better and that I want to help you?"

"Yes'm."

"Well, I can't do it all by myself, you know. I really *can't.* You have to help a little, too. Are you listening, Garner?"

"Yes'm, Miz Wagna."

"Garner, *please* look at me. Don't you like school at all?"

"Yes'm, ah likes school okay."

"Well, you simply can't do good work here if you don't pay attention in class. Are you listening to me?"

She tried to lift his head to face her, gently touching his face. He let her raise his chin, keeping his eyes down, fastened on her gray skirt.

"Will you try a little harder?"

"Yes'm. Jes' lazy, ah guess."

"You don't *want* to be lazy, do you?"

"Naw. Ah try betta."

She put her arm around his shoulders and cradled his chin on her forefinger. "Garner, is that a promise?" she asked, staring earnestly into his face.

He averted his eyes. She smelled funny. He liked that smell. Her touch was gentle, and he liked it, but his arm was getting tired, and he was embarrassed. He couldn't look at her, either; he wanted to, though. He wanted to stare at her. She sparkled and glowed as the light touched her hair and seemed to soften the cream and pink of her skin. The impact of her closeness moved him profoundly. He looked down at his own small, black hand and wiped it unconsciously against his dungarees.

"Garner, do you promise?"

"Yes'm, Miz Wagna."

"Very well then. I'm glad. Will you help me erase the blackboard?"

"Yes'm," he said eagerly.

He went to work, grinning, happy that she wasn't angry with him anymore and that she liked him again. Tom Ryan, another teacher, came through the door; Terry was with him.

"Miss Wagner, I've a young fella says you won't let his brother go home. Is that right?"

"Well," she laughed, "that's not *exactly* the way I'd put it. How are you, Terry?"

"Okay," he answered, his face, impassive. He watched Garner finishing up with his chore.

"Still at it, huh?" Tom chuckled, picking some lint from the sleeve of his dark overcoat.

"You hush up!"

"All done, Miz Wagna."

"Good, Garner, and thank you. Better get your coat; your brother's waiting for you."

"Yes'm."

"Terry," she began carefully as Garner ran to the cloakroom. "Does Garner stay up late at night?"

"Huh?"

"I asked if Garner stays up late," she repeated, glancing anxiously at Tom, who stood grinning at her.

"Garner sleep jes' much's ah do, ah guess."

"Well, do *you* stay up late at night?"

"Naw. Goes ta bed early, same's Garna."

"Well, I wish you'd try to get him not to sleep here in class. Maybe if you mentioned it to him, he'd try a little harder because you're his big brother."

"Naw, ah ain'."

"What?"

"Ah ain' tha big brotha; ah's his little brotha. Lutha' tha big brotha."

Tom laughed. Barbara gave him a sharp look of disapproval. She bent over to smile at Terry, her hands on her knees. "Well, mention it to him anyway. Okay, Terry?"

"Yes'm," he mumbled, his face still impassive.

The boys left. Tom Ryan watched Barbara slip into her coat and gather up her books, an amused smile on his face.

"Don't say it," she said.

Tom laughed, shaking his dark head as he followed her out of the room.

"You know, Barbara," he began as they walked along the dim old corridor. "You're wastin' your time with that Hawkins kid. Headed for trouble, all of them."

"I'm only trying to communicate something to the boy. And I *don't* believe I was completely unsuccessful either."

"Don't bet on it, darlin'. You know—you should've had his brother. He would've had—"

"Terry?"

"No. Name's Luther. Before your time. A bad kid. Wally Burke told me he caught him fighting again just yesterday Beat a kid up pretty bad. Damn shame. I know the boy, Mike Reardon. They should put that Luther away."

"He can't be all *that* bad."

"Listen, that kid ran an extortion racket right here when he was nine years old! *Protection!* Kids had to pay him their milk money. Well, I stopped that. I'm tellin' ya I wore my stick out on the kid."

"I'm not sure whipping a boy is any help."

"You'll learn, darlin'. You can't spare the rod if you wanna have order. Toughest kid I ever saw, I'm tellin' ya. And Garner's just like him—maybe not as mean yet, but give him time. You know, it's a shame in a way, too. Could've been a whale of an athlete. Run like the devil. You know, Garner even looks like him."

They stepped outside and walked down the steps to the parking lot. "Well, darlin', gotta go. See ya Monday. Take care, hear?"

Barbara nodded soberly, her head almost hidden by the heavy collar of her coat, and walked away.

Terry didn't want to go home. "Man, les' go down tha Boys Club."

"Naw, ol' man Thomas jes' throw us out agin."

"Man, he ain' gonna ketch us. Prob'bly won't even be theah." Terry leaned against a light pole and looked at the cars and trucks passing by in the street.

"Ah'm cold. Goin' home."

"Aw, c'mon, man. Why ya wanna go home? Ain' nothin' ta do. Ma jes' gonna be evil, shoot, man."

"Ah's tired."

"Man, you always tired. Sleepin' alla time. Miz Wagna say she don' wan no mo' that stuff, man."

"She nice lady," Garner mumbled. He kicked the base of the pole Terry was leaning on, chipping some ice loose. His eyes fastened covetously on the new, fur-lined jacket that Terry was wearing. It was a little big, but it looked warm. It was light brown. Terry wore the heavy fur collar up around his ears.

"Theah tha fuzz," Terry muttered.

Garner watched a police wagon pass in the street, "Yeah."

"Well, ah'm goin' down tha Boys Club. You comin'?"

"Naw."

"Sheet, man, *c'mon!* You comin'?"

"Naw. Goin' home."

"Aw, man," Terry grumbled in disgust, scuffing his shoe on the ice.

"Goin' home."

"See ya theah, man."

"See ya," Garner answered and watched him run off down the street.

He ran all the way home, not even stopping to throw snowballs, just loping along easily, despite the snow.

On the kitchen table, he saw two bags of food. Apparently, no one was home. He began to sift through them. Finding a box of cheese crackers, he took it out, wondering whether he should open it; he didn't dare. He put it down and continued searching the bags. There were eggs, bacon, beans, franks, chops, oranges, cereal, milk, jam, and bread. And he was hungry again. His stomach felt queasy. He knew he'd get a licking if he opened anything. Where was his mother? he wondered. Where had all the food come from? Maybe Uncle Charlie had finally come home.

"Whoozat in tha kitchen?" his mother called out.

Garner jumped away from the table. "It's me, Ma."

"What'cha want?"

"Nothin'."

"Well, g'wan outdoors."

She sounded angry, upset. Garner started toward her room.

"G'wan," she screamed then. "G'wan out! Ya heah me?"

He stopped, hesitating. "It's cold out, Ma," he whined.

She opened her door and stepped quickly into the living room, slamming the door behind her. Her hair was in disarray and she held her brown robe loosely around her. Garner stood in the kitchen doorway watching her.

"Ya heah what ah say, boy?"

"Yes'm," he replied, nodding vigorously, and started to back up into the kitchen.

She tried to get her robe closed, cursing bitterly as she walked toward him. Garner continued backing away.

"Gawddamn kids! Git tha hell outta heah! G'wan, g'wan out an' play, boy," she yelled, pushing roughly against his chest and knocking him into the table.

"Ah'm hongry, Ma."

"You always hongry! *Git outta heah!* Go 'head, g'wan! Git a piece a' bread a' somethin'. G'wan."

"Cold out, Ma."

She slapped him hard, sending him reeling along the edge of the table. A bag of food fell over. She hurried to catch the eggs as the crackers and two large boxes of cereal dropped to the floor. Garner's eyes watered as he backed up toward the door. His mother followed him, unrelenting, still howling, "G'wan, *g'wan!* Take a orange an' a piece a' bread a' somethin'! G'wan! Git outta heah!"

She ripped open one of the loaves of bread and shoved two slices toward him, then opened the oranges and gave him one. He held onto the food, watching his mother intently and fearfully as she stepped toward him. Reaching behind him, he opened the door and backed out into the hallway. She kicked the door shut, still cursing.

He didn't want to go outside. There was a short, twisting stairway to his right which led up to the roof. The door at the top of the stairs was locked tight, and it was dark up there, and it wasn't as cold as the outdoors. He could hide there and eat his food. He went up the stairs and sat down near the door. He ate hurriedly, his eyes still watery with tears. He kept peering anxiously around the corner, staring down at his front door. For a while, he could hear his mother arguing with someone, a man. He couldn't understand what was being said. It didn't sound like Uncle Charlie. Pretty soon, the noise stopped. He quickly finished eating and huddled up inside his jacket. Occasionally, he stole a look at the door down below. He started to doze off when the door opened.

Garner peeked cautiously around the corner. He saw a heavy white man step into the hallway and turn to say something to his mother. The man was wearing a black hat and a heavy, fur-collared overcoat. It was Sy Rosenthal. Garner watched him reach out and open up his mother's robe. Sy ran his hands casually over her body. Garner could see his mother's dark skin and Sy's thick white hands on her breasts. He pulled his head back, frightened, and without knowing why he began to cry.

His mother said, "Awright, honey, it's cold out heah."

"Wasn't cold a while ago, was it?" Sy laughed.

"Aw, man, g'wan. Git outta heah. Ya wife gonna wonda wheah ya at."

"Okay, Ella. I'll—uh, come over and collect the rest some other time."

"Yeah, you do that," she offered indifferently. "Ah be heah."

Garner heard the man going down the stairs. He sat stiffly, choking down the sound of his crying. He heard Sy call back up to his mother, "Hey, Ella, when are you people going to clean up the joint a little?"

She went back inside and closed the door. Garner waited a moment, then peeked down at the empty hallway. He listened for sounds of his mother moving around inside the apartment; he couldn't hear anything and sat back again, huddling up against the wall and pulling his jacket tighter.

He sat there for what seemed to him a very long time. Images of Sy and his mother flashed in his mind. Something akin to terror swelled in his stomach. The picture of his mother's naked body and Sy's hands touching her hung in his mind. Then he thought of Uncle Charlie. His yellowish, brown face and half-processed hair began to mingle with the images of Sy and his mother. The pictures blurred and ran together. Uncle Charlie, he thought, would be angry if he had seen Sy and his mother like that. Yes, and there'd be a fight. Suddenly, he saw Miss Wagner's face, then Uncle Charlie's and Sy's and his mother's breasts. Then he heard voices—*"Why do you sleep in class, Garner?"—"Did your mother send some money along to buy it with?"—"Aw, man, g'wan. Ah'm cold. Git outta heah!"—"What's with the money?"—"Do you believe me when I tell you that I like you?"—"Ah tol' ya boy, ah ain'cha daddy!"—"When are you people going to clean up the joint a little?"—"Ma jes' gonna be evil, man."—"Wuzn't sassin'."—"Wake up, Garner! Garner Hawkins, do you hear me?"—"Ah ain'cha daddy, nigga!"—"You're one of the Hawkins kids, ain'cha? Luther's gonna get inta real trouble one of these days."—"Naw!"—"Yeah, I'm keepin' my eye on him."—"You tell your mother there's not going to be any more free food. She doesn't look that good."—"Whoozat in tha kitchen?"—"Cold out, Ma."—"Where's the money?"—"Wake up, Garner!"—"Won't do it no mo'."—"Is that a promise, Garner?"—"Ah try betta."—"Git outta heah! Take a piece a' bread a' somethin'!"—"Tell your mother I'm coming over."*—Garner fell asleep then, hands in his pockets, huddled up on the stairs. He didn't hear the door open. His mother came to the foot of the stairs. He woke with a start when he heard her voice.

"Whoozat up theah? Garna, you up theah?"

"Yes'm."

"Come on down frum theah," she yelled angrily, starting up the stairs. "What'cha doin' up theah, boy?"

"Yes'm, ah'm comin'."

He came down slowly, frightened and ashamed. He hesitated, leaning against the wall as if to hide, looking at his mother. Tears crawled slowly down his cheeks. He kept his hands in his pockets, peering at her. She was dressed now, wearing clean, blue dungarees, slippers, and a man's black sport shirt hanging outside the pants. Her hair was pulled back from her forehead into a tight bun at the back of her head.

"How long ya been up theah?"

Garner turned his face to the wall, not answering.

She glared up at him and spoke again, her voice rising. "You heah me, boy?"

"Yes'm," he whispered.

"Well, how long ya been up theah?"

"Cold out, Ma."

"You come down frum up theah an' git in tha house."

He followed her down the stairs, wiping his eyes with his sleeve, listening to her scolding. They went inside and she slammed the door.

"What fa' ya sittin' up theah?"

"Ah's cold, Ma. Ah's hongry," he mumbled fearfully, looking down at the floor.

She sat down, hurriedly lighting a cigarette. Garner didn't look up. He began to fidget nervously.

"You kids gonna *drive* me crazy, ah sweah! Wheah's Terry?"

"Boys Club."

"Whyn'cha go wit'im? Ya shoulda gone wit' Terry."

"It's cold, Ma. Ain' paid no dues, an' ol' man Thomas don' wan' us in theah."

"Take ya coat off, boy."

He looked up at her then, frightened.

"Ah ain' gonna beat'cha. Git'cha coat off. Ah should, though. Tol' ya ta go 'head out, didn't ah?"

"Yes'm," he answered nervously, removing his coat and hanging it on the door.

"Set down, boy," she sighed wearily.

He did as he was told. She rested her elbow on the table, her head against her palm. She puffed her cigarette fitfully, staring at him.

"Wanna glass a' milk an' some bread an' jam?"

"Yes'm, Ma," Garner croaked as he nodded his head.

"Git a knife an' a glass frum tha sink."

She fixed his food, stealing glances at him through the smoke of her cigarette rising up from the ashtray. He had stopped crying. His mouth, bulging with food, worked furiously. She continued to watch him closely. She knew that he must have seen Sy in the hallway. What could he have thought, she wondered. What could he be thinking right now? And what could she tell him? What did one say to an eight-year-old boy? What had she told Luther—*so many times*—and Terry? She tried to remember. Had Garner any idea what she had done? If he did, did he also know why?

Garner was devouring his food voraciously. She peeked at his face, seeing the streaks left by his tears. Yes, she thought, he had been hurt. He knew something was wrong. *God.* And the welfare check wasn't due for two more weeks. She sighed and drew heavily on the cigarette. She continued to watch her son eat. She had to tell him *something!* She didn't want him to say anything to Charlie. He'd start another fight. He might even walk out on her again, especially if he had any money left. She sighed heavily. Garner glanced up, giving her a puzzled look, his mouth full of bread and jam.

Suddenly, she wanted to cry. No, Garner didn't really understand her relationship with Charlie. She wished that Charlie didn't have to remind him that he wasn't his father. Why couldn't he treat the boy more kindly? What did it hurt?

She was also afraid that Charlie might walk out for good. She remembered her husband, Ben. He had left her several times. The first was right after Luther was born. Then he had come home after a few months. But he left her again. She waited for months; a year went by, then two, then she decided he wasn't coming back. Then she had met Malcomb. He was married and had only been able to visit her occasionally. She had still been lonely, and started going out to the local bars, leaving little Luther alone, hoping he wouldn't wake up, then coming home with any man she could find. That had gone on for almost two years—*It was a warm night. It was late and the bar was closing. The place had been crowded, but she only saw a few single men, and they were drunk, or too old. She was still alone when she stepped out onto the sidewalk. She stopped on the corner under the street light, digging in her purse for a cigarette. She didn't have any. There was no money in it either. She scowled and started walking home. She was wearing her only good dress, one that Ben had bought her; it was close-fitting black jersey. Her hair hung down her back as she walked, head down, idly swinging her purse. Some men and women hurried by, black people, laughing and enjoying themselves. Out in the street a sleek, yellow Cadillac crawled slowly by her. She saw a white man behind the wheel. He honked the horn. She quickly looked away and started walking faster. The Caddy drove off. Then she saw the cruiser. It pulled up ahead of her and stopped. There were two white policemen in it. The driver was a young, hard-faced man, who sat watching her indifferently while the other one got out of the car. He was big, about forty years old. He walked up onto the sidewalk and stood there watching her come toward him. Ella walked closer to the buildings and quickened her pace. "Hold it right there, sister." "What?" she asked, watching him swagger over to her.*

The other policeman, still in the car, called out to his partner, "Leave it go, Jack. C'mon, let's get going." "Shut your mouth," he snapped back. The big cop stopped in front of her, hands on hips. His face was shadowy and dim under the visor of his cap. "What're you doin' down here, girl?" "What'cha mean? Goin' home, thass all." "I'll bet. What's ya name?" "Hawkins." "Hawkins what?" he growled. "What's ya first name?" "Ella. Ella Hawkins," she stammered indignantly. "Ella, huh? Ya got any identification on ya, Ella?" She opened her purse and fished around inside. The policeman snatched it out of her hand. She took a step back from him, watching him carefully. "Jack," the other officer yelled, "if she's one of Billy Ray's girls, you're gonna get your arse in a sling. Now, c'mon!" "Why don't you take a flyin'— are you workin' for Billy Ray, sister?" "Naw! Naw ah ain' workin' fa' nobuddy. Now you gimme back ma bag. Ah gotta—" "That's what I figured. Freelancin', huh?" "What? What'cha mean? Listen ah ain' workin' fa' nobuddy! Ah ain' hustlin', mister! What'cha think? Ah ain' no who'e!" "Yeah, sure, girl. You stay put right there." He walked over to a doorway, still holding her purse and looked through a window in the door. "Come over here," he ordered. "Look, mister, ah ain' no who'e now." "Yeah, sure, listen, sister, get over here and shut up, or I'll run you down to the vice squad. Christ, you ain't even got no I.D. Get over here."

He took her into a dark hallway, very much like the one in the building where she lived, and made her stand against the wall. "Sister, you got two choices. I run you in for solicitin' and vagrancy, or ya lift up ya dress." Ella cringed against the wall in terror. "Naw, naw. Ya leave me be now. Ah ain' no who'e. Leave me be." She was crying now, her voice breaking into sobs. "Stop the crap, nigger! Make up ya mind! Which is it gonna be?" "Please, mister, ah gotta baby home! Ah cain' be goin' nowheahs, please!" "Make up ya mind, goddammit!" Ella's hands reached slowly down to the hem of her dress. She held her head down. "Please, mister, ah ain' no who'e! Ah ain'! Leave me be!" "Come on, c'mon, stop the bullcrap, will ya?" he rasped. She pulled up her dress. "Yeah, nigger, you got a body on ya." He reached out and pulled her panties down, running his free hand up into her crotch. "Turn around and bend over," he hissed in a husky whisper. "This ain't gonna take but a minute." "Naw!" "What?" "Naw, mister! Ah ain' no who'e! Ah ain' gonna let'cha! Ah don' wan'cha! Ah ain' no who'e!" She put her dress down and started pulling up her panties. "Ah ain' no who'e," she repeated. "Ah ain' no—" His big fist smashed into her mouth, snapping her head back hard against the wall. He hit her in the belly, then in the face again, splitting her mouth open. She slid along the wall, holding her stomach, coughing and spitting blood. She took another blow on the back of the head. Then she couldn't see anymore; she fell slipping into a dark void.—Ella looked up at Garner and shook her head. Her face had been a mess after that and she had stayed home.

Malcomb left as soon as he discovered she was pregnant. Without warning, he simply stopped coming—*like Ben.* A few months after Malcomb left, Terry was born—*was he Terry's father?* Well, it didn't matter; Terry's name was Hawkins, too. After Terry was born she had remained at home, seldom going anywhere.

Looking at Garner now, she remembered the last time Ben had come home, eight years ago. After all that time she had still loved him—loved him now. Why hadn't he been able to see that? Ella sighed and put out her cigarette. *Big, black Ben.* He was a man—if only he had stayed. She was willing to work. Sooner or later he would have found something—some kind of work. Abruptly she thought of Ben's powerful body. His presence in her mind was almost overwhelming. Her pulse quickened. *Why?* Why her? Was having the man she loved too much to ask? And—*Ben had loved her. Why else had he kept coming back?* He had even understood about Terry. But just before Garner was born he left again. *Where was he now?* She folded her arms on the table and rested her head on them.

She still belonged to Ben, she knew. If he would come back—if by some miracle, she could have him again, she would welcome him home. But he wouldn't be back anymore. No. Now there was Charlie. And tomorrow, well, tomorrow she could only hope there'd be someone else. Finally, she knew, there wouldn't be anyone.

Ella sat up, fixing her eyes on Garner. She had to tell him *something.*

Her voice was soft. "Garna, is ya still hongry?"
"Yes'm."
"Kin ya make it till supper?"
"Yes'm, ah guess so."
"Garna?"
"Yes'm."
"Do ya love ya momma?" She hesitated then, wary and fearful of his reply. "Baby—ah mean, do ya *feel* fa' ya momma? Do ya know what ah'm tryin' ta ask ya, honey?"
He was unsure. "Yes'm. Yes'm, Momma."
She grasped his hands in hers, and he started to cry.
"C'mere ta ya momma, Garna," she begged, pulling on his hands as he stood up to walk around the table. She drew him to her and put her arms around him. "Gawd knows ah love ya, boy. Ya *knows* that, don'cha?"
He nodded vigorously, "Ah loves you too, Momma."
"Y'ain' mad at ya momma, then?"
"Naw! Ah loves you. Ah loves ya, Momma."
Ella held him close, and they were quiet for a moment. He put his arms around her neck. "Ah don' like Sy, Momma! Ah don' like him. Ah don'—"
"Ah don' like him, neither, baby! Garna, ah don' like him, neither. But—sometimes—" She felt tears coming now and hesitated. "Sometimes—ah needs—*he'p,* an'—ah mean, ah *gotta git it,* baby. Ya see? Frum wheahevah ah kin—an' don' matta frum who ya git it. Do ya unda'stan', Garna? Do ya? Are ya list'nin' ta what ah say?"
"Momma?"
"Yeah, baby?"
"Momma," Garner bawled. "Why Sy—ah mean, how come he touch ya like he done?"
Ella's breath nearly stopped. Fiercely, she clutched the boy against her, afraid to speak or look into his face. Her body jerked and shook with the force of her crying as she tried to keep from screaming. Garner's eyes slammed desperately around the kitchen. He was terrified, and he was ashamed. He had never said anything that made his

mother cry before. He remembered that sometimes Uncle Charlie made her cry.

"Don' cry, Momma! Please don'. Don' cry."

Ella tried to say something, but her voice broke and caught in her throat. God, she thought. How many times had she hurt her children like this? What could they think of her?

"Please don', Momma! Please don' cry! Ah's sorry. Ah *do* love ya, Momma! Please don' cry! Ah'm sorry."

She thought of Luther and his scorn for the various "uncles" in his life. And what about Terry? It was always difficult to figure out what he was thinking.

She seldom allowed her thoughts to dwell upon these things. She tried to blot out the reality of what she was doing. When she did think about them, she felt a kind of painful anxiety which she could not explain, not even to herself. Her stomach, her mind, her whole being, seemed to be caught up in a state of complete desperation. The pain which she felt then was almost unbearable. Her insides convulsed violently, and her mind was rent with near terror. The pain was erratic and uneven. It wouldn't stop, wouldn't peak, or subside, or increase. It was nightmarish, as if she were falling, plunging, putting out her hands as she tried to break her fall and finding nothing there. Unknown, unexplainable, and unspeakable horrors seemed to lurk everywhere, within, and without her being. The pain of her terror threatened to consume her; she tried to shut it out. But now, with her youngest son crying in her arms, his naive accusations, her thoughts were muddled and she was thrown into a storm of confusion. The pain cut deeply into her again, surging from the depths of her most terrible thoughts, and it was more frightening and more horrible. She trembled.

She held him away from her, speaking carefully, not trusting her voice, "Please, Garna, baby. Please, baby, will ya he'p ya momma, huh? Will ya he'p me?"

She waited momentarily, watching him jerk his head up and down. He wanted terribly to right whatever wrong he had done, to help his mother, to please her, and to stop her crying.

He didn't look at her though but stared down at her dungarees as she held his shoulders and spoke to him again. "Kin ya keep a secret fa' ya momma, huh? Kin ya—keep momma's secret?"

"Yes'm, Momma, ah kin. Ah kin keep a secret. Ah won't tell nothin'. Ah won't tell nobuddy nothin', Momma. Ah won't tell Charlie nothin', neither."

Ella kissed his hands and looked at him. "Bless ya, baby. Gawd bless ya," she croaked, burying her head on his shoulders as she pulled him to her again and hugged him. "Gawd bless ma baby. Gawd-a-mighty bless ya, boy."

"Ah loves ya, Momma," he whined as she sat back and wiped at her tears.

"Ah knows ya do, baby. Ah knows. Gawd-a-mighty, ah knows."

Supper was good that night. Terry and Garner devoured their food eagerly. They had bread and butter with fried pork chops and beans. They played while they ate, laughing at everything, chomping away all the while. Luther hadn't come home yet, and they didn't miss him. After supper, they stayed up late, watching television while their mother cleaned up the dishes in the kitchen.

When she was through, Ella came into the living room to sit with Garner and Terry. She wished Charlie would come home. She wondered where he was. He usually gambled when he had money but there were women too. She couldn't be sure where he was.

"Terry, wheah wuz that party Uncle Charlie went to befo'?"

"Ain' a party. It's a gamblin' place."

"Well, wheah's it at?"

"Corna Mass. an' C'lumbus."

"Ya sho'?"

"Yeah, Garna know wheah. He went wit' me, huh, Garna?"

"Don' rememba," Garner answered quickly.

Terry looked at his brother curiously. "What'cha mean, man? Don'cha rememba, Garna? Corna C'lumbus an' Mass."

"Don' rememba."

"Sho' ya do."

"Well," Ella interrupted, "it don' matta, prob'bly ain' theah anyways."

Garner heaved a sigh of relief. He recalled the place very well—*It was a cold night, no wind, only bitter cold. Some of the street lights were out. The streets were still busy with people and cars because it was fairly early. There was a lot of noise: horns honking, people chattering and laughing loudly, music from the bars and restaurants. And there were women in the doorways. Terry pointed them out. "See them, man. They who'es." "Huh?" "They who'es, man. Who'es! Sells pussy. Men pays 'em ta let'em fool wit'em." "What fa'?" Garner asked. His brother laughed, "Man, you sho' dumb. Don'cha know nothin'. Men pays'em, white cats. Then they takes off alla they clothes. Then they lays down an' them cats fool wit'em." "Ya mean they's nekkid?" Garner asked incredulously.*—He glanced up at his mother, thinking of her and Sy in the hallway, then looked back at the T.V.—*"Alla they clothes," Terry reemphasized. Garner thought it over, muttering to himself, "Alla they clothes? Naw. Don' b'lieve ya." Terry laughed again, "Man, you sho' dumb. Don' know nothin'. Ah knows what ah'm talkin' 'bout." "Naw, you lyin'." "Ain' lyin' ta ya, man. Look, see them big cars?" Garner's eyes followed Terry's finger. "Yeah, ah sees'em. So what?" "Ya see how slow they goin'?" "Yeah." "See'em stoppin'—theah, like that one ovah theah, see?" "Ah still don' b'lieve ya." Garner stood firm. "Man, you sho' dumb. Looka that now. See that? That lady goin' ovah ta talk ta that white cat in tha car. Theah now, ya see? Now ya b'lieve me?" Garner watched, without replying. "Do ya b'lieve me now?" Terry persisted. "How ya know?" Garner asked then. "Who tol' ya?" "Don' matta who tol' me, man. Ah knows, thass all. Ah seen'em befo', lotsa times.*
—Garner thought of Sy and his mother again—*Terry marched along triumphantly, still holding his brother's hand. "Theah tha fuzz," Garner whispered. "Sheet," Terry scoffed. "So what?" "Ain' they gonna say nothin'?" Garner asked. "Hell naw, nigga. Man, you dumb, thass all." Garner decided not to ask any more silly questions.*

"This the place," Terry announced, stopping suddenly. They were standing in front of an old apartment house. Garner looked around cautiously. "Wish Lutha wuz heah." "Man," Terry snorted. "What'cha skeered fa'?" "Ah ain' skeered." "Sheet, man, ain' nothin' ta be skeered 'bout." "Ah wanna go home," Garner whined. "Prob'bly he

ain' heah anyways." "S'pose he ain' heah, Terry? We could tell Ma we wuz heah an' couldn't find 'im. We could tell Ma he ain' heah." "Aw, man, c'mon," Terry said, starting down the icy steps. "We gotta go down theah?" Garner whined. "It's dark down theah, Terry." "Nigga, thass wheah tha place at. Now, c'mon."

A door opened at the foot of the steps and a man staggered out as a burst of noise and yellow light ripped into the dark. The door slammed shut, and the man, his overcoat half off, cursed as he slipped on the ice and fell. Terry backed up to the top of the steps. Garner pulled on Terry's arm. "C'mon, Terry! Maybe Lutha be home now, an' he kin come git Uncle Charlie! Ma kin send Lutha! C'mon, Terry!" Terry was staring at the man as he rolled over on all fours and tried to stand up slipping again and again, staring stupidly at Terry and Garner. "What—what's happ'nin'?" he mumbled. The boys didn't respond. "Gimme—thass ma money—got two pair. Ah got two pair, man. Thass—got ta be bes' hand. See—thass got—got ta be bes' hand. Gimme ma money, man—" His voice trailed off.

They were met at the door by a huge black man, hulking in the doorway. Beyond him they could see a crowd of people. There was a great deal of noise, laughter, and loud music. "What'cha want?" the big man demanded. "Uncle Charlie," Terry stammered. "Charlie who?" The boys gaped up at the man, riveted by the thick, ugly scar on his face which cut an oblique, uneven line from nose to jaw. Terry spoke fearfully. "It's our Uncle Charlie." "Charlie who, boy?" "Jes' Charlie," Terry blurted. Someone in the room yelled to the man to shut the door. "You kids g'wan home." He started to shut the door. Garner yelled, "Hawkins!" The man hesitated. "Who?" "Hawkins, Charlie Hawkins." "Don' know no Charlie Hawkins." "He's our fatha," Garner offered nervously, "Daddy Charlie." The man opened the door. "Ya daddy?" The boys nodded energetically. "Ya sho' his name's Hawkins?" Terry and Garner looked at each other helplessly then and he watched them, shaking his head. "C'mon in heah a minnit."

The room they entered was full of people. Thick, bluish-gray cigarette smoke hung in the dim light. The smoke stung their eyes, and they could smell liquor. A few couples were dancing, others stood at the bar. The men were all well dressed, apparently well-to-do. Garner had never seen so many pretty black women in his life, well turned out in expensive clothes. He saw tall, slender black girls, buxom browns and yellows, copper-colored girls and fair-skinned ones. He and Terry stood in the doorway, uncertain, uneasy, fascinated. Everyone appeared to be having a wonderful time, and they looked rich, like people in the movies. Some of the crowd watched the boys curiously, and with amusement on their faces. The man who had let them in motioned for them to follow him. "C'mon," he told them. "We'll take a look out back."

They followed him through the happy melee. Garner saw men with shiny black, straight hair. He whispered to his brother, "Hey, Terry, them cats got good hair, man." "S'a process, stupid," Terry answered in his all-knowing tone. "Ya git that at tha barba's." Garner nodded. The women smiled and someone yelled, "Hey, Willi, what'cha got theah?" and "Send them fellas ovah ta tha bar, Willi," and "Hey, man, did that gal finally catch up with ya?" Willi trudged through the crowd, smiling and waving them off.

The back room was set up for gambling, mainly for poker. There were three tables, all busy with cards and money. The room swarmed with players and people waiting to play. Willi asked, "Ya see'im?" The two boys looked around. A dark-skinned, nattily dressed young man came over to them. He had a wad of money in one hand and a cigar in the other. The boys' eyes bulged. The man had long, thick, shiny, black hair, processed like new with a pompadour in front. His clothes were expertly tailored and neat. "What's goin' on, Willi?" he asked. "Kids lookin' fa' they Uncle Charlie a' somethin'. Say he's they daddy, but they don' know his name fa' sho'." The younger man nodded thoughtfully. "Okay, baby," Willi asked again, "how 'bout it kids? He heah?"

Terry exclaimed, "Ovah theah!" He pointed across the room at the table in the corner. "Aw, ya mean Charlie Williams," Willi confirmed. The boys looked at each other, bewildered. "Yeah," Terry said nodding, "thass him." They walked slowly behind Willi.

He sat at the table, his fist full of money. A white woman in a black dress leaned against him, her arm draped casually over his shoulder. She was a big redhead, buxom, with a figure that had once been very good, but which was now beginning to show the effects of too much night life. She watched them come over, sipping her drink, unconcerned. Garner banged his brother with an elbow. "Whoozat wit' Uncle Charlie, Terry?" "Be quiet, man, ah don' know." "Ma gonna be mad," Garner went on. Terry wagged his head slowly up and down in agreement.

Charlie was a small man with yellow coloring. He had a two-day growth of beard. His hair was oily, half straight, half kinky, an old unkept process. He was wearing the greasy work clothes he wore in the junkyard. He gave no sign that he recognized the boys. "Ya know these kids, Charlie?" Charlie looked up at the man, his eyes half closed. "Wha'say, Willi? What's—what's happ'nin', baby?" "C'mon, Charlie. These yo' kids heah?" Charlie gave him a vacant smile. Some of the players and other people turned to see what was going on. The white woman smiled at the boys and laughed softly. They immediately averted their eyes. "What'cha say, Willi?" Charlie inquired. "Aw, c'mon now, man. Stop tha shit. These kids say you they daddy." Charlie smiled and buried his head against the woman's stomach, wrapping both arms around her. He looked up at her, grinning stupidly, and began to laugh. "Hell, naw, man. Ain' got no kids. Ah ain' got no kids, is ah Mary?" "I'm gonna get another drink," she told him. "Ya want one, baby?" "Yeah. Yeah, sweet thing, bring me one, too." She disengaged herself, picked up his glass, and went out to the bar. The boys watched her go.

Willi shook his head. "Come on, kids. You might's well go on home. Y'ain' got no daddy heah, an' thass fa' sho'." "He's our daddy, Uncle Charlie," Garner whined. Charlie's face took on an indignant expression. "Thass a gawddamn lie," he declared indignantly, pointing at Garner. "Ah ain'cha fuckin' daddy, nigga! How many times ah gotta tell ya? Ah ain'cha fuckin' black-ass daddy, sheet!" Garner stared at the man's finger. "Sheet, nigga, ain' no way in hell could ah fuck up an' put out nothin' black as you! Ain' nevah gonna git nothin' that black outta no bitch ah'm fuckin'!" The room suddenly became very quiet. Charlie threw his head back and laughed. Some of the men in the room smiled at each other uncomfortably. Garner dropped his eyes in shameful terror. "Sheet," Charlie continued. "Ain' thatta bitch? Ain' thatta bitch, Terry?" The boy looked away, his face blank, then he peeked at Garner and back to Charlie. "Ma say fa' ya ta come home," he almost whispered. Charlie scoffed, "Fuck that black bitch, sheet!" Willi cut in, "Awright now, man. Take it light. They only jes' kids, afta all, man." Charlie growled, "Fuck'em, an' you too, nigga! Sheet, they ain' ma kids! Ah got me a pretty white who'e ta buy ma likka. Yeah, man, ah gotta white bitch. Don' need no black-ass nigga woman ta fuck, sheet. Got me a white gal; ah'm good as any man, sheet. Don' need ta fuck no black woman. Got me a white gal now." He shook his head with gleeful, howling laughter.

Garner tugged on his brother's arm, his eyes hot with tears. "Les' go, man! Ah wanna go home!" "Man, ah'm gonna hafta put'cha out if ya keep on," Willi said. Charlie lurched angrily to his feet, stumbling against the table, sending cards, money, and glasses flying. "Gawd-damn," a heavy, black man bawled angrily, mopping off his suitcoat as he jerked to his feet, "git that nigga outta heah, fa' crissakes!" "Yeah," another man said, "send tha nigga an' his white who'e on tha fuck outta heah, Willi! Ah come ta gamble. Fuck all this heah bull-shit. Ah don' like no nigga ta fuck wit' ma money. Ah'm gamblin', shit. Git that black som'bitch outta heah."

Terry and Garner jumped out of the way as Willi grabbed Charlie and carried him out. Charlie struggled frantically, but his efforts were futile. He became hysterical, yelling at the top of his voice, his bearded, dirty face contorted with rage, "Lemme go! Lemme go, nigga!" He glared furiously at Garner, howling his outrage. "Ah ain'cha mutha-fuckin' daddy, gawddammit! Lemme go! Lemme go"—Garner tried to refocus his eyes on the T.V. screen. He remembered that Charlie hadn't come home for two weeks after that. He heard his mother talking to him and turned quickly.

"Boy, what'cha so dreamy 'bout?"

"Nothin', Ma."

"Don'cha heah me talkin' ta ya?"

"Yes'm."

"Well, whyn'cha answer then?"

"Yes'm."

"What?"

"Yes'm, Ma. Ah heah ya."

"Ya don' act like it," she scolded and tightened the bun in her hair.

Garner hesitated momentarily, wondering why she wanted to talk to him and started to turn back to the television set. He looked at his brother.

His mother spoke again, "C'mon. S'late. Y'all git on ta bed. You too, Terry. That Lutha's stayed out agin. Ah'm gonna beat'im good this time."

The two boys stood up reluctantly with woeful expressions of defeat.

"Ma?" Garner moaned.

"What'cha want?"

"Kin we see tha movie, Ma. Huh? Please kin we?"

"Yeah. Please, Ma?"

Ella groaned in resignation, "Ah s'pose so. What's the use? Go 'head. Ah'm gonna fix that Lutha this time, ah sweah. Gittin' bad's Charlie. Stayin' out alla time."

Terry and Garner sat down and began to elbow each other in the ribs, grinning happily, oblivious now to her voice.

Ella put her head back against her chair, sighing wearily. She was tired. She was often tired these days. But most of all, she was lonely. She wondered how long Charlie would be away this time. Probably until he ran out of money. She sighed again, listening to the wind outside. She could feel it getting colder as the temperature dropped. Idly, she fingered her shirt, thinking of Ben, remembering another time, Ben's hard body, sun, grass, the sweet smell of country air. Her eyes watered as she wished for those lost days of her young girlhood. What had become of all her pretty dreams—girl dreams? God almighty, *where was Ben now?* No longer a young girl, there weren't any more dreams. She wiped her eyes. The wind bawled fretfully outside, and it was cold.

BOOK

TIMILTY Junior High School sits high above much of the city, a sand-colored mass of bricks and mortar shaped like a huge square with one side missing. Garner leaned against the fence behind the school and looked through the flimsy, almost colorless, blue-white haze of early March at the city sprawling below. He was waiting for Terry, and he was nervous. This was a big day. He wished his brother would hurry. He had had too much time to think, to worry, time to wonder if he was afraid.

"Hey, Garna?"

He turned away from the fence and flicked some dirt from the pattern of X's pressed into his khaki jacket. "Yeah, man. Wheah tha fuck ya been, fa' crissakes?"

Terry ran over to him, his bright, orange face beaming. "Baby, ah got twenny-seven dollas heah. Ya kick Russo's ass an' we kin split *all* this change, man."

Garner stared uncertainly at the fistful of bills. "Russo gonna be tough, man. He—older'n me, man."

"Look, man? Sheet—ah'm tellin' ya, ah *know* ya kin kick 'is ass, man."

Garner turned back to the fence. "He big, Terry."

Terry fingered the money, frowning. "Man, fuck that white boy, gawddamn. He only a yeah older. Sheet, you kin kick that white boy's ass."

Garner didn't answer.

"Look, Garner—man, if ya whip this som'bitch, ya gonna be boss man, baby."

"Ah should fight Ellis."

Terry made an impatient gesture, angrily brandishing the money. "Man, mutha-fuck Ellis. That skinny nigga ain' shit. Fa' crissakes, ya awreddy got half tha seventh grade, man. Ya whip this paddy boy, an' ya automatic'lly git tha rest—an' ya git eight' grade 'long wit'it."

"Sheet. Russo ain' nevah been whipped, man. Ah could git eight' grade nex' yeah."

"Gawddamn," Terry protested through his teeth, "ya talkin' like this fuckin' gray boy could even whip tha Cross, fa' crissake! Ain'cha got no ambition? Ah tol' ya—Look, nex' yeah ya kin run tha whole fuckin' school, man. All tha protection gonna be yours. An' ya gonna be gittin' all that bread fa' 'notha' whole yeah too. Nigga, if ya skeered a' Russo—gawddammit, ah give this fuckin' bread back, thass all. Fuck it!"

"Ah ain' skeered!"

"Sheet!"

"Ah ain' skeered a' no fuckin' white boy, nigga," Garner said, scowling.

He knew Terry was right. There was a lot at stake. If he could lick Russo, he'd be on top. He leaned against the fence, smiling slightly as he thought about it. Luther was the only other boy he knew of who had taken over the protection racket on a schoolwide basis when he was in the eighth grade. And Luther had been kept back a year. Yes, he thought, when the ninth-graders leave, he'd be head man. He glanced at Terry; in another year he was going to quit school just as Luther had. Garner could be top dog for two years.

Terry took Garner's arm, pulling him along. "C'mon. We gotta git down theah. Russo'n evah'buddy gonna be down tha alley awreddy."

"Theah tha Cross," Garner muttered, pointing up ahead of them as they walked toward the street.

Terry looked at the tall, yellow-skinned youth. "Yeah. He hard, baby."

Garner stopped on the sidewalk just outside the entrance to the school, hesitating as he watched the Cross swagger along. He glanced at Terry, then out at the street as a big trailer-truck roared by them. A police cruiser followed it. Garner scowled.

"C'mon, Garna, we gotta git tha fuck down theah. Tha Cross headed down theah now. All tha hard studs gonna be theah. Gonna be wond'rin' wheah we at."

Garner followed him down the street, thinking about the fight. His blood was beginning to heat up. He felt quick and ready—*hard. Bobby Russo,* he thought, the only white boy in the school who collected protection money, a *tough* wop. Well, Garner would change that. "Hey, man," he yelled, catching up with Terry. "How much ya think Russo been payin' tha Cross?"

"Same's us, man. Half. An' nex' yeah *you* gonna git it."

"Yeah." Garner was grinning. "Ah'm gonna be bad. All these paddy boys gonna heah ma shit an' do like ah tell'em."

"Shit yeah, baby. Niggas too."

"Them paddies don' like niggas runnin' evah'thin' alla time."

"Fuck'em, man. Numbers don' mean nothin'. They got lotsa bodies, but they ain' hard. Ya gotta be hard if ya wanna be top."

"Russo hard, man," Garner said matter-of-factly. "A evil som'-bitch—fa' white boy."

"Yeah," Terry conceded. "But shit, he ain'—Well, jes' don'choo fuck up an' lose tha fight, fa' crissake. Lutha an' evah'buddy gonna be watchin'. Buzz'n Leroy an' all them cats, man."

"Don' worry 'bout it. Ah know what's happ'nin'."

"Shit, man, you lose an' ain' nobuddy gonna say yo' name fa' million billion yeahs. *A white boy*—hell naw, man!" Terry smiled and shook his head as he thought about what he had just said. "A white boy—*Jee-yee-sus!*" He paused, glancing quickly at Garner. "White boy? Naw, man, evah'buddy think you wuzn't nothin' at all. Jes' well shoot'cha'se'f."

Garner nodded thoughtfully. They turned a corner and went into an alley. There was a large crowd of kids up ahead of them near the fence where the narrow way widened behind the old buildings and opened up into a small, enclosed yard. Many fights were held there, especially "official" ones, like this. Garner could see Bobby Russo, a big boy, powerfully built and tall. His skin was dark olive and his black hair thick and shiny. There were also a lot of girls there; they outnumbered the boys. The black kids were all standing together on one side of the little yard, and the whites stood on the other.

Garner's stomach began to heave and turn. "Man," he mumbled, "thass a big stud."

"Sheet. Ain' hardly no bigger'n you. Anyways, he ain' no bigger'n tha last time ya seen'im, shit."

Garner's heart was racing now. His skin felt as though he was being pricked with a thousand needles all at once. He saw Russo eyeing him furtively. There was a cocky smile stamped across his dark, aquiline features. Garner met his eyes briefly, then looked away at the dirty brick walls and the piles of rubbish and debris which marked his approach. He tried hard to appear nonchalant. He licked his lips and looked at Russo again, trying to stare him down. *It's coming right at you, white folks.* Russo averted his eyes, then stared back at him. Garner shouldered his way in front of Terry and swaggered into the ring of kids.

Finally, as if by mutual consent, he and Russo stopped eyeballing one another, pretending to busy themselves with some kind of prefight ritual. Garner felt himself being jostled, backslapped, and pummeled. Laughing faces swirled around him. He saw Luther standing with Buzz and Leroy. They were all dressed up, wearing flashy suits and overcoats. The Cross stood talking with them. They laughed and looked at Garner, nodding their heads in a casual greeting. Garner forced a weak smile. Someone clapped him on the shoulder as he removed his jacket. He heard somebody else call his name, but somehow, he was only aware of Russo. Everyone else seemed to be apart—*out there*. The only thing he could feel was the immediate, desperate urgency of himself and Bobby Russo, alone, opposed, and *hard*. Garner looked at the boy. He had taken his coat off, exposing big shoulders under a gray sweatshirt. His black pants were tight, showing the bulge of his thighs. Garner, stripped down to his white T-shirt, was black, muscular, and lithe, unusually broad in the shoulders, with slim hips, like Luther.

They faced each other, fists up high, circling carefully. Garner was tight, nervous, moving stiffly. He snapped off a quick left, but Russo slipped under it and hit him in the belly. Garner swung angrily then, and Russo hit him in the mouth and skipped away. Garner went after him, boring in fast. Russo held him off with two quick lefts. Garner cursed and kept coming. But Russo avoided him, circling away, boxing skillfully, keeping him off balance and forcing him into mistakes. He rained blows on Garner's face and body almost at will, his fists hard and quick, bruising and cutting as they struck. Garner tried to keep from lunging so much, maneuvering, trying to land a solid punch. He saw Russo cock his right hand; he saw him throw it and moved forward quickly to get inside of the blow. As he stepped in, cocking his own right, he hesitated; in a brief instant, he knew that Russo had fooled him again. He was, again, off balance, moving the wrong way. A sharp, chilling shiver of fear cut into him. In that fleeting split second that was really no time at all, he consciously tried to direct his body to react to remove him from danger. But he couldn't move. He was helplessly off balance. Russo hurt him then.

The blow came from the other side, a very hard left that hooked in viciously, landing between his eyes, blinding him momentarily as his body gyrated grotesquely in a belated effort to avoid it. Another punch caught him flush in the mouth. The taste of blood filtered through a surge of intense pain as his teeth cut into his tongue and the inside of his mouth. And Russo kept on coming, relentless, boxing beautifully. He snapped Garner's head back, bloodying his nose with a straight left. Garner reeled, clumsily trying to avoid the blows. Russo threw his punches harder now, straight, bringing them right from the shoulder. Garner had never been in a fight like this one. He had never been hurt like this either. He was confused and dazed. Russo was too good. Garner couldn't get started. He ached all over, and he was beginning to feel sick. And Russo just kept on bringing it to him.

Terry knew, as he watched, that he had overmatched Garner this time. He fingered the money in his pocket and fidgeted nervously. Cursing, he stared through the blur of fighting boys at the crowd of white kids who were yelling and screaming, cheering Russo on. "How you hit'im, Bobby, baby!" "Keep it up, Bobby!" "C'mon, kid!" He looked helplessly at Luther who was howling epithets at Garner, "Ya stupid mutha-fucka, ya stupid bastid, c'mon!"

Buzz stamped his foot and pounded his fist in his hand in frustrated anger.

Luther yelled frantically, "Don'choo lose, gawddammit! Don'choo let that boy whip ya, ya som'bitch! Hit'im! Hit'im, gawddammit! Don' let'im whip ya ass. C'mon! C'mon, hit'im back." He wanted to step in and tear into Russo himself. But the rules were strict: no interference, no dirty fighting, and no ganging up on any one boy. The fight would go on until one of the boys quit. There were no rounds. He looked at Leroy, wondering why he wasn't saying anything.

Leroy's face was white with anger, tight and grim. He stood with his fists clenched at his sides. He didn't speak, but his guts churned with fierce rage.

As he watched the fight, Luther felt himself fighting in Garner's place. His eyes began to water. His breath came faster and faster. *"Don'choo lose,"* he bawled. "Don'choo lose, mutha-fucka! Whip'is ass, gawddammit! C'mon, git that mutha-fucka!"

Although neither boy could knock the other off his feet, they could punish and hurt. And Russo continued to give Garner an awful beating. Garner was badly hurt now, backing away along the wire fence, knocking over an ash can, lashing out blindly and feebly, crying, spitting up the blood he didn't swallow. One of his wild punches caught Russo high on the cheek. Russo charged forward then, punching furiously. Garner covered up against the fence. Russo swore and struck with renewed vigor even though he was tiring. He gasped and shouted, "Do ya give? Do ya give? Do ya?"

Garner didn't answer. He writhed in pain. It didn't occur to him that he might give up; his mind was no longer clear, anyway. He wasn't sure where he was or what was happening to him. Grating, aching hurt tore into him from all directions. Nausea mixed in the blood which clogged his throat; he swallowed it and spit it up. He reacted to the pain instinctively. He was hurt; he was fighting, moving, being hurt again. There was noise, yelling and screaming and the pain, pounding in his head. He couldn't stop—*couldn't lose.*

The intensity of the pain increased and became almost intolerable, and then Garner could feel it peak and hold steady. It began to numb him. He could see better. He could hear Luther yelling. He could see Russo in front of him. His blood was splattered all over the front of Russo's sweatshirt. Garner could see the punches coming too. He could feel them land but they didn't hurt as much. He moved his head in a jerky shudderlike movement, shaking some of the blood from his eyes. Russo's punches didn't seem to be coming as often or as hard. At times, the blows seemed almost halfhearted. Garner peered at the boy between his fists, circling warily, dodging some blows, taking others.

Russo went on hitting him, yelling at him in heaving, frantic gasps, "Give, goddammit! C'mon, give, and I'll let'cha go." He lunged at him again. "C'mon! Do ya give? C'mon, give up! C'mon, give!"

Garner said nothing.

Russo was amazed. The fight was actually over, wasn't it? He had won it long ago. He wished he could end it, knock Garner down and out like real fighters did. He was very tired. Shivers of fear crawled in his stomach. He watched, disbelieving, as Garner came off the fence and put up his fists. It was as if the last ten minutes meant nothing. He steadied himself then, circling to his left as he had learned to do at the Boys Club. He knew how to fight, and he knew that he could continue to give Garner a beating. But he began to worry, to think and plan. He thought about *how* to fight and tried to recall what he should do—*"Keep the left high"—"Circle left"—"Tuck that chin"—"Concentrate."*—He watched Garner spit up some blood. He felt fear then. Garner started plodding forward. He looked surer now, more determined and stronger.

Russo wanted to stop, but he knew the fight was only beginning. "C'mon," he gasped. "If ya wanna quit, I'll stop, too. And no hard feelin's."

He got no answer.

"C'mon—look, Garna—I hafta get home—c'mon—let's forget it."

Silence.

"You know I can lick ya."

Garner remained silent, his face streaked with dirt and blood. He kept coming.

Luther was yelling, "Don' pay him no mind, Garna! He skeered now! Don'choo stop, gawddammit! Kick'is fuckin' ass! C'mon, man, git tha som'bitch! Git'im, man! C'mon, git'im! Git'im, git'im, git'im, git'im!"

Russo looked around fearfully. The white kids were quiet. Garner punched him in the mouth and pushed him back. Russo's mind was no longer on the fight.

The black kids, especially the girls, started to scream, "Git'im, Garna, c'mon, git'im! Git'im, Garna, c'mon, git'im! Git'im, Garna, c'mon, git'im!"

Russo began to fight again, feinting, jabbing, boxing cleverly. But Garner ignored everything he did. He simply wound up and threw haymakers, taking two or three punches to land one of his own. He didn't care where he got hit himself or where his own punches landed. He hit Russo everywhere, in the mouth, on the arms, in the chest, on the shoulders, between the eyes, on the nose, and in the stomach. Russo was fighting defensively now. He could hear Garner's big brother yelling, "Thass it, Garna! Stan' still an' hit'im straight on! Thass it!"

Garner set his feet, throwing his punches straighter and harder. He began to punch more rapidly. Russo tried catching some of the blows on his arms and shoulders, but they hurt too much, and he couldn't get set to get off any hard punches of his own. Garner's savage, angry punching was beginning to reach his face more and more often, and he was getting hurt. Russo struck back desperately, but he was backing away now. His blows were not landing with as much force, and Garner ignored them. He smashed his way through Russo's defense and hit him flush between the eyes. It was a terrific blow. The pain was so sharp that, for a moment, Russo couldn't see. Garner wound up and fired again, banging him viciously on the nose. Russo's eyes watered; he was stunned. He backed away, swinging wildly, and took a hard blow to the ear and another to the mouth. Garner pushed him back and started to wind up again. Russo moved his hands to guard his face. Then Garner hit him very hard in the throat. The pain was nearly paralyzing. Russo couldn't breathe. He slid along the fence, clutching at his throat. Garner dug his toes in and hit him between the eyes again. Russo stumbled backward, swinging and missing with one hand, his eyes closed, face contorted with pain as he held up the other hand to ward off Garner's blows. Garner reached way back and belted him full in the mouth, ripping both of his lips open. Russo swung frantically, lunging in desperation, missed, and landed on hands and knees, cutting his hands on the glass in the dirt.

He looked up as Garner waited for him. The black kids were chanting in frenzied unison, "Git'im, Garna, c'mon, git'im!" All around him there seemed to be black faces, gleaming teeth, feverish screams, imploring Garner to keep it up, to hit him again. Russo got to his feet, staggering backward away from Garner. Then he held up his hand. "Hold it—hold it. Hawk—wait up," he muttered, keeping his head down, spitting blood.

The crowd immediately became very still. Terry started forward with Luther, Buzz, and Leroy.

"Do ya give?" Garner gasped.

"That's—that's it, Garna—Hawk. Okay?"

"Do ya give?"

"Look—I said, that's it, right?"

"Do ya give?"

"Look—Hawk. Okay. Okay, yeah. Okay, for crissakes!"

"Okay," Garner growled, looking down at the blood on his T-shirt.

A tremendous howl went up from his brothers as they bore him up on their shoulders. He tried to grin, but it was too painful. He felt sick, and he wanted to lie down somewhere. He watched Bobby Russo trudging slowly through the alley toward the street, head down, staying well behind his buddies walking ahead of him, alone, dragging his jacket in the dirt as he wiped blood off his face onto his sweatshirt.

After the Russo thing, Garner was referred to around the school as the "Hawk."

Black kids spoke of him with near reverence. "The Hawk is hard, baby." *"Nobuddy* fucks wit' tha Hawk, man." And the whites admired him equally, feared and respected him. "Hawk ain't afraid of nothin'," they said.

Bobby Russo became one of his closest allies. They feared and respected one another and they never fought again. Russo was the first white friend he ever had. Even the ninth-graders acknowledged Garner's newly won status, nodding to him when they saw him around the school. And the Cross sometimes walked with him in the schoolyard during recess, although this was usually business: a division of the week's take, or what to do about a youngster who failed to keep up his payments—a dime every week—or pulling a new kid into line, or an "execution"—beating up a youngster who fell too far behind with payments—or problems with the teachers.

Girls began to pay attention to him too—black and white alike. "Hello, Gar," and "Oh, there's Garna!" "Hi, Garna." They smiled and flirted. Sometimes, if he was alone, Garner would stop and talk to them, but if he was with his "boys," he just gave them a casual wave of his hand and continued on, walking in his own peculiar, hippity-hop way. The Hawk was cool; he had a reputation to uphold, and he did so. It was all heady stuff for a twelve-year-old boy.

Garner liked girls, but he made a great effort not to show it. He kept them at a distance, what he considered to be their proper places. This he did partly because of his status and partly—mostly—because, although he wouldn't own up to it, he was a little afraid of them. He didn't know anything about girls, and most of what he did know, he learned from Luther or Terry. But he had very little real experience.

Naturally, he knew some basic facts, how a guy did it to a girl. He tried masturbating, but he was unsuccessful because he didn't really know what he was doing or what to expect from it. When he danced with a girl, or kissed one, his stomach felt funny, first hot, then cold, up and down—but good. He would get warm; sometimes, he broke out in a sweat, and a warm, steady glow rose in his stomach. All this scared him a little, but it also fascinated him. He found himself sneaking looks at various girls around the school: black girls with tight skirts, neat, pear-shaped bottoms and dazzling variations of skin coloring which ranged from ebony to pink, and white girls with trim figures and light hair. Some of the girls were ugly, or too fat, or too skinny, and of course, the Hawk could have nothing to do with them. He had a reputation to maintain. And next year he planned to take his pick of all the prettiest of the girls just like the Cross. The Cross had the prettiest girl in the whole school. She was in the ninth grade. Her name was Loretta.

"Thass a pretty nigga theah," Terry said one day as he and Garner watched Loretta walking with the Cross in the schoolyard. "A pure fox."

"Yeah, she *real* fine."

"Yeah. She hincktey, too."

"Huh?"

"She *hincktey,* man. Think her shit somethin' special."

"Sho' is fine, though, man," Garner said staring after the girl.

"Yeah, an' she know it, too. Ain' nobuddy gittin' none a' that 'cept tha Cross."

Garner shook his head, trying to imagine what Loretta would look like without any clothes, but the thought of her dark, smooth skin naked before his eyes was too much for him. The only female he had ever seen without any clothes on was his mother.

"What say, Ellis?" Terry greeted the thin, black boy who strolled up to them.

"W'say, man? What's happ'nin', Hawk?" He was baby-faced, almost as black as Garner.

Garner inclined his head slightly, watching Loretta. Ellis followed his gaze.

"Hey, man," Terry said, nudging Garner. "Did Stevie pay up this week?"

Garner shrugged.

"Man, stop gawkin' at that pussy, will ya? We gonna hafta *buy* ya some pretty soon." Terry laughed. "This nigga crazy 'bout Loretta. Ah oughtta tell the Cross."

"Sheet," Ellis said. "Evah'buddy crazy 'bout that gal."

"Well, ain' no needa studyin' on her cuz she too fine fa' you niggas."

"Aw, fuck you, Terry. Ain' thatta bitch, Ellis? She too fine fa' *us* niggas."

"She *is* too fine fa' you niggas. Besides, y'all wouldn't know what ta do wit' it."

"Ah know what's happ'nin'," Garner protested.

"Yeah," Ellis mumbled.

"You niggas ain' nevah had none."

"Ah do awright," Garner said.

"Man, you niggas cain' bullshit me. This is Terry, shit!"

"You don' know evah'thin' we doin', man," Garner said, pretending nonchalance.

"Man, who you kiddin'? Who you—fa'git it, man. Look, did Stevie pay up this week?"

"Ah think he gonna be straight," Ellis said. "Bobby leanin' on'im now."

"Ya sho'? Well, he betta. Man, you niggas tickle me, though, ya know? Ain' had nothin' an' tryin' ta bullshit. You cats ain' shit."

Garner scowled. "Fuck you, man."

"Ain' no needa you niggas thinkin' on nothin' like Loretta, man. Ain' nobuddy but a hard stud gonna git hisse'f a pretty nigga like that. Them pretty niggas is hincktey."

"Heah come Bobby," Ellis mumbled.

Garner leaned back against the school wall, thinking about what Terry had said. *"Yeah, man, Loretta a fox. Cat hadda be hard ta git a fox like that. Hadda be bes'."* He frowned, remembering Terry saying, *"Ya cain' bullshit'em. Not them black bitches, man. They alla time know what's happ'nin'. Ya kin bullshit some a' these paddy chicks, but they mostly don' wanna fuck wit'cha afta school.* He looked at Terry then. *"White gals,"* he accused silently. *"Yeah, man, you dig them white chicks, don'cha? Snow fever—ya got snow fever."* He saw Terry looking at him and guiltily averted his eyes. He shoved his hands in his pockets, recalling what happened the day before—*They had kitchen duty again. Garner was happy that he had an excuse to be late for class—and that he had managed to fill his stomach with ice cream. Terry was standing behind Kathy as she bent over to put down a stack of trays. He placed his hand on her waist and offered her some help. Garner shook his head in awe as he watched his brother slide his hand down slowly and let it rest against her tight little bottom. Kathy's reddish-blond hair bounced lightly as she quickly straightened up and looked around the room, suppressing a giggle. "Terry, you're awful," she squealed, failing in her attempt to sound offended. Then Terry, to Garner's amazement, slid his arm around her waist and drew her close and whispered something in her ear. The girl's white face turned beet-red, and she pretended to try to take his arm away. Terry kissed her on the neck and cupped her breast. Garner almost gasped out loud. He glanced quickly about the room to make sure none of the cooks was returning, then stole a fascinated look at Terry's pants to see if they stuck out the way his own did; he saw the bulge and grinned slyly. Terry calmly disengaged himself from Kathy and sauntered over to him. "Listen, Hawk, ah'm gonna git this bitch ta come down the sto'room wit' me. Now ya gotta keep a lookout like befo', ya heah?" Garner nodded.*

Later, after some of the other kids had come in from the cafeteria to help them, Garner saw Kathy go over to Terry and whisper something. Terry grinned and looked around at some of the other girls. A coffee-colored girl blushed dark brown and poked a dark-haired white girl in the ribs with her elbow. The two of them began swiping guarded looks at Kathy, continuing to stack dishes in the sink as they watched her. Terry winked at Garner and went out through the back door and disappeared down the stairs. Kathy waited a bit, fiddling nervously with her piles of trays. A small, heavy woman in a white uniform, one of the cooks, stepped out of the kitchen office and looked around briefly, then went out into the cafeteria. The bell rang, and Garner could hear the kids yelling and laughing as they cleared the hall. He saw Kathy slip through the back door and go down the stairs.

Terry told him that he could do it to any white girl he wanted, and Garner almost believed him. He didn't know how carefully Terry selected the few girls, white or black, with whom he could play his little games. After he took any girl to the storeroom, Terry always boasted to him about his conquest. "She fucks nice," he'd say. And if Garner seemed unconvinced, he would hold up his hand triumphantly and say, "Smell, gawddammit. Go 'head, nigga, smell ma finga!" Garner would sniff away eagerly and nod his head in grudging admiration as the peculiar, pungent odor tickled his nose. This exercise became a ritual. Garner would watch Terry disappear with a girl and wait anxiously for the chance to smell that finger. He liked the musky, female smell that Terry held out to him on his hand. Sometimes, he would try to walk near the girl and smell her, too, and then, the heady scent of pubescent girl-sex tugged exquisitely at his groin. He started looking for the smell on other girls too, and grown women, even noticing it on some of the young, women teachers, mixed with perfume. This smell he knew from somewhere else; he couldn't remember where, but it pleased him. It was exotic, urgent, and compelling.

Finding that smell around other women and girls surprised him, at first, because he had learned to associate it with sexual intercourse. Sniffing Terry's finger confirmed the certainty that only moments before, a girl had invited, or permitted, the most intimate caress. Terry had put his hand under the girl's dress, under her panties, and touched her—*there.* The thought heated Garner's blood. He could feel the hot, quick tension between his thighs. He longed to take a girl down to the storeroom himself, but he didn't have the nerve to ask one. He thought that if a guy was really cool—like Terry, or the Cross, or Luther—he knew a rare and irresistible word ritual which just rendered any female helpless and sexy, simply overcome with passion. He didn't understand that girls liked boys, too.

Garner observed Terry's sexual activities attentively and questioned him at length: how was it? what was it like? which girl was better? why? He coaxed his brother, trying to get the details, as if in doing so he might actually know the experience himself.

Terry, of course, was glad to comply. He even dressed his stories up a little. Sometimes, he looked at Garner and laughed, "Man, you gotta git'cha'se'f some."

Garner would defend himself with something like, "Ah know what's happ'nin', man." Then sheepishly, starting with a whisper, he'd blurt out another volley of questions. "What else ya do, man?" or maybe "what'cha do then?" and "what she do when ya done that?"

And Terry would tell him. He talked about panties, and titties, and thighs, and skin, and soft pussies, and just everything that Garner wanted to know.

"Are white girls better'n cullid ones?" Garner asked Terry as they hid in the storeroom smoking one day.

"Sheet, baby, ain' no diff'rence. Sometime white gals is better cuz they ain' used ta gittin' it—'speshly like ah does it."

"Well," Garner ventured carefully as Terry listened at the door to hear if someone was coming, "white gals don' smell no diff'rent."

"Sheet, smell ain' got nothin' ta do wit'it, anyways. It's how ya moves, man."

"Yeah?"

"Yeah."

Garner puffed his cigarette, trying to imagine what it was like. Yes, Terry was cool. Then he decided to invite a girl down to the storeroom—but not right away. No. It was better not to rush things. Better cool it for a while. He would take his time.

The money that Garner received from his share of the protection racket, some eight dollars weekly, after splitting with the Cross and with Terry, brought a discipline into his life which had its disadvantages. He complained about this to Terry as they walked to school one morning.

"Man, hookin' school *one* day ain' gonna hurt nothin'!"

"Look, Hawk, now, ah been tryin' t'explain ta ya; hookin' cost money. If ya ain' heah, somebuddy gonna try ta do ya outta some bread. 'Sides, man, ya gotta keep tha peace, baby. Ya gotta keep things cool. Tha Cross don' want no shit ta start. First thing ya know, somebuddy might git ta thinkin' he bad an' squeal ta one a' tha teachers."

"Sheet, ah break his ass. Ain' nobuddy dare pull nothin' like that."

"Might if they don't see ya 'roun'. Git ta thinkin' ain' nobuddy watchin' out, maybe git ta talkin' wit' some other cat—"

"Man, is you fa' real? Ah whip his ass so bad—"

"Y'ain' gonna whip nobuddy if Murph heah 'bout this shit."

"Sheet."

"Sheet, ma ass, nigga! Nobuddy fucks wit' Murph. Ah mean, even tha Cross don' be fuckin' up in gym, man."

"You think Cross is skeered a' Murph?"

"Well—ah dunno. Ah know he don' mess wit'im, ah kin tell ya that."

"Sheet, man, he ain' skeered. He jes' takin' care a' bid'ness."

"Gawddammit," Terry snorted, "Cross ain' gonna fuck wit' Murph, man. Now, ah'm tellin' ya. 'Sides, top man gotta cool it; ya cain' make no bread if ya kicked outta school—Murph wuz a marine, baby."

"Yeah. Them cats is bad, man. Ya know what Ellis say? He say ol' man Tracy gonna quit, gonna be too ol' nex' yeah, an' Murph might git'is job."

"Sheet," Terry chuckled, "if *that* evil som'bitch git ta be prince-pul, you cats gonna be in *hell.* Ah'm sho' glad ah be up tha high school at Tech. Be gone frum heah, an' in Novemba ah kin quit, baby."

"Ah wish ah could quit."

"Wit' Murph in theah, *somebuddy* gonna hafta quit. He gonna kick you niggas' asses an' send ya all ta Dis-pee."

"Ah ain' goin' up *theah,"* Garner moaned with a shudder. "Not *me!"*

"They beat a nigga ta death up theah once," Terry stated matter-of-factly.

"Man!"

"Sheet, they ain' gonna git Terry. Terry gonna be gone frum heah."

"Man," Garner said unhappily as they turned into the schoolyard, "ah sho' wish ah could go ta tha movies."

"Yeah."

Terry loved the routine, the steady income, and the relative peace and order that came with Garner's new status. He spent more and more time with girls. After school he swaggered importantly as he walked with them, laughing, flirting, and telling jokes. Sometimes he'd stop and swing one of the girls around and dance with her on the sidewalk. Garner began to hang around after school, talking to Bobby Russo and Ellis Crawford. Very often, Garner and Bobby, lacking anything better to do, followed Ellis down to the gym to watch him work out with the basketball team. He was the only seventh-grader on the fifteen-man squad. Even though he was on the third team, he was proud of his basketball talent and liked to have his buddies watch him work out.

One afternoon in the gym, Mr. Murphy threw a ball out to Bobby and Garner. "Long as you're wearing sneakers, you can shoot awhile —till the team comes up—if you want."

Bobby grabbed the ball and ran toward the basket, dribbling once, and laid the ball up and into the basket. Garner followed on the run, picking the ball up under the net before it hit the floor. Murph sat down in the stands, his lean figure hunched forward, elbows on knees. A tiny smile played around his thin mouth.

"Let's have a game, Hawk."

"Ma ball first."

"You had it last time."

"You called the game, man."

Bobby shook his head and flipped the ball toward him. "Take it then."

"Winna's out, man."

"Yeah. Okay, go on."

They were well into their game when some of the boys on the team came up and started some casual warm-up shooting. Ellis Crawford jogged over to his buddies. "Ah got tha winna, man."

Neither boy answered, being too intent on their game.

"Hurry up, man. Coach gonna call tha lines in a minute."

Murph watched the boys for a long time. Finally, one of his players, a tall, black boy, stopped in front of him. "Wanna start tha lines, Coach?"

"Yeah. Yeah, start'em running." Murph shook his head and stood. "Bring it in, fellas." He watched Garner hesitate, then heave the ball angrily at Bobby.

"You guys interested in playing some ball?" Murph asked as he took the ball from Bobby.

"Huh?" Bobby answered.

Garner fed him an evil look and turned away.

"Why don't you come down and try out for the team?"

Bobby hesitated and turned to look at Garner.

Murph watched them, a frown knitting under his thick, blond crewcut. Then he smiled nonchalantly. "Listen, if you feel like it, come on down. Has to be soon though." He turned and walked toward his office without giving either boy a chance to reply.

They were back the next day and again asked for a ball.

Garner stood off to one side, scowling. "We ain' tryin' out, ya know. Jes' gonna—"

"We just wanna use a ball, Mr. Murphy."

Murph nodded thoughtfully, without letting his disappointment show.

The boys took off their coats and started to play. Murph sat down to watch.

A few days later, he asked them again. But they still weren't interested. Bobby stood looking at the gym floor shaking his head, Garner scowling.

"You sure," Murph asked.

"Well, Coach—uh—"

"Yeah, man, we sho'. Kin we use a ball a' not?"

Murph looked at Garner, trying to hold his temper. "That right, Bobby?"

"Huh? Yeah—sure. That's all—I mean, yeah, Coach."

"Okay, kid."

"C'mon, Bobby. Man, les' play."

Bobby Russo leaned against the fence in the schoolyard and dug a comb out of his dark-blue flight jacket. Garner watched him run the little comb through his thick, black hair. He envied Bobby for his hair. He stuffed his hands in his pockets and dropped his eyes, thinking of his own hair, cut short and close to the scalp. White boys were lucky to have hair like that, he felt. When his grew long, he couldn't comb it. He looked at Bobby again, noting the thick shock of hair which swung down from his pompadour over his low forehead. Cool, Garner thought, a good-looking, tough guinea wop.

"Ellis says he's goin' out for track," Bobby said, sticking the comb in his pocket.

"Sheet."

"Maybe it'd be fun, Hawk."

"Huh?"

"Goin' on a team. You know."

"Sheet."

"My brother likes it okay."

"Sheet, man, whyn'cha go on out, if ya think sports so fuckin' great."

Bobby scowled, thinking it over. "I dunno, Hawk, maybe it'd be awright. Shit, you should see all the stuff my brother won: trophies and stuff—and a beautiful jacket. Got his name and number on it, ya know? There's a big football on one side and a great big C right here," he boasted, poking his chest with a finger to indicate the spot on his jacket. "On the back it says *Catholic* in big letters too."

"Man, who tha fuck wanna go through alla shit—ya gotta go ta practice—evah' day. An' take a lotta shit offa Murph. Fuck that, sheet."

"Yeah. But, shit, Hawk, Mike's gotta lot of stuff. I dunno—Mike might make *All-City* next year. Coach's tryin' ta get'im a scholarship."

"Huh?"

"A scholarship. You know, ta go ta college."

"Sheet."

"Christ, it's for free," Bobby exclaimed peevishly.

Garner waved his hand in disgust.

Bobby squirmed uncomfortably, looking down at the asphalt and fiddling with the zipper on his jacket. "Shit, Hawk, I thought'cha liked ta play ball—I mean—what the hell, it's you that always wants ta play and—"

"Heah come Ellis."

Bobby turned to see Ellis coming toward them from the street. He glanced quickly at Garner and frowned. They were quiet for a moment, then Bobby nodded his head toward Ellis, "Ellis is gonna run track."

Garner picked up a rock and threw it down toward the end of the schoolyard.

Bobby watched it disappear beyond the lone, skinny tree which stood sentinel-like against the gray-blue of the sky. Beyond the tree, he could see the misty overcast which hung like thin, motionless fog in the damp air above the city.

"Ya gotta be a asshole ta take alla shit tha coach give ya," Garner continued.

"Huh? Shit, Mike don't have no trouble with the coach—he ain't no asshole, either. And Coach likes him."

Garner picked up another rock. "Listen, baby, if a cat's hard, he don' kiss nobuddy's ass fa' nothin'."

"Mike's hard as anybuddy, and he don't take shit from nobuddy, neither."

"Shit, man, Lutha nevah fucked around wit' none a' that shit. He hard. Use ta kick evah'buddy's ass, man."

"Bullshit; he ain't never kicked Mike's ass! Nobuddy ever beat him."

"Lutha coulda kicked his ass."

"In a pig's ass!"
"Man, fuck yo' brotha!"
"Fuck your brother, too!"
"Fuck you, too," Garner was yelling now.
"Aw, go pull ya prick!"
Garner stepped closer to Bobby and thrust his head forward, scowling at him menacingly. He howled at him. "You jackin' me up, man? You wanna start some shit?"
"Fuck you," Bobby hurled back, standing his ground, his face reddening with anger.
"You startin' some shit, man?"
"Aw, fuck you!"
"You jackin' me up?" Garner insisted, his face inches from Bobby's.
"Are you jackin' *me* up?"
"You wanna start some shit?"
"*You* wanna start somethin'?"
"Jes' watch it, thass all."
"Go fuck yourself!"
"Mutha-fuck you, Bobby. Sheet!"
Ellis strolled up and stopped a few feet away from them. A wide grin cut across his black, baby face. "Man, what'choo cats hollerin' 'bout? Heah ya alla way out ta tha street."
"Nothin'," Garner spat out. He scaled another rock as they started toward the gym.
Ellis looked, first, at one, then at the other. Bobby was walking, head down with a ferocious look on his face. Garner, hands jammed in the pockets of his chinos, stared straight ahead, his black face screwed up in an angry snarl. Ellis shrugged and shook his head.
Late that evening, Garner sprawled on the sofa, staring at the television set. On the screen, a sharpshooting cowpoke had just driven eighteen Apaches off his ranch. Garner wasn't watching; he stared at the screen, but he was thinking about his argument with Bobby. "Fuck'im," he muttered aloud. "Fuck Ellis too." He heard someone on the stairs. The hallway door creaked open, and he heard steps in the kitchen. He looked around to see Luther's tall, broad figure stand-

ing in the doorway. He grinned, jumping up from the sofa. "Hey, man, what's happ'nin'?"

Luther unbuttoned his topcoat and swaggered into the living room. "Wheah's Ma? She workin'?"

"Yeah."

"Harry too?"

"Yeah, man, they down Handy's evah' night. Be home in a while. Sheet, Ma be home now, if she knew *you* wuz heah."

"Shit, ah cain' stan' all that weepin' an' wailin', man. She alla time start that shit 'bout comin' home agin."

Garner nodded his head with a knowing air. "Yeah. What'cha been doin', Lutha? Wheah'd ya git them crazy rags?"

"Picked'em up, baby. You know how it is." Luther sat down on the arm of the sofa.

"Man," Garner whined as he fingered the gray topcoat, "you must *stay* wit' fuckin' bread. Them togs cost a whole lotta money. Gawd-damn!"

"Sheet, ya know ah likes ta keep a little change 'roun', baby. Coat ain' cost shit, though. Got it on sale—eighty bucks. Suit wuz neah two bills." Luther stood up and opened the topcoat to show off the dark, well-tailored suit.

"Man, you doin' awright. Wheah Buzz'n Leroy? They wit'cha?"

"Buzz down in the car. We goin' ta git Leroy now."

"Man," Garner exulted, hustling over to the window. "You cats always got a car. Which one yo' car?"

"Tha Caddy," Luther said with a triumphant smile.

Garner whistled low and hard. He turned to look at his brother, grinning broadly. "Jesus, Lutha, ya mean tha *new* one, tha con*vert?*" He watched his brother nod casually. "Man, wheah'd ya git it? That thing cost all *kinda* fuckin' bread."

"We sorta borrowed it."

"How much it cost?"

"Well, neah seven grand, ah s'pose—but it ain' exackly ours. We jes' usin' it."

"Man! Did ya boost it?"

"Well," Luther began slowly, "thass ma bid'ness, ya fuckin'—"

"Kin ah go wit'cha fa' ride? Kin ah, Lutha?"

"Naw, man, not ta-nite—say, ah got somethin' else ah could show ya, too, but ah better not cuz ya might git ta talkin'."

"Sheet, man," Garner whined in indignation as he ran quickly over to his brother, "you know ah don' fuck 'roun'! Ah know what's happ'nin', man! Ah ain' no sissy! What'cha got? C'mon, man. Lemme see."

"Ah dunno, Hawk. Ah don' want nobuddy ta know ma bid'ness. Ah cain' be fuckin' up, ya know."

"Hones', Lutha, ah ain' gonna say nothin'. Ah ain' nevah tol' nobuddy none a' yo' bid'ness, man."

Luther smiled and reached inside of his coat. "Look heah, baby."

It was a gun. Garner stared at it in awe. He was speechless. Luther turned the gun over slowly in his hand. It was a dark, bluish-black revolver with a short, thick barrel. The butt was heavy and black.

Garner finally found his voice, *"Jesus!* Hot damn, Lutha, thass cool! Wheah ya git that som'bitch, man? Gaw-awddamn. You a bad mutha-fucka, thass all, jesta bad som'bitch. Jesus Christ. Kin ah touch it? Kin ah hol' it?"

"Naw, man. You gonna fuck up an' hurt'cha'se'f."

"Naw ah ain', man! Naw ah ain'. Lemme hol' it. C'mon, man. Please, huh?"

"Heah, but jes' hol' it. Don' do nothin' else."

Garner held the gun gingerly. "Man, this thing sho' pretty."

"Be careful wit' it, now!" Luther's voice rose quickly.

"Gawddamn! Ah'm gonna git me one a' these. Gawddamn!"

Luther grinned broadly.

Then Garner, playfully, pointed the gun at him, his finger lightly on the trigger. "Wheah ya git it, man?"

"Hey, nigga—. Don' matta—ah mean, ah got it, thass all. Buzz'n Leroy gonna git them one, too. Gimme it back, man. *C'mon, now, nigga!* Don' play! *Don' do that, now!* Ah tol' ya. Gimme tha fuckin' thing befo' ya fuck up." With one large paw, Luther took firm hold of his brother's wrist. Garner smiled sheepishly and released the

weapon. Luther twirled it with careful nonchalance on his forefinger.

"Man," Garner howled.

"Nigga, ya tell anyone an' ah break ya fuckin' ass. Ya heah? Heah what ah'm tellin' ya?"

Garner nodded vigorously, staring at the gun. His eyes beamed in the dim little room. The T.V. droned quietly, its picture out of focus.

"Watch this, baby," Luther said calmly, breaking the pistol open to show Garner the bullets.

"Lemme see one, man."

Luther handed him one of the bullets.

"Man—this thing'd fuck a cat all up, wouldn't it, Lutha?"

" 'Sa thirty-eight, baby."

"Really?"

"Shit yeah, man." Luther took the cartridge away from the boy. He slipped it into its chamber, smiling as Garner stared at the gun. Then with a quick twist of his wrist, he flipped his hand sideways; the revolver snapped shut with a hard, crisp click.

Garner almost groaned as his brother shoved the weapon inside of his coat. *"Man!"*

"Ah gotta split, baby. Leroy be waitin' on us. Wanna come see tha car?"

"Yeah, man," Garner yelped and bolted for the kitchen.

Luther smiled, flipped his coat collar up, and followed along casually.

The car was a white convertible. Its shiny, new paint glittered in the light of the street lamp.

Garner raced gleefully around the automobile, exclaiming, "Thass tough. Man, thass tough."

"W'say, Garna," Buzz greeted him.

"Aw, man, she too much, thass all. Real fine."

Luther sauntered up to the car. Buzz craned his thick neck through the window, yelling, "Hey, man, we hafta split. Les' make it. Leroy gonna think we ain' gonna work ta-nite."

"Yeah. Gittin' late." Luther hurried around the car and slid behind the wheel.

"Cain' ah go wit'cha?"

"Naw, boy. Is you fa' real?"

Buzz laughed. "Sheet, we gonna be movin' fast ta-nite, chile. No time ta be fuckin' 'roun'."

"Cain' ah jes' git a ride, man?"

Luther started the engine and turned on the lights. "Naw, baby. We workin'. Gotta take care a' bid'ness."

Garner could see the dashboard glow in the dark inside of the car, then the shadow of Luther's hand switching on the radio. The sound of soft jazz wafted out from the dash lights. Then the Caddy dug out, tires squealing. Garner stared after it.

"Man! Gaw-aw-awddamn, man!" He stood on the sidewalk for what seemed to be a long time, staring after the car.

"Wheah tha fuck you cats been?" Leroy growled angrily as he slid into the back seat of the Caddy. "Ah been standin' on tha corna fa' fuckin' hour, gawddammit!"

The convertible rocked forward.

"Aw, man, take it easy. We stopped by tha house. Bullshitted wit' Garna fa' while," Luther told him.

"Wit' Garna?" Leroy yelled. "We gotta work, an' you fuckin' 'roun' wit' *Garna?* Now ain' thatta bitch? Fa' crissakes, man, tha fuckin' joint gonna be closin' soon! *Garna!* Gawddamn, you mutha-fuckas crazy, or what?"

"Take it slow, man," Buzz sighed. "Lutha know what he doin'."

"Gawddammit," Luther hissed, "we don' bitch 'bout comin' way tha fuck ovah heah to git'*choo,* shit."

Leroy sat forward quickly in his seat, his hard, white face reddening in the dark of the car. His voice shot up an octave. "Don'choo start no shit 'bout me an' Janice, Lutha, gawddammit! Don'choo start that shit agin, mutha-fucka! We talkin' 'bout Garna."

"Fuck you, man. If you kin go sit up in that gal's parlor like a fuckin' sissy, talkin' shit ta her folks all night, then ah kin stop off an' see ma mutha-fuckin' brotha, gawddammit!"

"Mutha-fuck you, Lutha! Gawddamn you *an'* ya fuckin' brotha! Shit!"

Buzz yelled his way into the argument. "Fa' crissakes, you guys gotta cut out all this fightin' an' yellin' an' shit! How we gonna work when ya fightin' an' yellin', fa' crissake?" Buzz shook his head. Luther threw him an exasperated look, his hands tightening on the wheel, then looked back at the road.

"Nawsuh, gawddammit, you niggas ain' gotta go nowheahs ta git Leroy. An' if ya wanna, ya kin stop tha fuckin' car right heah, an' ah git tha fuck out!"

Buzz and Luther looked at each other briefly. Nobody spoke for a while.

Finally, Buzz said quietly, "Evah' time we gotta work, you niggas wanna fight. What's tha matta wit'cha, fa' crissake. Ain' no needa alla this shit. You niggas ain' gonna *do* nothin' but yell an' git all evil fa' nothin'. Jes' wearin' out'cha fuckin' mouths, thass all. Jes' wearin' out'cha mouths. Ya *both* fulla shit, thass all. Don' mean shit. Jes' hard on tha ears. Ain' nobuddy mean a gawddamn word he say. An' ya sayin' it loud as ya kin on account a' ya *know* ain' nobuddy b'lieve ya, anyway—"

His voice broke off as he turned to look at Leroy who sat staring sullenly through the window. Luther sulked too. Buzz sighed. A slight smile, hiding itself in the dark, worked gently at the corners of his mouth.

The motor hummed quietly as the powerful convertible hurtled on into an endless maze of traffic and flashing, darting lights. They were nearing the outskirts of the city. The streets were crowded. The road stretched before them, opening up for the onrushing car. It seemed as though they had plunged into a tight channel which, from a distance, always appeared too narrow to admit them but continuously widened before their headlights. The lights of oncoming cars alternately blinded them and shot by, over and over again. In the silence of the car, they could hear and feel the rhythm outside, other people, other life, cars, trucks, horns honking, lights, the rush of the night air. It all seemed to hang together in a regular pattern. There was a constant beat, a sure, steady pulse that carried them forward. Their thoughts settled on their work now. They began to feel steadier. They were anxious, as usual, but confident.

Buzz broke the silence. "We should pick up some real bread ta-nite."

"At least a grand," Luther confirmed.

Leroy stared through the window, saying nothing, still sulking.

"How much ya figga, Leroy?" Buzz asked.

"No tellin'," Leroy muttered. "Don' know if we'll git a thou—ah mean—maybe two, three hunnerd apiece."

"Ah hope tha cat ain' cleaned out his cash yet," Buzz said.

"Naw," Luther was quick to reassure him. "They drops it in tha night deposit all tagetha."

Leroy frowned slightly. "Lutha, you sho' tha same man own tha likka sto' own tha gas station?"

"Shit yeah, man. Tha night manager drops two bags a' money same place evah' night. An' ta-day's Friday. Bigges' night a' tha week. Them bags gonna be fat, man."

Buzz laughed. "Yeah. Yestiddy wuz payday, but they ain' paid *us* yet. Tha eagle gonna shit 'notha load jes' fa' us, baby."

"He real nice fella," Luther muttered grimly.

"Say, Lutha," Leroy cut in. "Ya got'cha heat wit'cha?"

"Sheet, ya know ah got ta be heeled, man. Wouldn't wanna git caught wit'out it on a deal like ta-nite. Shit naw, baby. This be our bigges' score yet."

They were silent again. The traffic thinned. It was early morning.

"Theah it is," Buzz announced.

They saw brightly lit signs up ahead of them—OLD COLONY GAS—FAST SERVICE—LIQUORS.

"Yeah," Luther said, "thass it. Ah pull tha car 'roun' tha other side so tha cat won't see it. Now, you cats know tha deal, right?"

Leroy and Buzz nodded nervously. They could feel their guts tightening up. Leroy sat forward on his seat. Luther's palms were sweating and the steering wheel was slippery in his hands. Buzz fidgeted. The Caddy swung into the large parking area, now almost empty. A white man in an attendant's uniform came out of the gas station and walked over to an old Ford.

"Goin' home," Luther said. "Man in tha likka sto' oughtta be takin' his cash ovah tha station pretty quick now."

Leroy gripped the back of Luther's seat. "Yeah. He closes up first, man."

"Okay. Now, ah'm gonna pull tha car 'roun' tha other side. Boss man's car's out back. Buzz, you keep tha car runnin'. Leroy, stan' at the corna an' make sho' them other cats git in they cars an' move out. Look fa' tha fuzz. Ah meet tha man. Buzz, you watch Leroy fa' sign if somethin' wrong. An' evah'buddy play it cool."

They nodded, glancing quickly at one another. Luther pulled the convertible around behind the buildings and parked on the far side of the service station, away from the liquor store. They waited a few minutes. Then the big neon signs around the front of the parking area dimmed and flickered out. Leroy got out of the car and walked to the corner of the building. It was very quiet. He thought he could hear someone moving around inside the gas station. A door closed. Peeking around the corner, he saw a white man walking briskly toward the station. The liquor store was dark, except for the night lights. The man had a coat on and walked hurriedly. Leroy pulled his head back and signaled the guys in the car. His throat felt dry. He tried to swallow, but, as usual, when they were working, he couldn't.

Luther stepped out of the car and quietly closed the door. He stood there, awaiting Leroy's signal. Buzz leaned his chunky body forward and gripped the steering wheel nervously. His body was tense, muscles tight. His breath came in short gasps. He fixed his eyes hard on Leroy. Luther breathed in uneven, quiet grunts. Leroy peered around the corner.

A red Plymouth convertible drove into the parking lot and rolled by the gas pumps. The air hose on the ground set off the signal bell as the car went over it. Leroy yanked his head back and pinned his tall, lanky frame against the building. His brown topcoat helped to hide him in the dark. Buzz strained forward. Luther held his breath and reached for the car door. Leroy looked again, his heart racing. The Plymouth hesitated at the pumps and moved along again. Then it stopped. Leroy craned his neck, straining his eyes to see. A young blond boy got out of the car on the driver's side and stood staring over the convertible roof at the station. Leroy growled a curse under his breath and pulled his head back. This, he thought, they did not need. He took another peek. The boy was shaking his head. He bent over to say something to the dark-haired girl who was with him, then straightened up quickly and looked off down the highway. Then he looked back at the station. After standing there a minute longer, he got back into the car. Leroy watched, his eyes narrowed in his white face. The Plymouth pulled away from the pumps, slowly at first, creeping up to the edge of the road. Then it bolted out and sped away.

The man whom Leroy had seen earlier walking from the liquor store came out of the station and stopped to light a cigarette. Leroy could hear him breathing. He watched him flick his match away and walk over to a black Rambler. The lights inside the gas station went out, leaving only the night lights burning. Leroy signaled to his buddies.

Luther sucked his breath in sharply, turned quickly, and hurried around behind the building. He hesitated, then squatted down behind a new Country Squire, the only car there. He waited. He couldn't seem to hear anything. The uneven, intermittent bleat of traffic out on the road was low and quiet. It blended completely into the cool night air, unbroken, constant. It gave the effect of utter stillness. Nothing seemed to move. Luther's insides heaved in spasms of anxiety. Somewhere within himself, he could feel the touch of ice. He shivered and wiped the sweat from his face. He couldn't even hear the silence anymore. He felt almost deaf. No sound, and there seemed to be no end to the waiting. His knees ached from squatting. Then he heard footsteps, loud and sharp, snapping through the silence in clear, bold cracks. He reached hastily, jerkily, inside his coat and yanked out his revolver. He held his breath. The steps came around to the driver's side of the station wagon and stopped.

Luther jumped to his feet. "Don' move, mistah," he blurted in a husky voice.

"What? Who's that?" He was squat, heavy, and strongly made, with a square white face, wearing a gray trench coat and a battered black hat. He was carrying two heavy-looking, small canvas bags.

"Don' move! Don' move, mistah! Ah gotta gun! Ah gotta gun heah! Now, don'choo move!"

The man turned around slowly to face Luther. He didn't see Leroy creeping up behind him in the dark. Luther moved forward. The man squinted at him. "What is this? *Gun?* What the hell—what do you think you're doing? Who are you? What do you want?"

"Drop them bags," Luther ordered.

"What? I—won't," the man stammered. "Who the hell do you think you are? You can't get away with this." Suddenly, he lunged forward, grappling with Luther.

Leroy screamed, "Jesus!" He leaped toward the man, rabbit-punching him viciously from behind. The man grunted in pain and surprise, wrestling Luther's big body back against the car. Luther threw his knee up in a furious thrust, catching the man in the groin. The man's grip relaxed instantly. The bags of money dropped on the ground. Then the man jerked forward again, whining and sniffling, grunting in fear and anguish as he tried to bear-hug Luther. Leroy hit him again, harder this time, stretching his tall body, reaching way up and back, then driving his fist down into the man's neck with his whole weight snapping behind it. The man's heavy, powerful body jerked convulsively, but he tried to hang on, pulling on Luther's coat, grinding his face against the boy's body. The roar of Luther's .38 tore into the feverish stillness then. The man staggered backward, clutching his stomach. Luther swore, he hadn't meant to fire. He charged at the man, smashing the gun into his face. Blood gushed from the man's nose and mouth as he rocked backward into Leroy.

For a long, desperate instant, the three of them were locked in a weird, horrible dance, struggling frantically, gasping for breath. Luther and Leroy smashed at the man savagely, front and back. Then the man's legs began to buckle. Holding his stomach, he finally sank to his knees. Leroy hit him again. Luther flailed him viciously about the side of the head and face with the gun. Slowly, the man keeled over and fell on his side, wheezing and moaning in terrible, agonizing pain as he doubled up on the ground. Luther began to stomp him.

Leroy scooped up the bags of money and pulled hard on Luther's arm. "C'mon, man," he yelled, gasping as he pulled and tugged, trying to drag Luther away. *"C'mon!* Fuck that shit! We ain' got time! We gotta move, fa' crissake!"

They ran to the Caddy, hurled themselves inside, and Buzz dug out hard, burning rubber all the way out onto the highway.

"What happen, man? What tha fuck wuz tha shootin'?"

"Drive, mutha-fucka," Luther bellowed. "Jes' drive!"

Leroy's voice screamed over his, "Naw, man! Slow down! *Cool it!* Drive wit' tha other cars, man!"

Buzz braked the car, then eased his foot down on the gas pedal. The big convertible moved along with the thin flow of cars, and he held it at a steady, cruising speed.

Leroy looked through the rear window. "We *clean,"* he howled, pounding on the seat. "Ain' *nothin'* happ'nin' back theah! We *clean,* we clean! We gonna be okay! Evah'thin's cool!"

"Leroy, right, Buzz! Thass it, slow down. Cool it. Take it easy. We *in,* baby!"

They were all overheated and wet with sweat. Buzz turned to Luther. "What tha fuck happ'n?"

"Fuckin' asshole jumped Lutha, fa' crissake," Leroy answered, throwing the bags into the front seat.

"Jesus! Did ya kill'im?"

Luther switched on the map light. Leroy handed him a long razor.

"Don' know," Luther mumbled and cut into one of the bags.

"Hope not," Leroy said.

Luther cut open the other bag. "Fuck'im."

"Man," Buzz said. "Look'it all that pretty sugar. Gawddamn!"

"Leave tha fuckin' change," Leroy whispered quickly, sitting forward to look into the front seat.

"Yeah, Lutha. Jes' bills, baby."

Luther took out all the bills, leaving the change, and knocked the bags onto the floor as he started counting the money. Buzz was grinning happily. Leroy watched the count.

"Twenny-fo' hunnerd an' sevenny-two dollahs, baby."

Buzz gloated. "Thass ovah eight bills apiece! Did ya—"

"In small bills, too, man."

"—heah that, Leroy? Gawddamn, man! An' small bills, too! Lutha really put us on ta some shit this time."

Leroy didn't answer. He sat staring at the money. Luther divided it up and handed him his share. Leroy took it and put it in his coat pocket without counting it.

"What'sa matta, man?" Luther asked, handing Buzz his cut of the money.

"Ah jes' hope we ain' killed tha fuckin' man, thass all."

"Fa'git it, man," Buzz said. "We clean. Fuck tha man. Had no bid'ness jumpin' on nobuddy."

"Buzz is right, Leroy. Shit. Wuz his own fuckin' fault. An' he ain' tha last mutha-fucka we gonna hafta hit in his fuckin' head, neither. 'Sides, ah didn't mean ta *shoot* the silly som'bitch; he shouldn't a grabbed me."

Leroy lit a cigarette and sat back in his seat.

"What'cha gonna buy ya ol' lady, Leroy?" Buzz asked.

Leroy sighed in resignation.

"Hey, man, what'sa matta? C'mon, snap to it, baby."

"Shit, Janice don' want none a' this fuckin' money. If she knew what ah wuz doin'—well, ah dunno. Ah dunno, thass all."

"Who gonna tell'er?" Luther asked. "She don' hafta know nothin'."

"Ah dunno, man. Janice is sharp. Don' much git by her, baby."

Buzz laughed and lit a smoke. "She foxy as hell, man. Nothin' but a pure fox."

"Ain' she, though? Real fine, man."

"You like dark women, don'cha?" Luther said, turning to look at Leroy.

"You better b'lieve it, baby."

"She black," Buzz said, "but she pretty as hell, man. Ah mean, a nat'rul fox. Ain' but a damn few bitches, black, white, yella, nor no kinda way, lookin' that good. She got all that pretty, long hair an'—"

"She got a body too," Luther said. "You bes' git alla that shit that'cha kin, Leroy. That bitch got all kinda goodies theah, baby."

Leroy's voice took on a slight edge. "Muslim bitches don' fuck."

Buzz groaned. "Jesus, ya mean ta say that pretty mutha-fucka won't give ya none?"

"Naw. Won't git up off it. 'Gainst'er religion, man. Gotta be married first."

"Well, gawddamn! What'cha fuckin' 'roun' wit'er fa', then?"

"Tha nigga's in love. Sheet, don'choo know that shit. That gal got Leroy standin' on his head," Luther said, laughing.

Leroy puffed his cigarette thoughtfully. Then he sighed. "Ain' nevah met a gal ah couldn't fuck befo'. An' what git ma ass is, ah *know* tha bitch is *fa'* me, man. Ah mean this gal *loves* Leroy. Ya know?"

"Prob'bly wanna git married," Luther said.

"Yeah. She kinda religious. Wanna fam'ly an' evah'thin', ya know?"

"Jesus! Ya gonna do it, Leroy?" Buzz asked quickly.

Leroy didn't answer.

Luther smiled, mumbling, "Them Muslims kinda crazy, ain' they, man?"

"Huh?"

"Well, ah mean they wanna kill *all* tha white folks! Won't even eat po'k a' nothin'. Jesus Christ! They don' drink, *won't fuck!* Shit, Leroy, you don' wanna git messed up wit' them som'bitches."

"They ain' crazy, man. They know what's happ'nin', thass all. Know wheah it's at. Whitey ain' no mutha-fuckin' good."

"Thass fa' sho'," Buzz agreed quickly.

" 'Sides, Muslims don' wanna kill nobuddy. Don' fuck wit' nobuddy don' fuck wit' them. Religious, thass all."

"Christ, y'ain' gonna turn Muslim, is ya, Leroy?"

Leroy didn't answer. Buzz looked at him anxiously through the mirror. The car was filled with an awkward silence.

"Y'ain' gonna marry nobuddy, is ya?"

"Ah *dig* this bitch, man. Ah mean—she *so* fine, ya know? An' proud ta be black—*proud,* baby. All them Muslims is like that. Don' take no shit frum nobuddy—don' botha nobuddy, neither. She so fuckin' pretty an' proud, make me glad ah'm a nigga, man. She nice, too. Real people. An' decent-like—sorta—sorta pure. Ah mean, ain' nobuddy but me *even* had his hands on'er, ya know? Smart too. Wanna go ta college."

"Sheet," Luther guffawed. "Leroy, you too white ta be a Black Muslim. Them niggas too evil ta let a white nigga in."

"Don' matta, baby. Plenny niggas like me in tha Muslims. Leader shit-colored too—not bad as me, but *kinda* shit-colored. Nigga's a nigga ta them, black, yella, a' white. Make no diff'rence. Sheet, most niggas part white anyway. Ah bet'choo niggas even got some white blood in ya."

"Sheet," Luther howled, throwing his head back and laughing uproariously, "the blood a' tha white devil, gawddammit!"

"Yeah, well, it ain' funny."

Buzz and Luther exchanged smiles. Buzz flipped his cigarette out through the window. Luther shrugged, shaking his head very slowly.

Leroy watched him, frowning as he went on. "Ah want ma kids ta be black, gawddammit."

"Shit, Leroy, you cain' have no black kids," Buzz answered quickly. "Even if ya marry gal dark as Janice, ya kids still gonna be high yella —jes' like if me'n Lutha knock up a white gal. Shit. You white, Leroy."

"Ah'm a nigga, gawddammit! An' ah'm nigga jes' as much as you cats too."

Luther chuckled. "Okay, baby, okay, shit! Buzz right, though. Yo' kids gonna be light'n bright, man."

"They be niggas right on," Leroy shot back, "jes' like they daddy, jes' like niggas evah'wheahs."

"They be pretty too," Buzz said.

Leroy pressed a button to lower his window and flicked his cigarette butt out. He turned to watch the red ash dance along the road and die in the dark behind them. "Ah love Janice," he muttered after a while, "thass all." He sighed and relaxed in his seat. "Gawawddamn," he groaned then, speaking to nobody in particular.

They fell silent again. When they reached the city, Leroy got out and took a cab to their apartment. Buzz and Luther ditched the car and took a cab downtown to the parking lot where they had left Buzz's Oldsmobile. They drove to New York.

Sunday morning, Ella Hawkins sat quietly, sipping a cup of coffee as her eyes wandered over the newspaper. Terry hadn't come home the night before, and Garner gobbled one slice of toast after another as if trying to eat as much as possible before his brother arrived.

" 'Notha' man been robbed an' kilt," Ella sighed. "What the pole-leece doin', anyways?"

The article to which she referred was brief—ROBBERY VICTIM DEAD: "After lingering near death for eighteen hours, David Kaplan succumbed to a bullet wound in his abdomen inflicted by unknown assailants during a Friday night robbery. Police found Kaplan near death behind his place of business early Saturday morning. Dr. John F. O'Connor, of City Hospital, said the victim had been badly beaten about the head and neck and then shot. Mr. Kaplan was 41."

Ella didn't read the article. She finished her coffee and lit a cigarette. "Wheah Terry?"

"Don' know," Garner answered around a mouthful of food, shaking his head. "Hadda date. Went ta party."

Ella shook her head, puffing her cigarette irritably. She sighed with resignation. "He ain' nevah home no mo'. Always partyin'. Them parties—white girls, thass what. Ah sweah, ah don' know what's wrong wit'ch'all. Fine bunch ah got; Lutha, he gone 'bout his bid'ness. You alla time runnin' off somewheahs. What's tha use? Jes' what tha hell tha use—jes' like Lutha, thass all. Same foolishness all ovah agin."

"Ma?"

"What?"

"Ah'm goin' up tha park."

"What fa'?" she wailed, standing up, fixing an angry glare on him.

"Me'n Bobby gonna play baskitball."

"Ah don' know what'cha alla time wit' this baskitball fa'. Gawd know—. Yeah—yeah, sho'. Ah guess so. Jes' don' bang tha do' on ya way out. Don' wan'cha ta wake up Harry."

"Ain' nothin' wake him up."

"What'choo say, boy?"

"Nothin', Ma."

He stared down at his food and chewed vigorously. She went into the parlor on her way to the bedroom. Garner's eyes followed her. He didn't like Harry. He didn't like any of his mother's boyfriends. Harry was her latest, Garner's newest uncle, a heavy, black man of medium height, muscular and strong despite his thirty-eight years and balding head. He was one of a long line of uncles who had followed Uncle Charlie. Only now, Garner understood that uncle wasn't the right word. Old Uncle Charlie-daddy had taught him that—with Terry's help.

The exact distinction between fathers, uncles, and daddies continued to elude him. Terry had tried to clarify it for him, but his explanations were inadequate. Garner had been able to put together a few facts: fathers, uncles, and daddies all slept with their mother. A father became a father by first taking a mother to church. They were married, and they made babies. Uncles made babies with mothers, too, but because they hadn't been to church, they were not fathers but daddies.

Besides, Garner's uncles weren't real uncles, anyway. According to Terry, their mother just called them that when they were small. Real uncles did not sleep with mothers. They were brothers to real fathers. They didn't live in the house here, either; they lived far away. Real fathers, on the other hand, couldn't become daddies, and they lived in the same house that the mothers lived in. Also, they were home every night, and they dressed up quite often—like they did on television, or in the movies. Garner had often tried to imagine what a real father looked like and how he could tell one from an uncle, or a daddy, when he saw one. Not even Terry knew how to do that. Garner finished his food. He got up from the table, keeping a careful eye on the doorway, took one of his mother's cigarettes, lit it, and scooped up his basketball and went out.

Ella heard him leave and smiled, grinding her body against Harry's trying to pull him deeper into her, working with the smooth rhythm of his body. She kissed his neck and shoulder. His heavy, powerful body worked in a steady grind. He grunted rhythmically, contentedly, taking his breath in short, even gasps. Sweat stood out on his black skin. Ella arched her body, reaching for him. He picked up the pace then, driving harder with longer and deeper thrusts. She moaned, moving easily, gladly, and expectantly with him as he shifted gears. She felt his muscles tighten spasmodically. The pace and rhythm began to get away from them. They strained to hold it together, but their bodies shuddered, muscles and breath worked out of control. Then they gasped as the heat of his body exploded in her and met her own.

She held him tightly, kissing him tenderly, fulfilled and content. "That was good, baby," she whispered.

"Tastes like more," he teased, working his body slowly in hers.

She laughed. "Git me a cig'rette."

He reached over to the night table and took a cigarette from his pack. She kept her strong thighs locked around his while he lit her smoke.

He took a long drag from it and put it in her mouth. "Baby, you sure got a body on ya, and that's nothing but a fact."

Her eyes smiled up at him.

He watched her puff the cigarette. "Where's Garner gone?"

"Up tha park."

"To play ball?"

"Yeah."

"Doesn't like me much, does he?"

She turned her head away from him, not answering.

Harry took a puff of her cigarette. "Hey, girl. Hey, baby, c'mon, now."

Ella quickly shook her head.

"Aw—baby. C'mon. What's the matter?"

"Naw—ah guess he don' unda'stan'."

"Guess that's kinda—natural." He took another puff of the cigarette and offered it to her again. She refused it, and he crushed it out in the ashtray. Then he lay there watching her. Neither of them spoke for a while. Tears trickled down her cheeks. Gently, Harry wiped them away, his fleshy, black face pained. "Hey, there, now. Please don't do that, baby. *You* like Harry, don't you?"

She slid her arms around his neck, keeping her eyes away, and pulled him close, clinging to him, sobbing, nodding against his neck. She groaned, "Like ain' tha right word," and pulled her head back and kissed him fiercely, opening her mouth, driving her tongue between his teeth and sucking hard. Her body strained upward against him. He bore down, matching her strength, then overpowering her. She squeezed frantically with her legs. Then she felt his strength and heat rising within her. "Aw—aw-w-w, Harry—"

Afterward, Harry fell asleep. Ella lay beside him, thinking. She knew she was falling in love with him—a bad thing to do in her situation. She had no idea how long he'd stay with her. This fear lurked in her thoughts. It frightened her. He was the best she had known since—*Ben was dead now,* killed in a knife fight in Newark. She still had that letter, carefully folded and tucked away in her bureau. She had cried then. That was before Harry, and she had forgotten about love.

Love; that had become such a hazy thing, apart—*way out there.* Since Ben she had known only sex. Sex was her major source of satisfaction, ego-builder, her fun and relaxation. In a man's arms she found a temporary, elusive kind of peace. If only fleetingly, she was desired, alive—*feminine*—and creative. She found that good, swinging kick that made life bearable.

She sighed and took one of Harry's cigarettes and lit it. She remembered the last time she saw the white woman from the Welfare Department. She had found out that Ella was living with a man. The checks had stopped coming. Ella was scared out of her wits then. *Who was it she was living with then?* But three weeks later she had a job. *That's where she met Harry, too.* She worked as a waitress in a joint where he was the bartender and one of the bouncers.

She smiled slightly, puffing the cigarette as she recalled the expression on his face when she asked him—*told* him—to move in with her *—They were sitting in his car outside of her house one Sunday morning. It was still dark out, and cold. She could see traces of ice and snow beneath the headlights in front of the car. He had driven her home from work. When he kissed her, he whispered huskily, "I think I'll come up for a while." His hand slid under her skirt. She held his* *face in her hands and said, "Whyn'cha come on up an' stay fa' good, baby?" "What?" She dropped her hands and looked down at the seat. "Ah mean—ya been comin' up an' stayin'—jes' stayin' fa' while. Shoot, Harry, ah want—ah wan'cha in ma bed—ah mean, ah wan'cha heah—'roun' tha house, alla time. Ya see?" Harry listened to her quiet voice and sighed wearily. "Yeah. Yeah, baby. Sooner or later, you women always—Ella, look—I had it once with marriage—. Uh—baby, I dig ya, now. I mean, really. I really do, but—" "Harry, ah ain' said nothin' 'bout marryin'," she whispered, looking up at him. "Ah jes' wan'cha heah. Ah wanna do fa' ya. Thass what, Harry. Ah wanna—." He chuckled softly. "Baby, you get upstairs and warm my bed. I'll be right back.*—He had insisted on paying the rent and buying the food. He took her places, too, *remembered her birthday—bought her presents.* She propped herself up on her elbow and watched him sleep.

He wasn't a pretty man, homely really, but he was clean and neat, strongly made, and there was an unmistakable air of sexuality about him. Yes, she thought, and he cared for her, didn't chase around. *A man, that's all.* She feared losing him, feared also that he might be hurt in one of the fights that she had seen at the club—him right in the middle.

Looking down at Harry now, she could feel him somehow slipping away from her. She stifled the impulse to wake him up, to hear his voice, to feel his hands on her again. In her mind, her voice pleaded with him, *"Wake up, baby! C'mon! Lemme feel ya. Lemme know—."* Then her thoughts wandered, becoming incoherent.

Were her fears real or imagined? she wondered. Something was drifting, slipping, being taken away from her. What? A feeling of terror seized her. It was as if a part of her was being slowly, painfully, ripped from her body, or her mind, or both at once—a piece of her very soul, perhaps, splintering fragments of Ella Hawkins breaking up on the reefs of pain and despair which lurked in the dark waters of her life—life itself, perhaps. *Death?* But we all die. We all die. And then there was God, wasn't there? No. *No, not for her.* Where was that God she had learned to love—and fear—in that small country church

—that tall, fierce, black minister who so often stood above her, his voice filling the room, *"Ah'm talkin' ta you, gal, and you, sister, and you, brother"*—that she had known so many years ago?

All at once, Ella wanted to cry out, *"Gawd! He'p me; gawd! he'p me! He'p me, please!"* She shut her eyes for a moment, stifling the screams in her mind. She held her breath, looking down at Harry again. She wanted to sit on his chest, pin him with her knees and slap him until he woke up; God, she wanted to threaten him with *murder!* Was it absurd to dream of love, maybe—maybe, even of marriage? *"Naw. Ain' gonna marry me. Naw, Ella."* She put out her cigarette then and shook her head.

No. This tiny, happy moment of her life was trickling away, and she was sure that this was the last time, the last happy time for her. She was thirty-five now—suddenly that seemed very old. How long would her full-blown figure be attractive to men? And what men? No woman could expect more than two *real men* in her life, could she? Some women never had any, no real men. Was she luckier than they? Ben was dead. *Harry?* He would tire of her; he would leave, and she would be alone. She had failed herself in life, or something had, perhaps, failed her. Her boys were growing further away from her. Soon Terry would leave home just as Luther did. Garner would follow. Well—she could work. Yes. *Yes, she could!* Ella cried then, cringing against Harry, sobbing quietly until she fell asleep.

Spring was early that year, bringing a warm sun and the quick eager burst of life renewed. People crowded the streets. The pulse of the city quickened, and life seemed less desperate and more exuberant. It was good; spring was always good. It washed and cleansed the new days and seemed to filter away the harshness of winter.

Though Garner didn't understand the why of the seasons, he wanted to, without knowing there *was* a why, or that he even cared. Sometimes, staring out at the city through a classroom window, or sitting on his front stoop, or standing outside of the drugstore across from the school, he could almost feel, almost see, the why. An intense feeling would sweep through him then, and he was glad, grateful about nothing that he could explain. He felt so good that it almost hurt. He got an urge to get up and run full speed along the streets, by the people, darting in and out between the cars. Then he would wonder if there was something wrong with him, and he would hesitate, pondering, considering. Suddenly, the feeling would be gone, and he felt odd, lessened somehow. When he attempted, consciously, to recapture the mood, he couldn't. It was gone.

"Say, Hawk," Bobby said one Saturday afternoon. "What'cha lookin' at out there?"

"Huh?"

"C'mon, take a shot if ya gonna," Ellis complained.

Bobby idly dribbled the basketball and arched a long, one-hand push-shot toward the basket. The ball rimmed the hoop and bounded to the side. Ellis leaped up and caught it. Garner walked over to the fence behind the basket and leaned against it, pressing his black face against the rusty, chain-link mesh.

Bobby followed him. "You're always doin' that, ya know that, Hawk?"

"Doin' what, man?"

"Standin' there like that."

"Like how?"

"I dunno. Just standin', kinda."

"Sheet."

Ellis came over, dribbling the ball. "Track starts Monday," he said casually and began to move the ball in a circle around his body and behind his back, faster and faster.

"Who gives a fuck?" Garner said. He turned and bent down to pick up a rock and threw it across the playground, watching it clear the small, brick building which housed the park office. A tiny, black boy, who was shooting marbles with some other boys, stood up, following the flight of the rock, then he found one and threw it. Garner frowned and looked at Ellis.

Ellis caught his eyes momentarily and shrugged, flipping the ball into the air and catching it easily, first on one hand and then on the other. "Bet'cha ah could do jugglin'—. Sheet, you'n Bobby oughtta come on the baskitball team nex' yeah, man. Lotta cats leavin'. Evah'-thin' be wide open. We could have ourse'ves a ball."

"Aw, man," muttered Garner, heaving another rock. "Who wanna do alla practice an' shit?"

"My brother says I oughtta get on a team," Bobby whispered, watching Garner pick up more rocks.

Garner threw one. "Man, y'ain' gonna mess wit' none a' that shit, is ya?"

Bobby fidgeted and wiped some sweat off his face with the front of his sweatshirt. He stole a cautious look at Garner. Ellis sat down on the basketball. Bobby watched him scuff one of his sneakers in the dirt. "I'm goin' out for baseball," he announced in a loud voice that cracked with nervousness and the high and low, adolescent mixture of man and boy. "Coach says I gotta good chance of makin' the team."

"Tha hell wit' baseball," Garner grumbled. "What'cha wanna play baseball fa'?"

"Shit, Hawk, it might be fun, fa' crissake. Anyways, I like ta play. Mike plays. Me and him was playin' catch and—"

"Ah'm gonna run track," Ellis interrupted. "Murph say ah got tha build fa' it."

"Fuck Murph," Garner spat out. He stood, idly watching as a young, white woman with long black hair came out of the park office, followed by a group of small girls running to keep up with her. She walked over to the little boys who were shooting marbles. They stopped playing and gathered around her. She spoke to them for a moment, then they started yelling and jumping happily. She laughed as they pulled on the oversize man's shirt she was wearing. A little white girl hugged her from behind.

"Sheet, Ellis, *ah* kin run faster'n *you,* fa' crissake," Garner said.

"You fulla shit!"

The kids ran by them, laughing, pulling the young woman along. She glanced briefly at the three boys and smiled. It was an earnest smile of bright, blue eyes and rosy cheeks, dimples and flashing, white teeth. The boys' eyes followed her. She was pretty in blue shorts and the floppy shirt.

Bobby nudged Garner. "That's Carol. She's a neighborhood worker."

"Huh?"

"Works with little kids. Sadadays."

"Looka them legs," Ellis said.

They watched her and the children pile into an old station wagon parked out on the street.

Ellis looked up at Garner. "Bet'cha ah kin beat'cha down ta tha water fountain an' back."

Garner stepped quickly away from the fence and stared down at him. "How much ya wanna bet?" he yelped, his voice rising in a high-pitched squeal.

"I'll watch fa' the winna. You can race from the fence," Bobby said.

Ellis accepted eagerly. He was proud of his speed and had won prizes running for the Boys Club one winter. He was lighter and smaller than Garner, too. He grinned and did a little jig, then jogged back and forth a few times.

The distance was about seventy-five yards each way. The boys assumed sprinter's start positions, leaning forward on their hands, pushing against the fence with their sneakers. There were deadly serious expressions on their black faces. They tensed up, steeling themselves for the effort.

"I'll just say, one, two, three—go," Bobby said. "That okay?"

It was agreed. On Bobby's signal, they bolted from the fence. Ellis started fastest. He had experience and knew something about concentration. Garner lit out after him. His strides were longer than Ellis's. They tore across the playground almost neck and neck. When they reached the water fountain, Garner was ahead. They spun around, and he slipped. Ellis strained into the lead with Garner lunging desperately to catch him. He caught up and tried to go in front, but Ellis was running hard, and they continued sprinting together. Garner was tiring. He could feel his thighs thicken with fatigue and weaken as he reached for more speed. It was a long sprint for both boys. Garner kept jerking his head sideways to look at Ellis, and each time he did, Ellis inched in front of him. Garner stretched mightily. He was very tired, and his legs seemed to be slowing down even though he pumped his knees with all his strength. He saw the fence coming up fast and made a frantic lunge at it. They slammed into it together, breaking the force of their drive with their hands.

Bobby was yelling, "Ellis won! Ellis won! Ellis—"

"Aw, *naw,*" Garner howled, gasping violently. "Hell, naw, man!" He bent over, hands on knees panting and spitting.

Ellis sat down heavily, falling on his back in the dirt. *"Wow!* Thass a whole lotta runnin'."

"Ah won!" Garner gasped.

"Stop tha shit, now, Hawk," Ellis groaned, trying to suck air into his burning chest. Then he sat up abruptly and grinned at Garner. "Wuz a tie, man. Gawddamn, Hawk—you kin really go. Jesus—whew, baby. Gawddamn!"

"It was awful close," Bobby said uncertainly, "I dunno—"

"Sheet," Garner bawled.

Ellis fell backward to the ground again. He grimaced, pulling his knees up and down, scraping his heels in the dirt. "Baby, we wuz strainin'."

"You guys can really run."

Garner sat down, still fighting for breath. His lungs felt like they were on fire.

"Shit, Garna—we ran our asses off."

"Sheet, if ah wuzn't so tired, ah woulda whipped yo' tail bad, man."

"Shee-yee-yit! Is you fa' real, man? When ah git in shape, ain' *no* mutha-fucka gonna ketch me."

"Ellis is fast, Hawk. Wait'll he gets in condition."

"Fuck you, Bobby. Fa' crissake, he been playin' ball all winta."

"You come on out an' run, then, an' see if ah don' run away frum ya."

"Sheet—okay, man. Okay. Okay, gawddammit. Ah show ya. Ah show ya what's happ'nin'."

Bobby grinned. "Beautiful. We'll get us a whole *bunch* of jackets and shit."

When Frank Murphy saw Garner and Bobby sitting in the gym with the rest of his boys, he couldn't believe his eyes. Were they really coming out for spring sports? Why the sudden change? He turned away from the office window, chuckling. He looked at Bill Lasky, the baseball coach. "Wait'll I tell Collins about this," he gloated, chuckling again.

"About Garner?"

"Yeah. And Bobby Russo."

"I don't know, Frank. Maybe you better wait and see if they last the season."

Murph hesitated, looking at him seriously and frowned.

"Hell," Bill went on, "you know how some of these kids are."

"Yeah—well, we better get out there."

Ed Collins did not believe him, not at first. He had to go down to the practice field and see for himself. Later during the season, he walked up to Murph in the school corridor, fell in step, and walked along with him toward the teachers' room.

Murph grinned. "Coming to the meet Friday?"

Collins sighed and shook his head. *"Okay,* I told you before; you're hell on wheels."

"I told *you* that a long time ago."

"Seriously though, Frank, I don't get it. Russo—him I can figure, but *Garner*—well, that's just got to be the feat of the year. You remember Luther? Garner's—"

"I told you, I never quit."

"—just like him. At least, that's what I thought, anyway. Worst damn—nigger I ever had. Could never do a thing with him. He wasn't interested in *anything*—. Hell no. Boy, did I hate that black bastard."

"I think I know who you mean. Ninth-grader, wasn't he?"

"Yeah, when you came," Collins answered, nodding to two women teachers walking toward them.

"I remember. He quit school."

"Yeah. Great big kid, stupid. Must of stayed back at least—well, once that I'm sure of. Big boy, black as coal, looked like a high school kid. Garner even looks like him. Be just as big, too—and he's just as black."

"Garner's been staying out of trouble lately."

"Yeah. Hell, he's probably getting ready to burn the place down."

"I doubt that." Murph smiled.

Garner and Ellis were the only seventh-grade boys to play on a varsity team. Bobby was the catcher on the baseball team. "I got a arm," he told his buddies proudly after practice one day. "Coach says catchin's the fastest way to the big leagues."

Garner and Ellis stared at him incredulously, swapped grins, and then roared, falling to the ground, hugging each other and howling with glee.

"Ain' thatta bitch?" Garner screamed, rolling in the dirt with Ellis in their warm-up suits. "Ain' thatta bitch?"

Ellis was nearly in tears. "Gawddamn. Did ya heah'im? He talkin' 'bout tha big league! Ain' thatta mutha-fucka? Ain' thatta bitch?"

"Yeah—he gonna mess wit' tha Red Sox now!"

The two boys were helpless with laughter. Bobby watched them, trying to pretend anger, then, laughing with them, he jumped on them and began to wrestle, pummeling them furiously.

An intense rivalry developed between Garner and Ellis. The track team was loaded with fast sprinters, and they didn't have the experience to run with them, so they had most of their fun whipping each other. At the beginning of the season, they swapped wins and defeats evenly. Later, Garner started to win more consistently. "Ah got'cha now, Ellis, gawddammit," he boasted one day as they stepped out of the showers. "Ah'm gonna run yo' ass ta death."

"Sheet, you jes' bigga'n me, thass all."

"Sheet."

" 'Sides, Murph wan's me ta train fa' longer races, anyways. Says ah got good wind."

"Man, you crazy ta fuck wit' that long shit. Ah ain'. Ah'm gonna be a sprinta."

"You jes' ain' got tha wind fa' it, man. Ah got good wind."

"Sheet, you kin have that shit. Ah'm stayin' wit' tha dashes."

"Y'ain' got tha wind."

At the end of the season, all three boys received awards. Bobby earned his, but Garner and Ellis only got theirs because Murph gave all of his boys awards. Bobby hastened to make this point painfully clear, whispering to his friends slyly as they marched up to the front of the school assembly to go up and sit on the stage with the other athletes, "If you guys was on the baseball team, Lasky'd give ya nothin'."

"Fuck you," Garner hissed.

"Go to hell," Ellis said.

Bobby laughed and gave Garner an elbow in the ribs.

Garner scowled. He didn't enjoy Bobby's needling him, but he was proud and happy as he walked onto the stage. When his name was called, and he heard the applause, he scrambled out of his seat. A huge grin was frozen on his face when Murph handed him his school letter, a big T—for Timilty Junior High School—made of gold chenille with maroon trim. The ninth-grade boys received heavy maroon and gold athletic jackets. Later during the awards ceremony, Garner and his buddies sat together, grinning happily as they ran their fingers over the soft chenille letters.

"Man," Garner exclaimed in a whisper.

Ellis agreed. "Yeah."

"Man!"

Bobby smiled. "Didn't I tell ya, Hawk? Didn't I?"

Garner nodded, the broad grin still lighting up his black face. He had never won anything in his life before. He had never been applauded, either—especially by his teachers. "Man, nex' yeah, we gonna really show'em!"

Garner's protection racket was cut off with the long summer vacation, and he and his buddies found themselves hard put to dig up any money. They suffered in dire poverty for almost a week. Then, almost by accident, they found a new hustle.

It was late on a sticky, hot night. They were walking south on Washington Street. Their T-shirts and dungarees stuck to the sweat on their skins. There weren't many people about and the traffic on the street was thinning rapidly. Garner stopped to light a cigarette.

"Gimme one," Bobby said.

Garner handed him the pack. Ellis took one, too, and they lit up and started walking again. Then Garner stopped and stood staring across the street under the El structure.

"C'mon, Hawk," Ellis urged. "What'cha doin'?"

"How much ya figga them cats make?" Garner inquired, pointing his cigarette across the street at a newspaper boy.

"Who?"

"Them cats, man. Sellin' newspapers."

Ellis followed Garner's cigarette until he saw the newsboy. "Sheet, ah dunno. You know, Bobby?"

"Naw. Christ, Hawk, you gonna sell papers?"

"Shit, naw, man."

"Wait up a second, man. Ah mean—how many papers them cats sell a night?"

"Who gives a shit? C'mon."

Bobby spoke up, "Shit, I know a kid sells a hunnerd, maybe a hunnerd and fifty a night. He sold two hunnerd one night."

"Fa' dime each?"

"Yeah."

"Sheet, thass fifteen—maybe twenny dollas."

"So what?" Ellis sighed.

"He ain' very big," Garner pondered.

"So what, man?"

"So—so s'pose ah start some shit wit'im, and then he start some shit wit' me?"

"We'd hafta kick his ass," Bobby laughed.

Ellis came to life then. A wide grin spread over his face. They all stood on the edge of the curb, watching the newspaper boy. He started walking north at a brisk pace.

"What'cha gonna do, Hawk?" Ellis asked as they started across the street.

"Ah dunno—sheet, we gonna git some bread offa tha som'bitch, thass all."

Bobby was thinking it over. "Hey, Ellis can keep a lookout, and—"

"Yeah," Garner followed quickly, "an' ah start jackin' 'im up, an'—"

"I'll get him from behind," Bobby concluded.

It worked. They got eleven dollars from the boy, most of it in small change. Mugging newsboys turned out to be a good hustle. It was fun, too. The three boys prowled the streets at night like beasts of prey on the hunt, looking for an easy kill. A feeling of urgent, unbearable excitement came over them when they stalked a boy. It was as if they had the power of life and death in their hands. They felt hard, quick, and dangerous—hired assassins—gunslingers on the prod—pirates on the high seas.

Their operation became very sophisticated. They always looked for a boy who had only a few newspapers left, thus making sure the boy had sold enough papers to have some money. They also made sure that he wasn't too big, that he was alone, and then they followed him. When they got him alone, Garner and Bobby ran by the boy, bumping into him. One of them would then pick a fight with him while Ellis kept watch. Before the unfortunate boy could put his papers down, let alone put up his fists, or run, he got shoved from behind, then punched in his mouth, and before it was over, he was relieved of his money. Of course, they had to restrict the operation to areas outside of their own neighborhoods, and they couldn't do it every night, but it worked well for them. It was profitable and relatively free of danger.

One night, after a successful hunt, Garner left his friends and returned home to find Terry waiting for him on the front steps.

"Gawddamn, Hawk, wheah ya been?"

"What'cha mean, wheah ah been?"

"Man, ah been waitin' fa' ya."

"Ah been workin'," Garner said proudly. "Ah thought'choo wuz gonna party ta-nite."

"Been awreddy. Goin' back. Listen, man—"

"That tha suit ya got ta-day?"

"Yeah. Listen, Hawk, ya got any change?"

"Huh? Naw! Naw, man."

"Ah thought'cha said ya been workin'."

"You been gamblin'?"

"What'choo care?"

"Ah tol' ya, ah ain' holdin' nothin'."

Terry stood up and spat out onto the sidewalk. He smiled knowingly and lit a smoke. Then he checked his watch. Garner started up the steps, nervously fingering the money he had jammed into the watch pocket of his dungarees.

"Wait up, Hawk."

"Ah ain' holdin' nothin', Terry."

"Sheet—look, nigga, ya wanna pick up a little change?"

"Yeah. How?"

"Ah got a ideah. You jes' come on an' do like ah tell ya."

Terry led him through an alley and across an open lot. They passed some unfinished construction. There was a sign—YOUNG MEN'S CHRISTIAN ASSOCIATION.

"Man," Garner said, "they gonna build 'notha church."

"Sheet, thass not gonna be a fuckin' church, nigga. It's a YMCA. C'mon, man. We gotta git this change."

"Ah'm comin', nigga, shit. How far we gotta go, anyways?"

"Jes' down Dudley way, thass all."

"Gawddamn, man, ah don' wanna go way tha fuck down theah, sheet. How much we gonna git?"

"Plenny," Terry promised as they came out of the construction site onto the sidewalk. "C'mon. Do ya want tha fuckin' bread or don'cha?"

"How much?"

"*Jesus!* Look—we might could git—maybe fifty bucks, but we ain' gonna git a mutha-fuckin' thing 'less we git goin', gawddammit."

Terry hailed a cab and gave the driver, a white man, an address four blocks from the store he wanted to nit. When the car stopped, he stepped out and looked up at a lighted window. "Ma's still up. C'mon, boy," he said to Garner. "Ma want us in tha house. It's almos' 'leven o'clock."

"Hey," the cabbie snapped at him, "you owe me a buck sixty-five."

"Ah know it, man, ma motha got tha money. Jes' upstairs."

"Well—make it quick, will ya?"

"Yassuh," Terry answered crisply, waving Garner out of the car.

Garner followed his brother into an old apartment building and out through the back door into an alley. "You a cool mutha-fucka, Terry," he laughed as they ran through the alley.

"Ah tol' ya, jes' listen ta Terry, an' evah'thin' be okay, didn't ah?"

They stopped near a small building which was a combination store and restaurant with a dairy bar. Terry adjusted his blue suit carefully and took out a handkerchief to wipe the sweat off his face. "Okay. He gonna be closin' soon. We gonna wait 'til ain' nobuddy in theah. Then ah'm goin' in. Now, you listen; ah show ya what ah wan'cha ta do." He took Garner's arm and pulled him around the corner. They stopped at the entrance to an alley behind the store. Terry pointed at the building. "Okay, now, nigga, ya see that winda wit' tha light?"

"Yeah."

"Okay, now theah's 'notha alleyway 'cross tha street. It go all tha way ta tha nex' street. Ah'm gonna go in tha sto' an' git a Coke. When ya see me go in, ah wan'cha ta throw a stone through tha winda. Then git 'cross inta tha alleyway an' stay. Ya got it?"

Garner looked at him. Then he looked up at the window.

Terry grew impatient. "Ya got it now?"

Garner nodded.

Terry looked around in the dark. He handed Garner a red brick. "Heah. Now, wait 'til ah go in, an' take ya time, gawddammit. Make sho' ya break tha fuckin' winda. Ya heah? Don' fuck up."

"Ah got'cha, man, gawddamn."

Terry waited until there were no customers in the store and went inside. He ordered a Coke. A short, thin, white man served him, and Terry gave him a dime. As the man was about to ring up the sale, the crashing sound of splintering glass came from the back room. The man whirled around. "What the hell was that?" he yelled. He ran to the back of the store and disappeared through a door. As soon as he had entered the back room, he heard the jingle of his cash register. He hesitated, looking up at the broken window and then at the brick and jagged pieces of glass on the floor. He cursed and ran back into the store.

Terry was already fleeing through the front door. He raced across the street and turned the corner into the alley. Behind him, he could hear the man howling curses, "You black bastard, you! You black nigger son-of-a-bitch! You lousy, nigger bastard!"

Garner got twenty dollars. He thought he had received half of the loot, but he hadn't. Terry had over forty dollars for himself. But Garner was happy. He couldn't wait to tell Ellis and Bobby. They would have plenty of money now.

Leroy was drafted into the army that summer. Luther got the call, too, but he couldn't pass the written test. Leroy didn't want to go. His white face was grim as he packed his suitcase the day he was to leave. He was thinking about Janice and the night before—*They were standing in the hallway in the building where she lived. He kissed her long and hard. She was crying. Her slender body felt light in his arms, and he could feel her breasts pushing against his chest. She moved her head and smiled at him. Tears glistened in the dim light and trickled down over her ebony face. Lord, he thought, this girl is beautiful. She's beautiful, and she belongs to me. She kissed him then, whispering against his lips, "I love you, Leroy. I love you. Please write. I'll write every day; I won't be able to stand it otherwise." He had never written a letter, but he kissed her neck and whispered, "Ah write." She sighed and tightened her arms about his neck. "Ah—ah loves ya, gal," he groaned. "Ah loves ya."*—Leroy scowled and cursed under his breath. He wished her parents had allowed her to take the day off from work. Why did she have to work, anyway?

Buzz sat on the bed watching him pack. Luther leaned on the bureau at the other side of the room. They were all very quiet. It was raining outside. Luther looked away from his friends and shook his head. Buzz lit a smoke and walked over to the window. He stood motionless with his back to the others, staring out at the street. Everything was shining, gleaming with water. The wind drove the rain against the gray and red and brown buildings and swept the water along the glossy black street.

There were tears in Luther's eyes; he wiped at them quickly, glancing warily at the others to make sure they weren't watching him. He crushed his cigarette out and lit another, shaking his head helplessly, puffing without inhaling. Leroy finished packing and checked his watch. Luther kept shaking his head.

They took Leroy downtown in Buzz's car. Buzz drove idly, listlessly, as though he wasn't sure where he was going. Luther sat in the rear, staring at the back of Leroy's head. Leroy watched the windshield wipers, barely noticing the buildings they passed or the people hurrying through the rain along the sidewalks. The El train thundered overhead, momentarily drowning out the sound of the rain on the roof. Nobody said anything during the entire trip.

They got out of the car in front of the Fargo Building where Leroy was to report. Buzz got the suitcase from the trunk and walked around the car onto the sidewalk to stand with Leroy and Luther in the rain. After a while, Luther mumbled, "Shit, baby—ah mean—like this is *it,* ain' it?"

Leroy fidgeted uneasily.

Luther started to say something else but didn't because something knotted his stomach and clamped down hard on his voice. He looked at Buzz, who kept his head down, muttering in a low voice, "Say, Leroy—cool it, will ya? Ya know, man? Ya know what ah mean—don' be fuckin' up, will ya?"

Leroy tried to smile, but he had to avert his eyes. He began to blink and squint.

Luther looked down at his feet. Slowly, gingerly, he held out his hand through the rain. "So long, man."

"See you cats, man," Leroy said in a whisper, shaking Luther's hand and then Buzz's.

He picked up his suitcase and walked rapidly toward the building.

He heard Luther yelling to him, "Hey, Leroy. Hey, man—." He turned to look at them again.

Luther was standing with his fists clenched at his sides. He lowered his eyes, shaking his head, then he looked up and tried to grin through his tears. "Ain' this a *bitch?*" he yelled. "Ain' this a bitch, man?"

"Yeah," Leroy called to him, nodding his head.

Luther yelled angrily then, *"Leroy?"*

"What, man?"

"You take care, gawddammit! Ah mean—aw, fuck you, Leroy."

"Yeah," Leroy murmured against the rain. "Yeah—fuck you, too, baby." He smiled gently as Luther held up his hand to wave, then he turned and walked through the door into the building.

On the way home, Buzz and Luther bought two fifths of scotch. They had finished over half of one of them when they got back to the apartment.

"Hey, cool it, you guys," Ellis whispered hastily. "Heah come Lasky."

Garner and Bobby stopped talking when they saw Mr. Lasky striding purposefully down the aisle from the front of the assembly hall. He stood in the aisle beside their row and peered angrily at them over the heads of the other students. Bobby and Garner stared straight ahead. Ellis fiddled with his fingers, grinning.

Mr. Lasky put his hands on his hips and shook his dark head in disgust. "You'd think that you guys would be able to keep your mouths shut—that you could observe school regulations just *once* a year."

Some of the boys and girls sitting nearby turned to grin at the three boys. Garner and Ellis struck out with vicious glares all around them.

"Get up out of there, Bobby," Mr. Lasky ordered.

"Me?" Bobby asked innocently, pointing at his chest and looking around with an expression of feigned bewilderment on his face.

"Your name's Bobby, isn't it?"

"No, see? My name's Robert."

The other students snickered openly and nodded to each other as though Bobby's answer was a perfectly reasonable one.

"Okay, wise guy, get up from there."

Bobby thought of inviting Mr. Lasky to come and get him, but Ellis nudged him in the ribs. Bobby looked up to see Murph move away from a group of teachers clustered near the stage and take a couple of steps in their direction.

"What did *I* do?" Bobby asked with exaggerated surprise.

"Go over and sit with the rest of the ninth grade where you belong."

"First day of school," Bobby muttered sullenly, glancing briefly at Garner and Ellis, "and they're on our backs awreddy."

"Is there something wrong here?" Murph inquired, coming up to stand next to Mr. Lasky.

"No, Mr. Murphy, not really. I'm simply trying to find a way to make Bobby understand that he's been promoted."

"Do you find that hard to believe, Bobby?"

"Awright! Okay, awreddy. I'm comin'. I'm leavin', okay?"

Murph grabbed Bobby's arm with one strong hand as the boy attempted to shoulder his way between the teachers in the aisle. Murph's voice was hard and low. "You—uh, hold it nice and steady. Want to be careful not to muss your new suit. Understand, Bobby?"

"Yeah, yeah."

"Well, that's fine. Now, if you want me to move, just say so, in a polite way, see? Simply excuse yourself, and I'll be glad to step aside. It'll be easier on all of us that way. I'm wearing a new suit, too, see?"

"Well," Bobby mumbled, looking around at some of the other students and shrugging his big shoulders, "excuse me, then. Okay?"

Murph smiled. "Certainly."

"Very glad to," Lasky said.

Bobby threw one last grimace of exaggerated disgust at his two buddies and swaggered over to the middle of the hall to sit with the ninth grade.

As the two teachers turned to walk to the front of the hall, Ellis groaned in a low voice, "Man, this place gonna be a bitch wit' Murph fa' prince-pul."

"He ain' gonna be no prince-pul," Garner snarled.

"Thass tha shit *ah* been hearin', Hawk."

Garner saw Murph stop to look back at them. He gave Ellis a sharp elbow, and they both shut up quickly. Murph continued down the aisle.

Fidgeting uncomfortably in his new, light-brown suit, Garner dug a finger inside his collar and adjusted his tie. He hated assemblies, especially long ones. And assembly was always long on the first day of school. Looking around, he saw a whole host of new teachers. His eyes fastened, momentarily, on a short, black man wearing a navy-blue blazer and gray flannel pants. He was a handsome man, in a rough-featured way, compact and powerfully made. "Hey, Ellis. Who tha—cullid cat up theah? He gonna be a teacha' heah?"

"Ah dunno."

"Shit, he evil-lookin' stud, man. Cat looks hard."

"Theah go Moran. Why the fuck we alla time gotta listen ta this ol' bitch fa'?"

"Yeah—ah dunno, man. Bitch been heah so fuckin' long, seem like nobuddy kin do nothin' wit'out 'er talkin', fa' crissake."

"She so fuckin' ol', she wuz a teacha befo' they built tha fuckin' place, man."

"Yeah. Looka tha nose on tha bitch, will ya?"

Ellis had to put a hand over his mouth to keep from laughing out loud. Some of the other kids began to titter restlessly. Garner and Ellis kept cautious eyes on Murph seated on stage and went on entertaining the kids with their banter.

As usual, Mrs. Moran spoke for a long time. Garner and Ellis barely listened; nobody did, not even the teachers. "Now," she said finally, her voice ringing like hard, thin metal, "I'm extremely proud to introduce your new principal, Mr. James F. Sullivan."

A tall, thin, white man stood up and walked to the speaker's stand. Garner and Ellis elbowed each other at the same time. Garner was grinning happily. "Sheet, man, Murph ain' gonna be prince-pul."

"Thass tha bes' news a' tha fuckin' day, man."

The new principal had just said something, and Murph stood up and took a bow. Garner's face grew serious, and he quickly sat forward in his seat. "Hey, Ellis, what that cat talkin' 'bout?"

"Huh?"

"What he jes' say—somethin' 'bout Murph, man?"

"*What?* What he say?"

"Ah dunno. What tha fuck's a assistant ta tha prince-pul?"

"Jesus, Hawk, ah dunno. Almos' same's a prince-pul, ah *think*. Why?"

"Gaw-aw-awddamn! Man, thass what tha fuck Murph gonna be."

"Aw, *Jesus!*"

The short black man stood up and sat down again.

"What he say *now?*"

Ellis screwed his face up in a frown as he listened attentively. "Somethin' 'bout—thass tha new gym teacha."

"Sheet."

"Man, things been all shook up 'roun' heah."

Assembly was finally dismissed. School was recessed early. Garner and Ellis hung around the schoolyard, waiting for Bobby. Ellis kicked idly at a brown leaf which floated along the ground. Some girls went by and spoke to them. "Hi, Garna." "Hello, Ellis." The two boys nodded casually.

"Heah come Bobby now," Ellis announced and turned slowly to watch the girls walk across the busy street.

"That little blond bitch is fine, Ellis."

"Yeah. She tough. Hey, Bobby, what's been keepin' ya?"

"Yeah, man. Wheah ya been?"

"Down the fuckin' office, that's where!"

Garner and Ellis looked at each other, puzzled for a moment. Then they began to laugh.

"First day a' school," Ellis cried.

"Yeah, ain' this a bitch?"

"You guys think it's funny, but it ain't, goddammit. Murph pulled me in the office, says he's gonna drive me home after the teachers' meetin' so's he can talk to my folks."

Garner scowled, staring at Bobby with a pensive look on his face. "What tha fuck ya done, fa' crissake?"

"Nothin'! Shit, they're on my ass 'cause I give Lasky a hard time this mornin'."

Ellis's mouth fell open. "Jesus, they call ya in the office fa' *that* shit, man? Ah knew Murph wuz a prick, but Jesus Christ—ain' thatta bitch, Hawk?"

"Yeah. Yo' ol' man gonna kick yo' ass, Bobby."

"I *know* it, goddammit! I just hope he ain't been drinkin', that's all."

"Maybe he won't be theah," Ellis offered feebly.

Bobby angrily kicked at a pebble and jammed his hands in his pockets. Garner and Ellis shifted their feet around, stealing guarded peeks at him. Across the street, Garner saw the same group of girls who had spoken to them before, coming out of the drugstore eating ice cream. "What'cha gonna do, Bobby?"

"Yeah. Yo' ol' man is *evil!"* Ellis said.

"I dunno—get my teeth kicked in, I guess. What else?"

"Shit, man, don' go home, thass all," Garner suggested.

Bobby laughed bitterly. *"Balls!* Are you shittin' me, fa' crissake? My old man'd send my brothers afta me, and my Uncle Julio, too. Christ—they'd drag me home by my balls. Beat me ta death, fa' crissake."

The next day, Thursday, Bobby did not come to school. Garner and Ellis didn't see him over the weekend, either.

Garner felt uneasy, going to school on Monday. He felt worse when he discovered that Bobby had failed to show up again. Something was wrong, different, out of kilter. His chain of command was disrupted. He wanted to go right ahead and reorganize the protection racket, but he felt unsure about it. Things didn't seem the way they should.

During those first few days at school, he began to notice changes. The school had been freshly painted and scrubbed clean. Mr. Sullivan and Murph were all over the place, talking to students, teachers, and custodians. The teachers stepped smartly about the school. And every student offense received the immediate, personal attention of Mr. Sullivan and Murph. Garner didn't like it at all.

On Thursday, Ellis cornered him in home room before the first bell. "Hey, Hawk, ya heah 'bout Stevie?"

"Huh? Naw, man."

"Burke an' Lasky caught'im afta school smokin' down behind tha gym. Murph kicked him outta school."

"So what? Sheet, all he gotta do is git his motha ta come."

Ellis shook his head vigorously. "Naw, man! Stevie tol' Marie he's *out,* man! Goin' ta Dis-pee!"

"Gawddamn, ain' nobuddy git sent ta Dis-pee jes' fa' smokin', fa' crissake."

"Thass what Marie said."

"Man, fuck Marie, shit."

"Ah dunno, Hawk. Ah mean—what tha fuck's happ'nin'?"

"Sheet. Fuck all that shit, man. Ya seen Bobby?"

"Naw."

"Gawddamn."

Bobby was back in school the following day. Garner and Ellis stared in awe that morning as his brothers pushed and dragged him across the schoolyard and through the door. Bobby didn't acknowledge that he saw them. He looked scared.

"Did ya see his fuckin' face, Ellis?"

Ellis nodded gravely. "Yeah. Somebuddy whaled tha livin' shit outta him, man."

"Yo' fatha evah whip ya ass like that, man?"

"He only my stepfatha."

"Huh?"

"Stepfatha. He my stepfatha. Ma got married befo'—ta ma real fatha. *He* cut out. It's Ma kicks *ma* ass. She ketch me wrong, an' she really lay on, baby."

"What'sa stepfatha like?"

"He okay. Pain in tha ass sometime, though. Ma make me call'im daddy."

"What *he* say?"

"What'cha mean?"

"When ya call'im daddy."

"Nothin'—what'cha talkin' 'bout?"

"Nothin'. Shit, now Bobby back, we kin git goin' an' start tha collections, git movin', fa' crissake."

"Shit, Hawk, ah dunno. We bes' cool it, see what's happ'nin', man. Ya know? Things ain' right. Ah mean—Bobby ain' gonna wanna be fuckin' 'roun'."

"Man, what tha fuck ya talkin' 'bout?"

"Nothin', man. Jes' think we oughtta cool it fa' while, thass all."

"You skeered, Ellis."

"Naw, man—"

"Yeah, you is, nigga. Them mutha-fuckin' teachas an' shit done skeered tha shit outta *you.*"

"Naw, Hawk. But, shit, man, Sully'n Murph ain' playin'. They makin' tha teachas go ta meetin's evah'day, man. Ah seen'em."

"Fuck'em. You skeered, nigga. Y'ain' shit, Ellis."

"Jesus Christ, Hawk. What'cha gotta say that fa'?"

Garner didn't answer. He sulked until the school bell rang. Ellis followed him into the school, looking at him sheepishly.

They saw Bobby in gym class. The kids were lining up to play bombardment.

Bobby, his face swollen and discolored, was in a bad mood. "Fuck this shit, fa' crissake. Too many goddamn kids."

"It's betta' wit' lotsa kids," Garner said.

"Yeah," Ellis added. "Theah's mo' fun. What'sa matta? Ah thought'cha like ta play, man."

"Too many kids, goddammit. We shouldn't be in here with the eighth grade, anyways, fa' crissakes."

Garner gave him a sharp look. "Fuck you, man."

"Go pull ya prick." Bobby turned and walked away from them.

The physical education teacher was the black man who had been introduced during their first assembly. His name was Mr. Rollins—Shorty, the kids called him. He came out of his office and picked up six eight-inch playground balls and walked out to the center of the gym floor. He had a massive build. Huge, black arms bulged from the sleeves of his gray T-shirt as his muscles flexed to cradle the light, but awkward, load of balls. He placed the balls on the center stripe, spacing them evenly, about three feet apart. Then he divided up his class. There were forty-five eighth-grade boys and thirty-nine ninth-graders. He made teams of forty-two on a side, mixing grades on both teams as equally as possible.

The boys played the game avidly. The object of it all was to hit opposing players with the balls without hitting anything before hitting an opponent, and without crossing the center stripe. Each player hit was out of the game unless he caught the ball on the fly, in which case the person who threw it was out.

Garner found himself playing against Bobby and Ellis. At first, following an unspoken agreement between them, they avoided taking each other on. But Bobby was playing in a rage. Each time he threw a ball, he let it go with all of his considerable strength. When he wound up to throw, his swollen, purplish face twisted into an ugly grimace. He was head-hunting, too. One of his vicious heaves bounced off the top of Garner's head.

Garner glowered at him, amazed and angry, holding one hand against his head. Then he yelled, "You simple mutha-fucka," and ran toward him, fists clenched. Bobby stood his ground and put up his fists. Shorty Rollins leaped between them, and with a furious flurry of quick, powerful thrusts, he shoved them over to the side, then pinned them to the wall, holding them by their necks while they grasped his arms and peered frightened down over his arms.

Shorty's eyes were blazing. Enormous cords of muscle stood out in his neck. The rest of the boys gaped in amazement. Bobby Russo was the biggest boy in the school and Garner wasn't much smaller. The muscles in Shorty's back flexed and knotted as he nearly lifted them off the floor. "Now, let me establish something right away," he stated in tight, even tones. "Nobody fights *anybody* in here until *after* he whips *me!* Believe this, now. I won't say it again. Keep the peace around me, or I'm going to throw you right through those gym doors. Does everybody read me?"

Being unable to speak, both boys tried, heroically, to nod, but only managed to grimace painfully.

Shorty released Bobby and stretched Garner a bit higher and jammed one stubby, black finger against his nose. "Nobody," he continued to squeeze off the words as Garner tried to focus his gaze, "but *nobody* uses that kind of language around *me!* The next time you do, I'm going to take you by the neck and stuff a box of soap powder down your foolish throat!" He let him go then, and turned away to get the game going again.

Garner and Bobby sat on the floor against the wall, holding their throats and looking at each other stupidly.

During the rest of September, Garner tried to go about the business of reestablishing his protection racket, but his authority had begun to deteriorate. He and his buddies could not set a routine. If they threatened a boy, they very often received a counterthreat, something like, "I'll tell Murph," or "Ah tell Sully." Ellis and Bobby were both caught, on separate occasions, threatening boys. Murph immediately gave each of them a ride home. He didn't even wait until after school. Bobby couldn't come back to school for eight days, and Ellis couldn't leave his house after school for three weeks.

"Christ," Bobby despaired one October day as the three of them left school, "Kevin and Charlie're goin' ta Dis-pee, too."

"Thass five awreddy," Garner complained.

Ellis spoke gloomily, "An' two tha bitches. Did ya heah what Murph said in assembly, man?"

Garner nodded. "Yeah. No this an' no that—Jesus Christ!"

"Charlie and Joanne wuz caught fuckin', man. Unda' tha wood shop."

"Somebuddy musta squealed on'em," Garner said.

"Naw. Sully seen 'em sneakin' down theah afta lunch."

Bobby scowled. "Balls, that cocksucka's everywheres, fa' crissakes!"

Garner spat out into the street. "Rotten mutha-fuckas. Fuck'em, man. Les' go ovah tha sto' an' git a smoke, see some bitches, man."

The problems with school continued. Garner was dazed. He began to sulk. To make matters worse, Bobby and Ellis went out for basketball. Garner joined the team two days later.

Shorty drove the team hard. The first week of practice was run, run, run, ball-handling drills, rebounding drills, passing drills, dribbling drills, and shooting drills. Bobby and Ellis didn't seem to mind. They actually competed for leadership when the team ran. But Garner didn't like it.

"Man, this shit too much fuckin' work," he said to Bobby at practice one day.

"Gotta be hard ta play ball, Hawk."

"Sheet. Man, what tha fuck alla this shit got ta do wit' bein' hard, fa' crissake? All this runnin'—an' takin' a lotta shit frum Shorty—sheet. He pain in tha fuckin' ass."

"Shorty knows his stuff," Bobby replied calmly, moving up in line to await his turn to shoot foul shots.

"He ain' shit."

"Knows his stuff."

"He ain' shit, man."

"Don' take no crap off nobody, neither."

"Sheet, he's a fuckin' teacha!"

"Yeah. But he's a coach too, goddammit, an' a good one."

"He's a teacha."

"Christ, Hawk, why don'cha quit?"

"Sheet." Garner waved his hand in disgust.

The following week was better; practice became more fun. Shorty scrimmaged the team regularly. Garner liked that; he was a good basketball player, a big boy with speed and a lot of experience. In his part of the city, nearly every boy could play basketball, and he had few peers. He made the first team along with Ellis and Bobby, and he began to feel better.

His biggest headache, now, was Shorty: "C'mon, Hawkins; stop running on your heels. Pick it up, or I'll give you ten extra laps." The other players would laugh then, and, always, Garner would look up to see Ellis and Bobby, running way out in front, grinning at him over their shoulders. And it continued that way; Shorty wouldn't let up:

"Run on the balls of your feet, Hawkins. What are you trying to do, go backwards?" Garner didn't like Shorty. He didn't understand him, didn't like being nagged. All he seemed to hear from him was criticism: "Move the ball, Hawkins!" "Stop taking these foolish shots, boy!" "Don't force the shots; take the good ones!" "Take *your* shot!" "Relax out there!" "Aw, you had a man open! Why didn't you give him the ball?"

In their first competition against another school—a practice scrimmage on their own court—Garner was benched. He felt as if he was the victim of the most perverse kind of injustice. They had been losing that game; Garner had been shooting a lot and missing. Shorty yelled at him when he came to the sidelines: "What are you trying to do, play the whole offense out there? Why aren't you covering your man? Sit down. Sit down, for pete's sake. You need a rest."

Garner walked to the end of the bench and sat down, sulking, bitterly angry. Then, as if he didn't feel bad enough already, his team started to play better. They picked up momentum as soon as he left the floor. Garner was furious. Ellis and Bobby kept glancing at him as they hustled up and down the floor. Garner had to keep his head down. Some of the girls were watching the game, too.

They won the game without him. The following day, right after school, Garner raced down to Shorty's office and announced that he was quitting the team.

"Sit down and shut up," Shorty ordered with an impatient growl.

"Ah don' hafta, if ah don' wanna!"

Shorty glared at him and started to get up. Garner sat down hastily and stared at the floor. Shorty settled back into his chair. "Where'd you learn to play ball?" he asked gruffly.

"Ah dunno," Garner muttered sullenly. "Picked it up—ah kin play—"

"Play what, boy? Hell, you just came in here to quit. What the hell can *you* play? What are you ever going to be able to *play,* or do? I mean, well—I don't know. You hate my guts, don't you?"

"Huh?"

"You heard me, boy. C'mon; tell me to my face. *You don't like me!*"

Garner quickly looked at the wall, near panic chilling his insides. He heard Shorty sigh heavily and peeked at him out of the corner of one eye.

"Okay, what's wrong? What's your beef? Basketball too tough? These little boys whip you so badly yesterday that you have to give up the game?"

"Naw! Them cats cain' outplay *me!"*

"They made an ass out of you yesterday."

"What? Ah kin blow they eyes out, man! Them cats cain' play no ball! They wuzn't nothin'. They cain' play no ball."

"Okay, forget all that for a minute. Tell me why you want to quit."

Garner fidgeted and began to shuffle his feet around. He wanted to tell Shorty, in no uncertain terms, just what he thought of him, but he was stopped by the very real fear that the man would break him in half. So he simply said, "Coach, ah don' like a whole lotta——stuff—" He looked up, hesitating. Shorty's face was impassive. Garner dropped his eyes and went on with it. "You alla time—messin' wit' me. Ah kin play. Ah know what's happ'nin'. Ah mean—ah kin play. You always jumpin' on me. Ah don' hafta take alla that——stuff." He stopped, peeking carefully at the man, expecting him to explode in anger. But Shorty just sighed and sat back in his chair, staring at him pensively. Then he started to chuckle low and soft. Garner gaped at him, amazed.

Without looking at the boy Shorty began to speak again, very quietly, "Why do you think I get after you so much, Garner?"

Garner sat wagging his head back and forth, squirming in his seat and staring at the floor.

"Why do you think I do it?"

"Sheet—shoot. Shoot, man, ah dunno. Ah dunno. Cat don' like somebuddy, he jes' nat'cherly git on'im. Ah mean—thass all."

Shorty laughed out loud. Garner's head jerked up quickly; he was astonished, struck dumb. Shorty's black face sparkled at him; his eyes gleamed impishly. Then he became very serious, looking at Garner earnestly. "Boy," he said in a soft tone, *"I love you, for pete's sake!* I mean—do you understand me? You know what I mean, boy? You're—well, I dig ya. Okay? See? No, I suppose you don't. Hell, you're—" He stopped and fixed his eyes on the boy, pointing his finger at him. Garner squinted at him curiously, confused. Shorty pressed on, "Look, when a coach expects a lot from a boy, he puts more pressure on him. See?"

Garner's face was blank.

Shorty stood up and walked around the desk. He stopped in front of the boy, bending over to look at him. "Garner, you could be the best ballplayer I have out there. Somehow you've developed good basketball skills, I mean—dribbling, with both hands, slick passes—too slick. You have bad habits, too. You can be *too* fancy, too cute. You have to hustle more. And you like to hog the damn ball. Oh, for pete's sake, stop acting like I'm a cop trying to pin something on you, will you? Look, boy; *I love you!* If I sound like I'm putting you down, I'm not. I love you, Garner. You hear me talk basketball, but I'm talking about *you.* Sure, I'm talking about hustle and passing, but, dammit, boy, you don't hustle for *me.* That's not what I mean. I'm talking about *you;* hustle for Garner, man. Hustle for yourself. I've never seen a boy—not at this level—with as much physical ability as you. But ability and performance don't necessarily go together. It takes work and practice. And, Garner, you're *black*—. Dammit-all, sit still; I'm not a white man calling you a nigger—and that means sports aren't just sports anymore, see. You're playing for your *life!* How do you think I went to State? Football, that's how. I wasn't nearly as good an athlete as you are, but I knew I was playing for my life, and I played for blood." Shorty straightened up, looking down at Garner's frowning, black face. "Don't quit, man. *Don't* be another quitter. Hang tough, boy; *be hard.*" He paused and pounded his fist into his hand. "You have to pass off more. You have to get up on those boards and play defense. Scoring isn't the whole game. *Rebounding*—you can't score without the ball, can you?—and passing and defense. It doesn't matter *who* scores. Feed the guy with the hot hand. Garner, you should run things out there. You ballhandle better than anyone, but you're too big to stick back there with Ellis. But you can still make the plays, boy. And, listen; a forward who sets up plays winds up with more good shots than anyone. Well—look, if you want to quit—I mean, I can't stop you—." He stopped talking and wiped his brow.

"Huh?"

"I said—are you a quitter or not?"

"Ah kin play," Garner whispered.

"Well—go down and dress. Go on, beat it. Get out of here."

Garner stood up in a daze. He didn't hear the team going into the locker room. As he was leaving Shorty's office, he turned to look at the man. Shorty's back was turned. Garner shut the door and walked slowly down to the locker room to dress for practice.

He didn't understand everything Shorty told him, but after their little talk, Garner didn't fear and hate him anymore.

But that talk about love puzzled him considerably for several days. After all, a man didn't love men or boys. Men loved girls; girls loved boys. Only mothers could love everybody. In all of his thirteen years, no man ever told Garner that he loved him. He simply could not grasp the concept of a man loving a boy. *Shorty wasn't queer, was he?* No. No, Shorty wasn't queer; that much, Garner knew for sure.

As he thought it over, he finally came back to what Shorty said about expecting more from him. Shorty wanted him to be a better basketball player. *That was it;* Shorty liked him and wanted him to play good ball. That's all he had been saying. This conclusion, laboriously constructed, was as far as Garner could go with this love business. It did not leave his curiosity wholly satisfied; he merely found it acceptable, palatable.

Except for basketball and his buddies, school was an agonizing experience for Garner. With his exalted status in the school shaken and his authority undermined, the low quality of his work in academic areas became more and more painfully evident. He couldn't read. He couldn't spell, or count, or seem to remember important things which his teachers stressed. He had always been an indifferent student, but now he hated school. He had no idea that his inability to read was not entirely his fault. He couldn't read; that's all he knew—*stupid!* So he hated reading, too. He told himself that he didn't *want* to read and refused to admit, even to himself, that it bothered him. "Fuck school," he told himself. "Who needs this shit, anyways?" He recognized teachers and books as enemies, and he loathed them. And school books he hated most of all. These mauled his image of himself, terrified him more than anything he had ever faced. They told him things about himself that frightened him, angered and shamed him.

"Please open your book to page one twenty-six," Miss O'Donnell said. She was a handsome, white-haired woman of fifty. She taught geography.

Carefully, Garner and the other black kids opened their books. Ellis sneaked his foot across the aisle and poked Garner's leg. "Look, Hawk," he whispered frantically. "Jesus Christ! Looka this shit heah, man."

Garner looked. Then he and the other black children slid down in their seats as they peeked at the snickering white youngsters who kept glancing at them, then back at page 126, then at each other.

Garner tried desperately to hide in his seat, but he couldn't. He wanted to close the book, but he couldn't do that either. His eyes riveted themselves to the page: the image of an unspeakably ugly, black African leaped up at him. His hair was white and kinky; his face was very old, and wrinkled. His head was small and shapeless, set upon narrow, skinny shoulders over a sunken chest and a bloated, shiny, black stomach. The arms and legs were thin and formless. On his face and body there were scars, and there was a bone through his nose. There were other pictures, too: a handsome Englishman, impeccably tailored, surrounded by his peers in the House of Lords; a Chinese nobleman attended by his servants, a Brahmin Indian at Cambridge University, an American Indian chief signing a peace treaty with a white American general.

Garner tried to go deeper into his seat as his eyes raked over the page—NEGROID—MONGOLOID—CAUCASIAN—and the face of an alien black girl with gigantic lips made by large discs inserted in the flesh around her mouth. She wore metal rings which elongated her neck and head. Garner wanted to cry. He felt sick, thoroughly, utterly crushed—and the smiling, blond American girl beside the black one seemed to stare into his eyes and on into his mind.

"Ellis Crawford, please read from the top of page one twenty-six."

"Mam?"

"Read from the top of the page."

Ellis shot a terrified look at Garner. The white students giggled gleefully.

"Miss O'Donnell, ma stomick hurt!"

"Nonsense, Ellis," the woman scoffed, tapping a pencil on her desk to quiet the other students.

"Hones', Miss O'Donnell, ah gotta go tha basement! Ma stomick hurt *bad!"*

She stood up, annoyed, and came around to the front of her desk. "Ellis, you stop this nonsense immediately. Come here. Did you hear what I said? Bring your book up here with you."

Ellis hung his head and marched to the front of the room as the white kids fastened their eyes on him, smiling knowingly. Ellis wanted to vomit. He was angry with himself, too. Had he not kicked up a fuss, he might have enjoyed the relative privacy of reading from his desk in the middle of the room. He wouldn't have had to face the class, and he would have had Garner beside him to share his misery. But *now*—

He read: "Tha—sharpes' diff'rences between major—racial group-in's are—observed in tha——Caucasian an' Negroid types—Tha typical Caucasian is tall an' broad, very fair—wit' blue eyes, a high fo'head——aquiline features, an' light hair. Tha Caucasians are a proud an' handsome people. They are gen'rally—aggressive an'——resourceful. Most of tha people who live in our country are of tha Caucasian race. Tha Negroid peoples, found almos'——exclusively in southern Africa, are———*black*———wit' broad noses an' large nostrils. Typically, these people have coarse———*woolly* hair an' thick———black lips. Some Americans are of Negroid stock."

"Thank you, Ellis. You read fairly well when you want to. But I do wish you wouldn't hesitate so much. Try to read more fluidly and easily. You may return to your desk."

Miss O'Donnell paused, looking around the classroom as Ellis walked quickly back to his desk and sat down. Garner did not look up. He clenched his teeth, cringing as he anticipated hearing the teacher call his name next. He felt almost happy when she waved a hand around the room and said, "If we look about our own city, we can see why America is called the Melting Pot. Does anyone know what *cosmopolitan* means?"

"Wuzn't that a mutha-fucka?" Ellis whispered as they filed out of class. "Shit, that fuckin' bitch do that shit on purpose, man."

Garner just shook his head and stared at the floor as they walked.

Ellis casually acknowledged the exuberant hellos of three girls.

"That fuckin' Odie—you right, Ellis; she do that shit on purpose, gawddammit."

"Yeah. Fat-ass ol' bitch!"

"Yeah."

"Sheet, Hawk, we ain' Afrikin, man! We's *Amerikin!*"

"Well, ah sho's hell ain' no Afrikin," Garner snarled, stopping to face Ellis in emphasizing his point. "An' nobuddy betta not call me none, neither!"

"Yeah. Them fuckin' paddies bes' watch what they laffin' at."

"C'mon, man, les' go downstairs an' git us a smoke."

"Shit, Hawk, ain'cha goin' ta Collins's room?"

"Fuck Collins! He jes' gonna tell us how lucky we is cuz Mr. Lincoln love us niggas an' alla that shit. We git us a smoke. Then we kin tell tha nurse we wuz sick in tha toilet an' git a late pass."

"Ah dunno, Hawk. S'pose Murph's 'roun' somewheahs?"

"You skeered, Ellis?"

"Naw, man."

"Well, c'mon."

As soon as they were downstairs in the basement, Garner broke out a pack of cigarettes.

"Wait ta we git ta tha boiler room, man."

"Fuck tha boiler room. Safer in tha back shithouse. An' we kin take our time wit'out worryin' 'bout tha janitors jumpin' on us."

"Man, it's dark down heah."

Inside the lavatory, Ellis opened the window to let the smoke from their cigarettes escape. There was very little light in the small room.

It was rarely used for toilet purposes and the fluorescent bulb overhead wasn't working.

Garner puffed his cigarette, watching the bluish-gray smoke float out through the window. "Say, Ellis? Tell me somethin', man."

"What?"

"Man, if you wuz a slave would ya love ya master?"

"Naw, man."

"Me neither. Ah don' unda'stan' how niggas could like bein' slaves, man."

"Shit, Hawk, Mr. Collins say tha slavemasters treated'em real good, so they wuz happy, ah guess. Anyways, we ain' slave no mo'."

"Yeah, thass fa' sho'. But, man, ya know them fuckin' niggas wuzn't *shit!* They wuz stupid, man."

"Yeah."

"Ah mean, them niggas ain' said nothin' 'bout all that shit till white folks frum up heah went an' tol'em what wuz happ'nin'. Sheet."

Ellis leaned against the wall and tried to blow smoke rings, but the current from the open window made them mushroom into puffs of shapeless smoke. "Ah don' like Collins, neither," he stated in a flat, simple tone.

"Man, ah jes' cain' figga, thass all."

"Collins *hate* niggas, man. What'cha say, Hawk?"

"Ah said, ah jes' cain' figga, man."

"Figga what?"

"Them niggas."

"Sheet."

"Ah *cain'*, man."

"Man, what'choo worryin' 'bout them niggas fa? They wuz *crazy*. Them cats didn't know nothin'. Sheet, they wuz hardly out tha fuckin' jungle. Gawddamn, Hawk, even when they wuz freed, them niggas couldn't read a' nothin'. They wuz dumb."

"Sheet, ain' *nobuddy* that dumb."

" 'Cept niggas."

"Yeah. But—shit, Ellis, ain' nobuddy gotta tell nobuddy bein' slaves pain in tha ass. Right, man?"

"Niggas diff'rent, Hawk. 'Sides, man, wuzn't *all* bad. Ah mean, wit'out slav'ry, we be still in Africa wit' fuckin' spears."

"Sheet!"

"What'cha mean, *sheet?*"

"Sheet, thass what. All niggas ain' dumb, man."

"Fa' crissake, Hawk. It says right in tha book theah wuzn't nothin' in Africa till afta slaves!"

"Sheet."

"C'mon, Hawk, now, you jes' don' wanna heah tha troof, thass all."

"Ah ain' no Afrikin," Garner blurted angrily. "Niggas ain' all *that* fuckin' dumb!"

Ellis sighed and waved his hand at him. "Aw, man, it says right in tha book niggas nevah had no cities, a' armies, a'—nothin', shit."

Garner blew a hard, thin stream of smoke. He knew that Ellis got fairly decent grades and that he should drop the subject, but he didn't want to. In what he hoped was a superior voice, he said, "A white cat wrote tha fuckin' book, man."

"Aw, c'mon, Hawk. A book's a book. Books don' lie, man, not school books."

"How ya know?"

"Sheet."

"How ya *know?* S'pose ah wuz a liar, an' ah wrote a book? Then what?"

"Man, ain' no niggas kin write no school book."

"Well—s'pose ah wuz white, an' ah wrote one then. An' s'pose ah wuz a liar, an' s'pose ah hadda country, an' ah owned a big school. An' then s'pose ah didn't like niggas, an' *then* what if ah wrote a book?"

"She-yee-yit," Ellis croaked, beginning to laugh. "Man, you gone ta s'posin' like a bitch now. Gawddamn, man! Thass all *crazy* shit! S'pose this, an' s'pose that—fa' crissake, man."

Suddenly Garner laughed, too. It was absurd. Pretty soon he'd suppose that he was God almighty, or that he owned the whole world. "Yeah. S'pose ah had alla tha money in tha worl'?" He laughed harder as Ellis choked on his cigarette.

"Shit, Hawk, now, you know ah git good repo't cards in hist'ry, an' ya know alla that shit'choo talkin' is jes' talk, man."

"Yeah," Garner conceded, his laughter subsiding as he continued in a more serious tone. "But ah jes' proud ta be cullid, thass all."

"Me too, man. Me too."

"Ah hate fuckin' school."

"Yeah."

Terry didn't like school, either. Two weeks after his sixteenth birthday, he quit. He hadn't been attending with any regularity, anyway. His mother didn't want to let him quit, but after a long and steady flow of letters from the school and visits from truant officers threatening court action, she gave in.

Terry was free to do anything he wanted after that. He was a man. Overnight, he was shorn of the last official trappings of childhood. He hung out on street corners and down at the local pool hall, talking to all the hard guys. At night he went on the prowl, looking for girls—or work. Soon, Luther and Buzz took him in as a partner and he worked steadily with them. They invited him to parties at their apartment; he was having the time of his life.

"Ah wish ah could go on a job wit'choo cats," Garner begged one morning as he dressed for school.

Terry moaned sleepily and rolled over in the bed. "Sheet, you jesta kid, man. We don' want no kids 'roun' when we workin'."

"Ah ain' no kid."

"You in *school!*"

"Yeah."

"Well, shit, then!"

"You a lucky som'bitch, Terry. Ah wish ah wuzn't in school no mo'."

"Well, you jes' keep on wit'cha—wit'cha school an' ballplayin'—an' play it cool. We take ya 'long sometime when ya git a little bigga."

"Ah'm bigga'n *you,* sheet!"

Terry sat up on his elbow in the bed. He grinned triumphantly, tapping a finger to his head. "Ya don' *know* nothin', baby. You *young.* Jesta kid."

"Sheet."

"Man, ah gotta sleep. Git on up ta school, will ya?"

Garner was lonely, too. Ellis and Bobby were acting peculiar. They were seldom on the streets at night anymore.

Ellis said his mother wanted him to go to Classical High School. And he didn't seem to mind. "Ah'm gonna hafta go ta summer school," he told Bobby and Garner.

Bobby stared at him incredulously. Then he leaned against his locker, shaking his head as he buttoned up his shirt.

"Gawddamn," Garner squawked in amazement. "What tha fuck ya wanna do that fa'?"

Ellis shrugged and picked his basketball togs up from the bench and hung them in his locker.

Garner sat on the bench in front of the lockers, squinting at Ellis as some other members of the team said goodnight. "What'cha wanna go ta summer school fa'?"

"Gonna go ta Classical," Ellis said weakly.

"You ain' shit, Ellis."

"Aw, man—it's Ma, Hawk. She—"

"She gonna *make* ya go ta summer school?" Bobby asked.

"—says ah gotta go ta Classical—what?"

"Is she gonna *make* ya go?"

"Huh? Well, ah—"

"Ain' thatta bitch?" Garner said.

"My old lady wants me ta go ta Catholic," Bobby muttered, "but I don't think Pop's got the bread. But she never said anythin' about summer school. Jesus Christ!"

Ellis didn't look at them. "Ah *gotta* go, man."

"Man, this is a mutha-fucka," Garner said.

"Huh?"

"Fa'git it, man. Gaw-awddamn."

Bobby, Garner figured, had some excuse for not being out at night. After all, his father wouldn't let him out of the house!

"I can't get inta no more trouble," Bobby complained to them after basketball season ended. They were standing in the drugstore across the street from the school. Bobby mashed his cigarette out on the floor and checked his watch. "That's why I gotta get the fuck home now. My old man's been mad as a bitch ever since Murph drove me home, and he hadda go up the school."

Garner looked at Ellis sipping his Coke. He could understand Bobby's reasons, but Ellis not at all. "Say, Ellis, whyn'cha come up Tech wit' me? Ah mean—what'cha wanna go ta Classical fa'? Ain' nothin' up theah but faggots an' sissies, fa' crissake."

"Ma says Classical's good school."

"A good school?"

They went out onto the sidewalk. Garner faced Ellis, hands on hips, glowering. "What tha fuck ya talkin' 'bout, Ellis? Ah mean—*a good school,* fa' crissake?"

"Ya kin really learn somethin' up theah, Hawk—. Uh, ah mean, Ma say—it ain' bad. See? Ah mean, it ain'—" Ellis let the thought flutter precariously.

Garner shot an imploring look at Bobby.

Bobby lowered his eyes and shook his head sadly.

Garner faced Ellis again. "Shit, man, you git all that crazy shit frum ya motha an' ya fatha!"

"What'choo talkin' 'bout ma folks fa', man?"

"Yo' whole fam'ly acts kinda funny, anyways."

"Fuck you, Garna."

"Fuck you too, sheet."

"Why don't you guys quit it. Christ, Hawk, Ellis gotta right ta—"

"Sheet."

"Well, look, you guys, I gotta get home. My old lady'll tell Pop if I'm late. See ya."

"See ya," Ellis answered.

"Cool it, man."

Ellis had to leave, too. Garner walked home feeling lonely, cut off from his friends. And how was he going to keep money in his pocket? he wondered.

Terry had plenty of money, but wouldn't part with any of it. He was busy buying clothes and chasing girls. "Ah need ma fuckin' bread, man," he said, laughing. Garner stopped asking for handouts and asked, instead, to go on a job. But Terry wouldn't help him there, either. Garner was disgusted. He started combing the streets alone at night, working where he could, picking up a few dollars here and there.

He had little success working on stores. He needed an accomplice for that kind of work. His best hustle was still mugging newsboys—still the easiest way he knew to get hold of a decent amount of money. Some newsboys had over fifteen dollars when he intercepted them. He became very adept at his little racket. He always struck from behind, and he was fast. He was careful to pick a small boy, too, somebody he could overwhelm quickly. As he grew more confident, he became cockier, and a little careless.

One night, he went out as soon as it was dark. It was cold. Pedestrian and machine traffic were heavy. He picked out a small, chubby, white boy and began tracking him. It took almost twenty minutes to isolate the boy. He had only a few papers left. That was good. As the passers-by began to thin out, Garner moved in closer. His breath quickened. His stomach swam with the compelling excitement of impending violence. The boy paused at a corner street light. Garner slowed down and began looking around idly. He was almost ready to take the boy, only hoping that he would turn the corner and make it easier.

The newsboy turned around slowly. He looked at Garner briefly and disappeared around the corner. Garner grinned and closed in fast. Before he could strike, he saw a shadowy form leaping at him from a doorway. Then something struck him from behind. Somebody tripped him then, and he was falling. He hit the pavement hard. The boy he had been stalking dropped his papers and kicked him in the belly. He heard a boy yell, "Hey, there's only one!" Another boy screamed, "Kill the prick! Beat his ass!" Garner groaned in terror.

All around him, as he groveled on all fours, trying to get up, he could see legs moving, feel feet crashing into him. Someone hit him on the back of the head, and he went down again. He took a fierce blow to the groin, and blazing colors burst in his head. Then the blows came more rapidly, to his head, face, and back. They seemed to tear into him from all sides. There was blood in his mouth.

He tried to fight back, striking out with his fists and kicking his feet. It didn't help. Everywhere he moved, regardless of what he did, something else smashed into him, into his mouth, or his groin, or his ribs. And he couldn't regain his feet. Someone he couldn't see kept kicking his legs out from under him. A horrible fear seized him as he realized he was badly hurt. He dove forward, desperately grabbing at the air. He crashed against some legs, and his face smacked into a knee. He wrapped his arms around the legs and pulled frantically. A boy fell on him. Another boy fell over both of them and then another. Garner hung on, burying his face against the softest thing he could find. The kicks and punches became fewer. Then he wriggled and twisted and lashed out with his fists and kicked his feet. Now and again, one of his feet, or a fist, hit something solid. He struck about him again and again, swinging blindly, yanking, pulling and hitting anything he could grab. He heard more yelling: "Hold the bastard still." "Git'im; git tha mutha-fucka, man." *"Thass me, fa' crissake!"*

Then Garner's eyes dimmed. He tried to keep kicking and punching, but he was tired, weak with pain. The blows stormed in on him again. His body sank and he was flat on his back. He could barely see. Through a shadowy dim light, the blows ripped into him. Then he could see only pitch black. He couldn't hear anymore. Then the pain was gone. He could feel his body being shoved and pushed as the kicks and punches buffeted him from side to side. He seemed to be floating in deep, pure black. Then he felt nothing.

The first time he opened his eyes, he saw a policeman bending over him. *The cops had him!* His eyes flickered and opened again. The policeman was still there. Garner groaned and grimaced in pain as he tried to see where he was. His mind was shrouded with confusion, fright, and hurt. He tried to look at the policeman. He was a young white man, but Garner could not make out his features. "How're ya feelin', boy? Sorry I didn't get here sooner. Goddamn kids lit out before I could get my hands on them."

Garner didn't understand. He couldn't hear properly. His ears were ringing. When he blinked, he saw explosions of streaking colors and bits of light erupting somewhere behind his eyes. *The cops had him!* He saw the policeman's mouth moving. "Look, kid," he was explaining, "I'll be right back. Don't worry, hear? Gotta get help. Just take it easy, now. I'm comin' right back."

He closed his eyes, then opened them to see the policeman running toward the corner. Garner blinked as he rolled over. He had to get out of there. *The newsboys had left him for the cops!* He got himself up on one knee. Severe pain knifed through him. Using the wall of an old tenement building for support, he dragged himself to his feet. He felt sick, sure that he was going to vomit, aching everywhere. He had to get out of there. He peered down toward the corner. The cop would be back any minute. Icy dread shot through him. He stumbled toward an alley next to the tenement, his mind's eye fixed on the policeman's uniform. Glancing fearfully over his shoulder toward the corner, he saw that the cop hadn't reappeared.

He staggered into the alley, sliding along the brick wall, and fell over some barrels. He crawled on hands and knees toward an abandoned car, reached it, and dragged himself into the back and curled up on the floor. The dark flooded in on him.

When he awoke, daylight poked uncertainly into the car. He didn't move. His whole body throbbed with pain and cold. There was a strong stench of refuse, animal waste, dirt, and—*rats*. He jerked his head up, listening carefully, holding his breath. There didn't appear to be any rats about. He put his head down and found himself trying to read the label of an old, discolored package. Then his mind began to distinguish between the cold and the aching discomfort which wracked his body. He tried to move, but had to wait a moment. Finally he sat up in the car with his feet sticking out and began to shiver violently. The new day looked dull. His gaze wandered over junk cars, rubbish, and debris. The snow was almost gone. There was a dead dog frozen in a patch of ice. He shivered and looked himself over.

He was a mess. His pants and jacket were torn. Dirt and dried blood had crusted on his hands. The skin around his neck and face felt stiff and swollen. He struggled to his feet and looked around, wondering which way to go. His watch had stopped and he didn't realize it was too early for people to be up. He decided to use back alleys as much as possible. He wanted to get to Luther's place. It would be easier to explain himself to Buzz and Luther than to his mother.

The girl who opened the door was white. She was tall, even in her bare feet, and a long mane of snow blond hair spread over her shoulders. She was wearing a man's shirt.

Garner gaped at her bare legs. "Wheah my brotha?"

The girl took the cigarette out of her mouth and trailed a long stream of smoke into the hallway. "Well, hon, I'm not sure I know. Just *who* is your brother, anyway?"

"Wheah Lutha?"

"He's asleep, hon. What happened to *you?* You look like you've been in the war. I guess you're Luther's brother. You look like him, anyway. C'mon in."

She stepped back out of the doorway. He hesitated, staring at her legs. She laughed and spun around prettily, and he followed her inside.

She ushered him into the bathroom. "Get cleaned up, if you want. What the hell happened to you?"

"Nothin'."

"Well, that explanation is about as good as any, I suppose."

"Huh?"

She talked funny, reminded him of someone. He dabbed gingerly at the distended, dirty skin around his nose and mouth. She stood, arms folded across her deep bosom, watching him, a quiet smile on her face. Garner could see her reflection behind him in the mirror. Suddenly he was very warm.

"Look, hon, you may as well take that piece of a jacket off—your shirt, too."

"Ah'm doin' okay," he mumbled.

She threw her head back gracefully and laughed. Then she stepped around him and closed the toilet seat. "Sit down; I'll help you."

He didn't respond.

"C'mon," she urged gently. "I know what I'm doing."

He let her guide him to the seat and sat down. He couldn't keep his eyes from her. It was obvious that she wasn't wearing anything under the shirt. It was only casually buttoned, anyway, and constantly appeared about to open and reveal what was moving underneath.

"Here, let me help you with your shirt, hon. That jacket looks like it's been through hell."

"Who you?" he mumbled, watching her legs as she moved around him.

She slipped his jacket and shirt off. "Oh, you *are* Luther's brother, aren't you? You're Garner. I've heard about *you*."

"Huh?"

"You're Luther's little brother," she said and carefully began to wash his face. "Hon, these lumps are all over you. Nasty cuts there, too. Aren't you going to tell me what happened?"

"Ah ain' little."

She backed up a step and smiled at him. "No, you're not—just a figure of speech. Look, hon, I'll run some water in the tub for you. You need a nice, hot bath. And if you're nice to me, I'll fix you something to eat."

"What'cha name?"

"What? Oh. Well, I'm Pat," she replied, amused.

"You Lutha's gal?"

"Sometimes."

"Huh?"

"Hon, nobody is Luther's girl."

"Huh?"

"You wouldn't understand. There, your water is running."

She bent over and ran a hand through the water. The back of her legs yanked at his eyeballs. Something hot moved quickly in his stomach. Her legs were good, long and well-made. She reminded him of someone, but he couldn't remember who. He was nervous. Her coloring was creamy and pink, and she smelled funny. Suddenly, he wanted to touch his hand to her skin, but he only stared at her.

"C'mon; get undressed. You can't take a bath with your clothes on."

"Naw! Naw, man. Naw."

"Do you want me to *leave?* Or do you want me to help you undress?"

"Naw. Ah ain' no little kid."

She reached out and poked her finger at his chest. He fell sideways, getting to his feet and bumped against the cabinet and backed in between the sink and the toilet. Pat held her hand to her mouth and giggled. "You're adorable." Touching a hand to his face, she bent forward to kiss him softly on his cheek, and he cringed against the wall. "You wash. I'll get you some breakfast."

The hot water bothered him at first. It made his cuts and bruises smart. But after a while, he began to relax. The soapy warmth soothed him and made him a little sleepy.

The door flew open and Buzz was standing there. He was naked. "Well, gawddamn. What'choo doin'—what tha hell you doin' heah, Garna?"

Garner stared up at him from the tub, unable to find the words to explain. He looked at Buzz's naked body, the squat, chunky muscularity.

"How ya git'cha head all fucked up like that?" Buzz asked.

"Theah's a gal! Theah's a gal, man!" Garner gesticulated wildly with his hands. "She gonna see ya!"

Buzz laughed, picked up the toilet seat, and squatted down. "Sheet. Who care, man? They loves it, anyways. What'choo doin' heah, boy?"

Garner's voice was desperate. "Shut tha do', man!"

"Aw, fa' crissake, Garna, take it easy. How come you heah? How come you all fucked up, man?"

Garner looked anxiously toward the door, then back to Buzz.

"Pat let'cha in? White gal? Light yella hair?"

Garner nodded.

"She real fine, ain' she?" Buzz said, taking some toilet paper to clean himself.

"Man!"

"She wit' Lutha. What'cha do ta ya face, Garna? What'cha been doin'?"

"Aw, man, ah got messed up. C'mon, Buzz; close tha do', will ya? C'mon, will ya?"

"Man, you gotta stop bein' so skeered a' women. Hurry up an' git outta theah. You kin meet Edna."

"Who that?"

"A fox. C'mon, git outta theah."

Pat's snowy head appeared in the doorway. "Food's ready."

Garner jerked backward, trying to sit down too fast and splashed water, cracking his head on the edge of the tub. Buzz and Pat howled laughter.

"Shut tha do'! Shut tha do', man! Shut tha do'!"

"Easy," Pat laughed. "For the love of God, I'll leave, okay? I'm leaving."

Garner ate his ham and eggs in silence, his eyes darting from Pat to Luther to Edna to Buzz. Edna was a petite black girl with an exquisitely formed body, and cute, dimpled face. Her skin looked like wild, black honey. She wore only her panties and bra. Garner had never seen a black girl dressed like this, as pretty as Edna. Her startling beauty shocked him. Through her delicate panties, he could see a soft mound of black hair between her thighs. He squirmed in his chair as a slow, hot tightening drew up between his legs. He looked around guiltily, hoping no one would notice. Edna was small, but her legs were long and tapering, her breasts full and round. Garner gawked at her.

"Look at poor Garner," Pat laughed. She moved behind Luther and put her arms around his thick neck.

Garner watched her long, white fingers slide over his brother's powerful shoulders. Luther was clad only in undershorts; an enormous musculature rippled upward from his flat belly, over the broad chest, spreading thickly into his arms.

"Aw, leave the kid alone," Edna murmured gently putting an arm around Garner's shoulders. He could feel the cool, smooth skin of her body against his face. "Garner likes me, don't you, baby?"

He didn't answer. Buzz and Luther were laughing. Pat kissed Luther on his neck, and Garner averted his eyes, embarrassed.

After the girls left to wash and dress, Luther and Buzz made Garner tell them what happened to him. At first they didn't say anything. Then Luther broke out laughing. "Man, you been had."

Buzz smiled. "Sheet, them gray boys ain' *all* crazy, ya know."

"Some a' them wuz niggas."

"Ma gonna pitch a bitch when she git'cha home," Luther said.

"Ain' goin' home."

"Christ," Buzz exclaimed, "ya gotta go home sooner or later, Garna. Ya cain' quit school yet. So what'cha gonna do?"

Garner stared at the floor touching his face gingerly.

Luther said, "Well, he kin stay heah fa' 'while if he want." He pointed at Garner. "One thing ya gotta learn, baby, is don' run a good thing inta tha ground. You fucked wit' them newspaper boys too much, an' got'em evil, an' now they fucked wit'*choo.*" Buzz chuckled. Garner kept his head down, ashamed. Luther continued, "Ya kin stay heah ovah tha weekend, an' ah take ya home Sunday night. We'll make up somethin' ta tell Ma. But, baby, jes' don' try none a' this silly, kid shit agin."

Garner pouted. "Ah needed some bread, man."

"Kee-ee-rice, nigga, ain' nobuddy need bread that bad."

Buzz spoke up, "Yeah. 'Sides, ya didn't git any, anyways."

"Ah mos' times do."

Luther laughed. "Shit, boy, you come 'roun' heah once'n a while, an' maybe me'n Buzz'll put'cha on ta somethin'. But, fa' crissakes, quit fuckin' 'roun' on ya own. If ya don', ya gonna git'cha ya'se'f fucked up fa' real. Ya jes' lucky you wuz fuckin' wit' little kids."

Garner nodded slowly. He was quietly proud that his brother had asked him to come around to visit once in a while. He tried not to make his happiness too obvious. After all, Luther was hard.

That night, there was a party. Garner was fascinated by the people, the noise, and the intensity of it. He moved uneasily around the apartment, trying to hide his face in the dim light and watch without getting in the way. All kinds of people—black, white, and some he couldn't classify—came and went throughout the night. Garner saw beautiful women of all colors—and some ugly ones—peeling off their clothes in any one of six rooms, including the bathroom. The music didn't stop. Sometimes it was loud and raucous, then quiet and easy, and always sensual and provocative.

He stood stupefied as a beautiful oriental girl slithered up onto the kitchen table and started to strip while she did a writhing, twisting dance to the music coming from the phonograph. Some of the people in the other rooms crowded into the kitchen to watch along with the others. They began to clap and chant with the music. Garner's mouth hung open as the girl lowered her glistening, naked body backward and down to her knees. He gaped at the smooth sinew of her thighs. Beads of sweat rose up on her bright gold, satiny skin. She leaned back, and her straight, black hair tossed and bounced in a flowing mane that swirled halfway to the floor. Then she sat on her heels, full breasts quivering, nipples erect, glowing in a sheen of pearly moisture in the kitchen light. Her legs were parted and Garner's eyes fixed on the mixture of soft, black hair and pink, reddish flesh between her thighs. His belly hurt and he was beginning to sweat. His eyes seemed about to rip themselves from his head.

The girl seemed to be anchored to the table as her body rocked back; thighs, buttocks, stomach, and crotch shook and jerked, quavering in a paroxysm of power, sex, rhythm, and sweat. Her upper body swayed and shuddered like a sapling bending under a wind. Onlookers stepped up the chanting and the shouts. Garner wiped the sweat out of his eyes and stared between the girl's legs. The dampened, hairy flesh there tightened and opened in a series of spasms as if shivering from pain.

The ache in his stomach spread to the rest of his body. Then the dancer began to moan and curse. Her voice rose in high-pitched, ragged caws as her arms twisted snakily above her into a fog of blue-white cigarette smoke and the hot glare of light burning through it. Then she began to scream. Others screamed with her. More people attempted to shove their way into the kitchen. A slender, coffee-colored youth stood up suddenly, and in quick, jerky movements, tore off his clothes and crawled up on the table. The noise was deafening. The dancer offered herself wantonly to the youth. His hands swarmed over her sleek skin as he crouched above her. She raised her head and ground her mouth in his as he slid between her thighs and into her body. The noise stopped. Couples were embracing fiercely now. Some people collapsed to the floor in the kitchen and hallway. Others drifted toward one of the other rooms, disrobing along the way.

Garner was physically spent, emotionally overwhelmed. He was sweating freely, and there was something sticky on his legs. His bellyache hurt so much that it began to frighten him a little. Someone called him. He turned to see Pat reaching for him. "C'mon," she whispered. He let her pull him along, stepping over people on the floor.

She dragged him into Luther's room and gave him some rum and Coke. He gagged, but she made him drink it. He tried to kiss her, and she laughed and pressed him backward onto the bed. He fumbled at her breasts under the robe and pulled at her silky hair. "Hey, that hurts!" Then she kissed him full on the mouth, pushing her tongue between his teeth. Before he could grab her, she spun away from his clutching hands and stood up. "Wow! I have to hurry back to Luther." She gave him some more rum. "You lie down and sleep, hon," she whispered huskily. "There's not much you can do for Pat, right now." Then, smiling, she pushed him down on the bed and switched off the light.

He woke up on the floor beside the bed. A white man and a black girl lay sleeping in the bed in each other's arms. Garner rubbed his eyes and peered at the girl's naked body. His stomach hurt again. He was hungry, too. He heard music and laughter, but the apartment was quieter now. There were empty glasses on the floor near him, and someone had spilled a bottle of liquor on the night table.

He stood up and went to the window. It was dark outside. He walked over to the door and peeked into the hall. Young men and women in varying stages of undress were sitting on the floor against the wall. Others were dancing in the living room. Garner went back into the bedroom and put on his pants, then walked out into the hall and on down to the bathroom. A black man was sleeping in the tub.

He was fully dressed, in a dark suit and topcoat. Someone had run water into the tub, and an empty whisky bottle floated by his stomach. Garner hesitated, then went in. As he stood over the toilet urinating, he watched the man in the tub. The man's mouth was open and he snored loudly, his belly protruding above the water.

Garner found Luther in the kitchen, seated with his big body draped across the table. He was asleep, wearing a dirty, white dress shirt and his undershorts. Buzz and Edna were dancing. They had enclosed each other in their bathrobes and stood on one spot, knotted together, swaying to the quiet music, kissing one another gently. In one hand, Buzz held a drink which he shared with her between kisses.

Pat came in. "Well. Luther's baby brother has done woke up." She was very small in one of Luther's oversize sweatshirts. Garner tried to scowl as she grinned and took his arm in hers and escorted him to the table. "You slept all day and most of the night, hon."

Garner sat down and Pat snuggled up on his lap, kissing him playfully. His expression was a poor attempt at anger as he peeked down at her creamy thighs. Her body was heavy, but she felt soft and warm against him.

"You're going to drive that boy crazy," Edna chided.

"Garner and I have a mad crush on each other, don't we, hon?"

"He's terrified," Edna squealed, laughing with Buzz as Garner fought off a slight smile.

"No, that's belated, misunderstood, adolescent affection, that's all."

"Sheet. Thass a nigga wit'a hard on."

"Edna, tell Buzz not to be vulgar."

"Buzz, don't be vulgar."

"Sheet—say, did Garna git hisse'f a gal last night?"

"Of course not! I put him to bed *alone* this morning."

"Leave the kid alone," Edna said. "He's just a baby."

"Not after last night, hon."

Buzz guffawed, "Sheet! Baby ma ass! We gotta git that nigga a gal. If we don', he gonna be a sissy. Go 'head, Pat, take'im down tha bedroom."

Garner looked up in an embarrassed fright. Pat scrambled to her feet and tried to pull him up. He resisted with near violence, heaving himself and his chair over backward when she let him go.

Pat giggled through the laughter of the others, "We better leave him alone. He's had about enough from us this weekend."

"*You* leave him alone," Edna specified with a chuckle and helped Garner to his feet. She took his arm and slid it under the robe and around her waist, then bussed him lightly on the lips. "He's a good boy."

"He won't be for long, if you don't cut that out. Talk about me, for God's—"

"Am I bothering you, baby?"

Garner shook his head slowly. Buzz and the girls laughed.

"Look," Pat said, "let's throw all these bastards out of here. Edna, you feed the virgin while Buzz and I clean house." She put her arm around Buzz and they ducked out into the hall.

Garner was sorry when Sunday night arrived. He didn't want to go home. Edna and Pat kissed him goodbye.

"Keep cool, baby," Edna said. "Stay in school and keep at those sports. Maybe we'll see you again."

"Wheah ya goin'?"

"We have to get back to school, ourselves, hon. But don't worry, we'll see you again," Pat said.

Garner nodded numbly and climbed into Buzz's Olds. He turned and waved to Buzz and the girls as Luther pulled the car away from the curb.

"Hey, Lutha, what kinda school they go ta?"

"Huh? Oh. Pat'n Edna is college bitches, man."

"Them gals is *fine*."

Luther grinned. "You better believe it. They rich bitches." Touching a finger to his head, he continued, "They heavy, too, baby, cain' unda'stan' what they sayin' mosta tha time."

"You—ya done it—ya done it ta Pat, Lutha?"

" 'S'mo' like she do it ta me most times."

"*Man*—gaw-awddamn! She sho' fine."

"You like white bitches, Garna?"

"Huh? Naw—ah mean—they okay, ah guess. Sheet, tha—" Garner frowned and shrugged his shoulders noncommittally.

Luther stared at the road for a while, then looked thoughtfully at his brother. "Shit, evah' nigga got a touch a' snow fever. Even me—a little bit. We all got it—'cept Leroy—Buzz, too, man."

Garner didn't say anything.

"Jes' rememba, baby, white bitches likes niggas, too. 'S kinda nat'rul, kinda. Take Pat, now; *she* like niggas. Got what'cha might call *coal fever.* Sweah she won't fuck a white man, baby. Nawsuh! She say, 'They don' know how ta use that thing'—*coal fever!* Yeah." Luther started to laugh then, pounding a heavy paw on the steering wheel. "Yeah, man. Thass it; them bitches got coal fever—*nigga fever!* Shit, yeah!"

Garner sighed. "She sho' foxy, man."

"Yeah. Yeah, she a fox, awright. She ain' special, though."

"Ain' she ya gal, Lutha?"

"Shit, naw. Ah mean—Pat's fa' kicks, man. She fa' kicks fa' me same's ah'm fa' kicks fa' her. Ya know? *Ah* fucks who ah want, baby. Sheet, Pat do, too."

"She foxy, man. Ah sho' wish ah had a fine bitch like that."

"Sheet, man. You gotta learn, don' nevah git hung up on no one bitch, 'spesh'ly a white bitch. They wanna fuck ya, but on tha street, baby, they don' know ya."

"Pat seem okay."

"Yeah, Pat's good people—got a lot a' balls. But she *white,* man, and rich, too. Anyway, ah don' git too tight wit' *no* bitch. Ah got a pretty yella gal in New York, but she wanna git married. Bitches is crazy sometime, man. She-yee-yit! Ah mean, ya know ah ain' gonna let no bitch talk me inta *that* shit, baby. Right?" Luther looked at his brother, grinning.

Garner was unsure. He made a weak attempt to incline his head and look wise. "She foxier'n Pat?"

"Who?"

"That gal in New York."

"Oh," Luther said and thought it over. "Yeah—naw, man—ah

mean, not really. Pretty bitch jesta pretty bitch, see? Ah mean, Al is—name's Elvira—one a' them bitches so fine it kinda hurt ta look at 'er. Ya know? Foxy, man, like Pat'n Edna is."

"Man, how come ya don' wanna marry wit' a gal like that?"

"Sheet, ya kin fuck'em wit'out marryin' 'em, thass why."

"Ya mean, ya done it ta her, *too,* Lutha?"

"Shit, yeah."

"Man, Lutha, you sho' lucky. Ah wish ah had a gal like that. Ah even marry wit' 'er, if ah hadda."

"You ain' nevah fucked a gal, is ya?"

Garner didn't answer. The car stopped in front of the old building where he lived.

"Y'ain nevah been laid, is ya?"

Garner looked down at his lap, afraid to say anything.

"Well, baby, we be fixin' that, too. Okay? You come on 'roun' when ya ain' busy. Some weekend." Luther reached into his pocket and pulled out a large roll of money. He peeled off two ten-dollar bills. "Heah. Don' show this ta Ma—. Well, you ain' *that* crazy. Ya keep ya nose clean, an' ah put'cha onta some real bread. Whyn'cha come 'roun' nex' week?"

Garner nodded happily as he took the money. He started to get out of the car, then hesitated, looking back at Luther. "Ma gonna be mad."

Luther's eyes narrowed. Then he sighed. "Okay, man, c'mon. Les' go on up theah."

Ella Hawkins was surprised and happy to see Luther. She hadn't spoken to him in over a month. But she scolded Garner angrily, gripping his shoulders and shaking him. "Wheah ya been? What'cha done ta ya *face?* Ma Gawd! Wheah ya been since Thursday, boy? Been fightin' agin, ain'cha? *Ain'cha?"*

Harry intervened, stepping between her and Garner and throwing an arm around the boy's shoulders. Luther made up a weak lie about Garner's stopping by the apartment to visit him and then not feeling well, and he and Buzz had to keep him in bed most of the weekend.

Ella fumed. "Ah been sick ta death! Ah been neah outta ma head, thass what. An' ah don' b'lieve none a' *yo'* crap, Lutha! Y'ain' no good, no way! You g'wan an' git outta heah! Y'ain no good!" She was crying now.

Harry put his arm around her. Luther remained silent, and Garner was afraid to open his mouth.

"The boy's home now," Harry offered. "Take it easy, Ella. He's probably tired and hungry. He's home now. That's what counts, isn't it?"

"Look'it'is clothes," she wailed. "He's been fightin', thass why he ain' come home! Looka them cuts! He all swoll' up in tha face!" She moved away from Harry and gently touched her fingers to Garner's face. Garner cowered, fearing a blow. Then she snatched him to her breast.

Harry frowned and offered Luther a beer.

Luther stared at him incredulously, his flat, black face hostile, the peculiarly slanted eyes narrowed. He refused the offer, slowly shaking his head. He hated Harry. He didn't know why, and he never asked himself why, either. He knew very little about the man. His hatred was blind and uncompromising. "See ya, Garna," he growled sullenly, still glaring at Harry. Then he turned and stomped out.

Ella started toward the door. "Wait, Lutha! *Honey?* Wait a minute! C'mon an' eat somethin'—ah didn't mean alla what ah been sayin'—you wait, now, ya heah? *Lutha*—" Her voice broke into a sob as she held her face in her hands and wept. She wanted to ask him to sit down and talk to her, or simply to come and visit once in a while. But he was gone.

As Luther had promised, he solved Garner's money problems. Garner had new clothes again, and a new outlook. He was content. The excitement of working with Buzz and Luther was overwhelming. Having little success that he could measure in other ways, he was impressed by the money, the girls, and the clothes which were so much a part of Luther's life.

The new life gave Garner a new, peculiar, and perverted discipline. "Keep cool," Luther told him. "Keep ya nose clean. Don' give Ma no shit. Ya gotta stay outta trouble up at school an' keep tha peace. Ya know? Ya know what ah mean? Ya cain' be fuckin' 'roun'." And Garner learned the new order well. He kept the peace. He went to school, *did not* study, and ran track. He liked having new clothes and money in his pockets. He never showed his mother or Harry any money and explained away his clothes in his usual manner: they were gifts and hand-me-downs from Luther, or Buzz, or a boy at school.

He didn't tell Bobby or Ellis very much, either. Their questions concerning his newly achieved affluence elicited only evasive, mysterious answers, or seemingly hallucinatory, unbelievable stories of wild parties, which they liked to hear, but found hard to believe.

"Ya b'lieve that shit, Bobby?" Ellis asked one day as the three of them walked to school. Bobby looked cautiously at Garner who strode on, smiling importantly.

"They does it right on tha flo'," Garner repeated.

"You been gittin' any?" Ellis interrogated.

"Shit yeah," Garner lied with a grin and a casual gesture of his hands. "Gits all ah want. Evah'buddy do, man. We fucks till we gits tired an' then tha bitches fixes us up some food. Sometime, we swaps bitches an' starts all ovah agin."

Ellis and Bobby stared at him, awestruck. "Jesus Christ," Bobby exclaimed then, "I don't believe all that bullshit. Do you, Ellis?"

"Naw, man, shit."

By the end of April, Garner and Ellis were voluntarily prolonging their track workout in order to run extra laps together. Bobby came over to the track after baseball practice to run with them. "Gotta build my legs," he explained. For Garner, sports had grown into a serious business, a desperate, intense kind of fun. He and Ellis began to pester Shorty during practice, about timing their impromptu races by the stopwatch. "What wuz tha time?" Ellis would holler, running over to the coach after a race. "Who got tha bes' time now?" Shorty would tell them and remind Ellis that he was a half-miler and not a sprinter. "Shoot, Coach, ah'm all 'roun', man." Shorty told him that his head was all around then, and he and Garner laughed with some of the other boys while Ellis, cocky, and enjoying himself, shadow-boxed and grinned broadly.

Rivalry between the boys intensified the day Bobby ran over from the baseball field and announced that he had been offered a scholarship to Catholic High School. "I gotta good chance of bein' varsity catcher my first year. Don't hardly any soph'more play on the varsity," he said proudly. "Brother Halloran says the coach wants me to play Legion ball this summer." Garner and Ellis stretched their necks to see a short, barrel-shaped man in a black suit talking with Mr. Lasky over by the backstop on the baseball field. They shuddered with envy as Bobby grinned and ran back over to practice. After that, they began to drive themselves even harder.

"Bobby's a lucky som'bitch," Ellis told Garner a week later, sitting up beside him on the grass to watch Bobby jogging around the track in his baseball uniform. "Cath'lic's a good school, an' they don' give no schol'ships 'less ya kin really play, man. Ya gotta be hard."

"Sheet, man. What'cha mean, hard? Cath'lic's jes' like Classical. Bunch a' sissies."

"Fuck you, Garna. Some a' them cats is hard, man! Ya gotta be hard ta make a team at one a' them schools. You jes' jealous, thass all."

"Fuck you, Ellis."

"Fuck you, man. Shit. An' nex' yeah, Bobby gonna be up in high school, an' we be still fuckin' 'roun' in this gawddamn place. Ah wish ah could skip ninth grade."

Garner didn't answer.

"Bobby's lucky, Hawk. Ah wish we didn't hafta come back heah."

"Yeah."

"Man, ah wanna go ta high school right now."

"Yeah."

Three days before summer recess started, Shorty asked Garner to stop by and see him right after school.

"Want you to come for a little ride," he said when Garner stepped into his office.

"Wheah we goin', Coach?"

"Over to Sharon Street, to the Y."

"Tha new place?"

"Yes. Do you know where it is?" Shorty asked, closing his locker and slipping into a blue blazer. Without waiting for a reply he continued, "They've got a very fine athletic program going during the summer. Trying to get all the boys they can—good boys who'll do a job for them. I told them about you. Want to go over and look around—maybe meet a few people?"

"Sheet, ah dunno."

"What?"

"Uh, sho'."

"Beautiful."

They drove over in Shorty's black, five-year-old Ford. "It's a brand new building," he said. "They used to have a little cubbyhole office down near Dudley Station. Most people didn't know the place existed. But this place is big, right out where people can see it. They've got a new olympic pool and—" He paused and glanced at Garner; he was glad that the boy was neatly dressed. Expensive clothes, though, he observed, shaking his head.

"You ever been in the place, boy?"

"Naw."

"Well, you ought to join. Bill Chamberlain—he's the Physical Director up there—" Shorty hesitated, giving the boy a quick look and trying to gauge his indifference. "—has a summer basketball league going. Junior, Senior, and open. They've been city-wide champs three years running."

"Do ya hafta join ta play?"

"Not that I know of. They have a pretty fair track situation, too, if you're interested."

Garner looked at some winos sitting on the corner as Shorty pulled the Ford onto Washington Street. They rode under the El structure by Dudley Station and bent another corner onto Sharon Street. Garner scowled and nodded his head very slowly.

The YMCA building was a hulk of concrete and glass. It looked strange, modern, and yet old, like an ancient temple newly restored. It sat on a huge, open lot, which was cluttered with the debris of building demolition and new construction. There were brick and concrete rubble, bulldozers, scrapers, cranes, huge trucks, and construction workers scattered beyond three house trailers used as offices and a pre-fab, metal garage which stood behind the Y to its left. In front, beside the building, Garner saw a large, newly black-topped and lined outdoor basketball court with a chain-link fence around it. There was a volleyball net strung across one half of it, and a swarm of small, black boys were wrestling for control of a ball underneath.

Before they got out of the car, Shorty grabbed Garner's arm. "Listen, these people don't stand for any foolishness, see? So, uh, you keep the peace. I mean, if you don't dig any of this—well, say so, and we'll forget it. So keep cool. Okay?"

"Ah know what's happ'nin'," Garner muttered.

The inside of the building was small, but pleasant and bright. Shorty stopped in the glistening, new lobby to speak to a slender, black girl, who was working behind the front desk. "Garner, this is Janice."

Garner shook the girl's soft hand as though afraid of breaking it.

"Hi, Garner. Are you going to join our Y?"

He responded with an expression of flat-faced helplessness. She was pretty, a tall, graceful girl, beautifully made, with a proud and easy bearing. She smelled funny, too, reminding him of someone he couldn't recall. His eyes dropped to the twin mounds which filled out the front of her white blouse.

"Is Bill around?" Shorty asked her.

"He's in his office."

"C'mon, boy. Thanks, Janice."

"Okay, Mr. Rollins. Nice meeting you, Garner."

A crowd of small boys, colored every shade of black, ran by them, screaming and swinging wet bathing suits. One of them, a chubby, yellow-skinned boy, ran into Shorty. He snatched the youngster off his feet and swung him up over his head. "Whoa there, Eddie!"

The boy squealed, his round, yellow face beaming. Some of the other boys stopped and began pushing and pummeling Shorty playfully. "Swing us, too, Mr. Rollins! Swing us, too!"

Garner watched as Shorty gave each boy a turn.

"That's all, now!" Shorty barked finally and held up his hands. "That's all, fellas. Have to go." The boys went on tugging and trying to play, but Shorty just laughed and continued along, dragging Garner with him.

Garner stole a glance at his coach. Shorty seemed to be enjoying himself; his teeth flashed as he smiled and greeted different youngsters. He called most of them by name. Garner kept jerking his head about to look at the various people hollering to get Shorty's attention.

A tall, blond young man approached them, walking rapidly. "Hello, Mr. Rollins."

"Hi, Tommy. Still in school, boy?"

The youth shook Shorty's hand. "All done. Practice taught last fall."

"Atta baby! Bill down back?"

"Yeah."

"See you later."

"So long, Mr. Rollins."

"Bill Chamberlain white, too?" Garner asked.

Shorty smiled. "That worry you? Well—" He watched Garner shrug his shoulders in a guarded, careful way. "No. Tommy's not, either. Mother's German."

"Frum Germany?"

"No, boy, from Russia."

"Huh?"

"C'mon, boy."

When they arrived at his office, Bill Chamberlain was bent over his desk, working hard, his sleeves rolled up, shirt collar open, and tie bouncing at quarter-mast. He was a dark brown man, mustached, of average size and wiry build. He was the same age as Shorty, twenty-seven. "Well, for pete's sake," he sang out when he saw his two visitors. "How're you doing, Shorty?" He stood up quickly, and the two men shook hands.

"This is the boy I've been telling you about, Bill. Garner Hawkins."

"Glad to meet you, Garner. Heard a lot about you. Listen, you people pull up a couple of chairs and park. I'll be right with you." Bill snatched up a sheaf of papers and hustled out of the office.

"Come over here for a second, Garner. Look at this."

Garner looked through a large, glass partition at a busy swimming pool. "It's big."

"Beats that puddle you kids swim in down on Cabot Street, doesn't it?"

"Yeah. Cleaner, too. We don' go down Cabot no mo'. Who that?"

"Where?"

"That big stud."

"Oh. That's Horse. Plays football for State. He's one of Bill's assistants during the summer."

"Man, he really got a build!"

"Hasn't he, though? Six six and about two-fifty. Horse has been pushing weights for about five years. Wants to turn pro. All he does in his spare time is push those weights and run wind sprints."

"Kin he play?"

"Pros think so. Meanest black boy I know, that's for sure. He got a full ride at State."

"Huh?"

"Goes to college for nothing. The school pays for it."

Bill Chamberlain came back into the office. "Sorry to keep you waiting. What can I do for you people?"

"Garner here wants to play a little ball this summer," Shorty said as he and Garner seated themselves in front of the desk. "He thinks he's a sprinter, but he's really a basketball player."

"How about it, Garner? Are you a basketball player?"

"Ah kin play."

"We run a little track around here, too. Does he play for you, Shorty?"

"He's one of my aces."

"Do you think he can play down here? Senior ball is pretty fast, you know."

"He'd be playing with the Juniors, Bill."

"The Junior age limit is fifteen."

"Garner's only fourteen."

Bill gave Shorty a sharp, hasty look and stared at Garner, whistling softly. "Stand up, boy," he demanded excitedly.

Garner complied. He was a little embarrassed, but proud.

"He's a monster! You ever play football, boy?"

Garner shrugged, losing an intense struggle to stop the broad grin which was spreading across his flat, ebony face. "Jes' foolin' 'roun'."

"What do you do in track?"

"Bill, he sprints the hundred in ten five."

"Is that a *fact?"* Bill asked leaning back in his swivel chair. "Isn't that a city record for Juniors?"

"It equals the record. He did it in the Junior Regionals. Boy from Newton pushed him hard. He needed ten five to win."

"What's he weigh?"

"One-seventy."

"Six feet?"

"Just about."

Bill looked down at his desk and shook his head.

Garner sat with a silly grin on his face. He was mildly uncomfortable, but he was enjoying himself immensely.

Bill fixed a solemn look at Shorty. "Shorty, look—uh, I'm not sure I know how to say this, but—I mean—well, is the boy *yellow,* Shorty? I mean, I wonder if he—"

"Ah ain' skeered a' nobuddy," Garner blurted. "Ask anybuddy, man! Nobuddy fucks wit' *me*—ah mean—ah mean, nobuddy *messes* 'roun' wit' me. Ah mean—thass what ah mean, man. She—oot!"

Bill put up a hand. "That's not exactly what I'm talking about. It takes guts to play in this league. My boys are *hard,* boy! They do a job for me—all the way. They keep the peace, no matter *what* happens. They stay out of trouble—and they don't miss *any* games, or practices, either, see?"

Garner nodded slowly, casting an uncertain look at Shorty.

Bill leaned forward across the desk on his elbows, staring hard into Garner's face. "Boy, I'm boss man. Hear?"

"Ah knows what's happ'nin'." Garner squirmed uncomfortably and dropped his eyes.

"Okay," Bill relented, stroking his neat mustache as he winked at Shorty and continued in a gentler tone, "if you're interested in our program, you come on down here as soon as school's out."

Shorty stood up and looked at Garner, trying to determine what effect all this had on him. "Look, Bill, there's something else I'd like to talk over with you. Can I see you alone? Garner, do you mind stepping outside for a minute? I'll be right along."

Garner shrugged and started to leave.

Bill stood and offered the boy his hand. "Good meeting you, Garner."

Garner clasped the hand, glancing at Bill's handsome face. "Me too, man."

Shorty quickly shut the door behind Garner and sat down. "Well, what do you think?"

"He's beautiful, and that's a fact. That build—. Does he really run that fast?"

"He's going to run a lot faster. Hasn't got the strength for the quick start yet. Tremendous stride, though. Long and graceful and—Bill, he's worth a lot of sweat."

Bill lit a cigarette. "They all are. Listen, Shorty, I hope I didn't overdo it back there. I tried to—"

"No, man! That crack about being yellow surprised me, though. I had to fight to keep a straight face."

"Thinks he's hard, doesn't he?"

"He *is!* Believe me; he is. He runs Timilty. The kids're scared to death of him."

Bill frowned pensively, puffing his cigarette.

"I'm really worried about him, Bill. There's good stuff—real good stuff—in the kid. But—I have a feeling—that's all. He's got a mean streak in him a mile wide."

"Has he had any trouble with the police?"

"I'm pretty sure he's still clean. But he could have a run-in with the cops anytime. He doesn't work, always has plenty of cash, new clothes—I mean, he could get busted any day now. Probably been lucky."

"What's his home life like?"

"Aw, Bill, it's got to be bad. Both brothers quit school, no father—. Listen, there's violence in that kid, and anger. You should see—well, you *know* this neighborhood. Figure it out. All the signs are there. And, Bill, he's got this *great* gift, that speed—the hardest thing to find in an athlete—and size, and—I'd really hate to let this kid get away. I'd—well, it'd be a damn shame."

"I know what you mean, Shorty—but listen, you and I know we're going to do everything we can that the boy *will let us do.* We can bounce him around a little, work him along in the right direction, but—"

"I wish you'd come into teaching, Bill. Some of those white bastards up there are—"

"I *know,* buddy! We went to the white folks' school together, remember?"

"—the very worst. Don't give a *damn,* and those who do, don't know what there is to give a damn about."

"They're not black, Shorty."

"Yeah, and they make a big point of it, too."

"I know."

Terry left home. Ella came home from work one Saturday morning, and his clothes were gone. The house was empty; Garner was out with Luther. She had known that something like this was going to happen, just as well as she knew that she could do nothing to prevent it. Enlisting the help of the police was unthinkable. Terry was gone, that's all—just like Luther. *Ben.* And she could do nothing more than cry in self-accusing, frustrated anger. Two weeks afterward, Harry was still trying to console her, and she continued to disregard his advice. Then he made a well-intended, but hard observation to the effect that crying would not bring him home again.

"Ya don' *care,*" she howled at him over supper, knowing that he did. "Ya don' care, gawddamn ya! They ain' yo' kids! They mine!"

Harry clammed up then, flicking a what's-the-use look across the table at Garner before going back to his food. Garner stood up and picked up the small, black bag in which he carried his basketball uniform and sneakers.

"Wheah ya goin'?" his mother yelled at him.

"Got a game ta-nite."

"You wanna git'cho'se'f outta heah, too, don'cha? *Don'cha?*"

Garner started to say something, but thought better of it.

"Set'cha'se'f back down heah, ya heah? Do ya heah me talkin', boy? Do ya? Y'ain' goin' nowheahs! Evah since school been out, ya been findin' all kinda ways not ta be home heah. Mornin's it's runnin', afta'noons it's playin' ball, an' night-times ya on tha street, an' ah don' know what, gawddammit! Ah don'—"

"Ella, for crying out loud, what are you jumping on Garner for?" Harry asked quietly.

"You mind y'own bid'ness! Ya mind y'own gawddamn bid'ness. Ah'm talkin' ta ma son."

Harry took another bite of his food and shook his head.

Garner remained quiet, hoping that Harry would win this squabble. He wasn't particularly fond of Harry, but he had to get out, and he didn't want to have to sneak out. He had a ball game to play, and Luther wanted him to work.

Harry spoke patiently. "Look, the YMCA's a good place for a boy to be, Ella. Leave him alone, for crying out loud."

"Ah tol' ya," she screamed. "Ah tol' ya! They *ma* kids! Ah had'em, an' ah wuz raisin' 'em up befo' they *wuz* a YMCA, gawddammit! They ma sons. You ain' got no say heah. They *mine!*"

"Aw, for Christ's sake, leave the boy alone. It's not his fault Terry—"

"Don'choo say nothin' 'bout how ah run ma home, nigga! This *ma* house! This ma house, not yo's."

"Ella, I didn't say a goddamn word about you running this house. And remember, I help things out around here, too. So you might allow me an opinion. I've got—"

She jumped up from the table to glower down at him. "Shit, you kin take yo'se'f an' leave if ya don' like tha way things is heah! We wuz gittin' 'long befo' you come, an' we kin make out wit'out'cha, too. Go 'head if ya wanna. We don' need ya, nigga."

"Don't be too sure, baby. Sy sold that goddamn store—yeah, and those Portuguese niggers only take *money* for their—"

She slapped him savagely and doubled up her fists and began flailing away at him with all the strength she could muster. Garner leaped out of the way in a quick fright. Harry caught her arms and stood up, wrestling her down on top of the table.

"Aw, ya *bastid,"* she cried. "Ya black, *dirty* bastid!" She rolled back and forth in a rage, knocking the bread and Harry's beer and food to the floor, sobbing hysterically, yelling, "Lemme go, lemme go, ya bastid! Ya black som'bitch, lemme go! Aw, ya bastid, ah kill ya, ah kill ya! Ya mutha-fuckin' black bastid! Aw, *Jesus!"*

Harry yelled, "Go on, Garner! Get the hell out of here! Go ahead, if you're going, for Christ's sake."

Garner hesitated, watching his mother struggle with Harry. Her housedress had fallen open. Part of it was mashed in the butter. A carton of milk crashed to the floor along with the pot of black-eye peas and then the butter followed. Dishes clattered to the floor.

Ella cried a screeching wail as she hollered at her son, "Don'choo leave! Don'choo leave me, boy! Ya heah? You ma *son!* Don'choo leave me, now! Ah kill ya if ya go! Don'choo leave!"

Garner could hear someone downstairs yelling for them to stop all the noise.

Harry pinned Ella's arms, spread-eagling her on the table. Then he jammed his thigh between her legs, leaving her feet kicking futilely. "Go *on,* boy!"

Garner didn't move. He held his bag, staring at Harry and his mother, praying that Harry wouldn't hit her, that he wouldn't hurt her, and that he wouldn't have to fight him. He took a step toward them. "Don'choo hurt'er! Y'ain' gonna hurt ma momma, Harry!"

"Jesus Christ, boy, I'm the one getting *hurt!* Get the hell out of here! I'm not going to hurt this crazy woman, for Christ's sake!"

Garner fidgeted, feeling the water in his eyes and looking at Harry. He knew Harry had never raised a hand to his mother, but he was scared.

Harry peered at him with relative calm as Ella thrashed about wildly. He smiled. "Go ahead, Garner."

Ella collapsed on the table then, closing her eyes, her black face contorted with anguish. She wept and moaned helplessly.

Garner hesitated briefly, then ran out. He stopped outside in the street and looked back at the house, then turned and started running toward the Y.

The team had already started out to the basketball court when Garner ran into the building. Bill Chamberlain yelled at him in the lobby, "C'mon, Hawk. Move it, will you?" The locker rooms were in an uproar; happy black kids were opening and slamming lockers shut, rolling on the wet floors, yelling and throwing soap and snapping towels at each other. The tumult made Garner think of his mother and Harry. He felt guilty about leaving, but he was glad to be out of the house.

There was only a small crowd at the court. Most of the people there were black kids. It was a warm summer evening and Garner knew that the larger crowd would be coming later to see the Senior game. He wanted to stay and see that, himself, but he had to work. He took a place in line behind some of the other boys and watched a lithe, orange-colored boy take a pass and drive under the basket and lay the ball up on the backboard. Ellis came up behind him and bear-hugged him, lifting him up in the air.

"What's happ'nin', man?" Garner greeted him.

Ellis grunted and put him down. "Nothin'. Evah'thin's cool, baby. Ah passed Latin. Got a fat-ass B!"

"Sheet."

"Sheet ma ass! Ah wuz sweatin' that mutha-fucka, man."

"Ya seen Bobby?"

"He 'roun' heah somewheahs. He's talkin' a whole lotta shit ta-nite, man. They got'im battin' clean-up."

"Sheet, we gonna heah 'bout that shit."

"Awreddy did, man."

Garner jogged under the backboard and caught a rebounding ball. He passed it to a stubby little black boy and looked around the court as he skipped into the other line. There were more girls amongst the spectators than boys, black ones, brown, yellow, orange, near white, and white. Most of them wore shorts. Garner noted several pairs of pretty legs. Ellis ran into line behind him.

"What'cha doin', Hawk? Checkin' out tha foxes?"

"Yeah, man."

"Theah's a party ovah Quincy Street later. Ya goin', Hawk?"

"Naw. Be busy."

Ellis waited as Garner ran forward, taking a pass and laying the ball on the rim and turning to watch it drop through the chain net. Ellis followed, twisting gracefully under the basket to make a pretty, hooking lay-up on the opposite side. Bill hollered at him, "Learn to shoot a regular lay-up, will you, Crawford!"

Garner laughed. "Bill don' go fa' that fancy shit, man."

"Sheet, that wuzn't fancy. He jes' wanna git on somebuddy, thass all. Been bitchin' at me an' you evah since ya brought me down."

"Thass cuz we played fa' Shorty, an' Bill know we kin play."

"Sheet."

"Gawddamn, Ellis, when a coach 'spect a lot frum ya, he bitch at'cha mo', thass all. Bill want us ta *move* this wagon, man! Thass why he bitchin'."

Ellis gave him a pensive look.

Garner ran off to rebound the ball and pass it off.

Garner's team won the game easily. As soon as it was over, he started running for the locker rooms. He had to struggle to get through the boys and girls who crowded the court. The coaches and officials worked hard to clear the area for the next game.

Bill caught Garner by an arm. "Nice game, Hawk," he laughed, grinning. "We won't have it this easy Wednesday."

"Shoot, man, we'll blow them paddy boys' eyes out! See ya later, Bill. Gotta split."

"What's your hurry? Aren't you going to stay to see the Seniors play?"

"Gotta move, man. Hafta split."

"Where're you going?" Bill yelled after him.

Garner didn't hear him. Bobby and Ellis were hollering, signaling him to come and sit with them. "Gotta go," he shouted.

He slipped through the gate, waving, and ran toward the Y building, easily picking his way through the rubble and debris. It was getting dark now. The air was warm against his face. Glancing upward, he saw stars hanging bright and still in the flawless blue of the evening sky. He felt good, filled with the excitement of working with Luther and Buzz again.

They were working on a warehouse. It was a big job. Luther had even stolen a truck. Garner was nervous as he climbed into the cab and seated himself beside Buzz, who sat behind the wheel. Luther followed his brother in and shut the door.

Buzz eased the truck away from the curb. "What she say?"

"She ain' seen Terry, neither," Luther growled, trying to light a cigarette as the truck jounced them along and moved into the thickening traffic. "Bitch is lyin'."

"Sheet, ah tol' ya that, man. Terry got'er sellin'er ass! Thass why he moved in wit'er! Nigga don' wanna work."

"Fuck'im. You cats got'cha gloves on?"

"Yeah, man."

"Crazy. Les' go."

The inside of the cab grew quiet as Luther pondered his cigarette thoughtfully, blowing thick streams of smoke in the dark. Buzz concentrated on his driving. Garner wanted to ask what it was they were going after, but he didn't want to sound ignorant. He was a little frightened; he had only worked one warehouse before, and he found it a bit spooky.

Buzz left the heavy congestion of machines and people and maneuvered the light rig carefully through the narrow back streets of the city. Garner could smell the ocean. His mind wandered as he looked out at the dark, close buildings. Occasionally, a car's headlights stabbed at them through the darkness in scattered flashes of yellow and white. The sudden brightness seemed out of place, foreign to the drab buildings and narrow streets. Garner's mind began to work by itself then. He saw nothing, and everything. Lights and shadows seemed to be everywhere, first in front of him, then around him in the cab, and suddenly behind him. It was eerie. The shadows, lights, and darkness wove and moved one behind the other, touching again and again, then breaking one pattern to start another.

Garner's skin broke into goose bumps suddenly. He fidgeted and shivered, then cast a cautious look at Luther, then at Buzz. Abruptly, he wished he was somewhere else. "Naw, man, ah'm hard," he said to himself in immediate denial. He thought of playing basketball, then running track, then his mind floated, carrying him along, tugging gently as he resisted, then pulling him away in a rush—*The room was dark. He opened the door wider and peeked into the room. The hall light groped about in the dark room, leading his eyes. He followed it to the bed and saw Pat and Luther lying naked on top of the covers. Luther had passed out, drunk, and he was snoring. Pat's long, snowy hair was spread over her back and shoulders. Her head rested on Luther's chest.*—Garner jerked his head sideways, peeking at his brother. Luther was staring out the window. The cab was noiseless except for the raspy growl of the motor. Garner put his head back against the seat and looked up toward the roof—*Pat picked her head up quickly when the light touched her face. "Who's that?" she said. Garner didn't utter a sound. She sat up on the bed. Luther didn't stir. Garner thought he should shut the door, but his body was frozen still. He saw the light wash over her body. She slid quietly out of the bed. "That you, Garner?" she asked, still speaking in a low voice. "What are you doing there? Edna and Buzz back yet?" No, Garner thought, they aren't back yet, but he didn't say anything. His hand tightened on the door knob. His eyes raged over her milky skin and he told himself to shut the door, but all he did was grip the knob harder. He was, at once, terrified and entranced. Some great and urgent courage, which he didn't understand, spread through him. He felt weak, yet a surge of strength roared in his body. But he could not move. The full, exquisite shock of her nakedness overwhelmed him. He had seen her in all manner of dress and near nudity before, but now she was completely nude, tall, willowy, but full blown in a slender, graceful blend of pink and creamy white. Garner stood bewitched, enchanted, unable to move or speak, hoping she couldn't see the terrible, painful erection that bulged against his undershorts, stretching and pulling them tight against his naked skin. The effect of her, and his own fear, threatened to engulf him. She reminded him of someone. Sweet musk assailed him as she stood before him, hands on hips, legs wide apart, smiling. "Hello there," she whispered. "Why aren't you asleep? Did you come to play?" Garner gaped at her in silence. She laughed in a deep-throated whisper, "Come to play with Patty, hon?"*—The truck rocked as it slammed over a bump.

"Gimme a smoke," Buzz said.

Luther reached into his shirt pocket and took out a package of cigarettes. He lit one off his own and offered it to Buzz. "Heah, man."

Garner watched Luther's shadowy form in the dark, pressing himself back against the seat as Luther reached across his chest to hand Buzz the lighted cigarette. His stomach fluttered with excitement as he peeked at his brother out of the corner of an eye.

Buzz turned a corner. Garner started to relax again—*Pat moved against him and encircled him with soft, warm arms. He took his hand off the door knob. Her body was full and soft against his skin. His guts soared with blazing heat and sharp, biting cold. The deep swell of her breasts scorched his naked chest. Suddenly, he wanted to tear his shorts off. He wanted to be completely nude in her arms. His knees were weak, and his thighs were burning. He was certain that he was going to be sick, and he wanted to be. Her downy hair touched his face. He smelled her perfume.*

She pulled him into the hall and shut the door behind them. "Why are you standing there, hon?" she asked gently, holding him by the shoulders at arms' length and staring into his face. "Can't you sleep?" Garner said nothing. He stared at her, forcing the muscles in his neck and face into a fierce, gnarled, straining contraction, grimacing until his eyeballs bulged and hurt as though something was tearing them from their sockets. Before him, Pat's dazzling womanhood focused, then blurred, pink nipples on creamy globes of white flesh swirled in his head. "Garner—" she started, then she looked down at his body. "Oh," she chuckled softly. "Now look what I've done." Then she pulled his shorts down. "Yes," she murmured. "Oo-oo, yes, hon!"

She slid her hands over his shoulders and down on his chest. Her fingers touched his nipples lightly, then squeezed. "Hon," she croaked in a husky voice, "you're—you're gorgeous, beautiful." She leaned forward, still fingering his chest and kissed him gently several times. Her mouth clung hotly, wetly, to his, in quick, maddening thrusts. Abruptly, Garner clutched her to him in a fierce embrace, crushing her in his arms. With all of his strength, he lunged forward, hurling both of them backward into the wall. Pat cracked her head against the door frame. Garner rammed his mouth down on hers, driving her head back against the wall and thrusting his tongue into her open mouth.

She tore her mouth loose, gasping for breath, feeling his hand ripping frantically at her crotch. "Goddamn, you'll kill me!" Garner continued to clutch at her brutally. "Goddamn—" Then wrapping her arms around his neck and squeezing as hard as she could, she sucked her breath in hard and leaped upward, locking her legs about his body, and yanked desperately with her arms. Garner gasped, choking, and lurched forward. Together, they teetered crazily and slid along the wall, rubbing and scratching their skin. Pat sunk her teeth into his neck, strangling him with her arms and constricting her strong legs while he struggled to hold his balance. They hurtled to the floor. Pat fell on her back, dragging him with her. The fall slammed the breath out of her. She whispered a weak howl and grabbed his huge erection, arching her lithe torso upward in a frantic, squirming thrust.

Garner, not realizing or understanding what had happened, plunged into her. She thrashed beneath him, whining into his ear with each fitful heave and jerk of his body. "Go on," she squealed. "Go on, go on, go on, go on, go on—" He writhed and bucked feverishly, fighting for leverage against the desperate grasp of her arms and legs. She tried to steady him and increase the tempo. "C'mon," she groaned. "Oh, c'mon, give, baby, come on now, come on!" But Garner was too young. He was almost there, a second's instant away, dazed, swimming against the raging flood of his own energy and strength. His whole body was bursting with heat. He couldn't stop plunging and squirming. He fought, jockeying for better position. Pat's mouth caught his and clung. Then he couldn't breathe, and he couldn't feel his legs. He snorted and heaved like a wounded bull. Then a terrible, exquisite pain shot through his stomach and tore into his groin, thighs, and buttocks. He thought he was going to faint, or die. He heard Pat's grating moan, "Oh, Jesus, go on! Oh Jesus, Jesus, Jesus—" Awful heat and sweet, thrilling pain ravaged him, carrying his spirit and body soaring out of his control in a heaving rush that choked him, burned him, chilled and shook him with unbearable pleasure as the blessed agony mounted with a force that consumed him, peaking in a blinding surge of sustained, tortured delight. His powerful young body shook, convulsing violently as he tried to maintain the driving pace and failed. Spasms of pure pleasure wracked him, tearing the first great burst of his manhood from him and carrying it in irrepressible, staccato bursts down into her body. Then she wouldn't let him move, held him still, whispering, "I know I'm crazy now! Jesus Christ almighty—fourteen years old—." Garner stole a peek at Luther. He had never known. Garner struggled with his guilt, trying to sweep it aside, but it stuck with him. He looked down at his hands. They felt clammy inside of the leather gloves. He rubbed them together nervously.

"Theah it is," Buzz muttered.

"Stop heah fa' minute," Luther said.

Buzz hauled the truck to a stop at a corner. "We oughtta go on in, man."

Luther didn't say anything. Garner watched him intently, his heart quickening, stimulated by the excitement of the job before them and gnawing pangs of guilt. Buzz jabbed him in the ribs. "Theah it is, Garna."

Garner followed the turn of the older boy's head, squinting into the night.

Buzz looked at Luther. "What'cha think, man?"

"Les' git it done."

Buzz smiled grimly and drove forward.

The warehouse appeared huge to Garner. It hulked dimly amidst a mass of large, brick buildings, railroad yards, and freight cars. As usual, Luther and Buzz left him to keep watch, to warn them if he saw the police. Garner didn't like this; it was too dark. There were several trucks backed into the platform on either side of him. He half expected somebody to jump out of one of them at any moment. But there was no one around. It was quiet. He sat still, watching and listening. Looking out at the dark street, he saw some lights approaching rapidly. He held his breath and winced fearfully as a car shot by, its tires singing along the road, tail lights bright and red as it sped out of sight. He saw more lights coming. Another car whizzed by. His breath came in short gasps. He rubbed his hands anxiously along his thighs. More lights split the darkness, moving very slowly. Then they stopped and didn't move at all, then moved closer only to stop again.

Garner tried to stop breathing entirely. *Why didn't the lights keep moving and go on by?* He strained to hear something. The lights advanced again. He stared, exhaling quickly and choking down some air. He began to perspire. All at once, a loud, jagged voice knifed through the stillness out on the street. Another seemed to answer. He couldn't make out what was being said. He crouched, eyes riveted on the lights, and tried to hear. *What was out there?* Maybe he should go find Luther and Buzz. He heard another loud voice. What was that—*police?* A radio. *A radio?* Garner's heart was gripped with icy fear. *A police radio—cops!* In a frenzy he fumbled with the cab door. *Where were Luther and Buzz?* He wanted to scream, *"Tha fuzz, man, tha fuzz."*

He kicked the door open as the lights began to move again. He hesitated. A police car appeared behind the lights. Garner hastily yanked his legs back into the truck and shut the door. He crouched down and peered over the dashboard. The cruiser's lights dipped as it pulled into the yard. Garner gasped and chewed some air. His whole body felt tight. The cruiser stopped. A flashlight flicked a thin, yellow beam casually about the platform area. Then the car was moving slowly. Garner started to sigh in relief, but the cruiser stopped and backed up, then halted again. A policeman got out and stood beside it, looking toward the warehouse. Garner heard the police radio blaring. The police officer leaned over and said something to his companion, sitting at the wheel, then straightened up to look at the warehouse again. Garner gulped in some air and held onto the dashboard. Abruptly, the officer stepped into the cruiser. Then the car moved off and pulled out into the street.

Garner sat up relieved. He was breathing hard and sweating as if he had just run in a race. He braced himself against the back of his seat and tried, unsuccessfully, to relax. Myriad, ghostly shadows seemed all about the area now, lurking ominously in the dark, and they all looked like policemen. He had to blink hard several times before they slipped back into the night. The buildings across the street, pressed darkly against the sky, seemed to be staring down at him. One of the larger ones was shaped like a man. *What was keeping those guys so long?* He had to tell them about the cruiser. *Better go find them —quick!* Suddenly the truck door flew open. He sat forward with a start.

It was Buzz. "C'mon," he rasped, trying to catch his breath. "Move it, man! C'mon, les' go!"

Garner sprang from the cab and followed Buzz's leap up onto the platform.

Luther was yelling angrily, "Move yo' asses, gawddammit!" He was pulling a huge, flat cart from the building. It was loaded with bulky cartons. "You cats git tha stuff on tha truck. Ah gotta git some mo'."

"Tha fuzz!" Garner wheezed. "They—tha fuzz wuz heah!"

"Wheah?" Luther growled, grabbing his brother's arm roughly.

"Came right in tha yard!"

"We oughtta git our asses tha fuck outta heah, man," Buzz said.

"Fuck, no! They ain' seen shit, man! They gone! Sheet, evah' one a' them boxes is a hunnerd dollas, nigga!"

"Okay, Lutha, so we got two cartloads. Les' git tha fuck outta heah."

"Hell, naw, man! Fuck the fuzz. Ah got one mo' them carts loaded. Ah fuckin' sho' ain' gonna leave that shit up theah. You cats hurry wit' tha loadin'."

Buzz shook his head and went to work. "C'mon, Hawk. Les' git tha shit on tha truck. Ain' no need arguin' wit' tha nigga."

The boxes were awkward to handle, but they were light. The two boys loaded up quickly and stood waiting anxiously for Luther.

"What's in them things?" Garner wanted to know.

"Ladies' socks."

"Sheet, them things ain' worth nothin', man."

"You talkin' ignorant now, nigga. Five hunnerd pair ta box. Heah come Lutha. Les' load this shit an' git outta heah."

They hurriedly loaded the boxes and closed up the truck. "We ready now," Luther puffed. "Les' move!"

They hopped into the cab, and Buzz started the engine and shifted gears. Some lights splashed on the street before them almost instantly and started moving toward them.

"Don' move! Don' move, man! keep tha motor goin'," Luther said.

"Jesus Christ, it's tha fuckin' cops!"

Luther pushed Garner down in the seat. "Stay right theah! Don' move an' don' say nothin'!"

The cruiser stopped. It was partly hidden from view by a large trailer body which had been dropped to their left, away from the loading platform near the edge of the yard and the street.

"They gittin' outta tha car," Buzz croaked.

Luther opened his door and slid quietly out of the cab.

"What'cha gonna do? Gawddammit, nigga, what tha fuck ya gonna do, fa' crissake?"

"Shut up," Luther snarled. "Shut tha fuck up, gawddammit! Ah ain' skeered a' them mutha-fuckas."

Garner saw his brother draw his revolver. Buzz howled, "Naw, man! Don' do it!"

Luther cursed him and shut the door. One of the policemen hollered something.

Buzz whispered, "Aw, *Jesus!*"

Garner sat up, peering through the window. Buzz bolted out of the cab. One of the police officers squatted under the trailer and fired two quick shots. The first bullet knocked Buzz back against the cab. The second smashed into the body of the truck. Then Luther was shooting, using the hood of the truck to steady his aim. He fired three times; the officer under the trailer fell as his companion dove toward the ground, firing several times on the way down. One bullet crashed through the windshield and ripped through the back of the cab. Another came tearing through the door near Garner's face. Terrified, he threw himself down and huddled on the floor. He heard another shot, then abruptly, there was silence. For a long, agonized second, he heard nothing except the storm of his own heart and blood. Then there was a terrific burst of gunfire followed by a raging stillness. He held his breath, crouching in terror, unmoving.

He looked up as the door on the driver's side burst open. Luther dragged him over the shifting lever, under the steering wheel and out of the cab, screaming at him hysterically. "Git out, nigga! They got Buzz! They got Buzz!"

Garner scrambled as he tried to get his footing, fell down, got up and stood snapping his head around, trying to see what had happened.

Buzz sat on the ground slumped against the front wheel of the truck. One policeman lay face down under the trailer, not moving. The other one was huddled on his side nearby. Garner heard the police radio blaring, and a flashlight rolled slowly toward the platform, its light blinking uselessly.

"He'p me git'im in tha truck," Luther bellowed.

Garner got hold of Buzz's feet.

"Not like that, ya fuckin'—. Git out tha way. *Git out tha fuckin' way!*" He pushed Garner roughly aside and snatched Buzz from the ground and hurled him into the cab.

Garner stood in a stupor.

Luther jumped behind the wheel, then seeing him motionless, yelled, "Ya fuckin' dumb bastid, c'mon!" He vaulted from the truck, grabbed Garner's arm and threw him in a crazy, wild spin toward the other side of the truck. Garner fell down, and Luther was upon him again, dragging him upward and along, lifting him, thrusting him into the cab.

Garner was only vaguely aware of the insane, desperate ride through the narrow back streets of the city. Buzz lurched wildly about the cab, bouncing between him and Luther. The truck jerked and lunged on its way.

"Hang onta him, fa' crissake!" Luther hollered.

Garner tried to hold Buzz still, but his gloves kept slipping in something wet and slimy.

They ran into traffic and slowed down. Luther was cursing bitterly. Buzz threw his head back, groaning weakly. He coughed, and blood gurgled in his throat and spilled from the corners of his mouth. Garner stared as the wet, red goo drooled down the boy's chin. Buzz turned his head against the back of the seat and coughed. Garner shut his eyes, feeling sick as Buzz vomited red and yellow spume over him. The sticky mess slopped down the front of his T-shirt. Garner sucked in his stomach and tried to look out of the window. The truck hit a bump, rocking him and Buzz against the door. He could feel Buzz's hand grasping at him feebly. He felt something wet and scummy slither down his arm and wrist into the glove, oozing around his fingers. He tried moving his hand, but the gooey slime seemed to be everywhere. Then a foul odor rose up in the cab as Buzz urinated and defecated. He was suddenly still. Garner began to cry, holding onto Buzz fiercely and sobbing against his shoulder.

They rode for a long time. Finally, they stopped, and Luther leaped out and ran behind the truck. Garner heard voices in heated conversation. He clung to Buzz, tightening his grip.

A few minutes later, Luther came back. He examined Buzz for a moment. "Aw, *shit,*" he moaned weakly. "Aw—gawddamn, man, he—he *dead!* Jesus Christ—tha fuckin' bastids done killed Buzz." He cried then, tears coursing down his face as he climbed into the cab.

Garner hadn't really heard what he said. He squeezed his eyes shut and held Buzz as Luther cranked the engine. The slime was drying on his shirt and on his hands and arms. Luther drove back toward the city, his black face grim.

Garner sat dumbly when the truck stopped again. Then Buzz was wrenched from his arms. He didn't move, couldn't think. Luther got back into the cab. The truck lurched ahead. Garner stared at the windshield, seeing only his own tears. His hands were caked with the blood drying inside his gloves, but he was no longer aware of it. He was numb.

The truck stopped and Luther climbed out, then he was back, shaking Garner roughly. "Gimme a hand," he growled. Garner stepped out of the cab. They were on a bridge. It was very dark. There was no traffic. Luther pulled him along to the rear of the truck. "C'mon, ya black bastid," he demanded in an angry hiss. Dazed, Garner helped Luther drag Buzz's body from the back of the truck. The body was wrapped with ropes and weighted chains. Garner did not realize what they had done until he was back in the truck and remembered pushing Buzz out from the bridge and watching him plummet through the yawning black to the water below.

When they got back to the apartment, Garner started to wake up. He was sick. He threw up over the kitchen table and on the floor. Luther hauled him into the bathroom and watched him puke into the toilet. Garner's guts heaved long after he had emptied his stomach. He couldn't control himself. There was blood and puke all over him, and Luther, too. Garner cried and coughed, retching until he was exhausted. Luther stripped off his clothes and stuffed them into a cloth bag along with his own, then he stuck the boy in the bathtub, washed him, and put him to bed. . . .

Luther kept Garner in the apartment for three days, lecturing and instructing him about keeping his mouth shut. "Do evah'thin' like always!"—"Keep cool."—"Ya don' know nothin' 'bout nothin'."—"Don' nevah come heah no mo'."—"They ain' gonna find Buzz, neither, an' he paid tha rent. Tha man don' know who live heah."—"Ah be leavin' town."—"An' don'—"

Garner listened, nodding his head continuously. He would do exactly as Luther instructed. There was nothing to worry about. Keep the peace and keep cool. Luther gave him a hundred dollars and promised to send more. When Luther left him in front of his house, he was steady, mentally ready to follow instructions. He watched the big convertible dig out, wondering if Luther would be seeing Pat, wishing he were old enough to leave home. Then he turned and ran up the steps into the house.

"What's wrong with Garner lately?" Harry asked looking up from his evening paper at Ella and glancing quickly at Garner sitting in front of the television set.

"Ain' nothin' wrong wit'im. What'cha talkin' 'bout?"

"Hey, nothing! I mean—nothing. Home a lot, that's all."

"This wheah he live, ain' it?"

Harry frowned and went back to his paper. Garner pretended to ignore the conversation and went on staring at the T.V. His throat felt thick; he thought of Buzz and Luther and remembered the newscast—*"One policeman has been killed and another seriously wounded in a gun battle with hoodlums. Patrolmen John E. Burke and Francis J. Reilly were fired upon when they attempted to detain thieves who had broken into a warehouse off Atlantic Avenue. Officer Reilly was shot to death. He is survived by his wife, Margaret, and their five children—Officer Burke's condition is described as critical but doctors at City Hospital are optimistic about his chances. The officers' assailants may have been Negroes."*—Garner rubbed his eyes with the back of his hand and shook his head. He wished Terry had worked that night instead of him.

"Cops still haven't caught up with the boys who shot up those two cops," Harry announced. "Says here they've got police in a dozen states looking for them. Damn fools—shooting at cops. Now the other cop says he doesn't know if they were niggers or not! Isn't that something? Blame everything on the niggers. Well, I hope they get away with it. Better run fast, though, and far, too! White folks're looking all over—"—Garner shot an angry look at Harry—"—for those boys. Mr. Charlie better quit messing with niggers, I'm telling you that much. Colored folks're getting ready to tear this country *up!* Serves Charlie right, too."

"Well," Ella said, "it time cullid folks showed tha white man somethin'. They been beatin' our heads 'long's ah kin rememba."

"Says here curfew's been lifted down in Detroit. Man, I'm telling—"

Garner's thoughts dug in again—*"Police authorities in several states are combing this entire region."—"Killers continue to elude police."—"Commissioner Sweeney has vowed to continue the manhunt until the killers are apprehended."*—Garner heard Harry talking to him.

"Say, boy, you quit playing ball? *Hey,* boy, I said—how come you're not playing any more ball?"

"Leave'im be," Ella chided.

Garner shrugged and hung his head, staring at the floor.

"Shoot, Ella, I'm just—listen, there has to be a reason; maybe the boy's not feeling well."

"Jes' leave'im be, man."

Garner looked up at the T.V. and thought of the bridge and Buzz. Icy things wiggled in his belly. His face felt hot, and he kept his eyes away from Harry and his mother. He looked toward the window; it was still light out. Harry got up and fiddled with the television set, switching into the middle of a wild-west shootout. Garner grimaced, and walked quickly to his room.

The room seemed empty now, and, somehow, he wished that he could still share it with Terry and Luther. He sighed and fell across the bed. His thoughts drifted—*Buzz coughed and twisted his face against the back of the seat, vomiting red and yellow spume—Garner could feel the slime in his gloves—"They got Buzz!"*—He opened his eyes, trying to think of something else, but his mind worked against his will and kept coming back to the horror of that night—*It was very dark on the bridge. There was no traffic. Buzz's body was bound with ropes and weighted chains. The stench of urine and excrement was on him.*—Garner could smell Buzz's waste now, as though the corpse were in the bed with him.

He shook his head and rolled onto his stomach, burying his face in his hands—*"Police continue their search."*—*"Officer Burke said today that he is not certain that his attackers were Negroes."*—*"Burke said that it was difficult to see."*—*"The man he fired at may have been a Negro."*—*"Police Commissioner Sweeney has indicated that he may—."* Garner heard a knock at the door. He sat up quickly on the bed, his stomach crawling with fear. He held his breath, listening to voices. His mother was talking with somebody. He tried to understand what was being said.

"Garna? Garna, c'mon out heah, boy. Man frum yo' ball team heah fa' ya. Wanna see ya."

His body shuddered with blessed relief. He sprang to his feet, telling himself that he had known all along that it wasn't the police. How could they possibly find him? They weren't looking for *him!* Besides, he wasn't worried, anyway. He was hard. Nothing to worry about. Just keep cool. "Ah heah ya, Ma," he called out, and walked through the living room into the kitchen.

"Well," Bill Chamberlain said gruffly, holding out his hand, "it's good to know you're still alive!"

"Huh?" Garner grunted warily, not noticing the sharp twitch pulling at the corner of Bill's mustache.

"Where the devil have you *been,* boy?"

"Uh—"

"I thought somebody had run over you, or something, for pete's sake."

Ella left them and went into the living room. Bill sat down and loosened his collar and tie. "Don't you want to play ball?"

Garner didn't speak, but stood shifting his weight from one foot to the other.

The twitch around Bill's mouth stopped as he said through his teeth, "Couldn't you come by and *tell* me you've quit? Practice too hard? Get to be too much for you? Did—well, *have* you quit?"

Garner made a weak, meaningless gesture with his hands.

"Say, what *is* this?" Bill growled. "What the hell's going *on?*" He stood up, staring into the boy's face. "What have you been up to, anyway? What have you been—" He let the thought hang and sat down quickly. The devil, he reprimanded himself, with what the boy *had* done. What was he going to do *now?* That's why he had come. This kid had—problems—*big trouble,* he was certain, and this was no time to horse him. Watching him carefully, Bill's face tightened, masking a tremor of cold fear. *Something*—God, he could almost see it, the evil thing that crawled about the boy, bringing to mind a slithering snake, coiling itself a little tighter each time its prey takes a breath, slowly, relentlessly shutting out the precious air until the last gasp is taken and there is no more room for life. Bill wondered if he should get up and leave. "You—haven't been sick, have you?" he inquired gently, unable to think of anything else to say.

"Huh?"

"You been sick?"

Garner fastened his eyes on the man for a moment, screaming a wordless answer. *"Yeah, man! Ah been sick! Yeah, see?"* He lowered his gaze, continuing his bitter silence. *"Sheet. What'choo know? What'choo know, man? Fa' crissake, Buzz is dead! Man, Buzz is at tha bottom a' tha fuckin' Charles! Jesus Christ, man! What'choo know? Lutha—."* He picked his head up slowly, peering at the man through watery, hot eyes.

Bill saw the tears and looked down at the table. He spoke with quiet urgency, "Look, Hawk, this basketball thing is just about wrapped up, see? Football'll be starting soon and—well, we could really use you out there, Hawk."

Garner didn't say anything.

"I—I *need* you, boy. Been hoping—been counting on you."

"Huh?"

"Ellis and the other guys are all signed up already, Hawk. If we had *you*—hell, it could—make our whole season, boy."

Garner scowled against his tears and nodded in an unsure and unconvincing way.

Bill wanted to grab the boy and shake him as hard as he could, but he continued in the same quiet tone, "You're not *worried* about it, are you? I mean, football's a rough game. Kids out there're hard, boy, and they—"

"Naw, man! Sheet, ah ain' skeered a' none them cats."

"Well, then?"

"Ah could—ah could play, man."

"Most people can't take that kind of punishment and work, so just say the word if—"

"Man, sheet—*ah be out theah wit'em!* Gawd—*dawg*—it! Ah kin play."

"Well, okay," Bill said, getting to his feet and smiling. "I'm glad to hear it. You know, Hawk, it'll be good for you to learn the game now instead of waiting until you get to high school. And boy, sports—football is good for what ails you. Either you get it knocked into you, or you get it knocked *out* of you—*or else you quit,* that's all, boy."

"Ain' nobuddy gonna make me quit, man."

"Yeah. You'll like it, Hawk. It's a game for hard guys," Bill said.

They shook hands.

"See you later, okay, Hawk?"

"Yeah, man."

Bill left. Garner walked to the table and sat down, resting his head heavily on his hands. Shivering, he thought of Buzz, remembering the river—*It was dark, dull, and black. The night seemed to rise up out of the black water. Buzz's body was falling—.* He started to cry again. *Buzz was under there!* Glancing nervously over his shoulder toward the living room, he stood up hurriedly and went out. He paused in the hallway for a brief moment, then went up the short, dark stairs which led to the roof, and sat down, leaning against the wall as the tears rushed freely down his face.

BOOK

THREE

IT WAS raining. The downpour pelted through the cold night in a straight, needlelike torrent. Here and there, the rain glittered in uncertain light, falling in streams of watery beads. There was little wind.

Garner pressed his face against the bathroom window. The murky wet made him think of Buzz. A frown crossed his flat face. Two years had passed since then. Seldom now did he recall the horror of that night. Buzz, he stated silently, is dead. Drawing a towel slowly across his wide shoulders, he stepped back, turning to discover Harry leaning against the door frame smiling pleasantly and sipping a can of beer. Garner's expression darkened to a scowl, and he wrapped the towel around his waist and let the water out of the bathtub.

"What time's the party, Garner?"

"Anytime."

"Taking a girl?"

"Naw."

"How come?"

"Be plenny bitches theah, man," Garner replied irritably, searching in the medicine cabinet for the cologne.

"Terry picking you up?"

"Yeah."

"How come he doesn't come up when he stops by?"

"Whyn'choo ask'im?"

Harry's dark, round face took on a pained expression. "I didn't see him at the game this morning."

Garner rubbed some oil into his thick, tight hair and began to slide a large comb through it.

"I said, I didn't see Terry at the game today."

"Man, Terry don' go ta no games."

"Not even Thanksgiving?"

Garner finished combing his hair and sprayed some deodorant under his arms.

"Missed a helluva ball game. He ever see you play?"

"Ah guess so. Sheet, Terry's bid'nessman. Ain' got no time. He outta school, man."

"So what? His brother isn't."

Garner shouldered his way by Harry and started across the living room.

"*Businessman*—he's a pimp! He's—"

"Sheet! He makes mo' bread than you, man."

"He's still a pimp," Harry said, following the boy to his bedroom. "Just a punk kid, trying to play big shot."

"Aw, man, whyn'choo git off that shit. You ain' got half tha shit Terry got."

"Got what I need."

"Sheet."

Harry decided to change the subject. "Well, he missed a helluva game. I even took my radio so I could hear it at the same time. Lot of people—lot of newspaper people there, too. Hard to believe. I mean—"

"Sheet. Woulda been mo', if tha weather hadda been good. Tech'n Classical's bigges' game 'roun'."

"Tech almost lost it."

"Sheet, we kicked they asses."

A faint smile glimmered sardonically in Harry's face. "This the game ball?"

Garner cracked open a box of new, white shirts and tried to decide on a pair of cufflinks, his long fingers fishing around on top of his bureau.

Harry picked up the new football from the bed. "Helluva game. Lot of people. Boy, your mother—just scared to death. Every time you carried the ball, I thought she was going to have a fit. 'They gonna *kill'*im,' she kept saying."

Garner pulled some pins out of a new shirt.

"Who lettered it for you?"

"Huh?"

"Who lettered the ball for you?"

"Tha fellas."

"Wondered if you'd get it. Thought maybe an older boy, or the captain."

"Sheet."

"Helluva game. Too bad you and Ellis had to play against each other. He's a nice boy. He going to the party?"

"Naw, man."

"Why not?"

"Sheet, Ellis don' go nowheahs."

"Thought you were tight."

"Ellis okay. Simple, thass all."

"Nifty little runner."

"We whipped *his* ass."

"Must be a smart boy, too. I understand those kids at Classical are pushed pretty hard."

"Man, what'choo talkin' 'bout. Tha nigga don' *go* nowheahs. Don' *do* nothin'. *School*—alla time, school! Nigga simple, man."

"That's what I mean—smart boy."

"Didn't he'p'im ta-day, gawddammit."

"You were lucky to get the game ball," Harry attempted to compromise and skirt another argument. "Quite an honor."

"Man—wuzn't no choice, sheet. The Hawk is tough, thass all. Sheet—lucky, he say. *Man!*"

"Oh, I'm sorry."

"They ain' *nevah* seen nothin' like tha Hawk, baby."

"Yes. Well—of course, I didn't realize—I didn't know just how—"

"Lotta things *you* don' know, man."

Harry's brow knit in annoyance, and he flipped the ball back onto the bed. "Too bad Luther wasn't at the game."

"Fuck you, Harry," Garner yelled quickly.

"Now look, boy, you better watch your mouth. I'm not one of your—"

"Fuck you, nigga! *Fuck* you, shit!"

Harry took a step toward him. "Boy, I'll slap hell out of you!"

"Yeah? C'mon, fat man, c'mon! Ah break ya fat ass, ya som'-bitch!"

"Aw, I wouldn't lower myself. You and Luther are two of a kind—big, black—and stupid as hell."

"Mutha-fuck you, Harry! You ain' shit," Garner shrieked with tears in his eyes. "Lutha *kill* ya! He kill ya, if he heah ya!"

Ella burst into the room then, clutching her robe about her, curlers in her hair skewered with pins, swiveling her angry face from Garner to Harry and back. "Y'all stop alla this cussin'! What'ch'all fightin' 'bout?" she cried, stepping hastily between them and glaring up at her son. "What'sa matta? What'ch'all yelling fa'?"

"He startin' that shit 'bout Lutha agin. Ah ain' gonna—"

"Don'choo cuss at me, boy! Ah'm ya *Ma!* Ya heah?"

Garner turned away from her, his face pinched with distaste as he bent and picked up his jacket from the bed.

"Ya list'nin' ta me, Garna?"

"Yeah, Ma."

"Ya betta, ya heah?"

"Yeah, yeah. Ah heah ya."

"Yo' mouth got *awful* nasty, an' ah don' like it! Ain' gonna listen ta that kinda thing, an' you yellin' loud's ya kin. Heah me?"

"Yeah."

"What he needs is a swift boot right in his—black behind. That's what—"

Garner wheeled to face him, glowering. *"Sheet!* Who gonna do it, nigga? *You?* Ah wish you try! C'mon, fat man! you be bad! Sheet, talkin' 'bout pimpin'—you a lover, ain'cha?"

He dropped his jacket and started for Harry. The older man rushed to meet him, but Ella seized the boy at once, clamping down hard, mashing her face in his chest, and struggling to stop him.

"Let him come, Ella! Let the silly nigger come. He's big enough."

"Fuck you, fat man! Mutha-f—"

Ella's hand stung his face with an ear-ringing slap. She hit him again before he caught her wrists and held her. Her voice was shrill with indignation, "Lemme go! You lemme go, now! Ah—"

A horn sounded. Garner knew it was Terry. He pushed his mother away. As he bent to retrieve his jacket, she swung at him in furious outrage, missed and walloped Harry in the mouth, carrying both of them backward over the chair and crashing to the floor. Garner snatched his wallet and cigarettes from the bureau and strode into the living room, put on his jacket and stopped to grab his topcoat from the sofa. He quickly stripped the cleaner's plastic wrapping from the garment, listening to his mother raving at him from the bedroom as she fell again, trying to regain her feet, "Ya—ya come back heah—gawd-damn ya! Don'choo—don'choo go—"

But Garner was on his way, heaving the door shut behind him with a resounding slam.

The rain hadn't let up. Garner hesitated in the front doorway, watching the water sluicing along the gleaming red paint of Terry's new Buick convertible. Flipping his collar up and hunching his head between his shoulders, he ran down the steps to the car. Terry threw open the door and Garner slid into the front seat, glancing quickly at the three girls in the back.

"What say, Hawk?" Terry's thick mustache spread over a wide grin.

"Man, les' git tha fuck outta heah."

"Trouble wit' Ma?"

"Naw, Harry. He on Lutha agin."

Terry's thin, orange-colored face darkened. He wagged his head unhappily from side to side. "Lutha shoulda nevah went on that deal, baby. Didn't know them cats good. They wuz dumb mutha-fuckas, man. An' them New York fuzz is bastids. They hard."

Garner watched Terry switch on the dome light. "Sheet, man, fuckin' Harry gotta—"

"Fuck Harry, man. Looka heah, baby, wan'cha ta meet some pretty people." Terry turned in his seat and started pointing at the girls. They were pretty, and well dressed. One of them was white. "Thass Jackie," he began, aiming his finger at a girl with golden skin. "Thass, Shirley." He pointed at the white girl. "An' Carol," who was ebony-hued and full-bodied. "This ma brotha, Garna."

Garner acknowledged each of the girls with a slight nod of his head.

"Shirley knew Lutha in New York."

Garner focused on the girl. She was slender, with black hair swept up on top of her head and blue eyes set wide apart over a short, straight nose. "Ya been ta see'im?"

"Not after he went upstate," Shirley said in a quiet voice, "but I did see him once while they still had him in town."

"How he look? How wuz he takin' it?"

"Well, like a man, baby. Like—you look just like him, know that? Almost as big, too."

"You folks frum New York, too?"

"Sometimes, baby," Carol answered.

"We don't stay too long in any one place," Jackie said. She and the other girls laughed.

"Hey, Terry, when ya figga Lutha be comin' out, man?"
"Dunno."
"Well, what'cha figga?"
"Maybe five years."
"Gawddamn—. Naw, man, ah mean, wit' parole."
"Shit, Hawk, he gotta do least three years, man."
"Must be a bitch inside."
"It is," Shirley said grimly.
Garner looked at her with acute interest. "You been inside?"
She hesitated, then nodded slowly.
"Man, must be a bitch."
"Just don't be in a hurry to find out," Jackie said. "It's a drag, baby, a real drag."
Terry glanced at his brother. "Jes' gotta play it cool, thass all."
"Fuzz ain' gonna git tha Hawk."
"Sheet, ain' no fuzz kin fuck wit'cha, if ya know what's happ'nin'. Ya gotta git next ta tha people who *pays* tha fuzz, baby. Yeah. Like Billy Ray, man. Ain' a cop in tha worl' kin say shit ta him, gawddammit."

They fell silent. The rain had eased up to a steady drizzle now, working against the wipers. Traffic was slow and very heavy. Buzz loomed up in Garner's mind. Was he still under that river? What was left of him? There are, he thought, worse things than being inside.

They arrived at the party shortly after ten o'clock. Garner found himself in a large house in the oldest and most exclusive part of the city. As soon as they had left their coats, Terry whisked the girls away, telling Garner he would be back in a minute. Garner nodded and wandered over to a mirror to recheck his clothes.

The suit was dark blue; the shirt was white, with a full spread collar rolling gently under the lapels of his jacket. Yes, he thought, just enough of the white cuffs showed. He smiled and made certain that his tie was dead-center, then walked over to a doorway nearby.

He found himself looking into a very large room, filled with people dancing, drinking, and chatting. There were a number of middle-aged men in the room. Most of them were white. He saw a yellow-skinned youth and a white man holding hands. He scowled and lit a cigarette.

"Hello, there."

Garner turned to see a willowy, honey-colored girl in a short, wispy, black dress. His eyes worked over the good legs and shoulder-length hair. "How do."

She shoved a drink in his hand. "I'm Vicki."

"Yeah, uh—ah'm Garna."

"You're even bigger up close, Garner. *Garner*—I like it. Do you know anybody here?"

"Jes' Vicki."

"Beautiful," she purred. "That's Scotch, Garner. You're supposed to drink it."

"Huh? Aw, yeah." He raised the glass to his lips.

"Hey, not so fast, baby. Let it work a little."

She took the glass from him and began to sway gracefully to the music. "Vicki wants to dance now. Want to dance with Vicki, baby?"

Garner moved in front of her, picking up the slow, bouncing rhythm, and began to work with her.

"What'cha doin', Hawk?" Terry stood smiling in the doorway, fingering his thick, brand-new process. He was proud of his hair and had it done at least twice monthly, more often if necessary. The straightened hair gave him the look of a Spaniard or a Mexican, which pleased him and was, in his eyes, the best aspect of his appearance, and indeed, of what he fancied himself to be—a successful and fashionable young man about town, movie-style. "Hey, Hawk? Hey, man, who tha pretty people?"

"Man, be gone. Ah'm dancin'."

"Sheet, baby, you don' know *how* ta dance."

"Sheet."

"Honey, ah'm Terry, an' that impolite nigga you dancin' wit's ma baby brotha. How you?"

"Well, I'm Vicki, and I'm fine, baby, just fine."

"Yeah, man, an' we dancin', sheet."

Vicki reached up to kiss Garner lightly on the lips. "Yeah, baby."

"Hey, Hawk, c'mon upstairs, man. Bring tha people wit'cha. C'mon."

"They smoking yet?" Vicki asked, gyrating to a halt and fixing a hopeful look on Terry.

"Yeah."

"Well, let's go, then."

"That shit makes me sleepy," Garner said.

She laughed and slid one arm under his and the other under Terry's. "I'll keep you awake, baby. C'mon."

The upstairs was dark. Terry stopped in front of a closed door. Below it, a band of light shone, and they could hear muted voices laughing and talking. The door was locked. Terry rapped on it vigorously.

"Wheah ya take tha bitches, Terry?"

"Ta see Billy Ray."

"He gonna let'em work?"

"Yeah, man. Shit, yeah."

"Them bitches wuz fine."

"Ah got Shirley comin' up heah in a while."

The door opened, and a short white man hustled them inside to a dark room crowded with people. Overhead in the center, a weirdly colored chandelier tinkled softly as it turned, spinning flecks of dark and light, red, yellow, and blue through the smoke. Immediately under the chandelier stood a small wooden stage—the only well-lit spot in the room—around which the crowd had gathered. The girls, most of them of African descent, were in various states of undress, bra and panties, panties and skin, and skin. There was a strong smell of marijuana.

Terry lifted his face toward the ceiling, sniffing away with exaggerated enthusiasm. "Man, man, man-oh-man, we gonna *party* now!"

Vicki was delighted. She placed Garner's arms around her and kissed him hard, her tongue deep in his mouth, working her body against him

"Wait heah," Terry said with a grin. "Ah git tha shit."

A small blond girl stood up. She was naked. Her plump, white body shimmered under the light. She strolled up onto the low stage. Some cheers went up. The girl smiled dreamily and began a slow grind. She was short and powerfully built, with enormous, pendulous breasts.

Vicki laughed and turned in Garner's arms so that she could see better, leaning back into him with his arms folded under her breasts. Shirley came up behind them.

"Hi, Garner. Where's Terry? He said he'd be up here with you."

"He be right back."

"Hey, Billy Ray's really putting on a show, isn't he?"

"Yeah. Gawddamn, somebuddy oughtta put on a record or play—"

"I wish they'd put a man up there with her," Vicki giggled.

"Sheet, *ah* wouldn't wanna git up theah."

Terry came back with the smokes. Vicki and Garner each took one and lit up. Terry gave his to Shirley and buried his face in her neck.

Garner puffed vigorously, and Vicki burst out laughing. "Easy—slowly, baby." She pursed her lips around the cigarette and started a steady, long pull, dragging deeply, then holding the smoke in before exhaling. "Like that, see?"

Garner tried to imitate her but was distracted by the blond under the lights again. It made him high however he did it, anyway.

"Hey, Hawk, some a' tha cats downstairs gittin' theirse'fs fixed up wit' rooms, man. We oughtta grab us one befo' they all gone."

"Sheet, Terry, ah wanna see this."

"Me too, man, but—"

"Jesta coupla minutes, man."

"Gawddamn, Garna—sheet."

"Jes' be a minute."

Two black youths stood up, a girl, lissome and supple as a wild reed, her naked body glistening with sweat, and a thin young man, bare from the waist up. The girl joined the blond under the lights while the man sat on the floor at the right edge of the stage and placed a set of bongo drums between his knees. The room was very quiet now as the young man slowly and insistently began to stroke the drums. A quiet beat rose in the stillness, urgent and compelling.

Garner's eyes glazed, and a dreamy smile came over his face. Vicki pressed backward against him, taking his free hand from her belly and sliding it down between her thighs. Terry slipped an arm around

Shirley and she sagged against him, biting his ear through a glassy smile.

The girls under the lights, their bodies colored by the spinning chandelier, were dancing now, moving around one another. They came closer and closer together, then danced away, twirling their arms and shaking their breasts. The black girl, teeth glittering, skin shining, her sinewy figure coiling and uncoiling, moved like a cat around the blond. They circled closer, and their bodies nearly touched as they swayed in unison, wriggling their naked torsos and limbs, seemingly afraid to touch. The black girl's hard nipples brushed back and forth against the pale, bulbous breasts of her partner. The bongos grew more insistent, and the blond began to caress the black girl, white hands slithering over her dark skin as they weaved, nose to nose, staring into each other's eyes. Their bodies came together, bellies grinding, buttocks jerking and their skins quivering in sweaty spasms. Abruptly, their mouths locked, veins standing out on their necks. They sank to the floor.

"C'mon," Vicki whispered hoarsely, turning to face Garner. "I know where we can find a room."

Garner didn't remember leaving the party. He woke up in Terry's apartment the next afternoon. Laughter was coming from the kitchen. He was naked except for his watch and his socks. His mouth felt thick and dry. The bedroom was a mess. His stomach hurt with hunger pains. He flipped the sheet off himself and sat up on the edge of the bed. He wished he had some candy, or some ice cream. The door opened, and a dark-skinned girl, dressed in brassiere and skirt, stepped into the room. He blinked at her, covering himself with the sheet. She laughed. Garner's brow creased, and he blinked again and rubbed his eyes. He had seen her before. She was pretty, with a wide breadth of shoulders, and deep breasts.

"I'm Carol," she said with amusement. "Did you forget me that fast?"

His mouth swung open stupidly as he remembered the girls in the car.

"Want a cigarette?" she asked, sitting down beside him.

"Yeah."

"Hungry?"

"Yeah."

She lit two cigarettes and stuck one in his mouth. "Got some turnovers and milk in the kitchen. C'mon."

"Huh? Well—"

Giggling, she got up and pulled the sheet off him. "C'mon, baby. Carol doesn't bite."

He picked up his pants from the floor and tried to scowl.

"Your brother's in the kitchen," she said and took his hand, towing him behind her as he zipped up his pants.

Terry and Shirley were sitting at the table eating. Garner sat down and began eating his turnovers and milk. When he looked up, the three of them were staring at him.

"Didn't ah tell ya?" Terry cackled. "Nobuddy eat like this nigga."

"Are you really sixteen?" Shirley asked, her blue eyes glowing.

"Naw!" Garner growled, throwing a furious glare at his brother.

"He has to be," Carol said. "He's so bashful, you know he's got to be just a kid."

"Ah ain' no kid."

Shirley feigned surprise. *"Bashful?* After last night?"

Carol walked behind Garner's chair and put her arms around him. "He's only a kid. Just a baby."

"Sheet," Terry said, "tha nigga's a horse, man! Jes' like Lutha. Even got muscles in his head. Looka them jaws work."

"He's pretty," Shirley said, "and sweet, isn't he, Carol?"

"She-yee-yit, man. Thass tha uglies' nigga in tha whole worl', fa' crissake."

"Fuck you, Terry."

"Sheet. Man, air' nobuddy s'posed ta be that big. Looka tha nigga eat."

"Well, he's *growing,"* Carol explained with a laugh, hugging Garner and kissing his neck. "And *I* think he looks like a growing boy ought to look."

Shirley stood up from the table. "Looks like a *man* ought to look. I'm going to see if Jackie's up."

"Ah he'p ya." Terry got up and slapped her on the fanny and lifted her up from behind.

Garner watched Shirley's bare legs kicking in the air as her skirt rode up on her thighs. She squealed and twisted in Terry's arms.

Carol kissed Garner on the shoulder. "Want some more milk?" she asked as he finished eating.

"Naw."

"Want a cigarette?"

"Naw."

"Want Carol?"

"Yeah—naw—ah mean, ah'm sleepy."

She took his arm. "C'mon, I'll put you back to bed."

"Huh? No shit, Carol, now—"

"C'mon, baby—oh, c'mon. I'll let you sleep—for a while, anyway."

Garner stayed at Terry's place for a week. He even toyed briefly with the thought of quitting school and moving in with his brother permanently, but decided to wait a little longer. He had time, he figured. The basketball season was beginning now, and he looked forward to it with pleasant anticipation. He had been on the verge of quitting right after his birthday, but he had wanted to play football again, and afterward there was basketball and track. He was a junior in high school now, taking cabinet-making, although the idea of becoming a cabinet-maker had never occurred to him. He didn't know anyone who wanted to be a cabinet-maker, and that included the man who taught the course. Garner took it for the same reason everyone else did; it was easy, nobody failed, and most important, it meant he could play. However, despite the easy course and sports, he loathed school and hated to give up the good time he was having with Terry.

He wasn't happy to be going home that Friday, either. His mother would be furious at his week-long absence.

"Ma gonna be evil," he reflected as Terry drove him home.

"Yeah—. Fuck it, baby. She git too shitty, an' ya jes' git tha fuck outta theah, thass all, sheet. Time ya got out on ya own, anyways, man. Shit, yeah, ya could move in wit' me. That way ya be able ta work alla time, stead a' jes' part a' tha time, 'spesh'ly if ya quit alla that ball playin'."

"Aw, man—"

"Yeah, yeah, man—okay, fuck it. Nevah gonna grow up, gawddammit."

"Aw, fuck you, man."

"Yeah, yeah, yeah. What'cha gonna tell Ma?"

Garner didn't know what he would tell his mother, but when Terry dropped him in front of the house, he was prepared for a storm of anger.

The storm never came. When he stepped gingerly into the kitchen, she was cleaning the sink. There was some coffee working on the stove. She glanced quickly in his direction, but went right on with her work. Garner walked slowly through the kitchen, going around the far side of the table and peering at her cautiously. *Here it comes,* he thought, *right now.* But she didn't speak, just went on with her chores, her mouth set in a grim line. He hesitated as he came to the living room door, wondering, should *he* say something? He frowned. No, cool it. *Don't* get that woman started. Peeking hastily at her over his shoulder, he observed, she's hot now. Forget it. Better like this. *No noise,* and he went to his room.

Later, lying on his bed, he was uneasy. He could hear her working in the kitchen. He half expected her to come charging through the door, and his eyes were continually drawn to it. *Get it over with,* was his feeling now. Then it was quiet, and his senses sharpened with anticipation. But nothing happened. What was wrong with her? What could be—*had Harry taken off? No.* No, Harry wasn't going anywhere. He didn't understand it.

Suddenly, he didn't like it, either. A malaise caught in his guts and worked slowly up into his throat. He tried to shake it off, lighting a cigarette, directing his thoughts elsewhere, but it took hold, rooting in his mind. Then he saw Buzz's face. Goose pimples erupted on his skin. Hastily, he crushed out the cigarette. His hands felt clammy—

He felt something slimy oozing down his arm inside the glove. He tried moving his hand around, but the wet slime seemed to be everywhere. A foul odor rose up in the cab. Buzz had defecated.—Garner squeezed his eyes shut, and a feeling of gnawing loneliness washed over him, followed by an abrupt and terrifying plunge into an anxiety he didn't understand.

He wanted to go to his mother now and plead with her, "C'mon, Ma, les' heah it! Git it said!" Yes, that's what he would tell her—. No! Wait a minute, now. That wasn't it at all. He wanted *her* to say it, wanted to hear her voice, even in fury. Maybe she would say, "Wheah ya been, boy? Ya gone crazy?" or something like, "What's wrong wit'choo?" or, "Ma gawd, ma gawd, boy, wheah ya been alla this time?" *There,* that was it! Sure. His gaze fluttered at the door. He bit down on his lip. She wasn't coming. Well, maybe it was best that way. After all, what could he say to her?

Well, he'd say, "Look, Ma, ah been out wit' Terry, see?" and she would scowl then and say, "Terry?" "Yeah, Ma, ah been wit' Terry." "Ya been up ta no good, then," she'd say. "Aw, Ma—," and she'd hold up her hand, cutting him off with "Don' wanna heah it, ah don'. Terry ain' no damn good, thass all. Gonna wind up in jail!" "Aw, c'mon. Fa' crissake, Ma—" "Don'choo cuss me, boy! Ya heah? Ya—y'all crazy, thass what! Gonna wind up jes' like Lutha! Y'ain', none a' ya, no good, an' thass tha troof, an' ah—" Garner winced. No, he didn't want it to go like that. Maybe he could just sit with her kind of. Maybe she would—*yes!* Put her arms around him and hold him. *What's wrong with you, Hawk?* Well, just for *a while,* his thoughts scrambled on. Just quiet, easy, the way she used to—*"Do ya love ya momma?—Baby, ah mean, do ya feel fa' ya momma?"*—He grimaced, remembering.

He swung his feet over the edge of the bed and sat up, wondering if he should go over to the Y. No, he considered, no, Bill would be there, and Garner would have to listen to: "What's the deal, Hawk? Coach says you haven't been in school." He conjured up Bill's face in his mind; it was angry and hard. "How come?" is what he'd hear next. "Well, man—Bill—ah mean—see, man, ah been pooped—yeah. Football. Ya know, man? Ain' been thinkin' 'bout no roun' ball, ya dig?" But Bill, he knew, wouldn't dig it at all. He would look at him with those knowing eyes, his mustache twitching fitfully, the handsome, dark face steeling itself, working on a slow burn. *Forget that!* He couldn't con Bill. Garner smiled slightly then, remembering the time Bill threw him up against the fence in a fit of anger because he had been thrown out of a basketball game for swearing—*He towered over the man, scowling, and Bill glared up at him and said evenly, "Boy, don't you be crazy, now."*—Garner stretched his smile to a wide grin and chuckled aloud. Bill, he thought, would have killed him. Just like a poor, dumb dog. *Did Bill have any brothers?* he wondered. He lit a smoke then and began to relax as a feeling of warmth calmed him.

But when he climbed out of bed the next morning, he began worrying about his mother again and listened carefully, trying to find out if she was up. Then he heard muffled voices coming from the other bedroom. *Good,* he figured, she was still in bed. He looked toward the window, rubbing his arms. Outside, the day looked dull and cold. He dressed quickly, putting on some flannel slacks, a heavy, dark sweater and the navy-blue, crew-neck athletic jacket with the big football in white chenille on the front and TECHNICAL lettered across the back. He loved that jacket. HAWK was printed on its right sleeve, and his number, 30, was on the left.

He checked his watch. It was almost nine o'clock. He picked up his athletic bag, cocking an ear to find out if his mother had heard him. He wanted to avoid her, if possible, afraid that by now she had recovered her composure and was prepared to chew him out properly. Tiptoeing into the kitchen, it occurred to him suddenly to check his bag. Everything was there: sneakers, shorts, T-shirt, and jock. He made sure that he had two pairs of white athletic socks, too; he didn't want to start the season with blisters. The thought of eating fluttered briefly in his mind but was quickly rejected. He could eat on the way. There was plenty of time. The varsity wouldn't start practice until ten o'clock.

The air was cold and light as he walked briskly toward the high school. A number of people were about; women were already shopping for their groceries. Cars and trucks moved rapidly along the streets in a steady stream. At times, when buses passed, he found himself looking at the advertisements boldly lettered along the sides: bread—BUILDS STRONG BODIES 12 WAYS—with a picture of a handsome, young black family—COMING IN THE CITY RECORD: A DISCUSSION OF BLACK POWER—with a picture of four men, who all looked like great thinkers, one white and three black—SEE NBA BASKETBALL. Suddenly, Garner imagined that he was playing ball—*He was on the shiny floor of the City Gardens before a packed house of screaming fans; he was wearing white sneakers and moving with great speed, flashing in and out of swarms of opposing players with amazing dexterity, dribbling behind his back and between his legs and then scoring.* His face broke into a grin as he stopped at the curb and waited for the traffic to let up.

Across the street at a newsstand he saw two pretty girls wearing the dark-blue caps and coats of visiting nurses. One of them was white. He watched them for a moment as the traffic slowed, then he jogged to the other side of the street, up onto the sidewalk, and resumed his brisk walking pace. He passed by an old black wino drooling from the mouth, who was sitting on bundles of cardboard and newspaper near some barrels piled high with trash. Garner looked at him distastefully and strode quickly by. He stopped at Ma Jackson's restaurant and went inside.

Ellis saw him right away and grinned, hiding his face in his hands as Garner made his way over to the booth where he was seated with a small, coffee-colored young man.

Garner laughed, watching Ellis squirm. "You bes' hide. Sheet, afta tha way we whipped you faggots, man, ya know ah gotta put tha mouth on ya."

"You cats were lucky as hell," Ellis grumbled, making room for him in the booth.

"She-yee-yit, man! How ya figga, fa' crissake? You cats scored first."

"Say, Hawk, this here is Tobey Saunders."

Garner nodded to the young man across the table and continued with Ellis. "Ah thought'choo cats wuz gonna play some ball, man. What—"

"C'mon, Hawk, if we'd made those extra points we would've had ya."

The waitress came over to their booth.

"Sheet. Man, you know you cats didn't really 'spect ta win wit' tha Hawk runnin' against ya."

Ellis attempted a feeble smile. "What're ya goin' to eat, Hawk?"

Garner looked at the waitress. She was fat and very black. He smiled. "What's happ'nin', gal?"

She giggled and asked him what he wanted to eat.

Garner winked at Ellis. "What ah *really* want is you, baby, but'choo won't give me *nothin'*. When me'n you gonna party, gal?"

The girl giggled again and turned her head in an imitation of girlish embarrassment, bright teeth glinting as she touched a hand to her short, frizzy hair. "C'mon, boy," she tittered. "What'ch'all gonna eat, now?"

"You, baby, thass all," Garner laughed, slapping his thigh. "Ah need me some lovin'."

"You's awful, boy," she said with mock reproach.

Garner took her hand and patted it soothingly. "Baby doll, gimme double ham'n aigs wit' evah'thin'. Pile on tha grits an' corn muffins an' *all* that shit. Ya heah?"

She snickered, snatching her hand away and walked off in a slew-footed waddle, grinning broadly.

Ellis shook his head. "Man, I'm sorry, but that broad is *ugly!* Jee-yee-sus!"

They tried to choke down some of their laughter.

"Bitch takes ugly pills," Garner rasped. "Fat, black, an' ugly—*oogly,* man!"

This brought a fresh burst of laughter from them. Garner shook his head and lit a cigarette. After a while they calmed down.

"Say, now, Ellis," Garner said, "no shit, now, man—ah wan'cha ta tell tha troof, now—ain' Tech got a bitch uv a fullback? C'mon. Ain' they, now?"

"He stinks, man," Ellis said with a wink at Tobey.

"Sheet, nigga, you's crazy! Paper says—paper calls him *Tha Hawk,* ya know—says this cat is *hell,* man."

"Horseshit," Ellis chuckled.

"Aw, *man*—aw, you lyin' now, Ellis. You—you *wrong* now, man. Paper says this cat's bes' runnin' back in tha city. Sheet."

"I dunno, Hawk. Romano's the best we played."

Garner pretended pain. "Gawddamn, Ellis! Ah thought we wuz boys, man."

"Christ, he's been All-City twice!"

"Sheet, ah wuz too, nigga!"

"C'mon, Hawk. Catholic didn't have anythin' else and still won City. They beat Tech, fa' crissakes!"

"Sheet! Luckies' team in tha worl'," Garner complained as the waitress set his food in front of him. "Thank ya, sweet thing."

"Christ, the only other ball player they had was Bobby."

Tobey spoke up, "I think Ellis is right. Romano has to be good, baby. I know my school wants him bad. There was—"

"Wheah you go ta school?"

"Tobey goes to City College."

Garner frowned.

"Well, it's really a university, now," Tobey informed them.

"Tobey's finishin' his degree this year, Hawk. Goin' to be a teacher."

"Huh?"

"I may go right on to graduate school," Tobey added.

"Ya go ta school 'roun' heah befo'?" Garner asked, swabbing a corn muffin with butter.

"Certainly did, baby. As a matter of fact, I went to school with your brother."

"Oh yeah?"

"Sure thing. Luther Hawkins, a *hard* stud, I'm telling you. Toughest kid I ever met. I can—say, what's he doing now?"

Garner shrugged. "Ah dunno—ah mean, nothin' much. Ya know?"

"You know, I haven't seen him for years. For a minute there, I thought you were him when you walked in here."

Garner frowned and looked at Ellis.

"Here's my milk," Ellis interrupted the discussion. "Hand it here, will ya, Hawk?"

Garner shot a hard look at Tobey and leaned back to let the waitress pass the milk to Ellis. "Well—Lutha been outta town, see—ah mean, uh—we don' heah nothin'—much frum'im. Ya know?"

Tobey glanced at Ellis and caught a look which warned him away from the subject. "Uh, look, Ellis, I have to split, see? Stay cool and everything, you know?" He stood up. "Listen," he addressed Garner, offering him his hand, "nice meeting you. Next time you see—hear from your brother, tell him Tobey was asking for him, will you?"

Garner shook hands. "Yeah. Yeah, man, ah do that, heah?"

"So long," Tobey said and left.

"Whoozat nigga?" Garner grunted when Tobey had gone.

"Just told ya. Tobey Saunders."

"Fuckin' asshole."

"Tobey's a smart cat, man. Got a straight academic scholarship at school."

"Huh?—Sheet, man, what tha fuck—"

"I said, he's got—he gets free tuition and books—I mean, he goes to school—college—for nothin'. I mean—see, if ya get the marks—real good marks—in high school, you can go to college for free. Ya know?"

"Yeah? Sheet—well, he look like a nigga wanna go ta fuckin' school a' somethin'."

"Shit, Hawk, what're ya gettin' all excited about?"

"Nigga thinks he smart a' somethin', man. Sheet."

"For Christ's sake, he didn't say a damn thing. What're you talkin' about?"

"Nigga talk funny, man. Tryin' ta soun' like a fuckin' movie star a' somethin'," Garner chomped through his food.

"Oh, for Christ's sake, Hawk. Jesus—I mean, he has a right to speak English correctly. After all—"

Garner pointed his fork at him. *"Theah*—see? Now *you* doin' it! Jes' like that, thass how tha nigga soun'."

"I don't talk funny, man."

"Do sometime. But not like that nigga—ah mean, y'ain' bull-shittin' like he do. Ah bet'cha he talk that way alla time."

"What way, for Christ's sake?"

"Like a faggot—funny, man."

"Horseshit. He doesn't talk like a faggot—and neither do I."

"He soun' funny, now, Ellis. Seem like he *tryin'* ta talk that way."

"So what? I do too—Well, I mean, I—"

"Naw."

"Sure I do—sometimes."

"Naw, man. Sometime, you soun' regular, like evah'buddy else."

"Well, I try to—I mean, that's the way people are supposed to talk. Shit, ya have to speak properly if you want people to understand ya."

"Huh?"

"Well, I mean—nothin', man. Look, are you goin' to basketball practice? I got practice at ten. Gotta—have to cut out soon."

"Yeah, man. Me too. Goin' now."

"How's the team look? Pappas back?"

"Yeah. Ah ain' been out theah yet."

"What?"

"Ah ain' been ta practice yet, man."

"How come?"

"Sheet, baby, ah been partyin' ma ass off—all kinda bitches. Been gittin' all kinda pussy. Fuckin' an'—"

"Oh. But you're goin' out, aren't ya?"

"Yeah."

"Christ! With you and Pappas, Tech's gonna have a helluva team."

"Bet'cha ass, baby. Gonna take City."

"Don't be too sure, baby. We've got a wagon up Classical."

"Sheet."

"Catholic's goin' to be good, too. Bobby'll probably start up there this year."

"Huh?"

"Bobby, man. Remember, they had Driscoll last year?"

"Sheet, he gone! They lost fo' starters. They ain' got nothin'."

"They got Bobby."

"Ain' nobuddy studyin' 'bout him."

"That's what you said about football."

"Aw, sheet—fuck, Bobby, man. He put us niggas down."

"Horseshit. He's just goin' to another school—new friends, that's all."

"White cats alla same."

"Man, you're fulla shit. He ain't around, that's all."

"Fuck'im."

Ellis shrugged and decided to change the subject. "So how've you been doin', Hawk? Still hustlin' with Terry?"

"Yeah," Garner answered, lighting a cigarette.

"How's he doin'?"

"Crazy. Hustlin' his ass off. Makin' *plenny* bread."

"Sure got a pretty car. I saw him the other day—car *fulla* broads!"

"Man, Terry *stay* wit' pussy."

"They all work for him?"

"Shit yeah—well, Billy Ray—ah mean, yeah."

"You gettin' any?"

"Shit yeah, baby. You know *me.*"

"Gotta pay?"

"Hell, naw, man! You crazy?"

"White broads?"

"Shit yeah."

"Whores, huh? Shit, I couldn't mess with no broad who sells it, man. Leroy says—"

"Sheet. Mosta tha bitches workin' fa Terry is niggas, man. Wheah ya see Leroy at?"

"Over the Y. You know he and Janice are gettin' married?"

Garner smiled and took a long pull on the cigarette. "Leroy sho' hate white folks."

"Yeah."

"Gonna git married, huh?"

"Yeah."

"Janice fine, man, but shit—ah mean, ain' *no* bitch *that* fine."

"She's out of sight, baby. Hey, lemme up, Hawk. I gotta split."

Garner slid out of the booth. "Leroy crazy. When he gonna do it?"

"I dunno."

"Gonna be Muslim?"

"Dunno."

They paid for their food and walked out together.

"See ya later, Hawk."

"Cool it, man."

Garner watched Ellis hustle off down the street. It was warm now. He looked at his watch: ten o'clock. He crossed the street and started running.

Practice had already started when Garner walked into the gym. He stopped near the locker room door to watch the squad work. He counted twelve boys. Five of them were white. The team looked sharp, and there was a lot of chatter. Garner grinned. It sounded good. A tall, thin, white boy loped easily to the top of the key and took a pass from a small black boy who came from the other line left of the blackboard. Without dribbling, the white boy stepped down hard and sprang in the air and arched a soft, floating shot into the basket. Garner looked around for the coaches, feeling good, anxious to get working, and spotted them standing together talking at center court. He recognized Coach Connors, but he didn't know the other one. Connors was a towering, big-shouldered man with thick red hair. He was the head coach.

Garner started toward center court. Connors saw him coming and scowled. Garner hesitated then as the man turned away and threw a thumb toward him over his shoulder. The other coach, a thin man with dark hair, turned briefly to look at Garner, who saw him avert his eyes and say something to Connors.

A basketball came bounding toward Garner, and with one large hand, he plucked it out of the air and threw it to a yellow-skinned boy, who let it settle gently into his long, slender fingers and snapped off a hard chest pass toward the top of the key. The small black boy picked off the pass and bounded upward, his body momentarily suspending itself high in the air as he flicked a long jump shot off the top of his head. The ball swept cleanly through the net. Garner smiled and looked at the coaches. They had their backs to him now, their heads bent close together, and they were talking heatedly. He shrugged and went down into the locker rooms.

Matt Connors spun on his heel and strode stiffly toward his office. The other coach threw his hands up in futile gesture and walked slowly after him. Matt slammed into the small room and stomped over to his desk, stopping there briefly to fold his hands behind his neck, bending forward slightly at the waist as if in pain and sighing heavily.

"Gerry," he croaked, turning to face his assistant, "I'm tellin' ya—"

"Take it easy, Matt," the other man said, closing the door.

"Take it easy, my arse," Matt nearly shouted and then lowered his voice to an even roar. "Listen! Nobody—goddammit, I mean, *nobody* —comes out for *my* team the day after I cut the squad."

"Matt, the kid probably has a damn good reason. He—"

"What reason?" the big man shot at him, his face flushing red.

"Christ, who knows? He's a kid. How the hell do I know?"

"Look, the black bastard hasn't been in school since before Thanksgiving, for Christ's sake, and you wanna stand here and—" Matt picked up a cigarette pack from the desk. "Dammit-all, it's not fair to the other kids." He fumbled angrily with the cellophane wrapper. *"They* were *here!* They were out here every goddamn day. *They made the team!* And *now* what? We look up on a nice Saturday morning—*in December,* for Christ's sake—and Mr. Hawkins appears! Maybe we should be grateful, huh?" He offered Gerry a smoke. "Yeah. Maybe we should thank him for showing up at *all,"* he said and lit Gerry's cigarette.

"Matt, if this boy is as good as you say he is—"

"He's *not* good enough to play for me unless he's *out* here! I'll be goddamned if I'm gonna cut a boy who's been out here working his butt off for some—. Listen, I'll tell you somethin' else, too; we may not have this kid after marks come out, anyway."

"What?"

"Yeah. He's barely gettin' by the *shop* course!"

"Listen, at least give the kid—"

"And besides," Matt's voice rode over Gerry's, and he waved his hand at the gym outside, "I'm runnin' this show, and no hotshot nigger's gonna make me change my rules."

"—a chance to explain."

"Look, Gerry, I know all about the kid. I called Chamberlain. The boy's had problems, he says. Yeah? Well, so do I. Yeah, and *he* gets paid to hold hands with these kids. I don't, and I'm tellin' ya, the only excuse I'll listen to is *death!* Yeah. A death in the family, preferably a father."

"Matt, he's the best athlete in the school. You said so, yourself. So—well, *Jesus,* you can't just—cut this boy. I mean—"

Matt yelled then, "I *can't,* huh? I can't, huh? By Jesus, lemme tell you somethin' right now; that nigger's *not even on the team,* so I don't *hafta* cut him! See?"

"I'm not saying that you *can't* cut him. It's just—Jesus, you can't *want* to, that's all."

"Balls! I been nine years a coach. Five conference champions—we been state champs twice, four times in the finals—you just watch me, mister. Just watch." He heeled his smoke out on the floor and yanked the door open.

Gerry followed him into the gym, shaking his head angrily. Matt stopped just outside the office. Looking to his right, he saw Garner run under the backboard and jump for a rebound, spin off balance in the air, and squeeze off a crisp, sure pass behind his back to another player.

"Oh, boy," Matt grated over his shoulder to Gerry. "He's *fancy,* too!"

"Jesus, Matt—"

"Hey, you," Matt yelled, pointing at Garner.

Garner stepped out of the line and pushed his finger against his chest. "Who? Me?"

"Yeah! You! Come over here. Yeah, that's right. *You!* Come over here."

"Take it easy, Matt," Gerry begged.

Garner shrugged and threw a cocky grin at the other boys. "Sho', Coach."

"Who the hell do you think you are?" Matt growled, driving a steely gaze down at him.

Garner peered up at the man, a puzzled expression crossing his black face. "Hawkins, Coach. Uh—ah'm Garna—Hawkins."

Matt bellowed, *"What do you think you're doin' out there, Hawkins?"*

Garner's throat went dry. "Sheet. Comin' out fa' baskitball, thass all."

A look of amazement burst over Matt's freckled features. He leaned down toward the boy. *"What* did you just say?"

Garner tried to swallow. "Wanna play ball," he rephrased cautiously.

"No," his coach cried. "I mean that *other* expression!"

"Jes' wanna play ball, thass all, man."

Matt grimaced, his lips tight and thin. He spoke through clenched teeth. "Well, now, Hawkins, that's goddamn nice of you! You know that? Just when you decide all this?"

"Huh?"

"Oh, hell, take your time, kid. See, I'm only the head coach here. So don't pay *me* any mind. I mean—what the hell? Who gives a damn so long as a guy decides to come around sooner or later? Right?"

Garner took a step backward. "Huh?"

"Hey, I don't believe *this!* Is this a put-on or what?"

Garner took another step backward.

Matt's voice exploded then, *"Goddammit, boy, where the hell have you been?"*

The other players froze in their tracks.

The coach yelled again, *"Where the hell have you been, Hawkins?"*

"Well, see, Coach—uh, ah been—busy—ah mean—theah wuz football, an'—"

Matt threw his arms toward the ceiling and lowered his voice to a frantic whisper. "Why haven't you been to basketball practice, goddammit-all?"

Garner locked his eyes on the floor. "Been busy—kinda pooped—ya know? Ah mean—ah—ah ain' been ta school—ah—"

"Why?"

"Huh? What'cha mean? Been busy, thass all—What'sa matta? Bid'ness ta take care uv. Thass all—ah mean—"

"You're nuts," Matt said with cold fury. "Crazy! You get your arse the *hell* out of here! *Go on!* Get out of here before I lose my temper!"

"Huh?"

Gerry shook his head unhappily and stepped forward and took Garner's arm. He glanced at Matt's angry face, about to say something to him but spoke to Garner instead. "C'mon, kid," he urged, pulling him away.

Garner was baffled.

Matt looked at Gerry and said evenly, "Get him out of here."

Garner shook off Gerry's hand and backed away. "Don' be shovin' me, man! Don' be pullin' on *me!* You don' be messin' wit' me like *that,* man!"

Connors marched away toward his office.

"Go ahead," Gerry said. "Beat it. Take off, kid."

Garner turned toward the locker rooms. "Sheet, ah don' hafta take this heah shit, man. You white folks ain' sayin' nothin' ta tha Hawk, gawddammit."

"Go on, will you. Take off."

Garner attempted a smile at the other boys. "Ain' no flies on tha Hawk, man. Ah don' need *you!* Ain' this a bitch? Ah don' need you cats, white folks." He opened the locker room door and skipped down the stairs.

He sat down on a bench in front of a row of lockers and angrily began ripping off his clothes. A stifling, gigantic wrath mushroomed within him. He yanked his clothes out of the locker and dressed quickly. A tiny, brief thought of racing back upstairs to have it out with Coach Connors sped through his mind, but he remembered the size of the man and simply threw his stuff into his bag, zipped it closed, and headed for the stairs.

At the foot of the stairs, he hesitated, listening to the sounds of the team running through a drill. He could hear balls bouncing, chatter, running footsteps, and squealing rubber as the players stopped and cut. In his mind, he could see them flying up and down the gleaming hardwood floor, weaving in and out, changing direction, dribbling, shooting, and defending. He shut his eyes, his anger choking him, nausea welling up at the realization that he would not be a part of this team.

Suddenly, he imagined himself fighting with Coach Connors—*Connors was big and extremely powerful, but Garner was too quick for him. He whirled around the man, flicking punches at him, rending the flesh about his eyes and mouth while the other coach cowered in a far corner of the gym, too terrified to move. The whole team was watching. All his friends were watching. The coach's friends were watching. Everyone was watching, and all of them were too frightened to intervene. When Connors fell, Garner stomped him frantically. The coach's blood covered the gym floor. His face was swollen, discolored. He was swimming in his own blood. His tears, his terror and agony, were clear to everybody. Then he begged for mercy, but Garner only stomped him harder. Then, all at once, he was kneeling in front of Garner. The other coach knelt there, too. They begged Garner to return to the team. The whole school was begging him to return to the team. Garner refused and coolly lit a cigarette. After that he heard about the team losing games and then there was talk of firing the coach.*—Garner swore savagely and rubbed a hand across his mouth as he looked up toward the gym. Cursing again, he climbed the stairs to the gym door and peeked through the small window. The coaches were in the office. Garner looked quickly at his former teammates, took a deep breath, and opened the door.

As he walked across the court, his eyes tracked straight ahead, and he tried to assume an air of unconcern, swinging his bag easily as he walked toward the exit. The other boys stood watching him. The expressions on their faces were grim. Then one of them picked up a ball and yelled, "Let's work."

Outside, the rage within him was almost unbearable. He blinked his eyes ferociously, squeezing back the tears, his glowering ebony face set in a snarl. "Fuck you som'bitches," he rasped, looking back across the street at the school. "Mutha-fuck all you rotten, bastid, mutha-fuckin', cocksuckin', dirty bastids!"

He started walking aimlessly, but after a while he realized that he was headed for Terry's place. He stopped then and looked back, tears blurring his vision, and he couldn't see the school. Then he was walking again, picking up his pace.

Terry's car wasn't there. Garner ran up the stairs, hoping that one of the girls was in the apartment. No one answered when he knocked. He frowned. Momentarily, he thought of going home but turned and stared gloomily at the door. He didn't want to go to the Y, either. He sighed and put his bag down.

Later, that evening, he knew he could find Terry policing the girls on the street. After midnight, he'd be dealing poker at Billy Ray's. Garner scowled and moved over to the top of the stairs and sat down. He could wait. Terry was probably making numbers collections. He could have been anywhere. Garner rested his head against the wall and shut his eyes. Connors's face loomed up. "Rotten mutha-fucka," Garner muttered to himself. "Git tha hell outta heah, he say. Sheet! What make him so fuckin' bad? White mutha-fucka!"

He imagined himself standing over the man's corpse, that he was spitting and defecating on him. It occurred to him that Connors might have a wife. *Maybe she could die, too,* and he could spit and defecate on her—and his kids, too, and his mother and father. He would stomp them first. Then, when they were all dead, he would burn them. *No!* That was too easy on them. Abruptly, he laughed aloud. "Sheet, nigga," he berated himself. "How ya gonna burn dead people? They ain' gonna feel nothin'. How ya gonna do it?" He smiled and stuck a cigarette in his mouth. Slowly, his anger began to subside. Outside, a car door slammed. He listened carefully, wondering if it was Terry. The door downstairs opened and banged shut and then he heard a woman's high heels clicking on the stairs.

It was Carol. She smiled at him, her dark face sparkling with surprise as she stopped in front of him on the stairs. "Well, hi, baby."

"What's happ'nin', gal? Wheah Terry?"

"He's working. What're you sitting out here for?" She bent forward and rested her hands on his knees. Her dress was very short, her pretty black face laughing, "C'mon inside," she hummed.

"Wuzn't nobuddy theah," he complained, waving a hand toward the apartment.

"Hell, baby, the door's open. How long you been sitting here?"

"Little while."

"Didn't you try the door, baby? It's open. C'mon."

He stood up. The street door opened and closed again, and he heard tires screeching outside as he followed her into the apartment. He flopped down on the sofa.

Jackie came in. "Hey, baby. What're *you* doing here? Want a drink?" she asked, holding up two bottles. "Got some Teacher's here."

"Yeah," he said indifferently.

Carol went into the kitchen for some glasses. Jackie smiled down at Garner, her baby face dimpling. He noticed the light catching in the gold of her skin and lowered his gaze over the full turn of her legs filling the black stretch pants. She sat down across from him and lit a cigarette. Carol came back and Jackie broke a bottle open.

The Scotch warmed him, and he settled back into the sofa. Carol leaned against him, sipping her drink, her breasts cushioning his arm. She smelled good.

Jackie looked at them over the rim of her glass and laughed. "You two going to play?"

Carol smiled and lit a smoke. "You can watch if you want to."

"You gals know when Terry comin' back?"

"He'll be back tonight to pick us up," Carol said.

"Ya workin' ta-nite?"

Jackie smiled into her drink. "Have to work, baby."

Garner nodded.

Carol kissed him lightly on the cheek and bit his ear. "We have to get some sleep, too."

"Yeah." Jackie stood up, flashing a playful smile at Garner. "Want to tuck us in, baby?"

He grinned. "Shit yeah."

Terry found them sleeping naked, a tangle of arms and legs. He pulled the covers off them. "Hey, git up niggas! Ain' this a bitch? C'mon, gawddammit!"

Garner rubbed his eyes and reached for the blankets. Carol sat up, her globular breasts jutting out high and firm under broad shoulders. Terry's eyes wandered over their nude bodies.

Carol drew her legs up and hugged her knees. "What time is it?"

"Time ta work," Terry said, trying to shake Jackie awake.

Jackie frowned and snuggled up closer to Garner.

"Ain' this a bitch?" Terry said. "Looka these niggas. C'mon, niggas, git tha fuck up. What'choo doin' heah, Hawk?"

"What's happ'nin', Terry?"

Terry put his hands on his hips and started to laugh, watching Jackie roll over and yawn. "What's happ'nin', tha nigga say. Ain' thatta bitch, now? *What's happ'nin'*—. You gals may's well roll on outta theah. We gotta work. Wheah Shirley?"

"Bill Ray's," Carol answered him.

"Sheet, that nigga cain' leave a white gal 'lone."

"Christ," Carol muttered sleepily swinging her legs out of the bed, "nigger men're all the same."

Garner sat up and took a cigarette from the night table.

"C'mon, git up! Git tha fuck up." Terry swept the covers from the bed.

While the girls were getting ready for work, Garner told Terry what happened at school.

Terry closed the refrigerator. "Man, thass the bes' thing coulda happined. Ah nevah could see alla that runnin' up'n down an' bustin' ya ass, anyways." He opened the other fifth of whisky. "Want some?"

"Naw, man. Fuckin' head hurt."

Terry dropped some ice in his glass. "That shit's fa' kids, Hawk. Sheet, ah learned long time ago, ain' nothin' worth shit if it don' make ya no bread—'cept maybe some pussy. Hey, you stayin' heah ta-nite, man?"

"Guess so."

"Theah s'posed ta be a whole lotta shit happ'nin' ta-nite."

"Wheah?"

"Sheet, all ovah. Coupla parties right heah on tha hill, dance down tha social club. Lotta shit happ'nin'."

"Man, ah don' be fuckin' 'roun' wit' them kids'n shit."

Terry picked up his drink and started unbuttoning his shirt. "Gotta git dressed," he muttered and walked into his bedroom.

Jackie was sitting on the bed in her bra and panties, pulling on her stockings. Carol was almost dressed. Terry set his drink on the night table, went to the closet, flipped his shirt off and unbuckled his belt.

Garner dug some cheese and sausage out of the refrigerator and walked over to the bedroom door. "Terry, you gonna be workin' all night, man?"

"Shit yeah. Big night, baby," Terry replied, taking a gray suit from the closet and strolling over to the bed to sit down beside Jackie. "Move ovah, gal."

"Kiss my ass."

Terry bent down to comply. She laughed and hopped up.

"What'choo gonna do ta-nite, Hawk?" Terry inquired, grinning at Jackie.

Garner shrugged, "Ah dunno, man."

"Why doesn't he come with us?" Carol suggested.

"Sheet," Terry snorted stepping into his pants, "ah'm gonna be busy—an' so you, gawddammit."

"I don't mean with me and Jackie for Christ's sake. He could make the rounds with you."

"Wanna come, Hawk?" Terry offered.

"Shit yeah."

It was a cold night. Terry dropped Carol and Jackie in front of a restaurant on the busy corner of Massachusetts and Columbus Avenues. The girls scrambled out of the car and hugged their fur coats tightly to them.

"Cold out here," Carol said, shivering.

"Sheet," Terry said. "Stop bullshittin'. See ya in a while."

Jackie waved her handbag at him. "Not if we see you first, honey-chile."

Terry laughed. The big Buick dug out.

"Rememba'," Terry told Garner, after they had cruised a few blocks. "Y'ain' gittin' paid, now. This yo' idea. You jes' ridin'."

"Sheet, nigga, ah ain' worryin' 'bout'choo givin' no bread away, man."

Terry stopped the car for a red light. "Ya fuckin' right, baby. Ah works fa' ma fuckin' money. Anyways, you got no bitch comin'; *y'always* gits paid when ya works fa' Terry, gawddammit. Ah'm a bid'nessman; ya works, ya git paid, ya rides, an' ya git shit."

Garner leaned back against the seat with a laconic smirk as the car started forward.

"Ya goin' ta school Monday?"

"Ah dunno. Why?"

"Thought'cha might wanna pick up some change."

"What doin'?"

"What'cha mean, what doin'? Ya wanna coin some change, or what?"

"Shit yeah."

"Awright, then. Crazy."

Garner sighed and looked out of his window.

Terry stuck a cigarette in his mouth and grinned at his brother as he shoved in the lighter. "Gotta git a package, thass all."

"What ah'm gonna git?"

"Sheet, nigga, ah dunno—twenny, maybe."

"What Billy Ray payin' *you* fa' tha deal?"

"Now, see that shit! Give a nigga a chance ta make some fuckin' bread, an' he gonna start a whole lotta shit. No wonder Whitey don' wanna hire you niggas, fa' crissake." He lit his smoke. "Man, don' be askin' me 'bout ma bid'ness. If ya don' wanna work, jes' say no, thass all."

"Nigga, fuck alla bullshit; ah work. Sheet, ah don' wanna heah all that shit, man."

Terry pulled the car over to the curb and leaned over to look out of the window. A small white woman stepped out of the shadows near the dark building and strolled over to the car.

"Hi, honey," she greeted Terry.

Garner peeked at her behind the glow of her cigarette. She was round-faced and looked about forty years old.

"What's happ'nin', baby?" Terry answered.

"Trying to keep warm. Things're slow right now. Got a job for me?"

"Naw, baby. Jes' cruisin'."

She laughed. "Look, honey, give me a couple of hours; things'll be picking up. It's early."

"Okay, doll. Dig ya later."

The Buick rocked forward.

"Listen, Hawk. Ah gotta run a errand. Ah drop ya back at Billy Ray's, okay?"

"Huh?"

"See ya in a while."

"Wheah ya goin'?"

"*See?* Theah ya go agin! Fuckin' wit' Terry's bid'ness, man!"

"Sheet."

"Look," Terry sighed, trying to soften his voice, "ah gotta take care a' somethin'. See? Anybuddy ask ya, ya tell'im ah'm cruisin', thass all. Ya dig?"

"Yeah."

Billy Ray's club was an old tenement building of dull, red brick. As Garner stood on the sidewalk, looking up at the place, it appeared dark and lifeless. It could have been the house he lived in.

Two black men stood talking near the front door. A woman was standing under the light on the corner. She was black, well groomed, and attractive. A taxi pulled up and she got into it.

Garner walked down a dark hallway, feeling his way and knocked on the door at the end. A thin black man opened it a crack and squinted out at him.

"What'cha want?"

"What's happ'nin', Sam?"

"Oh. What say, boy? Come on in heah."

Garner stepped into the small, dimly lit vestibule. Sam shut the hall door and opened another one behind them. There were a few people, mostly men, lolling about the door and in the corridor into which it opened. Garner could hear muffled voices coming from nearby. He walked down the corridor to his right and turned into a parlor-size room. There were three poker tables there. Two of them were working. He looked at his watch. It was ten-thirty.

An enormous black man with a thick scar across his face walked up to him.

"Evenin', boy."

"W'say, Willi."

"Gonna play? Ah git'cha seat."

"Maybe later. Anybuddy upstairs?"

Willi shrugged and scratched his stomach. "Coupla people. Goin' up theah?"

"Yeah."

"Crazy. Tell Marie ta fix some coffee. Ah be up in a minute."

The bar was almost empty. Garner pulled up a stool and sat down.

John, a short, yellow-skinned man sporting a huge, shining process, was squatting behind the bar.

"Willi want some coffee, man."

John shoved a tray of glasses in place and stood up. "Say, boy. How ya doin'? Where's your brother?"

"Cruisin'," Garner lied easily, spinning around on his stool and picking out two white men seated at a table in the back of the room.

"Hey," John hollered. "Hey, Marie?"

He waited for an answer, leaning on the bar and looking at a door behind him. Garner stared at the swirls of processed hair on top of his head. It reminded him of Terry. *Terry?* he pondered. What was he doing now, anyway? He shrugged.

The door behind the bar opened and a fat, yellow, old woman poked her grizzled head out. "What'cha want, nigga?" she asked in a gruff voice. Her gaze fell on Garner then and she shuffled through the doorway. "Hey theah, big fella. Terry heah? He s'posed ta be cruisin'. What he doin'?"

"Willi wants some coffee," John told her. "Sam'll probably want some, too."

She waddled over to the bar. "Fuck Willi."

"Terry's on tha street," Garner answered her.

"Oh."

Marie was an ugly, wrinkled, disheveled, old woman of about sixty. Her left arm was withered and shorter than the other.

"Want somethin' ta eat, boy? Ah got some po'k chops 'n black-eye peas out theah."

"Shit, he didn't ask for no food, woman," John said. "Why you always wanna feed the nigger for?"

"Cuz he always hongry," she cackled. "Ain'cha, boy?"

Garner grinned.

"See, nigga. Young boy that size gotta be hongry. Gotta git his vittles." She patted Garner's arm. "Ah git'cha somethin', boy."

"Shit. Goddammit, woman, why don't you just fix the fuckin' coffee like you was told to do?" John said.

Marie's good arm wagged disdainfully in the air. "Listen, nigga," she said with mock anger, "fuck *you,* an' *Willi,* an' *Sam,* an' Billy *Ray,* an' yo' *mothas,* an' yo' *brothas,* an' yo' *sistas,* an' yo'—"

"Okay! Okay, okay!" John doubled over the bar laughing. "For crissakes! Jesus! *Okay,* gal."

She winked at Garner and toddled off.

"Hey, John, who them white cats?" Garner asked.

John was still laughing. "That old woman will put the mouth on you in a minute."

Garner shook his head and chuckled quietly.

John straightened up and pointed quickly with his eyes at the two white men. "They fuzz," he whispered. "Waitin' for Billy Ray. Probably wanna handout, man."

"Sheet, they ain' gonna git shit frum Billy Ray."

"Hell, no, man. They're just a couple of assholes hopin' to catch a fool, that's all."

"Sheet, baby, Billy Ray ain' no fool."

"You better believe it. The big stud's name's Cronin. He's a sergeant with the vice squad. Him and baldy, there, go around the whole South End, tryin' to play like they're bad. You know, tryin' to shake down everybody. Don't get nowhere, though, because the bitches all know they ain't shit, anyway."

"What they fuckin' wit' Billy Ray fa'?"

"They ain', man. Shit, he ain't even in yet."

Marie came back with a plate of food.

"They're gonna sit there, now, and make out like they're checkin' on how much business we're doin'. Ya know? Then try to worry somebody about jackin' up the price downtown, see?"

Garner smiled and went to work on the black-eye peas and pork chops.

"What'ch'all talkin' 'bout?" Marie asked.

"Man, as much sugar as Billy Ray's spreadin' around," John was saying, "there ain't no way in hell them cats gonna get any bread."

Garner jerked his head toward the two white men. "Talkin' 'bout them fuzz," he informed Marie.

"She-yee-yit. What fa'?" She trudged back to her kitchen.

After eating, Garner went downstairs and sat down to play poker. There were five men at the table. One of them was an old white man. There was a woman there, too. She was short, almost as black as Garner, and very thin. The dealer was a medium-sized, chestnut-colored man, with close-cropped, dark-brown hair, named Marcus.

While Garner carefully scrutinized the inside of his wallet, Marcus told him that the table stakes were ten dollars.

"Gawddamn," Garner said closing the billfold and staring at the man. "Ah thought it wuz five, man."

Marcus leaned across the table and pointed a finger at him. "Five-dollar table ain't workin' yet, boy. Are you playin'?"

Garner took out two fives and put them on the table, pulled out his cigarettes and watched Marcus deal. The man had short, stubby fingers and wore a big diamond set in a thick gold band on the ring finger of his right hand. He dealt the cards with astonishing speed and dexterity. The diamond glittered as he spun the cards around the table.

"You got a quarter?" he demanded of Garner.

"Naw. Theah's a quarter out tha piece," the boy replied, pointing to one of the fives with his cigarette.

"First ace bets," Marcus noted impatiently, flicking a finger at the white man.

He was a wizened, ashy-white old man, thin, with lank, white hair. His hands shook as he fiddled idly with his money. "Four bits," was his bet.

The woman called. Garner checked his cards. He had a king face up with a deuce in the hole. He called.

"Everybody's in," Marcus announced in a hurry-up tone after the last player threw in his money. "How about hole cards?"

The woman turned up a four. Garner flipped over his deuce. The cards flew around the table. Garner caught another deuce and fidgeted nervously. He didn't like small pairs.

"Ace ten," Marcus snapped at a squat, yellow-skinned man.

"Dollar."

"Dollar to you, boy," Marcus said to Garner, pointing at him urgently with the deck of cards and lighting a cigarette.

Garner peeked at his hole card again and pushed one of the fives into the center.

The dealer covered the bill immediately with his free hand. "Dollar six out the piece. Dollar to you, pop."

The old white man threw in a dollar.

Marcus gave Garner two one-dollar bills and five quarters. A chubby black man turned his cards down. Marcus raked them in and pointed at the woman. She dropped four quarters in the pot. The rest of the players called. Marcus cut a dollar and twenty-five cents from the pile of money—the house cut from any pot in excess of five dollars—and squeezed it into a slit in a tin box which was buried in the table in front of him.

The cards came around. A seven was added to Garner's cards and his face clouded. The yellow-skinned man picked up another ten and bet five dollars. Garner squirmed. The woman called, and two players dropped out. The white man had ace, king, jack up.

"Raise," he said calmly and jacked the price up to ten dollars.

Garner checked his hole card again.

"Cost you all ya got," Marcus hurried him, puffing his cigarette with agitation.

Terry sauntered into the room and stood beside his brother's chair. "How ya doin', Hawk?" He slipped out of his dark cashmere topcoat and nodded hello to Marcus.

Garner shook his head slowly and gazed despondently at the deuce he had in the hole.

"Bet's ten dollars." Marcus made no effort to conceal his annoyance.

Garner counted his money. Terry peeked at his hole card, his face remaining expressionless.

"Got seven an' a quarter heah," Garner said, inching his money forward.

The white man smiled. Marcus put Garner's money to one side. The woman called, and the yellow-skinned man threw in another five.

Marcus added a dollar bill to Garner's money and made a second pot of it. "Four players. Your money stops here, boy," he told Garner, spreading his hand over the bigger pot in the center of the table. "The lady and the other gentlemen can go all the way."

The cards moved. Splinters needled Garner's insides when he caught a third deuce. A black club demolished the woman's garden of hearts, an ace fell for yellow-skin, and Garner almost wept as the white man paired kings and bet twenty dollars. Yellow-skin and the woman folded.

Marcus shoved the second pot of eight dollars and twenty-five cents over to the white man. "Everybody turn out," he ordered and ground his cigarette out in the ashtray.

Garner turned out his third deuce and prayed. The white man folded his hand, shaking his head, and smiled. Marcus opened up both hands, exposing the white man's two pairs of aces and kings and pushed forty-two seventy-five at Garner, who, relieved and jubilant, raked it in and thanked him with a seventy-five cent tip.

Marcus grinned. "Thanks, baby."

Terry chuckled. "You ain' nothin' but a lucky som'bitch. C'mon, les' split, man."

Garner hesitated. Marcus called for the antes.

"C'mon, Hawk, we be back, man. Ah be dealin' later, anyhow."

Garner shrugged and got up from the table.

"Sheet," Terry said as they climbed into the Buick, "ya win a hand like that, man, an' ya always git tha fuck up. Them som'bitches kin take back that lil' bit a' bread in no time."

"Naw, man. Ah ain' *that* crazy."

"Sheet, ya called open tens wit' a pair a' deuces, nigga. Thass *somethin'* like crazy ta *me!*" Terry nosed the red convertible into the street.

"Sheet."

"Sheet, ma ass. Ya git broke in a hurry, fuckin' 'roun' like that, baby."

Terry made his first stop. Two women emerged from a dark doorway and walked leisurely over to the car. Terry rolled his window down.

"What's happ'nin', gals?"

One of them was tall and fair, wearing a fur coat. The other one was shorter and brown-skinned. They were pretty, in their late twenties.

The tall one answered, "How you, Terry? Who ya got wit'cha?"

"Ma brotha."

"Well, hi, there, Terry's brotha," she said, peering into the car at Garner lighting his cigarette. "Ah'm Jo, an' this heah's Rosalie."

"How do? Ah'm Garna."

"How's bid'ness?" Terry asked.

Rosalie feigned annoyance. "Checkin' up, huh? Earnin' ya money."

"Gotta do it, baby."

"Well, ya kin tell Billy Ray, evah'thin' gonna be awright. Ya heah?"

"Ah tell'im, baby. Any fuzz 'roun'?"

"Naw. Cruiser wuz by. Corelli wuz sittin' up in the back seat all done up in brass, tryin' ta look impo'tant. They bullshitted wit' us fa' while an' went on."

"Well, keep cool, chickens." Terry gunned the engine, and the Buick lurched away.

Garner relaxed into a sprawl in the soft leather seat and pulled on his cigarette. "This tha way ta live," he mused silently. "Terry cool nigga. This wheah tha shit *really* at, man. *Fuck* tha rough stuff. Gotta play it cool." He smiled, his thoughts focusing momentarily on Billy Ray. " 'Notha' cool stud, baby. *Stays* pretty, got a Cadillac car, don' nevah git dirty, all kinda fuckin' money, an' tha fuzz cain' tell'im shit. Jesta bad mutha-fucka, thass all."

He looked out at the amorphous mass of buildings hovering in the cold night. Suddenly, he felt like playing poker again. Yes, he thought, maybe he could make some more money, and turned his head to look at his brother.

Terry's face was pensive as the car rustled quietly through the traffic. Garner admired the sheen of his luxurious process in the passing lights and rubbed a hand over his own hair. Maybe he would get a process someday. Well—no, he debated, he wouldn't look good with hair like that. Terry looked good. Terry was handsome, light-skinned, with features like a white boy's.

Garner frowned and cracked the window to toss out his butt. Then he put his head back against the seat and closed his eyes—*He was on a dark street. It was very cold—there was a lot of noise, horns honking, people and music—there were women in the doorways—. Terry said, "See them, man? They who'es."—"Sell pussy."—"Men pays 'em."—"You lyin'," Garner said.—"Man, you sho' dumb."—They were met at the door by a huge black man. He had a thick, ugly scar on his face.—"What'cha want?"—"Uncle Charlie," Terry stammered.—"Charlie who?"—Garner yelled, "Hawkins!"—"Don' know no Charlie Hawkins."—"He's our fatha," Garner offered nervously, "daddy Charlie."—"Ah ain'cha fuckin' daddy! How many times ah gotta tell ya, nigga? Ah ain'cha fuckin', black-ass daddy!"—"Sheet, nigga, ain' no way in hell could ah fuck up an' put out nothin' black as you!"*—Garner opened his eyes.

"Hey, Terry, you evah know Big Willi befo'?"

"Ah dunno. Mighta seen'im somewheahs. Why?"

"Ah seen'im befo'—you too, man."

"So what?"

"Shit, man—ah mean—nothin'. Jes' wond'rin', thass all."

"Huh?"

"You rememba Charlie?"

"Charlie who?"

"You know. *Charlie,* man. You rememba Charlie. Cat use ta be wit' Ma."

Terry's eyes narrowed as he thought it over. He shook his head. "When, man?"

"We wuz little, man. *Charlie!* Rememba. *Charlie,* man."

"Yeah," Terry drawled, "yeah, ah s'pose so. Why?"

"Thass wheah we seen'im."

"Who, man? What tha fuck ya talkin' 'bout, Hawk?"

"Willi, man. Big Willi."

"Sheet, Hawk, ah don' rememba Ma bein' wit' no Willi."

"Naw, man. Willi he'ped us find Charlie one time. We wuz lookin' fa' Charlie, man. One night, rememba? Ma said, go ovah theah an' git Charlie, an' we went ta this heah dark place, an' Charlie wuz theah an'—"

"Yeah, man! Wuz cold's a bitch out. Yeah. He open tha do'. Shit yeah."

"Thass it!"

Terry started laughing. "Man, we didn't even know tha cat's *name,*" he said excitedly, pounding on the steering wheel. "Dumbes' niggas in tha worl', man."

"Yeah. Now ya got it. Thass it."

"Charlie had a white gal wit'im. Ol' Charlie. Sho' wuz glad when Ma got rid a' *him,* man. Wonda if that nigga's still starvin' babies."

"He wuz a rotten som'bitch."

"Aw, he wuzn't no trouble."

"He wuz a rotten black mutha-fucka, man."

"Well, he wuzn't much, thass fa' sho'."

"Black mutha-fucka."

When Terry and Garner drove back to the apartment, it was nearly eight o'clock, a gray, cold Sunday morning. A chilly wind swept through the city, and they could see tiny flakes of snow in the air. The streets were nearly free of traffic. Occasionally, some old newspapers floated along the sidewalks. Terry parked the car. Garner saw a scrawny tiger cat run across the street in front of them, stop on the curb, then slip into an alley. Hungry, he thought, and cold, too.

Upstairs, Garner stopped in the kitchen and started eating what was left of the cheese and sausage.

"Anybuddy heah?" Terry called from the living room as he shut the door and took off his coat.

"Dunno."

Terry went down to his bedroom. He came back to the kitchen, laughing.

"What'sa matta?" Garner asked, his jaws working vigorously.

Terry snatched a piece of sausage. "Shirley back. Laid out on tha bed, snorin' ta beat hell."

Garner walked down to the room to have a look. Shirley was draped carelessly across Terry's bed, her nude body tangled in the sheets. Most of the covers were on the floor. He switched on the light, and she rolled over and groaned sleepily, her mouth slackening open as she slept. Her black hair buoyed against her face, contrasting sharply with her white skin. He started to wake her, but Terry touched his arm.

"Let tha bitch sleep, man," he whispered and started to undress.

Garner grinned at him.

Terry sat down on the bed and pulled off his shoes. He caught his brother's look and waved his hand in protest. "Aw, nigga, fuck you," he sighed wearily. "Ah'm beat—wasted, man."

"Sheet."

"Sheet, ma ass, nigga. Ain' evah'buddy no big-ass, black horse, like you, man."

"Watch that shit, nigga!"

"Huh?"

"Jes' cuz you light—"

Terry slid into bed. "Aw, nigga, fa' crissake—fuck it. Shut off tha light, will ya?"

Garner dawdled sulkily.

Terry smiled contentedly and closed his eyes. When Garner switched off the light, he was already asleep.

Monday morning, Garner awoke to find Carol and Jackie sleeping beside him. Terry opened the door. "C'mon," he said roughly. "You gonna work, or what?"

Garner scowled and climbed over Carol and sat on the edge of the bed. "Ah'm tired," he yawned, reaching for his pants.

Terry pulled on a turtleneck sweater. "C'mon, nigga."

Garner shoved his feet into the pants and stood up, dragging them up with him. "Sheet. Lost *all* ma fuckin' bread last night, man."

"Ah tol' ya not ta play agin. C'mon. Git tha fuck up."

Garner swayed to his feet, muscles tightening in massive bunches under his skin as he stretched. "Ah'm comin', man. Be wit'cha in a minute."

They hurried downstairs and piled into the car. Terry cranked the engine, and the red convertible was off and running.

"Kin we stop somewheahs an' eat?" Garner suggested hopefully.

"Hell, naw. We be late then, man. We gotta move."

"Ah'm hongry's a mutha-fucka."

"Sheet, nigga, we workin' now. Gotta drop tha car at Billy Ray's an' git goin'."

"What'cha mean? What'cha—what fa'?"

"What *fa'?* Look, we gonna ketch tha subway downtown. Then we gonna pick up a car. Jes' set tight, man, an' do like Terry say. Awright?"

They left the Buick in front of the club and set out on foot toward the subway.

"What car we gonna git?" Garner asked suddenly.

Terry groaned and stopped walking, turning to face his brother. " 'S'a sports car, see? Yeah. An' it's hot, ya know?"

Garner looked baffled.

"C'mon, man. You be askin' too many questions an' shit ta be workin' wit' *me.* Gawddamn! *See,* nigga, the car's yella. Gonna be parked frunna thirteen fifty-seven Washington Street. We gonna use it ta make tha pick-up."

"Huh? How come?"

Terry threw his arms skyward in disgust. "Nigga, what's *wrong* wit'choo? B'cuz ah *don'* want that shit in ma fuckin' car. Thass how *come,* gawddammit."

"What we—we pickin' up some snow, man?"

Terry frowned and lit a smoke, holding up a hand as if to check his brother's questions. "Terry don' ask nobuddy shit, baby. Ah gits paid ta work, thass all."

Garner's stomach began to writhe with excitement. Up ahead of them he saw a policeman standing in the middle of an intersection, holding up a hand to stop the traffic. A crowd of people crossed the street. A small black boy charged by them, running full out, despite a heavy load of school books. Garner looked at his brother. Terry strolled along, his gleaming process bouncing with each step. Garner grinned, and they turned into the subway.

The yellow sports car was where Terry said it would be. Across the street, a wrecking crew was tearing down a block of old tenements. A line of heavy dump trucks waited to be loaded by a huge crane. Terry and Garner stopped a few doors away from the car and looked over the scene carefully. Two police officers stood near the trucks talking to a man in a steel helmet.

Terry tapped Garner's arm. "Les' go, baby."

The car was unlocked. Terry dug the keys out of the ashtray. Garner twisted his head halfway around so that he could keep an eye on the policemen. Terry started the car, turned on the radio, and tuned in some music. Garner shot him a glance of astonished admiration and quickly looked back at the police officers. They were still talking. Then one of the men looked toward them, and a chill slid up Garner's spine.

"C'mon, Terry, les' go, man. Shit."

Terry smiled at him and pulled the car into the busy street. The policeman, who had been watching them, started toward them. Garner's heart raced. The officer interrupted the stream of cars and motioned Terry out into the street. Terry waved his hand to thank him and pulled out.

Garner beamed.

"Ah gits 'long good wit' tha fuzz," Terry gloated. "They real gennamens down heah."

Garner relaxed, laughing softly as Terry cruised leisurely through the early morning crush of machines carrying people to their jobs. "Wheah we goin' now?"

"Down by tha shipyards, man."

"Down tha docks?"

"Naw. Look, jes' cool it, baby. All we gonna do is stop at a garage an' git our spare tire fixed, thass all."

"Huh?"

"Man gonna fix our spare. Soun' too hard?"

"Sheet, man—she-yee-yit—ah mean—ain' thatta bitch? Ya mean, thass *it?* What *ah* gotta do?"

"You gonna git tha tire out tha trunk an' take it in tha garage. Then ya gonna bring it back out when ah come back fa' ya."

"Wheah *you* goin', nigga?"

"Now, cool it, man. Ah be right down tha way."

"Wheah?"

"Up tha street."

"Why?"

"*Gawddamn*—awright. Tha man don' want no hot car in his fuckin' garage, thass why. Sheet. Ain' gonna take long."

They rode under the elevated trains in City Square, and Terry turned into a short, narrow street. They could smell the ocean now. The traffic was very slow moving. There were a number of servicemen about. Garner searched the sidewalks for policemen. He didn't see any. Terry followed a long line of cars up onto a bridge and stopped to pay a toll. Then they were moving again, faster now. Below them on both sides Garner could see City Harbor, the ocean, and gray, rust-spotted ships berthed at the docks. The water looked shiny, dark, and cold under the blue-gray morning.

Staring at the water as the yellow sports car swept across the bridge, Garner thought again of Buzz. A cold shudder ran through him. He looked at Terry and saw that his face was calm. The traffic had loosened up a bit and Terry drove easily now. Garner looked back to the harbor. The city curled away from it on both sides, a dense, concrete wilderness that stretched out endlessly into the distance.

As the bridge lowered them swiftly into a thicket of brick and concrete, Garner saw billboards sprouting up before his eyes, howling messages at him—COME TO MARLBORO COUNTRY—he didn't smoke Marlboros—FLY SOUTH THIS WINTER—he had never been on an airplane, and he wasn't really interested in going south, either—READ THE CITY NEWS—what for? he wondered—WANT A GOOD JOB? GET A GOOD EDUCATION—he scowled and puffed vigorously on his cigarette—COMING: INTERCOLLEGIATE BASKETBALL—*basketball,* he reflected irritably. No more. That was all over. He might have been good enough to play for a college team, mightn't he? Sure. But that was all over. All *over.* And he didn't miss it at all, he told himself. *Kidstuff,* that's what it was. *Well, wasn't it? Yes,* was his angry retort. That's a lie, now, Hawk. What? *It's a lie!* Listen, now—why not—why not forget it—forget the whole thing. *That won't solve anything.*

He looked over at Terry, trying to stop his thoughts. *Yes, school was the worst. Sports were—.* Then he remembered playing basketball and football for Bill Chamberlain. He thought of Shorty then, and Ellis, and Bobby Russo—well, that was all over. That was—what was the point in worrying about it, anyway? *Coach Connors.* Garner swore silently. *You were wrong then, Hawk.* What? Wait a minute, now—. He shrugged uneasily then and flipped his cigarette out of the window.

They left the bridge and headed down a narrow cobblestone street. The car's tires sang along the stones as Terry steadied his pressure on the accelerator. The dull red buildings on either side of them were close to the street—a narrow sidewalk between. Occasionally, Terry slowed the car in order to avoid hitting the children playing there.

"Man," Terry said, "these white folks heah ain' got *shit.*"

Garner looked closely at the children. Their clothes were dirty, nair unkempt, faces pinched. They looked hungry. He thought of his home—*He sat up in the bed, listening for the rat. He didn't like rats.*— He wondered then if Terry remembered the rats.

"Theah it is," Terry announced, braking the car and pointing to a gas station two blocks further up the street.

Garner's insides began to heat with excitement.

"Awright. Go down tha station an' ask fa' Mario. Now, ya heah? Thass all. Ask fa' Mario an' come right back heah."

Garner nodded quickly. Terry stopped the car, and Garner stepped out onto the sidewalk and strode away briskly toward the station.

A young, white man, wearing grease-stained, blue working clothes, was in the gas station working on a car. He looked up from the car's engine when Garner walked into the shop.

"What can I do for ya, buddy?" he asked pleasantly.

"Mario heah?"

The man's eyes narrowed slightly under a shock of unruly, reddish-blond hair. He pulled a grimy rag out of his back pocket and very deliberately wiped his hands. "Ya talkin' to him," he answered and fished a pack of cigarettes out of his shirt pocket.

Garner turned and walked back to the sports car.

"Mario theah," he informed his brother as he climbed into the car.

Terry smiled and drove down the street and into the station. "Heah," he muttered, giving the keys to Garner. "Git tha spare."

Mario hurried over to the car as Garner opened the trunk and unfastened the spare. Mario reached in, hauled it out, and rolled it inside. Garner started to follow him.

Terry growled at him, "Close tha trunk, man, an' gimme tha keys."

Garner did as he was told. Terry pulled out of the lot and drove off down the street, disappearing around a corner. Garner went inside.

Mario put the tire on the repair machine and broke it down. It was tubeless. He lifted it off the machine, leaving the wheel, and carried it into a small room in the back of his shop. Garner followed.

"Shut the door," Mario said brusquely.

Garner carefully eased the door shut and watched the man pull a long cylindrical package from another unmounted tire and stuff it into the spare. He stepped hastily out of the way as Mario hustled through the door into the shop. The tire was placed carefully on the machine and hurriedly remounted and filled with air.

"Take off," Mario ordered.

Garner grabbed the tire and walked out to the pumps, looking around for Terry. The sports car was pulling into the station. As soon as the car stopped, Garner snatched the keys from Terry, opened the trunk, and threw in the tire.

"Hurry it up, man," Terry yelled.

Garner slammed the trunk shut and jumped in the car. Terry dug out. Garner looked back at the gas station and saw Mario on the phone. Terry turned into a side street that appeared to run right into the sea. At the end of the street, he turned and headed back toward the city.

"Ain'cha gonna use tha bridge?"

"Ain' done yet, man. Set tight. Jesta few mo' minutes."

They stopped at a toll booth. Then they were racing through a tunnel, part of the wave of speeding cars. Terry's face was grim now. Garner sat up straight and squinted ahead. The tunnel was poorly lit, and the noise was deafening. He rubbed his hands nervously along his thighs, wishing they had already unloaded the package. This was a dangerous business, he knew. It was exciting, but it was dangerous.

They came out of the tunnel in the heart of the City Market district. Terry stopped for a red light, and a police cruiser drew alongside of them next to Garner. Two white policemen sat in it, talking quietly. Garner looked away from them and stared through the windshield. For a moment, he thought he was going to be sick. He scowled as Terry started whistling. The light changed. Terry calmly eased the little car forward, letting the cruiser move ahead of them. Abruptly, he swung the car onto Atlantic Avenue, which ran by City Harbor past the wharves. Garner saw a clock on a billboard—TIME TO CHANGE TO GAS HEAT—it was nine o'clock. He looked at his watch. It was two minutes slow. He reset it. Terry switched on the radio. Another cruiser passed them. One of the policemen in it cast an idle glance their way. Terry pulled the car around a corner and hurried it up a ramp into a big garage. An old man, sitting in a booth just inside the door, waved them along. Behind them the garage door rolled down and shut with a metallic crash. Garner heaved a long sigh.

Terry stopped the car between two long rows of parked cars. "Outside, baby."

A tiny, bald-headed white man, wearing coveralls, ran over to them. "Gimme the keys."

Garner had never seen such a small man. He banged his brother with an elbow. "Gawddamn, man," he whispered. "What tha fuck is *this?* What'sa matta wit' this cat? Why he so—fuckin' little, man?"

"Shut up," Terry warned, handing the keys to the man.

The man threw a vicious look at Garner as he took the keys. "Pick up the black Ford. It's down on the right. Keys in the dash. Leave it at eleven thirty-three Tremont."

Terry nodded.

The tiny man got into the sports car. He slammed the floor shift around angrily, grinding the gears. Then the car hurtled forward, tires screeching, and disappeared down a ramp on the left.

"Les' move," Terry barked.

They found the Ford, and Terry pulled it out between the rows of cars. The old man let them out.

"What a shitbox this is," Terry complained. "Ah don' like no little car. People see me an' think ah ain' hustlin' no mo'."

"When ah git paid, man?"

"Ah git tha bread ta-morra night."

"Sheet."

"Nigga, ah give ya tha twenny when we git back, if ya cain' wait."

"Crazy."

Christmas passed into a new year. Garner barely noticed. He still hadn't been home. Terry, in addition to taking him along on odd jobs, taught him to deal poker. He showed him how to deal eight hands of five-card stud to players betting eight different amounts of money and avoid making mistakes. Garner learned the basic skills very quickly. Occasionally, Terry let him deal for him. The cold winter nights usually brought a large crowd to the club, and Garner soon found himself with a steady job. Willi paid him a dealer's full share—twenty percent of the house cut for every hand he dealt. Garner earned between forty and fifty dollars most nights. Sometimes he made more. Terry also taught him to gamble less often and more cautiously, so he learned to hang onto his money long enough to spend some of it.

He bought clothes, expensive suits, slacks, shoes, and handmade, monogrammed shirts. Of course he partied, and even after the girls moved into their own apartment, he still had all the women he could use. "Sheet," he told his brother one evening as they dressed for work, "ah gotta git Ma ta sign tha paper so's ah kin quit school. This tha only way ta do it, man. Jes' keep on hustlin', thass all."

"Ah tol' ya that shit long time ago. Terry know what' *shakin'*, baby. An' this jes' tha start. Ah got a real *good* thing workin' fa' *me*. Cain' talk 'bout it yet cuz it ain' set. 'Sides, you talk too fuckin' much. But Terry gonna make it big. Ah know wheah tha shit's *really* at, man."

Garner smiled, staring at his brother in awe. "Yeah," he thought, "Terry know what's *happ'nin'*, gawddammit. Ain' no flies on *his* ass."

Sometimes he did think of home though, or Ellis, or even basketball, but only briefly. Home was a pain in the behind, Ellis was square, and basketball meant school. He was a businessman now. He was making it. Not even the police could touch him. At times, he laughed about it all, unless something reminded him of Luther—or Buzz. Well, he thought, those things happened, see. Luther had to learn to keep cool, that's all. *Buzz?* Well, he was dead now. *Wasn't he?* Buzz had been unlucky. So now he was dead, dead, that's all. But the *Hawk*—well, he was something else again.

Had it been possible, Garner would have ordered time to stop right there and drop him where he was. Life was good. No teachers yelled at him; he wasn't cold or hungry. No, sir. He had his hands on the controls now. He was moving, and he knew where he was going.

One afternoon, after making collections for Billy Ray, Terry and Garner stopped at Ma Jackson's restaurant. While they ate, Terry kept checking his watch.

"What'choo fidgetin' fa', man?" Garner asked, spearing a forkful of collard greens.

Terry bit into a piece of chicken and gave his brother a blank look. "Ain' nobuddy fidgetin', nigga."

"Sheet, you awful worried 'bout tha time."

"Bullshit."

"You gonna cut out somewheahs?"

Terry laughed. "Man, when you gonna git'cha hair fixed and git rid a' that woolly shit?"

Garner's brow furrowed as he ran a large black hand over his hair. "Stop bullshittin', nigga. Ah ain' fuckin' wit'cha gawddamn bid'ness. Sheet, you alla time playin' it *cute*. Ah don' give a *fuck* 'bout'chore bid'ness, man—. Talkin' 'bout ma fuckin' hair—. Ain' thatta *bitch?* Sheet—sheet, man, ah'm *prouda* ma hair."

"You a fuckin' liar, nigga."

"Fuck you, man! Ah don' want no process shit on *ma* head."

"Aw, man—you so black, process be no he'p, anyways."

"What'choo say? What'choo say, nigga?"

Several other patrons turned in their chairs to look in their direction.

"Aw, boy, cool it, will ya. People lookin' at'cha."

"Watch ya fuckin' mouth!"

"Aw, fuck you, man. Ah ain' said shit ta you."

"Sheet! Shit-colored nigga think he jesta 'bout a bitch. *Fuck* you, Terry!"

"Yeah, yeah, man. Eat'cha food. People lookin' at'cha."

"Gawddamn, man," Garner muttered. "Ask a nigga a simple fuckin' question, man. An' he gotta start a whole lotta shit, fa' crissake. Sheet. Ah don' give a fuck what'choo doin', man. Got ma own bid'ness ta take care uv."

"Fa' crissake, Hawk! Cool it, will ya! *Awright!* Ah gotta errand ta run. *Okay?* Gawddamn, man! Ah got bid'ness ah gotta do! Awright now? Gawddamn!"

"Whyn'cha jes' say so then, 'stead a' startin' some shit?" Garner said and chomped away at his food.

"Look," Terry whispered, carefully sweeping his plate clean with a piece of bread, "you right, see? Ah'm gonna split—what'choo gonna do?"

"Huh?"

"Ah mean, ya goin' up tha club or what?"

"Shit, man, ah thought'choo wuz gonna ride me home."

"Cain', man."

"Y'ain' even got time ta ride me home, man? 'S'cold out, man."

"Look, Hawk—c'mon, now, man. Now, if ya see anybuddy—"

"Yeah, yeah, ah know. Don' know wheah ya at."

"Jes' say ah'm wit' a bitch—yeah. Yeah, thass all." Terry stood and dropped a five-dollar bill on the table. "Heah, baby. Pay fa' tha food. Dig ya later."

Garner waved and finished his food.

When he left the restaurant the murky sky had darkened. The wind was colder. As he trudged along, he felt the hard snow and ice crunching crisply under his feet. A number of cars moved slowly through the streets. Some of them were spotted with ice. People were making their way home from work. He watched a group of children throw pieces of ice and snow at each other. A yellow-skinned boy knocked a dirty chunk of snow loose from some barrels which were heaped high with frozen rubbish and threw it at a little black girl. It hit her in the face, and she began to cry. Garner kicked at some ice and stomped on his way, pulling his sweater down under his jacket. His eyes narrowed as he looked ahead into the brisk wind and banged his fist in his palm. The wind whipped sharply around his face and worked its way through his heavy slacks. He scanned the street, looking for a taxi.

Ahead of him, he noticed a tall white man with a heavy beard walking quickly toward him carrying a black satchel. Garner glanced at him idly and started to cross the street. The man looked very young. His clothes were old and shabby. Around his neck he wore a heavy, red scarf tucked inside his long, shapeless coat. Garner smiled to himself and shook his head as he jogged over to the opposite curb. He stepped up on the sidewalk and hesitated, turning to look back at the man. He thought he had seen him before. *Sure.* He knew the guy. He squinted across the tops of the passing cars as people passed him on the sidewalk. "Yeah. It's Leroy, fa' crissake."

He walked quickly out into the street. "Hey, man," he shouted. "Hey, Leroy!"

Leroy stopped and turned to see Garner sprinting toward him. He stared at the boy momentarily, then threw his head back, laughing loudly. "I don't believe it," he cried.

A broad grin stretched across Garner's face as he offered his hand.

"Garner," Leroy exulted, clasping the proffered hand. "How *are* you? How're things going? For a minute, I thought it was Luther. How've you been? I've been meaning to come by the house and see you—I mean, so *many* times, baby. I'll be damned. How's your mother? What do you hear from Luther? How's Terry? How's—"

Garner cut him off. "Hold up, man! Wait up a minute! Ah been 'roun', sheet. Evah'thin's cool." He hesitated then. "Ah mean—ain' heard nothin'—*much*—frum Lutha, man. Ya know? Ah mean—what'*choo* been doin', Leroy?"

"Too much, Hawk. Working too hard and sleeping too little. How is everything?"

"Crazy, man." Garner nodded quickly several times as Leroy continued to pump his hand. "Evah'thin's uptight, man. Been hustlin' ma ass off. What'cha got in tha suitcase?"

"This—I use this to carry books."

"Huh?"

"Books, I've been—"

"Books—man, you bullshittin'! Stop tha shit, now, Leroy, gawddamn."

"I'm for real, baby. Leroy's not kidding. Look." He opened the satchel, and Garner stared incredulously at the books inside. He looked at Leroy and shook his head. "Carry work clothes in there, too," Leroy went on, lifting some books out. "See there?"

Garner stared at the young man in disbelief. "Gawddamn, Leroy, what tha fuck—you in *school?"*

Leroy smiled and closed the satchel. "I'm afraid so, Hawk."

"Gaw-awd*damn!* How long ya been fuckin' 'roun' wit' school, Le-roy?"

"Couple of years now. Summers too."

"Gawddamn." Garner kicked a piece of ice and jammed his hands into his pockets. A black woman, holding a little brown boy by the hand, passed them and walked out into the street. A car horn honked, and the woman turned to glare at the driver. "Sheet, man. Ah *quit* fuckin' wit' them books, man. Fuck that shit, baby. Ah'm *really* makin' it now."

Leroy's face grew serious then, the light-blue eyes hardened. He spoke in a low, even tone. "Bill told me."

Garner shrugged and smiled weakly. "Yeah, ah gotta git ovah ta see ol' Bill. But, sheet, ah dunno—Bill, man, he kinda funny. Ya know? 'Sides, ah been kinda busy, see? Ain' had tha time." He stopped talking and watched a pretty, copper-colored girl tramp by carrying a bag of groceries. Her short boots slapped against her legs as she walked. Garner shivered. He was aware of the cold again, and the wind snapping through his clothes.

"Bill would like that," Leroy said quietly.

"Huh?"

"I said—"

"Aw, naw," Garner said weakly, then hesitated, glancing at Leroy's face. "Naw," he repeated, wondering why Leroy was looking at him like that. "Well—yeah. Maybe. You know—maybe sometime. Bill's okay, but—well, you know what ah mean, man. 'Sides, ah'm workin'."

Leroy rubbed his beard and fixed his gaze on the boy. Garner had to avert his eyes. He tugged at his sweater and shuffled his feet on the ice.

"You haven't been going to school at all, then, have you, Hawk?"

Garner shook his head and looked across the street. An uneasy feeling pulled at his insides. "Naw."

A touch of weariness softened Leroy's tone a bit. "Well, white folks win again." He grimaced and shook his head. "Just like they do in the movies."

Garner glanced at him. "Huh, man?"

"What happened, Hawk? Why did you quit?"

Garner looked down at the snow. His face took on a sullen expression. "Sheet. Cat started *fuckin'* wit' me. First day—yellin' an' holl'rin' cuz ah missed coupla days. Sheet. White som'bitch started cussin' an' raisin' all *kinda* hell. Ah don' needa take no shit offa *no* white mutha-fucka, man."

Leroy grabbed Garner's arm, his eyes flashing. "Look, that's what they *want!* Don't you under*stand* that?"

"Huh?" Garner was embarrassed as well as baffled. He looked cautiously around at passers-by to see if anyone was watching them.

"Look, man, come by and see me. Stop by, and we'll talk." Leroy paused, watching Garner jerk his head about. "Look, Hawk—it's cold now, see? But—let's talk sometime. Sometime soon. Come by. Okay?"

The boy fidgeted uncomfortably and shrugged. "Sho', Leroy—sho' —but see, ah'm—ah'm kinda in a hurry right now. Kinda late, see? Ya know? Ah mean, ah got bid'ness, see?"

Leroy's face whitened and hardened. He watched Garner shift his weight from one foot to the other. "Terry, huh?"

Garner shrugged and quickly nodded his head.

Anger blazed in Leroy's face. His voice was low, almost a whisper. "Don't you realize—Hawk, what kind of *business*—selling black women to—*white perverts*—how can you call that *business?* Why— you and—" He checked himself and uttered a long sigh.

A look of pure amazement was in Garner's eyes—and some apprehension. He began to move away. Leroy reached out and caught him by the shoulder, staring hard into the boy's eyes, squeezing him firmly. "Look, baby," he pleaded, *"please*—please come and see me. Say—hello. Afternoons I'm up Freedom House." His grip on the boy's shoulder tightened.

"Sho'. Sho', Leroy. Ah do that. Yeah—yeah, man. Ah stop by. Ah be 'roun', heah? Okay? Ah gotta split now, though, man. No lie, see. So ah be 'roun'. Yeah, ah see ya, man."

Leroy watched him walk away and scowled. He cursed and kicked some snow out of an icy rut. Then he went on his way. It was dark. The headlights of the passing vehicles were shining in tattered, uneven patches of light on the street. He turned to look back at Garner, but he couldn't see him any longer.

The encounter with Leroy troubled Garner for several days. *What was he talking about?* There was no sense to it all. After thinking it over, he felt sorry for Leroy. Then he tried to dismiss their conversation from his mind, but the memory hung on. It was irksome, unsettling. He told Terry about it.

"You fulla shit, Hawk." Terry sat on the sofa, his face twitching with amusement.

"Ah ain' bullshittin', Terry."

"Stop tha shit, now, man."

"Ah'm tellin' ya—then he start talkin' ta hisse'f, an' he say we wuz—*sellin'*—colored—black gals ta white folks, man."

Terry exploded into laughter then. *"You a fuckin' liar, nigga!* Ain' thatta bitch?"

"Man—ah ain' bullshittin', now."

"Naw, man! *Naw*—no shit, man?"

"No lie, Terry, ah'm tellin' ya, man."

"Nigga's crazy, man!" Terry cried.

Garner laughed, too, then, listening to his brother howl.

"Sheet, that nigga's head's *all* fucked up! Them Mooslims got his head all fulla *crazy* shit, man!" Terry doubled up laughing and collapsed onto the floor and rolled back and forth, yelling. *"Gawddamn!* Say ah'm sellin' black pussy ta tha white devil, do he? Ain' thatta *bitch?"* He held onto his sides, pounding the floor with his feet. "Ain' thatta mutha-fucka, now? Sheet, that nigga ain' *well,* man! Need he'p, he do, no lie!"

Garner chuckled and leaned forward in his chair to pour himself some Scotch.

Terry sat up on the floor and giggled and rubbed his eyes as his body shook with laughter. "What else tha nigga say, man? What else he say?"

Garner wagged his head sadly from side to side and sipped his Scotch. "He goin' ta school, man."

"What?" Terry croaked.

"Ain' really funny, man."

"Huh?"

"Ain' funny."

Terry blinked at him. "Nigga, what'choo talkin' 'bout?"

"Sheet, Ellis say Leroy gonna git married, too."

Terry broke into laughter again. *"Holy Jesus!* Holy fuckin' Jesus Christ-a-mighty! Great gawd-a-mighty, ain' thatta bitch?" He struggled to hold back some of his laughter. "See theah, now? *Thass it!"* A look of realization passed over his face. "Sheet, that nigga gonna git hisse'f put in tha funny farm, fa' crissake." He pounded his feet on the floor again, then rubbed his eyes. "Gawddamn, Hawk, man, gimme 'notha drink, will ya? Ah *gotta* git a drink now! Holy fuckin' Jesus."

Garner poured some Scotch into Terry's glass and handed it to him.

Terry shook his head and stood up. "C'mon, les' go, man." He emptied the glass in a quick gulp and grinned at Garner. "Sheet, ah wuz *you,* ah go see tha nigga jes' ta heah some mo' that shit, gawd-damn."

Garner threw on his coat. "Naw. Not me, man. Don' wanna heah no mo'. Ain' funny ta see cat's head all tore up like that."

"Say, Hawk," Terry chuckled as they left the house, "how come ya didn't tell me this shit befo'?"

Garner shrugged and skipped down the steps, fastening the buttons higher on his coat. Terry followed, mumbling and laughing to himself.

Ella Hawkins stepped out of the car and looked up at the stone and glass building before her. She had never been inside of the YMCA before. It was a handsome structure of reinforced concrete, set in a wide flat area which was cluttered with piles of debris, the leftover rubble of the old slum buildings that had been demolished. Most of the residue of brick, mortar, and iron was covered with dirty, hard, crusty snow. The Y looked out of place there—it looked new, as if it had a future.

Harry shut the car door and took her arm. "That outfit looks good on you, baby," he said, smiling at her.

She leaned against him for a moment.

"C'mon," he whispered, carefully adjusting his tie.

Ella hoped that Bill Chamberlain was in. She was nervous and didn't want to wait around in strange surroundings. When she called to talk to him, the girl who answered the phone had assured her that he would be there.

"What time ya got, Harry?"

"Quarter of four," he replied, watching her face. "Stop worryin', will ya? These people are used to meeting people. Relax."

They went inside. There were only two people in the lobby, a young man, who lounged against the front desk, and a girl, standing behind the desk near him.

"Good afternoon, Mrs. Hawkins," the young man said when he saw her.

Ella smiled uncertainly at him. He looked white and wore a beard. She tried to place him.

He grinned and held out his hand. "I'm Leroy. Leroy Collins. Remember?"

She nodded slowly and let him shake her hand. She thought of Luther then. "Well, sho'," she acknowledged suddenly. "Yeah, Harry, this Leroy. Him an' Lutha be friends."

"Oh. Sure. Pleased to meet you," Harry said, extending his hand.

Leroy shook hands. "Have you heard anything from Luther?"

"Well," Ella began, "ah ain'—"

Harry cut in, "Not really. See, we haven't seen him in a long time. Guess he keeps—pretty busy."

"If you're ready, I'll take you down to see Mr. Chamberlain," the girl said, smiling. She was dark, pretty, her manner easy and confident.

They followed her along a brightly lit corridor to the office. Bill looked up from his work and stood. "Mrs. Hawkins, it's good to see you again." He nodded quickly to Harry and pulled two chairs over in front of his desk.

"What can I do for you?" Bill asked when they were seated.

"Mistah Cham'blin'," Ella began nervously, "what ah wanna talk 'bout is ma boy. Ah ain' seen'im in so long, an' he ain' come home, an' ah thought—ah mean, ah hoped'choo might be able ta he'p—he'p me find'im."

Bill glanced at Harry and tapped his pencil idly on the desk. "You mean Garner."

"Yeah."

"Well, I know he's around. Of course, he hasn't been by here for some time, but I know he's staying around here somewhere."

"Do ya know wheah at?" Ella begged. "Man frum tha school wuz gonna put tha *law* on'im! Ah hadda beg'im not ta do it."

"I thought Garner had left school—officially, I mean."

"Naw. Naw, he jes' plain ain' *goin',* thass all. Tha man lef' some papers. Said ah could sign'em, an' Garna be *outta* school. Said, ah don' sign, an' he gonna git tha *law!"*

Bill rubbed a hand slowly across his forehead and sighed. "I see." His small mustache twitched as he thought it over.

Harry spoke. "The boy just up and walked out of the house one day and didn't come back, see? No reason, no warning, either. Just walked on out. Haven't heard from him since."

Bill frowned. "Yes, I heard something about it. Shorty—I mean Mr. Rollins said something about it the other day—Garner played ball for him, too, you know, same's he did for me. The people up at Tech are pretty upset. Garner hasn't been in school since November. Basketball coach told me the boy came out late for the team, and he had to throw him off."

"Don't understand that," Harry said. *"I* always thought sports meant a lot to the kid."

"He wuz alla time playin' ball," Ella said, a pained expression on her dark face.

"Well, I'll be glad to help in any way I can—even if I can't guarantee the results."

"Ah jes' wan'cha ta talk wit'im, thass all," Ella blurted. "Jes'—talk ta ma boy." She began to cry.

Harry put his arm around Ella's shoulders. "Listen, we really would appreciate it. I mean—I know you're a busy man. But we figured—

hell, you know the boy. And maybe you can help us find out where he lives. I mean, we can't go to the police, and the school—what do they know about it? And what do they really care? Let's face it, they want to write the kid off, get him out of their hair. Garner's just another black kid—and they've got other things to do. They lose lots of kids—glad to see them go. Maybe if he was the right color and religion, came from the right neighborhood—I don't know. Do you think you can help us, ask around—find out where he's staying?"

"Well, I heard he's been staying with his brother. Shouldn't be too hard to find out where he lives." Bill hesitated and looked at Ella. She reached in her handbag for a handkerchief which she used to dry her eyes. "I'll do everything I can," Bill said and stood up to offer his hand to Harry.

Harry stood and took the hand, clasping it solidly. Ella thanked him. Bill smiled and watched them leave.

Ella felt better when she left the Y. As she and Harry drove home through the cold winter afternoon she was immensely relieved. A great burden had been lifted from her shoulders. She looked through her window. It was almost dark. A lot of people hurried along the sidewalks, bundled warmly in heavy clothes. Some paused at the corners, or on the edge of a curb, then hustled across the slippery streets. She saw children running and playing. A group of boys were wrestling on a hill, trying to keep each other from reaching the top. She peeked at Harry; thank God for him, she thought. She felt snug and warm now. Harry was intent on his driving, puffing a cigarette. Ella eased herself over carefully on the leather seat and slid against him. He chuckled softly.

It was ten o'clock when Bill left the Y that night. A chilling, gusty wind smacked him as he stepped from the building. He hunched up his shoulders inside the heavy topcoat and ducked his head, walking quickly to his Ford. He started the car and lit a smoke. Outside, the wind whistled by, dying in the distance, then starting anew from another direction. Bill turned on the radio. Loud, raucous music burst into the car. Quickly, he punched a button and found something softer. He wasn't really interested in the music, just killing time while the engine warmed. Besides, there was no real hurry. Leroy had told him that Garner was working with Terry for Billy Ray. He sighed and checked his watch. It was ten past ten. He set the clock in the dashboard and sat back against his seat, smoking and drumming his fingers on the steering wheel, mixing his thoughts.

What was he going to say to the boy, anyway? Something like, "Why did you quit school, kid?" Sure, and the kid would laugh at him. His brother was a pimp, certainly making twice what *he* earned at the Y. *Well, who wants to be a pimp?* Garner? Maybe. Well, why not? It paid well, didn't it? Bill grimaced and shut the radio off. Suddenly the cigarette tasted bad. He lowered the window and flipped it out. So just what *do* you say to a boy who's making that kind of money, a boy who never had two cents? *And the girls!* The boy was probably having the time of his life. Bill shrugged, switched on the headlights, and pulled the car away from the curb.

The club was crowded. The downstairs was jammed with people, playing poker, shooting craps, or standing about, talking, laughing, and drinking. Many of the men were white. Bill heard music coming from the rooms upstairs. He scowled and eased himself in and out of the crowd.

He found Garner dealing poker. He watched him zip the cards around the table, snapping them off the deck with the ease and confidence of a professional. There were two other tables in the room, both full with players. There was chatter, laughter, smoke, and a lot of money on the tables. A feeling of helplessness came over Bill. But he waited and watched. Garner's face was shiny with sweat. Black, muscular arms bulged from his light, short-sleeved shirt. His shoulders looked gigantic as he bent over the table, fully engrossed in his job.

"Stan' outta tha do'way, man."

Bill turned and saw a huge black man, his face cruelly scarred, standing behind him. He stepped back into the corridor to let him pass.

"Lotta people 'head a' ya, fella. Gotta wait'cha turn."

"Uh, I didn't come to play. Just want to talk to the dealer."

"Which one?"

"The kid there. Hawkins."

The man looked at his watch. "He be up fa' break 'bout twenny minutes. Stay heah if ya wanna, but try not ta block tha do'. Okay?"

Bill nodded and thanked him. Looking back into the room, he saw Garner squinting at him and frowning. Bill inclined his head as a greeting. A puzzled look crossed the boy's face and he averted his gaze and went back to his work.

A while later, a thin, fair-skinned man with red, processed hair pushed his way through the crowd to Garner's table. He was carrying a metal box with a large coin hole in it. Garner lifted another box just like it out of a hole in the table and stood up and jostled through the people to the doorway.

"What's happ'nin', Bill?" he said, nervous quickness touching his voice.

"How are you, Hawk?"

"Cool, man. You know—evah'thin's cool."

"Yeah—well, uh, can I talk to you for a minute, Hawk?"

Garner looked down at him and tried to smile. "Well, sho'. Uh—sho'. Jes' lemme check this. Be right back."

When the boy returned, Bill suggested they step outside and talk in the car.

"Well, we kin go up tha kitchen," Garner said.

"Fine," Bill quickly agreed and followed him down the corridor.

Garner smiled a greeting to the policeman at the foot of the stairs.

Upstairs, the music from the juke box was louder and there was less lighting. It, too, was packed with people. Garner and Bill shoved their way into a dimly lit room. Some couples were dancing and the short bar was busy with people. A pretty, golden-colored girl stopped Garner and fed him some of her drink. Bill waited while she slid a plump arm around the boy's waist and snuggled up to him. Garner kissed her lightly on the mouth and gently eased her aside. "Back in a minute. Keep it warm, chicken."

Bill shook his head. *By all means, keep it warm! When did she ever let it get cold?* Then he realized that he was more than a little jealous.

Well, the girl *was* pretty. He cursed silently and followed Garner behind the bar. What was the use? Why should this kid listen to *him?* Garner led him through a door behind the bar.

They were met in the kitchen by a fat, yellow woman, old and with a withered arm. "Hey theah, big fella. How's ma baby ta-nite? Ya sneakin' up heah ta steal some mo' ma food, ain'cha? Whoozat wit'cha?"

"He's a fren'. Come up ta talk, thass all."

"Sheet. Meanin' tha *hell* wit' ol' Marie, huh? Don' need *nothin'* frum *me,* do ya?"

Bill smiled and looked down at his feet.

"Aw, c'mon, baby," Garner soothed, slipping his arm around the woman from behind. He laid his cheek against hers. "Ya know ah cain' live wit'out'cha."

"Sheet. Git away, boy." She handed him a piece of fried chicken. "Git away, nigga. Take ya fren' ovah theah an' set if y'all gonna talk. Marie got work ta do, gawddammit."

"Where's Terry?" Bill asked as they sat down.

Garner gave him a carefully guarded look. "Aw, he cruisin'."

"What?"

"Cruisin', man—workin'. He busy."

"Oh."

"What'choo doin' down heah, Bill?"

"Just wanted to see you—talk to you, I mean. Well—I haven't seen you in a while—so here I am." Bill studied the boy closely for a moment, then abruptly he said, "No. No, that's a lie. Your mother came to see me. She asked me to talk to you."

Garner sat up attentively. He regarded Bill briefly, then relaxed, slowly munching the chicken. "What Ma want?"

Bill put his elbows on the table. "Hawk, I—Your mother is worried about you. Now, I suppose it's none of my business, but—anyway, I said I *would,* and now I *am*. Garner, she doesn't even know where you're living. See? I mean, she came in and—started crying. She says, 'Talk to my boy.' Some guy from the school department wants to send the police out after you, for God's sake. So—I'm here. Go see her, boy. Tell her not to worry, or *something*—I don't know. Jesus, if you're not going to go to school, go by and tell her so. The guy left some papers to sign, and he—"

"Ma got tha paper, huh?"

"What? Yes. Guy says she better sign it soon, or he's calling the cops. Your mother's worried, Hawk."

"Whyn't she sign, then?"

"Well, *Jesus,* Hawk, I suppose—"

"All she gotta do's sign tha paper?"

"Well—*yes.*"

"Well, thass cool, man. Sheet, tell'er ta sign, then."

"What?" Bill's voice was sharp.

"Tell'er ta sign, man. Thass all. Sheet, she don' need me fa' that."

Bill stared at him, trying to control his temper. "How—how do *you* know *that?* For the love of—look, go by and see her. *Jesus!* She wants to see you, Garner!"

"Man, ah dunno. Pretty busy, man. Ya know? Ah mean—what she want, man? Sheet, ah gotta—"

"What does she want?" Bill yelled. He glanced over his shoulder and quieted his voice. *"Jesus,"* he hissed into the boy's startled face. "That's a stupid question! What do you think she wants? She's your mother—I mean—dammit-all, boy, what do you think she wants?"

"Aw, man—"

"Aw, man? Aw, man, *what?* I wouldn't be *too* surprised if she wanted to know whether or not you're still *alive!* Damn—are you crazy or something? She hasn't seen you since—since *football* season! Now you sit there and want to know what she *wants!*"

"Now look, Bill, you ain' got no bid'ness yellin' an'—comin' down heah an' messin' wit' me. Sheet. Ah don' mess wit'*choo.* Y'ain' got no bid'ness wit' me. You ain' ma *daddy,* ya know."

Bill lunged across the table and grabbed the front of the boy's shirt with both hands.

"Sheet," Garner bawled, banging down at the man's arms. He tried to stand and rocked up and backward into the back of the booth with a crash. His shirt ripped. He yelped, "What tha fuck—what'cha

doin', nigga? Leggo, gawddammit! Leggo! Who tha fuck ya think ya fuckin' wit'? Leggo!"

Marie waddled over to them quickly, her wrinkled, yellow face flushed red. "What'ch'all *doin'?"* She glared at Bill. "What'choo doin', man? Leggo that boy! *Leggo!* C'mon, dammit, turn'im loose, now. Ya heah?"

Bill released his grip on the boy's shirt. Marie's eyes blazed furiously as he sank slowly back into his seat.

"Y'all gonna fight, ya git on outta heah wit'it! Ya heah me?" She railed at them. "Gawddamn niggas is *crazy!* Y'all take ya fightin' outta ma kitchen, thass what! *Ah* don' need it! Ah don' need it, heah?"

" 'S'awright, Marie," Garner grunted as he rearranged the booth.

"Ain' awright, neither! This *ma* kitchen, so it ain' nowheahs *neah* bein' awright! Niggas is crazy!"

"Awright, okay," Garner groaned, holding up his hands as if to cushion the impact of her words. "We sorry. We sorry, Marie. Okay?"

Bill shivered in a spasm of disgust and peered up at the boy watching the old woman leave. He dropped his eyes as Garner gave him a quick, hostile look. Bill was ashamed. His temper was too quick.

"Sheet, y'ain' s'posed ta be puttin' ya hands on *me,* man. Ah don' let *nobuddy* put they hands on *me,* gawddammit. Ah ain' no kid. Ah ain' playin' ball fa' you no mo', man."

Bill nodded his head jerkily. "Yeah," he croaked in a whisper. "Yeah. Look, Hawk, I didn't mean to—I'm sorry. Look, Hawk—sit down a minute, will you?"

"Ah gotta git back, man."

"Just—please, Hawk. Just for a minute."

Garner slid into his seat, sulking.

Bill's voice was quiet now. "Go see her, Hawk. Say it to her, yourself. Say, 'Sign the paper, Ma. I want to quit school.' "

Garner looked at him, then averted his eyes.

"Hawk?"

"Huh?"

"What do you say, man?"

"Aw, man—yeah, mebbe, man."

They sat in silence then. Slowly, a cold tremor way down in Garner's bowels started to expand and grow in him, chilling his insides. He fidgeted and lit a smoke. The cold in his guts squeezed its way through his pores. He goosepimpled with a series of quick shudders as it rippled along his skin. He was ashamed, but he didn't know why. Looking at Bill now made him feel this way. His eyes darted away as Bill looked up. *What was it?* He didn't understand. As he thought about what he had said to this man, he shook his head. *And that look on Bill's face!* Why was he fighting with this man? Why? He sensed that Bill was feeling miserable—perhaps ashamed? But, of what? Their little scuffle? He liked Bill, so what were they fighting about? He grimaced as if in pain and dropped his chin dejectedly. And Bill had to come over here for his mother, too. Was that why he looked uncomfortable—ashamed?

"Look, Hawk," Bill said, standing up, "I'm sorry about all this, see, sorry for sticking my nose in here and—." Bill hesitated, staring uneasily at the boy, wondering what to say next. Why was Garner hiding his eyes like that? What was wrong with this kid? He frowned and walked to the door, half expecting the boy to say something. He didn't, and Bill left.

The cold winter washed away in a rush of spring rain. Then the sun came out, and suddenly it was too hot. The city grew damp and sticky. A foul stench rose up from trash and refuse rotting in the heat. Heavy, moist air pressed in on the city then, and it seemed harder to breathe.

"What'cha thinkin' 'bout, Hawk?" Terry asked one night as they cruised the streets.

"Nothin'."

"You real quiet ovah theah."

"Huh? Yeah—thinkin' 'bout things, thass all."

"What things, man?"

"Jes'—things. 'Bout'choo—Lutha an' evah'thin'—Ma, too."

"How tha ol' gal doin'?"

"Okay—keep askin' when ya comin' by."

"Well, prob'bly be a while. Too busy, man. What Harry doin'?"

Garner shrugged. "Nothin', bought a new car."

"Yeah? What kind?"

" 'Notha' Olds."

"Yeah?" Terry pulled over to the curb and rolled his window down. Carol and Jackie approached the car.

Carol leaned into the window. "Hey, baby."

"What's happ'nin', gal?" Terry answered.

"How're you, Garner?"

"Cool, baby. How do, Jackie?"

Jackie laughed. "The Hawkins boys're here again!" She peeked into the car. "Hi there, baby."

Garner grinned and lit a smoke.

"Evah'thin' shakin' awright?" Terry asked.

A soft chuckle came from Carol. "Don't worry about it, baby. You just keep cruising. We're working."

"Awright, baby, long as ya workin'." Terry laughed and waved a hand. The Buick dug out.

"Wheah Shirley?" Garner asked.

"Huh?"

"Wheah Shirley?"

"What'cha mean, nigga? What'*choo* care?"

"Huh, man? Sheet, fuck you, Terry. Jes' askin'."

"What fa'?"

"Sheet, ah know ya steady fuckin'er."

"Fuck you, man."

"Gawddamn, ask tha nigga somethin', an' he gonna—"

"She busy, nigga, sheet. What tha hell ya care? She busy, thass all."

"Fuck it then, man. Sheet."

Terry sighed wearily. "Ma still wan'cha ta come back home?"

"Yeah, she alla time talkin' that shit, man. She say, 'Why cain'cha stay heah?' an' ah jes' listens an' don' say nothin'."

"Maybe ya oughtta."

"*Who?* Shee-yee-yit, man, ah ain' stayin' back home no mo'. Is you crazy? What's wrong wit'choo? Gawddamn."

"Look, Hawk, ah'm gonna be—well, ol' Harry still 'roun', anyways."

"What'cha say? Oh. Yeah, that nigga act like he run tha place, man."

"Yeah. Man been 'roun' fa' long time. Ma must be treatin'im *real* good." Terry laughed then. "Sheet, nigga ain' careful, Ma gonna git'im up in frunna tha preacha, man."

Garner shot his brother a quizzical look. "Naw," he said, wondering.

They stopped to talk to a white woman, then they rode in silence for a while.

"Sheet, Terry, then Harry an' Ma be married, huh?"

"Huh? Oh—yeah."

"Yeah. Say, man, do that make him a *real* uncle then?"

"Naw."

"Thass what'choo said."

"Huh? Naw, man," Terry laughed. "He be a daddy then—be Ma's husbin'."

"Sheet, nigga, how he gonna be a daddy? He ain' *ma* fuckin' daddy!"

"Naw, man. Be a stepdaddy, thass all."

"Whazzat, man?"

"Ah mean—he ain'cha real daddy, man—takes his place, thass all."

Garner laughed. "Well, gawddamn. Ain' thatta bitch?" He settled back in his seat, mulling it over. That was a good one, he thought, and smiled to himself. He put his head back, staring up at the dark interior of the convertible roof. Suddenly he thought of his mother—*She stood up from the kitchen table, looking at him in surprise. "Harry," she called toward the other room, "Garna's heah." Harry came to stand in the doorway. He looked older in his robe and slippers, his dark, round face seemed heavier. He had a day's growth of beard, flecked with bits of gray. "Well," he declared quietly as Ella moved slowly around the table and walked over to her son. She stopped and glared up at the boy. Garner saw tears glistening in her eyes. He quickly looked away. Harry came into the room and leaned heavily against the new refrigerator. "Terry downstairs?" he asked. Garner shook his head and glanced at his mother again. Why was she looking at him like that? She was just standing there, staring at him and rubbing her hands in the folds of her housecoat. Garner looked at the floor. Then she started yelling at him, "Wheah ya been? What'cha do alla this time—weeks and months? Ah could kill ya, boy. Ah could kill ya, thass what." Her voice broke with sobbing, "Ah could—jes'—jes' kill ya," and she threw her arms around his waist and hugged and squeezed as she wept against his chest. Without understanding why, Garner felt his own eyes watering. He fought against it, but, slowly, the tears trickled out. Then his arms were around his mother—.* Terry stopped at an intersection. He saw his brother looking at him curiously.

"You a dreamy nigga," he chuckled, an uneasiness quieting his voice.

"Huh?" Garner grunted.

"Nothin', man."

Terry pulled the car to a halt in front of Billy Ray's. "Dig ya later," he said as Garner stepped from the car. " 'Memba, now, man—"

"Yeah—"

"—ah'm jes' cruisin'."

"Yeah, yeah, nigga, see ya later. Sheet."

Bill Chamberlain was at his desk, working. It was early afternoon, and the building was quiet. It was a good time to work. Later, when the schools got out, the place would be mobbed. There was a knock on the door. Bill smiled. *Naturally.* "C'mon in," he said.

Garner walked in.

"Well, I'll be damned," Bill exclaimed. "How've you been, Hawk?"

"Okay, man. Evah'thin's cool. You know."

"Good. Listen, pull up a chair, for pete's sake. I'll be damned. How's your mother?"

Garner sat down. "Uh—okay. Yeah, she's good, Bill. That's how come ah stopped by. Ah mean, ah jes' lef' theah, see, an' Ma said, 'Ya been by tha Y yet?' So ah said, ah ain', an' then ah told'er ah might walk on ovah heah. Uh—" He stopped talking and crossed his long legs, looking down at his hands.

Bill nodded pensively and pushed back in his chair. "She called a while back and told me she had seen you. I was glad to hear that, Hawk."

Garner fidgeted in his chair. "Yeah—well, ah hadda git tha paper signed, anyways, see? Ya know? Hadda git some clothes an'—"

"She said you'd been by a *couple* times."

"Uh, yeah, man—ah mean, she keep tellin' me ta stop by an' say hullo—eat a good meal, a' somethin'. So—jes' keepin'er happy, thass all."

Bill fought off a slight smile. "Think that's important, do you?"

"Huh?"

"I asked if you think keeping your mother happy is important."

"Ah dunno. Wit' Lutha inside—an' Terry alla time busy an' all, ah mean—ah dunno."

"She fill you full of food when you visit?"

"Oh, yeah." Garner's face brightened.

"Beats sandwiches and restaurants, huh?"

"Yeah, man."

"Yes—are you still with Terry at Billy Ray's place?"

"Yeah. Ah mean, ah deals. Ya know? An' he'p Terry out."

"With the girls?"

"Huh?"

"Do you help your brother with the girls?"

"Huh? Naw! Ah mean, a li'l bit—sometimes—ah mean—ah mean, ah jes' deal—an' stuff, thass all. Terry deal, too, 'cept he gotta lot ta do—ah mean—he make mo' than me, see?"

"Do you have a girl, Hawk?" Bill asked, lighting a smoke.

"Naw, man." Garner attempted a weak laugh. "You kiddin'? Ah mean—well, sho', ah know some—broads, but ah don' be lettin' *no* gal git a hol' on *me,* man. Ya know?"

"I see." Bill leaned forward across his desk. "Hawk," he went on in a quiet, careful tone, "I'd like to ask you something."

"Huh?"

"Do you love your mother, boy?"

"Huh? What'cha—"

"Take it easy, now. It's a simple question. I'm not trying to be funny. I'm asking you if you love your ma."

Garner hesitated—*"Do ya love ya momma, baby?"—"Baby—ah mean do ya feel fa' ya momma?"—"Yes'm. Yes'm, Momma."—His mother grasped his hands in hers—she drew him to her and put her arms around him. "Gawd knows ah love ya, boy. Ya knows that, don'cha?"*—He scuffed his feet on the floor and shrugged. "Ma's okay, ah guess."

"Do—you—*love* your mother? I'm not asking if you think she's *okay.*"

"Well—Ma's awright—sho'."

Bill mashed the cigarette out, put an elbow on the desk, and rested his chin on his palm. The fingers of his free hand drummed slowly on the desk. "Hawk?"

"Huh?"

"My mother's older than yours. Sometimes she stops by the house, or my wife and I visit her, and we con her into fixing us up a batch of food. Then we sit back and watch her cook while she talks all over the place. I mean, she just chatters—and sings a little—all the while. And sometimes, watching her like that, I feel so much—*love*—know what I mean?"

"Huh? Well—ah dunno—uh—ah guess. Ah dunno."

"Do you ever feel that way about *your* mother?"

Garner stared at the man in awe. "Man—"

"Do you?"

"Huh?"

"Do you love her?"

"Ma—Ma's straight wit' me, man. Ma's cool an'—evah'thin'. Ah likes Ma—ah mean—ah loves'er okay."

Bill frowned and lit another smoke. He offered one to the boy. Garner took it and lit it off Bill's lighter. He was glad for the cigarette and hoped that the painful interrogation was over. He wanted to get out of there, but he settled back in his chair and tried to relax a bit.

"Hawk, I want to ask one more question. Now, I'd like an honest answer. Of course you don't *have* to answer, but I wish you would. Take your time and think about this: I want to know if you would want *your* mother to work for Billy Ray—for Terry."

Garner bolted straight up in his seat. "Man, what'choo—talkin' 'bout?"

"Think about it."

"What'cha mean, man?" Garner blurted, his voice getting louder.

"Take it easy, now! *Cool* it! I'm not putting your mother down, boy. I'm asking you a question about her—and *yourself*. Would you want her at Billy Ray's place working?"

"Sheet," Garner whined irritably, "ah—ah ain' got nothin' ta do wit'—none a' that shit—them gals. Ah mean, they ain' *ma* bid'ness."

"I didn't ask you that."

"Gawddamn, man, me'n Terry jes' *works,* thass all. Ah mean Terry cruise—an' *ah* ride sometime, thass all. *Ah* deals poker!"

"Look, Garner, I just want to know how you think you would feel if your mother worked for Billy Ray."

Garner stared at him fixedly. His thick mouth quivered. He ducked his eyes.

"Well, then, maybe you *would* like her down there! Maybe you *would* like to see your mother on the street." Bill studied the boy intently.

Garner's head rose up slowly, his eyes blinking several times. He began to shake his head, slowly at first, then vigorously, in quick, jerky movements. "Naw," he said in a grating tone. "Naw. Naw, man."

Bill stood up and put out his cigarette. He took out a handkerchief and wiped his face. "C'mon, boy," he whispered. "Let's go across the street and get a cup of coffee and a sandwich or something. I'm buying. What do you say?"

That night things were slow at the club. Garner sat at the bar, smoking a cigarette and nursing a highball, listening to a steady flow of chatter from John as he worked the bar. "Yeah, baby, that's what niggers got to do, hit some of these white folks in the head. Know what I mean? Shit. I mean, Charlie's been fuckin' with us a *long* time, and niggers been takin' it. Time now we get started beatin' somebody's ass. We need another riot, that's what we need—we're goin' to get one, too, I'm tellin' you. Only this time we ought to fuck up Charlie's *own* neighborhood—shoot some white cops. White man won't listen if you don't hurt him. And I mean hurt him *bad,* too, tear up his house, hit him in the head. Shit, *kill* a few!"

Garner smiled idly, watching the little man stack some bottles of liquor. John kept right on talking. "This town never had a riot, man. We've got to give them one—like we been doin' other places. That's what niggers have to do, man, beat Charlie's ass. You should have seen what this brother said last night on the T.V., man. 'If a honky puts his hands on you,' he said, '*kill* him! Don't demonstrate and don't hesitate! Just kill the fool!' Yessir. Now, *he's* makin' sense." He stopped for a moment and rubbed a hand over his shiny process. "Shit, man, that nigger told those reporters like it is. One of them says to him, 'Do you believe in violence?' and this soul brother says, 'Man, violence is the American *way,* and baby, I'm a *good* American.' Then the cat gets evil and says, 'If you had a gun would you kill all the white people?' Guess what the brother told him." John was laughing now. "He says, 'I don't know about all that, baby, but if I got a gun right now, I just might kill *you!*' Well, gawddamn, man, this white cat was hot as a bitch then. Could hardly talk. Kept sayin', 'Yeah, boy. *Yeah,* boy,' over and over. He wanted to say somethin' else, but this nigger caught him right at the end of the show."

Garner laughed and sipped his drink. "Sheet, ah ain' nevah let no white cat fuck wit' me, man."

"Can't do it, baby. You should have seen this white reporter, man. Gawddamn, was he *evil!* I'm tellin' you!" John shook his head, chuckling as he leaned across the bar.

"Sheet, too bad that nigga *didn't* kill the mutha-fucka."

"Yeah. That's the truth. Yessir, baby, that's the natural truth," John agreed and mixed himself a rum collins. "Man, you know, white folks ain't shit. Got to come down here and buy black pussy. Scared to ask a white bitch, no lie. And you know white women like to fuck, too, man. Drop their drawers in a *minute!*"

"Sheet, evah'buddy like ta fuck, man."

"Shit, yeah, baby, but white folks're scared to admit it! That's why they buy it, see? That way they can *use* the pussy and forget about the woman. Don't even have to *admit* they're buying a woman, then. I guess white folks don't feel like they can live unless they buy whatever they want. Christ, they don't want to *fuck* a woman, they want to bust their *nuts!* See, if you really fuck a woman, you have to treat her right —like a woman—a *person*—see? She has to bust her nuts, too. You have to make love to a woman, can't just pop your nuts and roll over." John held up briefly and took a long pull from his drink. "Course, you got to be *able* to love a woman if you want to make love. Have to love to fuck, see, and be glad to admit it, *proud* of it, man. White folks're ashamed to fuck; that's why they have to buy it, like I said before."

Garner ground his cigarette out and finished his drink. "Say, John, you gotta gal, man?"

John smiled. "Hell, boy, I got a *wife!* Are you kiddin'? Got a Jap gal straight out of the land of the rising sun. Love that woman, too, baby. Shit, she loves me so strong, I couldn't have a gal if I wanted to. Leave that to you youngbloods."

"You got a motha?"

"*What?* Watch that shit, now, boy," John laughed. "You and me'll have to wrestle here in a minute. Why you gettin' on my family, man?"

"Naw, man, ah ain' bullshittin', fa' crissake."

"Well—*yeah,* man, course I have a mother. What kind of a question is that? Naturally, I have a mother. Jesus Christ!"

"You love'er?"

"Shit yeah."

"Yeah."

"Why?"

The puzzled look on John's face stopped the boy. Embarrassed, he slid off the stool and pretended to yawn. "Guess ah bes' see what's happ'nin' down below, man." He walked quickly out of the room.

Garner's thoughts were in a turmoil. He remembered Leroy's angry words—*selling black women*—and John talking about white men buying black women—and Bill. *Would you want your mother to work for Billy Ray?* That was a *lousy* thing to ask a guy, Garner felt—and

Leroy. Well—Leroy was a little crazy. Wasn't he? Sure he was. He was crazy. And he talked funny, too, and he was going to school, going to get married. *Selling black women.* He was nuts. Garner scowled as he started slowly down the stairs. Bill talked funny, too. But it didn't sound funny coming from him. Well—sure, it sounded funny, but that was how he talked, that's all. But he wished Bill hadn't asked him about his mother like that. After all, he wasn't selling anybody. No. He was a dealer.

Time and time again, during the days that followed, while he worked, or cruised the streets with Terry, or when he woke up in the middle of a bad dream, made love, even while he was eating, he caught himself thinking about *selling his mother!* Then he transferred that idea to black women—girls in the street, at parties, or a girl whose body he was about to enter—had entered, and he'd howl silently that *nobody was selling anybody's mother!* Then: and nobody was going to sell his, either. He argued that Billy Ray's girls were *working.* That's all. And what of it? They were well paid, weren't they? Maybe it was worth—*"Ah don' like Sy, Momma."—"Ah don' like him, neither, baby."—"Momma, why Sy—how come he touch ya like he done?"*—Why did Bill have to ask him that? A *lousy* thing —*"Ah jes' deals, thass all."* Making money, too. *Yes!* Billy Ray was making plenty of money, too. What did Leroy make going to school and talking like a sissy? What did Bill make? What did they *have?* Nothing, that's what. Right. There it was. Nobody sold anybody's mother, anyway. That's what Bill was talking about. *Selling black women* to white men like Leroy said. Okay, Billy Ray—*sold*—some—women. *Okay!* That was Billy Ray's business—*"Ah jes' deals!"*—Terry? Well, Terry—Well, he worked—worked *with*—the girls. *He's a pimp*—No! *You work with him—"Ah jes' deals!"* Well, maybe—maybe selling girls was better than buying them. *You work with Terry* —would Terry sell his mother? *That* was a lousy question to ask. A *lousy* question. Garner thought of Carol, Jackie, and the others—they aren't mothers. *They aren't even girlfriends!*

Sometimes when he and Terry went to a party, Garner would stop and stare at some of the girls. He might imagine a white man fondling

Carol's breasts—*The man's fat, white hands passed over his mother's breasts*—and he got an uneasy feeling in the pit of his stomach. Billy Ray *did* sell women, and Terry helped him—*and you*—no—and John—so what was *he* talking about?—and Sam, and Willi, and Marie. Even the cops were in on it—*everybody!* Would they sell *his* mother? No—*liar—you know they would!* Bill and Leroy shouldn't talk like that—a lousy thing to say. Leroy was crazy—Bill didn't have to say that—John—

"Hey, man," Terry laughed one night as they drove up to the club, "you dreamin' agin, nigga."

"Naw ah ain'."

"Sheet. You ain' heard a thing ah said all night, nigga."

Garner frowned, resenting his brother's intrusion into his thoughts. "Sheet," he mouthed without knowing it and continued his mental struggles.

"Hey, nigga?" Terry cried impatiently, banging the steering wheel and shaking his head. "C'mon, wake up, man! Git wit'it, fa' crissake."

Garner got out of the car. Using—*mothers?* Using mothers, girls who might—or should—become mothers, or lovers, whose bodies had been used, handed around in return for a few dollars? *Now there it is*—the same thing John talked about—*you have to be able to love a woman if you want to make love.* You have to love—*woman.* Woman was special, woman was female—what made life so special just by making it *possible!* Woman was—*would you sell your mother?*

"Gawddammit, ah'm talkin' ta you, nigga!"

"Huh?" Garner grunted, bending over to look into the car.

"Nigga, ah said, ah got bid'ness! Be busy fa' 'while, see?"

"Yeah, okay, Terry. Ah know what's happ'nin'."

"No, ya don', man."

Garner tried to focus on what Terry was saying. "Huh?"

"Whyn'choo stay by Ma's ta-nite?"

"Man, what tha fuck ya talkin' 'bout, fa' crissake?"

"Ah'm talkin' 'bout bid'ness, man! Gonna be busy ta-nite."

"Huh? So what, man? You alla time got bid'ness. Why ah gotta move home? Wheah you gonna be?"

"Gawddammit, y'ain' gotta move home, nigga. Jes' fa ta-nite—fa' 'while, ah'm sayin', thass all. Ah tol' ya, ah be busy."

"So fuckin' what, Terry? Fa' crissake, go wheah ya want, man! Ah wanna git me some pussy ta-nite, anyways. Man, what's wrong wit'-choo?"

"Nigga, ah tol' ya not ta be askin' 'bout ma bid'ness."

"Aw, fuck you, Terry," Garner growled and walked around the car and up onto the sidewalk.

"Fuck you, nigga. Look, ah tol' ya ah wuz onta somethin' big. Well, ah'm right *in* tha shit now, man. May be 'way fa' 'while, see?" Terry shifted his weight around to look out at Garner, sighing in exasperation. "Ah cain' be tellin' ya nothin' else, now, man. Jes' do like ah tell ya. Ah ain' back, ya jes' go on up ta Ma's, a' some place."

"Ain' thatta bitch?" Garner said, staring down at his brother. "Man—ain' thatta mutha-fucka, now? Sheet."

"Anybuddy ask ya anythin', tell'im ah'm cruisin'—ah wuzn't feelin' good, head all tore up, an' ah mighta gone home. Ya heah?"

The Buick dug out hard. Garner shook his head and went inside.

At four o'clock the next morning, Terry hadn't returned. Garner got up from the poker table and went out to check his box with Willi. While the big man counted the money and paid him his share, Garner watched the girls drift in off the street. It was late. Business was dropping off sharply. The white hunters were going home. Garner counted his money idly, then pulled a healthy roll of bills from his pocket and added to it the eighteen dollars he had just collected. Where was Terry? he wondered. Well, who cared, anyway? He left Willi and started down the hallway.

"Hi, baby," Carol called to him. "Where's Billy Ray Jr.?"

"Huh?"

She laughed and took his hand. "Where's Terry?"

"Who gives a fuck?"

"What're you so mad about?"

"Nothin', girl."

"Well, what're you barking for?"

"Sheet, girl, what'choo talkin' 'bout?"

"Aw, don't let's fight," she whispered softly, pressing against him, her pretty, dark face aglow with a smile. "Carol doesn't want to fight. Business was good tonight, baby. Carol feels good." She kissed him on the cheek. "Feel cuddly. Wanna cuddle with Carol? Carol wants to cuddle. Okay? C'mon, turn off the deep freeze. You're going to hurt my feelings, baby. Shoot, I thought you like to be with Carol."

"Naw. Terry—ah dunno wheah Terry is. He cut out. Tol' me ta stay somewheahs else ta-nite."

"Well, so what? We'll go up our place." She moved her body tighter against his, sliding her soft arms around his neck, and kissed him lightly. Then her arms tightened. He felt her breasts and thighs straining against him. Her mouth began to work insistently on his. Some of the people coming through the hallway smiled at them. Garner closed his eyes, wrapping the girl in his thick, long arms.

"There," she breathed huskily. "Wait a minute. I'll go get Jackie." She disengaged herself. "Just be a minute, baby." She headed for the stairs.

"Shirley workin'?" he called after her.

Carol turned to look back. "What?"

"Wheah Shirley?"

"I don't know. Shoot, she's hardly ever on the street anymore. Why? You got snow fever tonight?"

"Sheet, girl—git Jackie an' c'mon."

That afternoon he took a taxi back to Terry's. He looked for Terry's convertible, but it wasn't there. When he turned to watch the taxi drive away, he saw a sleek, black Lincoln parked across the street. Two men, one of them white, were sitting in it. The white man looked over at him and said something to his companion who quickly turned to take a look, himself. Garner frowned and glanced about awkwardly. He finally noticed that his fly was open, and grinning foolishly, he spun around, looking up at the sky, and zipped it closed. Behind him, a car door slammed, and then another. He turned and saw the two men who had been sitting in the Lincoln standing beside the car talking and smoking. They were tall, lean men, nattily attired in dark suits and topcoats, their light hats sitting forward on their heads at a jaunty, careless angle. Garner smiled, turned, and jogged up the stairs.

Wondering casually where Terry could be, he paused in the living room and threw his sport coat on the sofa. Then he went into the kitchen and opened the ice box, looking for something cold to drink. He found some milk, but it was sour. After pouring the milk into the sink, he drew himself a glass of water. There was a knock at the door. With a shrug, he walked through the living room and opened the door.

Hard steel smashed into his face, knocking him backward into the room. Another blow slammed him between the eyes, blinding him, and something else hit him in the mouth. He felt himself falling and tried to right himself, but his body wouldn't obey. Lights whirled and popped inside his head as quick, grinding bolts of pain shot through him. He fell on his back and something hit him in the groin. His head cracked against the floor as he struck out instinctively with both feet, his fists flailing. Another blow to the groin sent terrible shivers of agony knifing through his stomach and legs and forced him to double up. A reddish haze spread before his eyes, then dimmed and buried him in darkness.

A flood of cold water revived him. He blinked, trying to see through the blood and water in his eyes. The pain was worse now. His groin and thighs throbbed with an ache that burned white-hot, and there was blood in his mouth. The first thing he saw was the muzzle of an ugly, black .45 staring between his eyes. Instantly, he froze on the floor, his body jerking and quivering despite his efforts to lie still. His heart trip-hammered in his chest. The police had him, he screamed silently, the *fuzz!*

He stared at the gun, squeezing his eyes in an attempt to focus on it. The bore looked enormous, black and deep. It was a thick, heavy automatic. A hard, black face smiled down at him. A voice behind the face said, "There's no one else here." The voice came closer and Garner saw a white man, pale, with a thin, cruel mouth. He was blond. "No clothes in one of the bedrooms," he hissed.

"Well, that figures," the black face answered calmly.

"That's a *big* bastard right there, you know that?"

"Yeah. But he's smaller now."

"Looks like a sensible fella, too—reasonable sorta."

The black man laughed. "Yeah. Now, he's gonna get up—aren't you, baby—and be real sensible." He stood up and motioned to Garner to do the same.

Garner rolled over on his side and struggled to get his legs underneath his body as needles of pain worked into his spine. The two men pulled him up roughly. Garner thought he was going to vomit. Blondie picked the sport jacket up from the sofa and threw it at the boy.

The black man gently clicked the hammer down on the .45. "Relax, baby," he chuckled. "Just relax and don't be in a hurry to do *anything,* see? We're all going down the stairs and into the car, and then we're going to go have a talk, see? You keep cool." He waved the gun casually, then, with a shrug, he slid it out of sight under his coat and grinned at Garner. "Now you see it, now you don't."

"Shall we go?" the white man asked and opened the door.

"Wheah we goin'?" Garner gurgled, swallowing blood.

A terrific blow behind the ear knocked him across the threshold to the floor.

"Aw, gee, now you've hit him again," the black man said.

"Well, he don't know how to relax."

"Aw, sure he does. Don't you, baby? C'mon now, let me help you up from there." The black man yanked him up and made a great to-do about smoothing the boy's clothes. Then he spun him around and hurled him through the door. Garner stumbled and caught at the railing to keep from falling. After escorting him down the stairs, they led him out to the black Lincoln and shoved him inside.

Blondie drove. The other man was in the back seat with Garner. It was quiet in the car. Garner stole a look at the man beside him. He averted his gaze when he noticed the smile working at the corner of the black man's mouth. His blood raced, and he ached all over. He wondered what the police wanted with him—*something Terry did, maybe?* What? Where *was* he, anyway? He set his face straight ahead, his eyes flicking about the car. Momentarily, he thought of jerking the door open and leaping out. *But, no,* he tried to calm himself. *Take it easy.* The Lincoln stopped for a traffic signal. Garner stared at the light blond hairs on the driver's neck, then he scowled and continued to look over his surroundings.

His thoughts were muddled now. The car was beautiful, roomy, with all leather seats, cigarette lighters in the ashtrays, and curtains on the windows. *These men aren't policemen!* Cold fear crawled in him. Where was *Terry?* This looked bad—*well, at least the police didn't have him.* Carefully, slowly, he turned his eyes toward the man sitting next to him. An impassive, hard, black face met his gaze. Quickly he looked away. Suddenly, he hoped they *were* policemen, because—but they weren't. Garner sighed and looked through the window. It was nearly dark, but he didn't notice, didn't see the cars passing close by on either side, lights in the windows, or the people hurrying along the sidewalks.

He began to refocus his thoughts when the Lincoln wheeled by Billy Ray's club and shot into an alley beside the place. Blondie stopped the car with tires squealing, jumped out, and opened the door for him, making a grand, polite gesture as he said, "Outside, fella."

The black man pushed the boy out. They walked by a row of empty rubbish barrels to a small door. Blondie opened it and shoved Garner into a dark passageway. Garner could hear voices as he followed the black man through the narrow hall and Blondie pushed him along from behind. They went up a short flight of stairs and into a well-lit suite of rooms. Garner was deposited in a chair in a large room, and Blondie and his companion stood on either side of him.

A white man who was standing by the window, watching them, called out, "They're here," and was joined immediately by two more white men who came from an adjoining room. Garner didn't recognize any of these men. A tall, yellow man, wearing a mustache and a new, very conservative and neat process, followed. Garner recognized him; it was Billy Ray.

He heaved a sigh of relief, he was glad to see someone he knew.

"You work for me, don't you?" Billy Ray stated matter-of-factly, unconsciously fingering his elegant clothes as he stood before the boy and stared down at him.

"Yeah," Garner answered quickly. "Yassuh."

Billy Ray frowned and sat down in a large sofa, facing the boy. The man who had been near the window and the other two white men stood just behind the sofa staring at Garner. One of them, Pat, a heavy, ruddy-faced man with thinning brown hair, asked, "This is the kid's brother?"

Billy Ray nodded. "You're Terry's brother, aren't you?"

"Yeah," Garner said nervously. "Wheah he at?"

A short, thin man laughed, "We expect to know that directly."

"We want to know where Terry is," Billy Ray explained to Garner. "When did you see him last?"

"Ah ain' seen'im," Garner said in a voice he barely recognized.

Billy Ray shook his head unhappily and stroked his mustache. Then he nodded to Blondie who immediately dealt the boy a vicious smash to the back of the neck. Garner's eyes watered quickly as the pain exploded in his head.

"C'mon now," Billy Ray urged gently. He smiled and stuck a cigar in his mouth. The short, thin white man pulled his lighter out and lit it for him. "Thank you, John," Billy Ray acknowledged. "Now then, let's approach this thing logically, young fellow, so we can get everything clear in our minds. Pete and Georgie there are going to work on your foolish head until you tell us what you know. Do you understand that?"

Garner nodded dumbly, a sick feeling spreading through him as he looked furtively around the room. His gaze focused on a petite blond lounging against a doorway to his right and behind Billy Ray and the three white men. She was smiling and smoking a cigarette, her filmy negligee offering an arresting view of her body underneath.

Billy Ray stopped talking and turned to follow the boy's eyes. He scowled when he saw the girl. "Leave us alone and shut the door," he ordered.

She shrugged and turned to go.

Garner stared at her white legs moving under the thin dress.

"I said shut the door," Billy Ray ordered, his voice rising. The door closed quickly. "Now," he continued, "did you understand what I said, Hawkins?"

"Yeah," Garner whispered, and then he attempted to strengthen the quality of his voice, "but—but, ah ain' seen'im, ah tell ya! Ah ain'!" He cringed in his chair as he spoke, peering nervously up at the thin-faced blond man, who had raised an arm to strike him again.

"Easy, Peter," Billy Ray cautioned. "Now, Hawkins—it's Garner, isn't it?"

The boy's head bobbed up and down quickly.

"Okay, Garner, didn't Terry bring you to work last night?"

"Yeah."

"All right, then. Where did he go after he dropped you off?"

"Ah dunno!" Garner croaked, his heart pumping furiously.

Billy Ray sighed and spat a bit of cigar tobacco. Pete slammed his fist against the side of the boy's head and knocked him out of the chair. Georgie kicked him in the belly and drew his foot back to do it again, but his boss's voice checked him.

"Garner," the man started again as he smoothed a wrinkle out of his well-tailored suit. "This could become extremely unpleasant. Now, I realize you want to protect your brother. This is only natural. Certainly we don't wish to, in any way, alter your loyalty toward him. He's family. But let's try to look at this—philosophically. A great deal of money has apparently been misplaced. And one of our girls—a very attractive girl, I might add—has suddenly chosen to leave us. Coincidentally, Terry is gone, too. Now, we don't *have* Terry, Garner, but we do have *you,* see? And, as you can well understand, we are somewhat disturbed about all this, and—we would appreciate it if you would give us whatever assistance you can in locating your brother."

Pete and Georgie picked Garner up and pushed him back into his chair.

"Hones'," Garner pleaded with tears in his eyes, "ah ain' seen 'im since last night!" He hesitated, seeing the blank look on Billy Ray's handsome, yellow face. "No lie, Mistah Ray, ah ain' seen 'im!"

The man smiled and said, "Call me Billy, please."

"Jesus, Mistah Ray—uh, Billy, Terry don' tell me *nothin'!* Ah don' know wheah he at!"

Billy Ray wrinkled his brow thoughtfully and looked around at the three men behind him. "What do you think?"

John shrugged. "I don't know. Terry *was* pretty close-mouthed."

A tall man, who had not spoken before, cut in. "If he knew anything, he'd probably be in on it, and if he was, he would have taken off."

"Aw, for Christ's sake, he's lying," Pat snarled. "Jesus, if you'd just let some of *my* boys work on the—boy, *we'd* find your money, and that whore, and her boyfriend, too."

Billy waved his cigar at him. "Listen. If we ran our affairs as inefficiently as you cops, we wouldn't be in business five minutes. I don't think he knows anything," he declared impatiently.

"Okay, then."

"I agree."

Billy Ray shook his head. "Okay, get him out of here."

Pete and Georgie hauled the boy to his feet. Garner groaned; he felt sick.

"Want us to lean on him some more, or lose him, or what?" Pete asked in a flat, calm voice.

Garner looked up in panic.

"Don't be ridiculous," Billy Ray snapped. "Just let him go—and, Hawkins?"

"Yassuh?"

"You don't work here anymore. Understand?"

"Yassuh!"

"How old are you, boy?"

"Sixteen."

"What? You're six*teen?"*

"Yassuh."

"Dammit, that's not what Terry told Willi. Sixteen years old—well, how would you like to see *seven*teen?"

"Huh—Mr. Ray?"

"How's your memory, boy?"

Garner hesitated, looking around fearfully at the others, feeling Pete and Georgie gripping his arm tightly. *"Bad,"* he whispered.

"What?"

"Ah don' know *nothin'!"*

"Fine," Billy Ray said seriously. "You in school?"

"Huh? Naw."

"You quit?"

"Uh—yassuh."

"Well, go back, Hawkins, hear? You go back. Keep your nose clean. You're O.K., Garner. Don't get yourself into any trouble. Understand?"

"Yassuh."

Pete and Georgie dropped Garner in front of Terry's place. He stumbled groggily from the car and stood on the sidewalk, his back to the street, hands at his sides, staring at the pavement as the black Lincoln pulled away. He stayed there for a while in the cool night, shaking his head in bewilderment. Occasionally, a passer-by hesitated as if about to help him, then walked hurriedly by. He didn't see them. He simply stared down at the ground, head wagging from side to side.

The pain had calmed to a steady throbbing. His face was puffed and swollen, but his mind wasn't on that, or the pain. He was thinking of Terry. Where was he? What money was Billy Ray talking about? How much?

He wished Luther was back. He thought of Buzz then, and cold nausea tightened in his belly. "Gawddamn," he muttered weakly aloud. "Wheah's Terry, fa' crissake? What's tha nigga *done?*" He remembered the ride back with Pete and Georgie and the way they had laughed and joked, chatting amiably as he cowered silently in the back seat alone. A shudder swept over him. *Where was Terry?* He stepped uncertainly toward the dark apartment building and started carefully up the stairs. All at once, he realized that he felt very tired.

Monday morning, Bill Chamberlain's phone rang. He stuffed another piece of bacon in his mouth, looking wonderingly at his wife as she put her fork down, reached up behind her, and took the receiver from the wall. Bill watched her plump, pretty face as she spoke into the phone.

"Hello?" A smile flashed quickly across her dark features, then a look of fear, and disbelief, was in her eyes. Wordlessly, she thrust the phone at her husband.

Bill frowned and took the phone. "Yeah? Hello. Yeah, Shorty—what? Oh, *Jesus!* Are you sure? Jesus, God—yeah. *When?* Jesus Christ almighty! Look, let me get the paper. What? Yeah—okay. Okay, Shorty, yeah." He dropped the receiver on the table and ran to the front door, yanked it open, and grabbed the newspaper.

He found what he was looking for near the bottom of the front page—TWO SLAIN. And he read: "The bodies of a man and a woman were found by state troopers late last night in an abandoned convertible on Route 2-A. The man has been tentatively identified as Terry Hawkins, a Negro, 19, of this city. The woman, white, is believed to be Shirley Noonan, 24, formerly of New York. The pair are believed to be the forty-third and forty-fourth victims of the underworld's violent and macabre form of jurisprudence. Police authorities say that no leads as to the identity of the killer, or killers, of Hawkins, or Miss Noonan, have as yet been found. The killing was executed in typical gangland style: each victim was gagged, hands tied behind his back, and shot once through the head—" There was more, but Bill didn't read any further. He reread the victims' names and folded the paper with great care and went back inside the house.

Terry Hawkins, Bill pondered, sitting back down at the kitchen table. Well, if it wasn't the police, it had to be somebody. He looked at his wife; she was staring at him, her face stricken. God, he thought—*and Garner?* A ripple of fear trickled up his back, bringing him out of his seat on the run.

His repeated and insistent thumping on the door of Ella Hawkins's apartment brought no response. He continued knocking, however, even though he realized that nobody was home. Finally he stopped and looked at his watch. It was nine-thirty. He frowned and turned around, shaking his head in a helpless way, and headed slowly down the stairs. Nobody home, he fretted. Well, they probably knew about it by this time. But where was Garner? Was he all right? God, he must be. What had his brother gotten himself *into?* What did he get *Garner* into? According to the police, there were no leads. What a laugh *that* was. As long as the cops got their slice of the pie, there *wouldn't* be any leads, either. Well—he cursed himself for not finding out where Garner and Terry lived, then his thoughts rambled on. He hoped the boy was safe. *He had to be!* "Dammit," he said aloud, "I've got to get him out of that *zoo* down there." He hustled down the front steps and strode quickly over to his Ford.

Late that afternoon, Leroy burst into Bill's office. "You heard about this thing, huh?" he blurted, pulling up a chair, his bearded, white face taut with anger.

Bill nodded quickly. "Yes, I have. Damn shame. Cops in this town are nothing. We'd have less problems without them. Have you seen Garner?"

"No. Mrs. Hawkins is going nuts."

"Yeah—I'll get over and see her tonight. Damn shame."

"Yeah—well, with one dead and one inside, and Garner headed the same way, what can you—"

"Just a goddamned shame."

"The fuzz fingered them, you know."

"What?" Bill asked incredulously.

"Sure. The word was on the street before they were even found."

"That's the payoff, for pete's sake!"

"These honkies are low, Bill. You know that."

"Yeah—you know—sometimes I just want to—I get the feeling that all hell is going to bust wide open around here. Honest to—"

"You *know* it, baby! Black folks're getting evil."

"Ought to be, man. I wish I could find Garner. I'm worried."

"What about?"

"What about?" Bill cried. "What're you talking about? Man, they just murdered his brother, didn't they? Garner worked with Terry, didn't he? C'mon, Leroy!"

"There's no sweat *there,* Bill. Garner's out of it."

"How do you know that?"

"The street. All they did to Garner was lean on him a little bit, that's all. He's okay."

"I'd still like to see him. Who was the girl?"

"A whore—white girl."

Bill lit a cigarette. "She his girl?"

"I guess so. She lived with him for a while, or something."

"Yeah? Well—I wonder what Garner will do?"

"What? Oh. I don't—"

"Think he'll go home?"

"What for?"

"What do you mean, 'What for?' "

Leroy shrugged. "What's home ever done for him?"

"I don't know—hell, nothing, but it's all he has."

"Yeah. But he's not going back home now."

"What makes you say that?"

"It's—not in the cards."

Garner heard it from the radio while he was eating a hamburger at a diner near the apartment. He wasn't listening at first. A local disc jockey had been playing a loud, pounding kind of music which threatened to make itself heard over the raucous din made by a mob of kids and truck drivers competing for a late afternoon snack. Except for some stale doughnuts, he hadn't eaten at all Sunday, and he told himself that he had to be hungry.

But he discovered that he *was* hungry. The smell of french fries and meat cooking licked deliciously at his nostrils, and a pretty, yellow-skinned girl worked behind the counter with buoyant enthusiasm. The man beside him, a black, slick-looking fellow with processed hair, kept up a steady patter of small talk.

"Hey, baby," he said to the waitress, his voice barely audible against the furious, driving music blaring from the radio and the noise of the people around him, "gimme piece a' that theah pie. Les' see's it sweet as you." He smiled at her when she gave it to him.

She turned away, rang up his money, and drew a cup of coffee for another customer while he grinned and stared at the taut roundness of her buttocks under the white uniform.

Garner was watching her, too. Then the music stopped. Through the sounds of cups and spoons, slamming doors and the cash register, Garner heard it: "—found shot to death last night. The youth, a Negro, has been identified as Terry Hawkins. The other body is believed to be that of Shirley Noonan, a young white woman—" Now he listened desperately. The bread and hamburger meat stuck in his throat. His mouth was open. A voice screamed in his head, *"Gawddamn, they done it!* Jesus Christ! They done it! *Them fuckin' bastids killed Terry!"* No—couldn't be. No way—and Shirley. He thought of Pete and Georgie, Billy Ray's handsome face and peculiar way of talking. In a fierce instant, he vowed vengeance, "Ah'm gonna git'choo mutha-fuckas, ah git'cha! You gonna pay fa' this!" He got up from his stool without paying his bill, hamburger in hand and pushed his way through the crowd. A happy jingle was playing on the radio, then came, "Next news at six o'clock," and Garner hurled the door open and charged into the street, not hearing the counter girl's voice, "Hey, Mistah—*hey!* Hey, man, y'all ain'—"

He raced on, fairly flying through the darkening shadows, over the cement and asphalt, hurtling between cars and honking horns and the angry curses of people he bumped into. He wasn't sure where he was going. Then he saw the police station lurking between two run-down tenements, its single, grim light above the entrance, glowing feebly in the faded afternoon—POLICE.

He had been running for nearly five minutes. He stopped, sprawling against a lamp post, gasping and staring at the place. Sweat poured down his black face as he hugged the post, trying to recover from the effects of his violent effort. His right hand felt sticky. Bits of onion and crumbs of bread and meat, mustard and relish, were plastered all over it. He wiped the hand on the post.

Garner had never been inside a police station, and now he was frightened. What could he tell them? Images from years past came to his mind—a red-faced cop, beating Terry to his knees—other cops hanging around the bookie joints, taking payoffs—and Billy Ray's cops, his associates—*Pat.*

Looking across the street at the police station, he knew he couldn't go in there. *No!* There was no way. They weren't there to protect *him* —or Terry! No, if he went in there, they'd beat his brains out, get word to Billy Ray, then turn him out into the streets. *Why, he'd be killed!* And he wouldn't accomplish anything. His eyes filled with tears. A sense of terrible loneliness cut into him. Billy Ray wasn't in on it, anyway. Neither were Pete and Georgie. No, it was a contract killing. *Forget it.* His body wilted against the lamp post. The weight of his sixteen years in the city seemed about to crush him. "Mutha-fuck tha whole worl'," he cried. *"All* you rotten mutha-fuckas should *die!* Gawddamn—ah wish ah could cut'cha balls off—an' ya tits, an' ya hearts, an'—ah wish ah could kill ya *all,* an'—" Abruptly, he thought of Carol's pretty, dark face, and Jackie. Then he was running again, slower this time, looking for a taxi. Soon he gave up that idea and just ran and ran and ran on, away from the thought of his dead brother, away from Billy Ray, and away from the police.

It was dark when he stomped his weary way up the stairs and knocked at the girls' door. There was no answer. He looked at his watch: six-thirty. Carol and Jackie should have been home. He knocked again, angrily now, beating the door with large, black fists.

"Stop alla that bangin'," a squeaky, irate voice called out. "Who down theah? What'cha want?"

Garner stopped and listened. It sounded like a woman. "Carol," he yelled, "an' Jackie. They lives heah."

"Naw, they don'," came the angry reply.

"Huh? What'cha mean? Sho' they lives heah."

A wizened, old black woman appeared on the stairs above him, clutching a shabby robe about her meager person. "What'choo mean, boy? What'choo makin' alla that theah noise fa'? Them gals is *gone!"* Then she cackled down at his sweating, puzzled face. "This town done got too warm fa' them hincktey who'es. They *gone,* boy! They gone, an' good riddance, ah say. Yassuh, comin' an' goin' alla time, day an' night wit' them fancy clothes. They who'es, thass what. Damn nigga who'es. Y'all git on outta heah befo' ah git tha law on ya."

"Huh? Sheet, woman—"

"G'wan, nigga. Git!"

"Aw—*fuck* you, ya black-ass, fuckin' ol' bitch!" Garner yelled up at her.

She screamed at him, "Git outta heah, nigga! Git'cha black ass outta heah!"

"Ah ain' black as you, *bitch!"*

She waved her arms frantically then, her thin voice crackling in a furious, birdlike wail. "Sheet, gawddamn you, nigga boy! Ah ain' no black nigga—ah'm Portugee! Ah ain' no nigga! Git on outta heah wit'cha! Nigga ain' shit, no way! Ain' *shit!*"

Garner started down the stairs. "Fuck you, woman! Yo' fuckin' pussy's so ol' an' black, an' nasty, wouldn't even a dyin' dog fuck ya, ya mutha-fucka, ya fuckin' nasty black bitch!"

He walked a long time, aimlessly. Tears came. He struggled against them, but they persisted, flowing over his swollen face, making dark streaks on his skin. Squinting ahead, he could see part of the city skyline in dark outline against the blue-black, starless night. Lights from dingy old buildings split the darkness. And he walked.

"This is a bitch," he whispered aloud. "Tha shit has hit tha fuckin' fan. Man—they jes' kilt'im like a dog, thass all. An' ain' no-buddy gonna do nothin' 'bout it—not even—*me.*" The tears poured freely then, and he didn't try to fight them.

He stopped walking in front of his mother's house. A number of cars were parked outside. Lights shone all over the building. He saw a police cruiser there. A policeman was sitting behind the wheel, sleeping peacefully. Garner started to go into the building, then hesitated, debating whether he should. His jaws tightened as his legs, almost involuntarily, carried him up the steps.

The apartment was crowded with people. Bill Chamberlain was there, and Shorty Rollins, Leroy and Janice. There was a policeman there, Harry—and his mother. She was crying hysterically. He heard her over the muffled voices of the others as soon as he entered the kitchen. Bill rushed over to him, ahead of Shorty and Harry, and took his arm, staring with astonishment and pleasure up into his face. Garner let himself be led into the living room.

His mother saw him and heaved herself up from the sofa and into his arms. "Thank *gawd,*" she cried. "Thank gawd-a-mighty."

Harry helped pay for the funeral. It was a modest affair. A minister whom Garner had never seen before spoke fire and brimstone, pain, love, and peace over the coffin. Garner was thinking of Buzz that morning as Terry sank into his deep, dark hole, and he wept openly in the warm sun which had followed the cold rain of the night before. He took no notice of the tiny cluster of black, brown, and yellow faces gathered around the gravesite, didn't see Leroy standing behind his mother as she wept in Harry's arms. Buzz's grave was dark, too, he noted, and like death, it was forever.

Later, his mother held his arm, and he walked with her and Harry back to the limousine. Garner's mind was full with death then. His thoughts grappled with the finality of it and the transient, flimsy nature of life, and people and their relations with one another. Shirley was dead, too. And Carol and Jackie were gone, vanished, running scared—perhaps to a new town. They'd find another place, live—play—their deadly, futile game. Then what? Garner felt his insides shriveling. Suddenly, he felt very small, tiny, less than an ant. A sense of helplessness came over him, and he knew he was terribly insignificant—minute, a leaf fluttering in the wind as it drifted away from a tree in a huge forest.

"Ah ain' shit," he cried soundlessly. "Ah mean, *nothin'*, jes' nothin' at all. Ah could die ta-morra, wouldn't mean shit, nothin'. All us niggas heah could die, git kilt, an' who gives a fuck? An' ain' none a' us gonna be heah long, neither—" He looked about the cemetery—"Sheet, trees live longer than people. Yeah, like that one, startin' ta grow agin, like it gonna do evah yeah—like nevah dyin'. Aw, Jesus."

He wiped at his tears as they approached the limousine, a long Cadillac, its black paint shining like still water. It stood between trees and shrubs which stretched their bare, thin branches skyward, their new buds glistening with the promise of rebirth. New life, new vigor, and energy were pounding vibrantly through every living thing around him—except the people. Soon, this quick, irresistible growth would be green, and it would thrive. And the trees and shrubs would be cared for, too, cultivated, nurtured, fed, and pampered in order to encourage the greatest possible strength and beauty from each. It wasn't like that with people, he thought, especially black people. No, when people got sick, or old, and their bodies withered, they died—and were only dead, cold and gone. There was no spring for people, no regeneration, no sun to drive the new sap of life through the human tree. They were dead.

Sunday morning, Leroy drove Garner over to Terry's apartment to pick up his clothes. It was a quiet morning, and a cool whisper of wind had preceded the sun's warmth. There were few people on the street, and as the Chevvy bore them on, Garner felt lonely. The city was very still. Nothing seemed to be moving. It looked different to him now. He had never thought about it before, but the city was dirty. It was old and grim. Some austere, mad architect had created this towering, ugly mass of brick and concrete while in an insane rage. He had jammed one structure into another just like it, setting them close to narrow streets which twisted and wound their way crazily across each other like a bunch of angry snakes.

"What are you going to do with Terry's stuff, Hawk?"

"Ah dunno, mos' gone. Terry took it wit'im."

"Yeah."

"Ah keep tha hi fi an' T.V. Don' need tha resta tha shit. Mebbe *you* find somethin' you want."

"Yeah, maybe. You going over Bill's this afternoon?"

"Ah dunno."

"Should go. Gail sets a good table."

"Ah don' really feel like goin', man."

"Well, you should go. It should be nice. Your mother going?"

"Naw, man. She don' wanna see nobuddy."

"That's understandable. What time did Bill say to come over?"

" 'Bout two."

Leroy glanced quickly at him then. "Are you still working for Billy Ray?"

"Naw."

"Good. I'm glad you quit that foolishness."

"Didn't quit. Tha mutha-fucka fired me. Black som'bitch. Wish tha nigga would die, gawddammit."

"Yeah. You know, Hawk, I never thought you'd move back home—"

"Ah wish alla them mutha-fuckas would die, gawddammit, an' alla they fam'lies, too—. What'cha say, Leroy?"

"I said, I didn't think you'd move home again."

"Aw, yeah—well, me neither. Ma kinda got on me 'bout it. An' what ah'm gonna tell'er? No? Sheet, she wuz *all* tore up, man. What ah'm gonna tell'er?"

"Yes—that's right. She's had a difficult time. I'm glad you didn't disappoint her." Leroy stopped the car in front of the building where Terry's apartment was.

"Say, man," Garner said as they got out of the car, "why you talk so funny?"

"What do you mean, Hawk?"

"Why ya talk so funny, man?"

"Why do you ask a question like that?"

"See, now, thass what ah'm talkin' 'bout. How come ya do that, Leroy, talkin' so proper, kinda?"

They went up the steps into the building. "Well," Leroy began thoughtfully, "it's hard to explain—I'll tell you about it sometime."

Garner cleared his belongings out of the apartment quickly. Then he and Leroy carried the record player and the television set down the stairs and loaded them into the back seat.

"Did you lock the place back up?" Leroy asked when they finished.

"Who gives a fuck? C'mon, man, les' split."

They climbed into the car, and Garner looked up at the apartment building. He frowned when he felt the tears coming. Pretending to have something in his eyes, he poked at them furtively with his fingers. Terry was dead, he thought, dead.

Some people walked by, a yellow-skinned man, a black woman and three small, brown boys. They were all dressed up for church. Garner watched them talking and laughing as they strolled along, and remembered his mother as she held him in her arms, her voice breaking with anguish and relief—*"Thank gawd! Thank gawd-a-mighty."*

Leroy pulled the Chevvy out into the street. "No," he was saying, half to himself, "I didn't think you'd go back home."

"Huh?"

"I said—I mean, I don't think Luther would have gone back."

"Oh. Naw, man—well, sheet, ah dunno. Lutha's a hard stud."

"Do you have any money, Hawk?"

"Yeah."

"Well, that's something, anyway."

"What'cha mean?"

"Well, you have to have a *little* dough, you know. You'll need something to tide you over."

"Huh?"

"Money, Hawk—green stuff—you're going to need it. Good you have some to keep you going."

"Sheet. Yeah, ah guess so. Ah'm home now, though. Ah ain' goin' nowheahs."

"It'll come in handy, Hawk. You'll need it to see you through while you're looking for a job."

"Huh?"

"You *are* planning to work, aren't you?"

"Huh, man? Sheet."

"Well, what else do you have in mind? You going back on the street?"

"Sheet—who gives a fuck, man? Ah dunno."

"Yeah. Listen, Hawk, my bag's on the floor in back. Can you reach it?"

Garner reached down behind him. "Yeah."

"Open it up. There's a paperback in there somewhere—soft-cover book. It's kind of beat-up."

"Don' see it."

"It's there. Keep looking."

"Ah got it," Garner announced, glancing casually at the book's title—*The Negro Past: A Renaissance*. "Man, this thing fallin' apart. Heah." He handed it to Leroy.

"Guy gave it to me back in the army."

Garner stared through the window, not answering.

"Listen, Hawk, how're you getting over to Bill's? Taxi?"

"Ah dunno if ah'm goin', man."

"Do you need a ride? I could come around about one-thirty and pick you up."

"Aw—don' sweat it, man."

"It's no sweat, baby. Janice and I are going out, anyway. We're celebrating."

"Huh?"

"Yeah. I murdered my exams, baby. Listen, how about it? I'll pick you up. What do you say?"

Garner moved his big shoulders in an indifferent shrug. "Ah guess so. Shit, yeah, Leroy. What tha hell."

After they carried Garner's things into the house, they stood on the hall stairs, talking. Leroy idly ran his long, white fingers over the broken plaster in the wall. He paused then, slowly rubbing his fingers together to flick off some dirt and bits of plaster.

"Thanks fa' tha ride, man," Garner said and lit a cigarette, watching Leroy pick at some bare lathboards.

"Listen, Hawk, I wish you'd do me a favor."

"Sho', man. What'cha need?"

"No big deal," Leroy replied, pulling the tattered old paperback from his coat. "Uh—man, I'd like for you to take a look at this—before I come back for you."

"Huh?"

Leroy frowned. "I'd like you to look at this book—just—kind of look it over."

"What'cha talkin' 'bout, man?"

"Nothing. Will you do it?"

"What fa'? What'cha mean, man?"

"Man, just open it and look at it, will you? Tell me what you think of it."

"Sheet."

"Here, man, take a look at the thing."

Garner finally accepted the book. He went up the stairs into the apartment. There was no one in the kitchen. He threw the book on the table, opened the refrigerator, and pulled out a cold piece of fried chicken and bit into it. Harry came in.

"Wheah Ma?"

"Lying down. Want some cold milk with that?"

"Naw."

"How about a beer?" Harry offered, tying his robe.

"Naw."

Harry shrugged and went to the refrigerator. He took out a can of beer. Garner watched him pop it open. He noticed the clock: ten-fifteen. He had plenty of time to clean up and get dressed. Still munching on the chicken, he stood up and went through the parlor to his bedroom. Terry's television set and his hi fi were on the bed. Garner finished the chicken and threw the bones in the waste basket. Then he put the T.V. on a small table near the window, hooked it up, and turned it on. The new clothes that he had brought back from Terry's place were on the bed, too. He started hanging them up in the closet.

Harry appeared in the doorway. "This yours?" he asked, holding up Leroy's book.

"Naw."

"Where'd it come from? It's a helluva book."

"Leroy," Garner replied and picked up the record player.

"Helluva writer," Harry said, putting the book on the bureau. "Knows everything about black folks."

"Huh?"

"Leroy marked some of the stuff. Guy says the Egyptians were black, the Moors, too. He says—"

"Huh?"

"—white folks don't want to admit it. Says black folks did everything white folks *think* they invented before a lot of white people learned to read and write! Isn't that something? Tell Leroy I have to read it. I'll buy it off him if he wants."

"Sho', Harry."

Shortly after one o'clock, Leroy walked into Garner's bedroom. "Hey, Hawk, get dressed, man. Aren't you going?"

Garner didn't say anything, but swung his feet onto the floor and sat up on the edge of the bed, his eyes riveted to the book. Leroy watched him. Garner was holding the little book with both hands as if he was about to wrestle with it. His eyes were narrowed to tiny slits, jaws tight. The thick, black mouth was set and grim. His eyes moved very slowly and carefully over the words.

Amusement flickered in Leroy's eyes and worked its way across his white face, tugging at the corners of his mouth and twitching in his heavy whiskers. He unbuttoned the jacket of his one good suit, a well-worn brown worsted, and checked his watch. "It's late."

Garner looked up at him, blinking. "Man—Leroy, you b'lieve alla this heah shit? This nigga *crazy!*"

"Why do you say that?"

"Man, who gonna b'lieve this shit heah?"

"What?"

"This shit, man. Jesus *Christ!* Heah—yeah—heah tha nigga say the first good fighter—baddes' cat, man—wuz a nigga. *Sheet!* An' *this* shit, man—'bout Africa—nigga armies beatin' peoples' asses, an' buildin' shit in tha jungle, schools, an' roads an' evah'thin'."

"Do *you* believe it?"

"Sheet, man—nigga crazy!"

"Do you *believe* it?"

"Man, ah ain' no asshole, gawddammit. Heah." Garner handed the book to Leroy. "Sheet," he continued as he stood up and looked at his watch. "Nigga fulla shit, man. Hey, ah gotta git dressed. Be wit'cha in a minute."

Leroy nodded and watched him go across the parlor into the bathroom. He walked over to the window and stood tapping the worn paperback gently in his hand. Below in the street, some children were playing tag. A thin, fair-skinned boy fell, sprawling on the dirty sidewalk i. his clean Sunday clothes. He was almost as fair as Leroy. A black boy jumped on the kid and slammed both hands down against his back, then took off on the dead run. The fallen boy leaped to his feet and lit out after him. The other kids scattered into alleys, up steps, and over and between the parked cars. Leroy watched them and scowled. He heard someone behind him and turned around. Garner sat on the bed and started tying his shoes.

"Look at this, Hawk."

A look of near disgust crossed Garner's face. He finished tying his shoes and then, with a gesture of exasperation, he snatched the book from Leroy's hand.

"Read right there—where it's underlined."

Garner sighed in resignation and started to read: "So as a white man, I began my—" Garner glanced quickly up at Leroy and then back to the book. He flipped it over and checked the author's name—Aaron David. Turning back to his place in the book, his flat, black face scowling, he read again: "So as a *white man*—" He stared at those words for a moment and shook his head, then he stood up and gave the book to Leroy without saying anything.

"C'mon," Leroy prodded quietly. "It's ten minutes of."

The afternoon was light and warm as they drove over to Bill's house. The bright, shining sun had heated the day, burning off some of the heavy moisture. Several people strolled along the sidewalks and cruised leisurely in their cars. The city seemed alive now, dirty and old, massive and ugly—but brimful of the people who lived in it. They passed a tall black man and a boy who were washing a red Mercury. A coffee-colored woman sat on some steps near them and chatted with a small, copper-colored girl.

Garner sat in the back seat of the car. He peeked at Janice's glowing, black skin. She was sitting up front beside Leroy. The sun washed brightly against her cheeks. She looked pretty in her elegant, light-blue dress. She smelled good, too. The car was filled with the heady scent of her perfume. It reminded him of someone. He thought of Carol. No, it wasn't her. Someone else, he decided, a long time ago. It was the same smell, gentle, disturbing, a clean, woman smell. What woman? He watched the girl's bright, dark face sparkle as she laughed at something Leroy said and punched him playfully on the arm.

"Hey, Leroy?" Garner started hesitantly. "Did Harry see ya?"

"Yeah. Why?"

"Nothin'. Said he wanna look at tha book. Harry *like* ta read, man. Nigga alla time lookin' at somethin'. You goin' back up theah, man?"

"Where?"

"Up tha house?"

"Oh. No—won't have the time."

"Harry say he wanna see it, man."

"Well, I told him he could."

"Harry wanna look at it bad."

"Well, okay, he *can.* I'll bring it by."

"Ah bring it back wit' *me,* if ya want."

"Well, I—"

"*You* don' hafta worry 'bout it, man. Ah see Harry git it."

"Well, okay. I mean, I don't see any reason—"

"Yeah, ah see he git it. Harry wanna read that book real bad. Ah kin give it ta him fa' ya." Garner paused then, his eyes darting quickly toward Janice who had turned to look at him, smiling.

Bill Chamberlain lived in a neat, red brick duplex on a quiet street near the Y. He saw the Chevvy drive up and looked at his watch: two-fifteen. "He's here, honey," he called out.

Garner was somewhat inhibited when he first sat down to eat, but when he saw Bill and his family dig in, he followed suit. He had never seen a spread of food like this; the table was covered with delicious food: roast beef, tossed salad, black-eye peas, rice, collard greens, and sparkling rosé.

"Man," Garner chuckled after sipping his wine, "this stuff fizzes."

"Like it?" Gail Chamberlain asked.

"Man!" Garner grinned and chewed away happily. Occasionally, he glanced around the table, making sure that no one was watching him too closely. At times, his eyes lingered on Gail Chamberlain. She had dark, rich, brown coloring, and a neat figure, plump and soft-looking. Her hair was black, cut short and carefully groomed. She reminded him of Janice—and someone else, too. Her breasts pushed full and strong against the soft pink and white of her dress. Garner felt uncomfortable when he looked at her body like that, particularly when he felt the quick warmth in his stomach. He kept checking to see if Bill noticed his furtive looks. He issued himself a silent warning, "Awright, now, nigga, this *Bill's* people heah. Gotta cool it, baby.

Nigga could git'is ass kicked ovah bitch like this." He grinned then. "Yeah, this man beat ma ass, if he heah me thinkin'."

The woman looked up at him, and he hurriedly shifted his gaze to the children, to Joelle, ten, slender and brown, and Billy, who was twelve. Joelle nibbled at the tiny bit of wine which she had begged from her mother and wrinkled her nose at him. Garner smiled, remembering how she held out her hand to him when he met her—*"I'm Joelle," she announced without a touch of shyness. "Jo. And this is Billy. He's my brother." Billy's thin face clouded with indignation, and he yelped, "I can introduce myself, girl!"*—Garner winked at Joelle, who giggled and went back to her food. The table was quiet, except for the tinkle of silverware against the dishes.

Then Garner suddenly saw Luther's face, the mirror of his own, and his mind started clicking like a strange slide projector, snapping off shadowy images of his mother, Harry—and Terry. *Terry,* he pondered, and Buzz. He paused, his fork halfway to his mouth. Leroy and Janice were probably eating now, too, he thought. He stole another look at Bill's wife and wondered if Leroy had ever slept with Janice. He tried to picture the girl without any clothes.

"Would you like some more wine, Garner?" Gail Chamberlain asked.

"Huh?"

"How about some wine?"

"Oh—yeah."

She took his glass and handed it to Bill. He filled it, and she took it back and put it down next to Garner's plate. Then she stood up. Garner watched her, and somehow, he felt sure that Janice had never been to bed with anyone. His black face twisted into a frown. *Who did she remind him of?*

"Still hungry, Hawk?" Bill asked as the children followed their mother into the kitchen.

"Huh? Aw——naw. Naw, man, ah—"

"Give me your plate, boy, and stop the foolishness."

A silly grin brightened Garner's face as he held up his plate. Bill dished him up some more black-eye peas, rice, and greens, then cut him some of the roast.

Garner cackled appreciatively. *"Man!"*

Gail Chamberlain came back and sat down. "The kids're having their ice cream and pie in the kitchen," she said.

Garner started peeking at her again. She caught him at it and smiled, and he looked away quickly and bent closer to his food. Then he thought of Bill making love to his wife—*anytime he wanted to!* Leroy and Janice would be like that. Suddenly he was conscious of the book in his pocket. "Say, Bill, man," he ventured.

"Yeah, Hawk?"

"Who wuz tha Moors?"

"What? The *Moors?* Well, they were Arabs, invaded and conquered Spain. Why?"

"Wuz they niggas—ah mean, wuz they cullid?"

"Well—yes, many of them, Hawk," Bill replied thoughtfully, glancing at his wife.

"Wuz they Afrikins?"

"Yes. Yes, they were. Who's been talking to you about the Moors?"

"Uh, Leroy. Uh—man, who wuz Homah?"

"Homer? Homer—was an ancient Greek writer."

"He was a Greek," Gail Chamberlain offered quietly, "a writer. Before Christ was born."

"Oh. Uh—did he write 'bout Afrikins? 'Bout niggas—cullid people?"

Gail looked at her husband and put her fork down. "Well, yes, I suppose he did—in *The Iliad*—yes. Something about Ethiopia. He wrote *The Odyssey,* too."

"Whuzzat?"

"Another book."

"Naw, ah mean, what he wuz writin' 'bout."

"Ethiopia?"

"Yeah."

"It's a country—a black country—in Africa. Homer had a very high opinion of the people there, as I recall."

"They do any fightin'?"

"I'm not sure I know what you mean."

"Did they fight wit' armies?"

Bill cut in, "Certainly. Why?"

"Ya mean, they hadda army?"

"Of course—still do."

"They ain' all dead?"

"No, man."

"An' they hadda army?"

Bill frowned. "Yes."

"An' they Afrikins, huh?"

"Yes. Listen, Hawk—*everyone* has an army. I mean, all countries—all peoples. See?"

"An' Afrikins, too, huh?"

"Of course! Hell, many of the most powerful countries in the ancient world were black African countries: Egypt, Nubia, Ethiopia, the Sudan—"

"Wuzn't them places white?"

"No! Why would they be white—I mean, in *Africa?"*

"Ah thought they wuz white. In tha movies—"

"Hawk," Bill said, "some Africans—well, okay, you asked about the Moors. Now, they were Arabs—Moslems, and as a matter of fact, Janice and her people belong to a Moslem sect, the Black Muslims—and, see—How can I explain this? Well, some Africans—African Arabs—look like Leroy, and some look like me—or *you."*

"What—*yeah, man?"*

"Garner, what Bill means," Gail said, "is that the difference in color and things amongst Africans—and the Moors—are like the differences between southern Italians and northern Italians, or Spaniards and Swedes."

"An' some a' them looked like Leroy—an' Bill, huh?"

"Yes," Bill breathed heavily.

"An'—an' *me,* too?"

"That's right, Hawk."

Reading Leroy's book was an arduous task for Garner. He had never read a book before, and his vocabulary was so limited that he seldom came across a sentence in which there weren't one or more words that he didn't know. He complained about this to Harry when he asked him if he had finished the book.

"Ah cain' read it fast."

"Why? What's the matter?" Harry asked and sat down on the sofa.

"Ah don' know alla words, man."

"So get a dictionary."

"Huh?"

"A dictionary."

"Oh. Sheet, man—ah ain' got none."

"Well, I do. Course it's only a pocketbook, but it's better than nothing. Hell, after three days you should have finished that thing."

Harry went into the bedroom. A minute later he was back with the dictionary.

Garner took it and leafed through it idly. "Sheet," he moaned after a while. "Ah cain' 'memba alla this shit, man."

"Hell, boy, you don't have to. When you come to a word you don't know, write it down and look it up, that's all."

"Man, ah be alla time lookin' fa' words then."

"So what? Look, if you can't read the book, let me see it, will ya?"

"Ah kin read tha fuckin' thing. Sheet."

Garner frowned and went into his room and started reading again. But the dictionary made it *more* difficult, and he found his efforts slowed from a walk to a crawl. Sometimes, the definitions of words were set down in language he couldn't understand. Then he had to look up the words in the definition. And he couldn't pronounce many of the new words, either.

As the week wore on, he discovered another problem: frequently, he couldn't understand or conceive of a word's meaning even if he could understand the words which defined it. These were things like: *polemic, a priori, mythological, metaphysical, empirical, viable,* and so many others. What was *objectivity,* or *subjectivity?* It was hard work. Too hard.

Saturday Ella and Harry found him lying on his bed, and there were tears in his eyes. "What'sa matta?" she asked, glancing down at the book on the floor with its pages falling out. "What's wrong wit'-choo, boy?"

"Nothin', Ma."

"What'cha cryin' fa'?"

Garner turned his face away. "Ah ain' cryin'. Ma eyes hurt."

"Ya gotta col'?"

"Naw."

"What'sa matta, then? Don'cha feel good, honey?"

"Yeah, Ma. Ma eyes hurt, thass all."

"Frum readin'?"

"Huh? Naw—yeah, Ma, frum readin'. Yeah, ma eyes hurt."

"Ya oughtta git some sleep."

Garner shrugged and closed his eyes. His mother left the room.

Harry sighed and sat on the bed. "What's wrong, Hawk?"

"Nothin'."

"Aw, c'mon, Hawk. C'mon, c'mon. Is it the book?"

"Naw, man—yeah—ah mean," Garner started in a whining, angry voice, opening his eyes to look at the man, and holding up his hands in a helpless way. "It's them fuckin' words, Harry, them mutha-fuckin' *words!* Ah mean—ah *wanna* read tha gawddamn—. Fuck it."

Harry nodded. "I see. Well, are you through with the book?"

"Fuck it."

"Yeah. Well, I'll read it, and if you want it back—"

"Ah don' want it back, neither. Ya kin keep tha fuckin' thing."

Harry gathered the book together and stood up. He walked over to the door and stood there, tapping the book against his leg. "Listen, Hawk?"

"What?"

"How about reading it together?"

"Huh?"

"We'll read it to each other—take turns writing down the words."

"Sheet."

It took Harry two weeks to drag Garner to the end of that little book. The work was painful, but it was done. When they finished, Garner held the book in his hands looking at it in awe. "Man, that wuz a bitch, ah'm tellin' ya. But this cat tells tha shit right, like it *really* is."

Harry smiled. "Why don't you read it by yourself, some of it, I mean? Use your word list. Review it first, then read a little."

Garner read the whole thing. During five tough days, he and his word list and Harry's dictionary made the trip again. Every morning, before he started reading, he reviewed those strange, tongue-twisting words. And he discovered, to his delight and amazement, that the further he went into the book, the easier his progress was made. When he came to the end of the book, he read it again. He learned to love it.

"Sheet," he told Leroy one day in front of the Y. "Ah read tha whole fuckin' thing in a day now, man."

Leroy laughed. "Like it, huh?"

"Man!"

"You can keep it if you want to, Hawk."

"Naw—ya mean it, Leroy?"

"I mean it."

"Man, don'cha want it no mo'?"

"I don't need it anymore, Hawk. Listen, I've got another one I'd like you to see. How about it?"

" 'Bout niggas?"

"Yes."

"Wheah's it at?"

Leroy opened his satchel and took out a brown, hard-cover book.

Garner gaped at it—*The Black Soldier*. "Gaw-awddamn!"

"I have to get this one back."

"When, man?" Garner asked, opening the book.

"Oh, don't worry about that. You can take your time with it. I just want to keep it, that's all."

Garner and Harry devoured that book in just three days. When they finished it, Garner went into his room and started rereading it. He finished it Monday morning. Then he reviewed his word list, had his lunch, and headed for the Y, swinging the book at arm's length as he walked. The book made him a little self-conscious, but he felt good, satisfied, yet strangely expectant.

Bill Chamberlain stood at the front desk, talking to Janice. "Just the man I'm looking for," he called to Garner when he walked in. "How're you doin', Hawk?"

Garner grinned. "What's happ'nin', man? Janice?"

"Hawk, I need a favor—some of your time."

"What'cha mean?"

"I need some help down here evenings. Mr. Lewis, the guy we have on the front desk, has had a little trouble with the kids—I mean, he's an old man, and the kids busted up a few things, see? I hoped you might help us out."

"Sheet, man—ah mean—"

"Are you busy evenings?"

"What?"

"Do you have something else to do?"

"How many nights ah gotta come?"

"Whatever you can spare. Of course the pay's next to nothing, but I'd sure appreciate it."

"When ah start?"

"Hell, tonight, man. How about it?"

Garner shrugged. "Sho', man, okay."

"Crazy. Come by about six. I'll introduce you to Mr. Lewis and show you what we want."

Garner nodded. Bill went down to his office. Garner leaned against the front desk, idly leafing through the book. A while later, he looked up to see Shorty Rollins coming. There was a slender, crew-cut white man with him.

"Hello, Mr. Rollins," Garner greeted him.

"What's happening, Hawk?" Shorty said. "Hi, Janice. Bill busy?"

"Hi. He's on the phone. Won't be long."

"Good. Oh, listen, Janice, this is Tom Peterson."

"How do you do, Janice," the man said to her, extending his hand.

"And this is Garner Hawkins. He's—"

"Glad to meet you—*Hawkins,* huh? You play football?"

"Yeah. Ah mean, ah use ta."

"At Technical High School?" Peterson asked, opening a leather folder he was carrying.

"Yeah," Garner answered.

Peterson ran his finger over a list of names in the folder. "*Right.* Hawkins, Garner. Brother, you're big enough, that's for sure. What do you weigh now?"

"Ah dunno."

"They've got you here at six two, one ninety. Must have grown some, fella."

"Take it easy, Tom," Shorty said, smiling. "Garner's only a junior."

"Hell, that'll change."

Shorty laughed and grabbed his arm, pulling him along. "Man, that can wait. Let's catch Bill before he cuts out somewhere."

Garner frowned and bent his body across the counter, wondering why Tom Peterson was carrying his name around on a list like that. He watched Janice step smartly about her cabinets and equipment, carefully appraising her fine legs. It occurred to him then that he hadn't been near a girl in weeks.

Leroy arrived. "Hi, baby," he greeted Janice and patted Garner on the shoulder. "How're you, Hawk?"

Janice smiled. "Hi."

"Say, Leroy, ah got'cha book heah."

"What, Hawk? Oh. Don't you like it?"

"Yeah, man. Me'n Harry finished it."

"Really? Crazy. You know, I've got some more, if you want to see them." Leroy opened his satchel and put the book inside. "But I don't have anything with me right now."

"When kin ah git'em?"

"Well—I mean—okay, *now*—couple of minutes, if you want to take a ride up Freedom House with me. Don't have much time, though. Have to be to work at five."

"Sheet—uh, shoot, man, les' go."

Leroy laughed. "Okay. Wait a minute." He took Janice by the hand and walked her down the length of the counter to the corner and leaned across to whisper something in her ear. She giggled and gave Garner an embarrassed look.

Seeing them like that, Garner fidgeted uncomfortably. He wondered where Carol and Jackie were now. Then it occurred to him that

Carol and Jackie did not have what he wanted—not everything he wanted, anyway. They were—*forms of recreation.* His relationship with them was a transient thing. There was no love in it—affection of a kind, perhaps, and fun, but no love. It was love-making, playing at love—playing at life, like getting high, or drunk, that's what it was, and the next day he could drop dead, they would vanish, run away and hide—find some other recreation. He thought of Shirley then, her sparkling blue eyes and finely chiseled face. And *Terry.*

Freedom House was in an old, worn building. Children, of various shades of black, brown and yellow, swarmed over the front steps. There were children inside, too. A few of them ran over to Leroy, yelling, and pushing their way between him and Garner. A small, brown girl threw her arms around Leroy's waist, peering up at him as they walked along the hall. "We gonna read another story?" she begged. "Huh, Leroy?"

"No, chicken, not now. C'mon, you run along. We'll read again tomorrow." Leroy started walking again. "Some of my kids," he said to Garner with a touch of pride.

They came to a bulletin board—ARE YOU BLACK?—Garner stopped—ARE YOU PROUD OF IT?—WE ARE—Garner stared at the board, fascinated—BLACK IS BEAUTIFUL.

A little yellow-skinned boy ran into Garner and careened away. "Sorry, Mistah." He looked over his shoulder, giggled, and started running again as two boys turned a corner, darted between Leroy and Garner and ran after him.

"Man," Garner whispered, staring at the board—FREEDOM NOW, BABY—FREEDOM NOW—FREEDOM NOW—. There were pictures, too: a magnificent black athlete, the angry face of an old, bearded, black man between two burning spears—*Jomo Kenyatta*—a beautiful black girl, with an Afro and a white bikini which glowed against her ebony skin—Garner smiled—BLACK POWER—SOUL—.

"Hawk, it's four o'clock," Leroy interrupted and pulled him away from the board.

At a quarter to six that evening, Garner skipped down his front steps and hurried over to the Y. Bill met him out front. "Now, look,

Hawk," he explained as they went inside, "I have to take off—be back later—so, briefly, let me give you the lowdown. Number one: no kids are supposed to be in here on weekday nights. At six sharp we clear them out. That's because of supper, school, and what-have-you. So, at night, it's only adults. Now, some of them will try to sneak back in. They're not afraid of Mr. Lewis, because he's old, and the Y's too big for him to track them down and throw them out. There're too many places to hide, see? That's *your* job. Number two—and this is important: Mr. Lewis is responsible for this entire building during the evening. He runs the place, okay? So, what he says goes. Understand?"

"Yeah."

"Any questions?"

"Naw."

"Okay, c'mon. I want you to meet Mr. Lewis."

"How long ah gotta stay?"

"Building shuts at ten. You can cut out about nine-thirty. How's that?"

"Okay, man. Thass cool."

"All I can pay you is a buck and a quarter an hour. Okay?"

"What?" Garner's tone was incredulous.

Bill stopped in the lobby and turned to look at him. "There's no money in the budget for this as it is," he said testily. "You don't *have* to—look, I could use some help, Hawk."

"Man," Garner groaned. Then he smiled.

"Well?"

"What? Oh. Okay, Bill. Listen, man, y'ain' gotta pay me nothin'—"

"No," Bill said, holding up his hand, "we'll pay you what we can. When things quiet down, you can find something to read, if you want."

"Ah got somethin' heah." Garner showed Bill the new paperback that Leroy had given him.

"Du Bois, huh? Great man. Another one of Leroy's?"

"Yeah—well, frum Freedom House, frum tha lye-berry."

"What did you think of the place?"

"Aw, man, that place is somethin' *else!* Evah'thin's black up theah. They got them signs all ovah. Black is *hell* up theah, man! They got—"

"Did you meet Andre?"

"You mean tha cat with tha beard, tha blind cat?"

"That's him."

"Yeah, man. Cat had them Afrikin' clothes on. But you shoulda seen this *gal,* man! Seck-a-terry a' somethin', big broad, too, an' fine. Almos' big as me, wit' them heels on. Chick was outta sight. Got a Afro, too, baby. She looked—"

"That's Chana," Bill chuckled and opened the door to the lounge.

Later, as Bill was leaving, two small black boys ran up the walk. He caught one of them and held him, calling the other one back. Garner caught the second boy in the lobby. The kid tried to break away, but Garner hauled him up off the floor. The boy kicked his legs and thrashed his arms about uselessly.

Mr. Lewis, a small, brown man, came to the corner of the front desk and stood watching them. "Okay, Gary, what're you gonna do now?"

"Lemme go," the boy wailed.

Garner toted him outside and set him down. He grinned at Bill.

The boy glared up at him. "What'choo *doin',* man? You lee-me 'lone! What'cha think ya doin'?"

"Now, look, boy," Garner said, "y'ain' s'posed ta be in theah now. So, git 'long, man. Take off, see?"

"Sheet! Who you, man?"

"He's the fella who just told you to get out of here," Mr. Lewis called from the doorway.

Garner looked up to see the boy Bill had run off peeking around a corner of the building. "Yeah. Now, split, ya heah? An' ah mean both a' ya."

The other boy ducked back out of sight. Bill shook his head and left.

Mr. Lewis yelled, "Go on. C'mon, Gary. Go on home."

The kid backed away from Garner and stuck his tongue out. Then he ran out to the sidewalk and yelled at them, "Fuck you, ol' man, an' you, too, ya fuckin' black nigga!"

Garner started for him then, but held up to watch the boy light out across the street. He frowned as the kid stopped at the entrance to an alley to make a face and give him the finger. Garner shrugged and went back inside.

By the time Bill returned, Garner had chased kids upstairs, downstairs, into the gym, and through a men's volleyball game, into the pool area and locker rooms, and even through the boiler room and maintenance area. "Man, this job is tough," he complained to Bill. "Them kids work ya ta death, fa' crissake—ah mean—well, shoot!"

That night, after grabbing a late snack, Garner sat on his bed to watch television. He hadn't looked at the tube for a long time. He wanted to relax for a while. Harry and Ella were at work. There was an old movie on, but he had seen it. He switched channels, and a pretty blond woman tried to sell him a television set. Garner opened up the new book and looked through it. Another commercial started on the T.V. screen, and a full-throated woman's voice told him that if she had only one life to live, she wanted to live it as a blond. He looked up and saw a tall, dark-haired man usher another blond woman into a sleek, new convertible. He shut the set off and lay back on the bed.

When Harry and Ella came home, Garner was reading. He could hear someone fishing around in the refrigerator. It was probably Harry, he mused, looking for a can of beer. Garner stopped reading and picked up his word list. A ton of words, he thought, pages of them.

The door opened, and his mother came in and sat down beside him. "You gonna hurt'cha eyes readin' so much, baby."

"Ah'm okay, Ma."

"Whyn'cha git some sleep?"

"Ah'm *okay,* Ma."

Harry appeared with his beer in hand. "You know it's going on two o'clock, boy?"

"Yeah. Any more beer?"

"Here, you can finish this. Why don't you put that book down and get some sleep. We can go at it together in the morning, get back to it bright and early."

Harry and Ella left the room. Garner took a long drink from the can of beer and continued reviewing his words.

He was still dressed when he awoke. The pages of his word list were on the floor, and his new book lay between his legs. He yawned and looked at his watch: seven-thirty. Outside, a car horn howled. Then a door slammed, and he heard tires squealing. Sitting up on the bed, he started in on the book again. Thirty-one pages done, he pondered, *it's getting faster now,* over ten pages an hour. A satisfied grin split his black face. He put the book down and lit a cigarette, his eyes wandering over his room. For a moment, he stared at Terry's hi fi. Buzz's face focused slowly in his thoughts. Garner closed his eyes, pushing the image from his mind. Terry appeared then. Garner shook his head and went into the kitchen.

Terry wouldn't go away. Garner leaned against the sink, drinking a glass of milk, and tried to think of something else. *Terry,* slick and smooth, the cool one, the guy with all the answers, was deep in that cold, dark earth. *Well, who's crazy now, you or Leroy?* Garner scowled.

Harry walked in. "Ready to get with it, boy?"

Garner nodded.

"Okay, just let me get some coffee working, and I'll be right with you."

Garner read the last one hundred pages of the new book in just under five hours. Saturday afternoon, checking his word list, he found that it had swelled to forty-six pages. Constant review enabled him to whisk through the words now, and his retention had begun to take a real foothold. Many of the words were a lot alike: *antecedent, precedent, recede, concede,* and others. Very often, he could determine the meaning of a word by the way it was used and by its similarity to another. But he continued to use the dictionary, because his word associations sometimes resulted in rather serious semantic problems: *primitive, prime, primary,* or *primordial.* But the list didn't overwhelm him anymore. His eyes flicked over it easily, and a buoyant, confident feeling rippled through him.

He finished the list and lay on the bed, stretching himself luxuriously. "Sheet, ah kin whip much ass now," he boasted to himself, laughing aloud as he thought about it. "Yeah, baby, ain' *no* book *ah* cain' whip. Ah be bad soon. Gotta see Leroy an' git me 'notha' fuckin' book, sheet. Ain' nothin' 'bout niggas ah ain' gonna know." He clapped his hands together, then jammed them between his knees and pounded his feet on the floor. "Shoot, man, anythin' ah cain' read, ah'm gonna fight wit' ol' Mr. Webster heah. Pretty soon, ah be fuckin' 'roun' like Leroy an' Bill. Yeah—*I* shall talk like them. Naw—I *will* talk in the way that they do." He frowned. It was hard to talk like that. His voice sounded odd, ugly and unnatural. Well, he decided, he didn't have to talk that way, anyway. He stood up and checked the time. It was three o'clock. He wondered where Leroy was. *Freedom House.*

Leroy was there. Garner found him sitting in the library reading to some children.

"How're you, Hawk?"

"What're you doing up here?"

"Nothin'. Jes' walkin'."

"Well, make yourself at home, baby. Take a look around. Want something to read? There's plenty here."

Leroy returned his attention to the kids for a moment, then excused himself and followed Garner over to the bookshelves.

Garner walked along the rows of books, running his hands over some of them—*The Black Soldier*—he smiled, saying to himself, "Yeah, baby, ah know *you."—Life With a Negro Regiment—A Brave Negro Regiment—The Black Cowboys*—Garner pulled that one down and opened it. Leroy stood beside him, watching, smiling faintly. It was written in simple language. After quickly reading a few pages, Garner noticed that he hadn't encountered a single word he didn't know.

A tapping noise came from the hallway. "Sounds like Andre coming," Leroy said. "That reminds me; I better find out what time he wants me to pick him up tonight."

A heavily bearded black man, with a cane, appeared at the door.

"Andre, what time do you want me to come by?" Leroy asked.

Andre was blind, a very black man, of average height and heavy, powerful build. He wore dark sunglasses and a flowing African robe and sandals. His hair was cut in an enormous Afro. The robe was simple, but elegant, colored light-blue. "Seven o'clock, baby. Didn't Chana tell you?"

"I haven't seen her today."

"Oh. Well, she ran a couple of errands for me. Who's that with you?"

"Hullo, Mr. Saint Pierre."

"Hawkins. How are you, man?"

"Good, Mr. Saint Pierre."

"You up here to steal some more of our books?"

"Yassuh, Mr. Saint Pierre—ah mean, ah'm lookin' at'em."

"Cut that out, man. What're you trying to do? The name's Andre. Okay?"

"Yassuh."

The exchange brought a smile to Leroy's face. "He was looking at *Cowboys*. I said he could borrow it."

"Well, that's cool, man. Listen, Garner, you come on down to the office, and you can look at some of my stuff. What do you say?"

"Shit, yeah—ah mean, yassuh."

Andre chuckled. "C'mon, baby."

The office was small and drab. There were books and papers everywhere: on the floor, on the shelves, the window sill, the chair in the corner, and even under the desk in the middle of the room. Only the desk top remained untouched by the disorder. It seemed to be the center of a powerful whirlpool of activity.

A girl sat at the desk typing. She was pretty, honey-colored like burnt-orange. "Hi," she sang out.

"Hello, chicken," Leroy answered.

"How's it coming, kid?" Andre asked. "Oh—you've met Garner here, haven't you?"

"Not really. How are you, Garner—Hawkins?"

"Garner, this is Chana Jackson. She's one of the kids who plays secretary around here."

"How do?" Garner said and went with Andre and Leroy over to a small bookcase.

"See if there's anything you like," Andre said, tapping the bookcase with his cane. "I don't use these anymore."

Garner squatted down to investigate, and Leroy leaned over his shoulder.

"Whuzzat about?"

Leroy followed Garner's finger—*Negro Philosophers.* "That's a little deep, Hawk. There's one though, *Negroes in the Ancient World.* That's history, easy reading."

"He can read them both," was Andre's recommendation.

"Yeah," Garner said.

"Okay, but you ought to finish the one you have, relax with something light before you get into this stuff."

"Aw, leave him alone, Leroy."

"Okay, boss. You heard the man, Hawk. Take them both." Leroy yawned. "I have to split, Andre."

"Okay, baby. Pick me up at the house."

"Right. Say, Hawk, can I give you a lift?" Leroy watched Garner stealing guarded peeks at Chana. "Hawk?"

"Leroy, why don't you bring him along tonight?" Andre said.

"Well—sure, if he wants. How about it, Hawk? Andre's giving a lecture tonight. Want to come?"

"Alla ya goin'?"

"C'mon," Leroy laughed and pushed the boy toward the door. "I'll bring him along, Andre."

Andre's speaking engagement was being held at City College. During the ride over there that night, Garner couldn't avoid pilfering furtive glances at Chana. She sat between him and Andre in the back seat. A luxurious African coiffure wrapped her orange and honey face in an abundance of shiny, black softness. Large metal rings dangled exotically from her ears. Her beauty amazed Garner. He sat stiffly, tight to his side of the car, trying not to put any pressure against her hip and thigh. He was extremely uncomfortable. He held his body rigid, muscles pulled tight, feet hard on the floor, knees together.

Whenever Leroy took the Chevvy around a corner, Garner pulled hard on the door handle to prevent himself from rocking against the girl. At times, lights from passing cars, buildings, and street lights quicksilvered through the car and danced excitingly along her legs, heating his guts and increasing his discomfort.

Leroy drove through a large, stone archway and continued up a narrow drive. Garner squinted through the window, trying to make out the buildings along the way. Leroy pulled the car over the hill and drove around a large fountain, by several cars, and people walking, and braked to a stop in front of a huge brick edifice. Garner vaulted from the car and stared up at the structure.

Bright yellow light splashed down from a balcony about halfway up in the center of the building. A steady stream of people, mostly white, moved up the long, wide steps which led inside. While the others climbed out of the car, Garner looked around wonderingly. Behind the building on both sides, he saw an ocean of cars, and men and women swarming amongst them.

"Man, Whitey's giving you a big crowd, Andre," Leroy observed.

"Well, if they want to hear it, baby, *I'll* sure tell it to them," Andre growled as Leroy and Janice guided him to the steps.

A noisy crowd filled the lecture hall. Most of the people there were white college students. Garner saw a number of blacks, too. A white girl, wearing a scarlet school blazer, seated them in the center of the hall, just three rows away from the stage. Four white men sat onstage with Andre. One of them, a tall man, partially bald, and graying, walked to the speaker's stand and blew into the microphone.

"Ladies and gentlemen—may I beg your indulgence? Ladies and gentlemen, please. Please—thank you. We are ready to start now. I'm Dr. Cohen—as some of you may know—from our College of Education, and with me on the stage, from the College of Liberal Arts, are my colleagues—"

When Andre was introduced, he walked carefully to the speaker's stand, assisted by Dr. Cohen. He whispered something to the white man, who then walked quickly offstage. A moment later, the lights dimmed.

Andre leaned on the stand in an unconcerned, almost casual way, and pulled the mike closer to his face. "It may appear to some of you," he began in a quiet voice, "that because I don't have any notes, I'm going to talk off the top of my head, so to speak. Well, I want to assure you that this is not the case. I—intend to earn my money, such as it is. I'm here to talk about social problems—race problems—in America. Yeah. Yeah, I'm going to talk about black people, and what I have to say is based upon the toughest, and the most thorough—if not scholarly—research available—experience. *Experience.* Yeah. Now, I want to warn you that you're going to find it difficult to understand what I'm talking about. This is because most of you are racists, see?" He paused to allow a ripple of surprise to spread in the audience. "Oh, yes, I said *racists!* Racists. Now, I'm not accusing you of anything; I'm stating a fact. Racist. A simple fact. I know you're racist, because if you weren't, I wouldn't have been paid to come here tonight and talk to you about black people. You'd already know, and—"

Garner listened in a stupor of admiration. Andre had tremendous, overwhelming stage presence. In his handsome African robe, with black stripes slashed zebralike against a white background, he presented an exotic, electrifying figure of a man. And Garner had never attended a lecture before. He stared at Andre and his great beard and African hair style, and he was awed.

Andre raised his hands in clenched fists and screamed, *"Black Power,"* then lowered his voice to an almost gentle, conversational level, "I say, is the only hope left to black Americans. Black Power is an interesting expression—*curious*—isn't it? Yeah. Take the two words apart and wait a few minutes, then say *black,* then wait a little longer and say *power,* and you have two harmless, do-nothing little words. Yeah. See, in America, power is a respectable enough word—but *black* isn't. No, *black is evil!* It isn't pretty, either, or handsome—*I mean, we all know that blonds have all the fun,* don't we?"—Andre paused to chuckle sarcastically then—"Yeah. Well, put those two words together and say *Black Power,* and someone calls out the National Guard, the C.I.A.—*the soldiers, man!* Oh, yeah. But the soldiers can't stop Black Power. No, sir—you know, the soldiers have been lucky, so far, because we haven't really set out to start killing you people—and them—yet. *But we will!* Yeah. We will, if we have to. And it looks as though we're going to have to. You know? Yeah. *We'll kill a whole bunch of you honkies, and your kids, and your mothers,* and—"

A collective gasp wriggled through the room. Garner smiled uncertainly, hanging on every word.

"—no, *the soldiers can't stop us,* and if you think they can, look and see what a handful of guerrillas can do to a city in Southeast Asia. Yeah. The big, bad white man, and some deluded, black idiots, all over there killing *colored people*—. Yes, you *should* die"—Andre stopped, momentarily, and drank some water—"You *should* die," he snarled, "and you will! And this stinking filth we call America will die with you. Now, I know that to some of you, these are the ravings of a weird-looking, mad, black extremist. Yeah. Well—I won't start on those guerrillas again—but mark this, white folks; your beloved America *will not survive—cannot endure,* unless this black-white thing *is* solved, *and the goddamn army can't do it,* see? Okay, I'll get back to Black Power—"

Garner sat up on the edge of his seat, leaning forward. Andre's voice began to soar, howling out of the mixed storm of dimmed lights and his own black manhood to come crashing down into the crowd from the speakers placed high along the walls. Garner inventoried his surroundings. A white girl sat mouth open, a film of shiny sweat on her forehead as she stared down at the speaker. A look of pure terror was on one white boy's face, and hatred on the face of another.

"—Black Power," Andre boomed, "means that black people have got to think black, act black, and *love* black. It is political, educational, sociological, legal, and economic. We will have political representation, educational representation—and the dignity and pride which you have taken from us with your vile folklore and your twisted and mythological history. Yeah, baby—*yeah.* We will have justice on the streets from your honkie cops and in the courts from your racist judges. And we will have jobs—*real* jobs: no more sweeping the streets, no more suckling your white brats, and no more will we shovel your manure against the tides or—we *will* burn this pesthole—

all of it—to the ground with you in it! Yes, we die, too! Yes—*yes!* But that isn't going to solve *your* problem! Yeah—yeah, Black—Power, baby. That's what I'm—"

Garner glanced at his companions. Leroy's white face was set, serious and hard. Janice stared down at the stage, entranced. Chana's face was calm, almost impassive, but her demeanor was serious and thoughtful. The audience was still. The only sound was Andre's thundering voice erupting from the speakers and slamming through the dark silence.

"—Black Power means that we blacks no longer wish to be integrated into your hostile, sterile, stagnant, *loveless* white America. Black people are no longer interested in being *white,* man. Yeah—no, baby, *you* keep all that. We don't want it—we don't want *you!*" Andre's hand swept out over the crowd as he continued. "Black Power *does* mean violence, *whenever* and *wherever* violence is required. If a white man puts his hands on a black man, intending violence to his person, the black man should kill him! *Kill him,* don't hit him! Don't talk! Don't come to City College and try to educate white folks! Just *kill* the bastard! Yeah. Black Power means black policemen in black communities in the same proportion as there are white policemen in white communities. *Yes, and black teachers*—we don't want your white teachers filling black kids' heads with hatred for themselves, either—and, above all, *Black History,* white folks, *Black Geography, Black Literature, Black Art, Black Music, Black Sculpture,* and with it all, *black—black—black* pride."

Andre stopped, drank some water, and wiped his brow. "Let's talk about violence again—*yeah.* Black Power has always been associated —in your minds—with violence. *Why?* Well—I'm going to tell you. See, when a black man insists that he's human, demands food for his children, demands decent housing, education, political participation, due process of law, or a job, white folks say he is *violent!* This is amazing, baby! Yeah—amazing. *You*—" Andre lowered his voice as if to tête-à-tête with the audience—"use violence, don't you? C'mon, now, *'fess up, baby. Say*—that you don't like to use violence, but *if* it becomes absolutely *necessary*—well—*aw, I'm probably wasting my time*. You folks don't want to believe *me!* Anyway—were *your* soldiers ever violent? Your police? How about labor unions? Oh, yeah—now you want to say that all that is in the past, *Mister*. You want to say that despite anything I might say, you've built a great country here, a great *civilization*—you want to say that you were intelligent, energetic, and resourceful. Yeah. *Well, I say you were violent!* The Indians caught hell, baby. You were violent. We blacks caught it, too. Most of you are immigrants, and you caught some of it. Then *you* learned violence, and black folks caught *more* hell, but you called it *'pulling yourself up by your bootstraps!'* See, in order to make progress in a society, people need supports, footing, traction, some base from which to work. *Well, in a human society, people use people for that base!* Now, at our lowest, and therefore, at the most fundamental, most crucial level of society, we blacks were used as that base, that level, below which *you* cannot fall. Yeah. I'm not just talking economics, either, baby. No. I'm talking about the psychological battering we took from your history and folklore in order to give *you* a vicarious thrill, a kick which you couldn't realize in fact. I'm talking about legal, moral, and illegal, and immoral oppression, man. *You were violent, baby*."

Andre paused briefly, folding his arms on the stand. Then he went on, his voice dropping the conversational tone to raise itself to a shout. "I believe in *violence!* I believe in *whatever* is required to get a positive, human response from your sick and insane white racism. *You* should be able to understand *that*. Violence is your oldest and most revered form of social process—certainly your most successful. Yes, *you* are violent. *You* are racist. You want to deny it, don't you? Yes, you'd tell me that isn't so. Well, let me say this then—I know that it'll be difficult for a racist to understand, especially, a *liberal, white* racist, but listen: it is an act of unspeakable horror—of savage violence—to deny a black child an education. It is an act of violence to imprison his father in a filthy, ghetto tenement. It is an act of violence to deny him a decent job. It is an act of violence to charge him high rents. It is an act of violence to send *white, racist* cops to police him. It is an act of violence to overcharge him for rotten food. It is an act of violence to allow rats to feed on his baby's flesh. It is an act of violence to teach that child to hate himself through your language, your books, your television, movies, and folklore—*this is violence,* white folks, white, racist violence. Yeah. Well, *I* believe in *black violence,* black violence and Black Power. Don't—imagine that you have seen black violence, white folks. Hell—" Andre's voice quieted then—*"Baby, you ain't seen nothin' yet."*

Andre stepped back from the speaker's stand. For a moment, the crowd remained silent. Then someone clapped, and, slowly, others joined in, hesitant, but courteous. The lights came on. Suddenly, three students, two black, and one white, stood up and pounded their hands together furiously, howling and whistling. Then another, larger group, joined them. The noise grew louder, rumbling about the hall. Garner saw Dr. Cohen walk to the speaker's stand.

"Your attention, please. *Please!* Ladies and gentlemen—may I have your attention?" Dr. Cohen pleaded. "Please. For just a moment. Ladies and gentlemen, Mr. Saint Pierre—*please be quiet*—our speaker —well, *thank you,*" he acknowledged as the noise subsided. "Our speaker has informed me that he must leave immediately, and we will not have time for questions from the audience, so we—"

A low moan swelled through the hall. The crowd milled about in angry frustration for a few minutes, then they grumbled their way to the exits.

Garner led the others out into the aisle, then stood with the girls while Leroy went up on the stage to get Andre. He was fascinated, still thinking about Andre's speech. He hadn't understood it all, but he was busy sorting it out, and it occurred to him that Andre had told these people a lot of things that he, himself, felt and had never been able to articulate, even in his own mind.

"Oh, there's Bill," Janice announced, waving a hand. "Hi, Bill. Hello, Gail. Hey, over here." She smiled as Bill pushed his way over to them, dragging his wife along behind him.

"Hello, you people, Chana, Janice—nothing but *pretty* people over *here.* What's happ'nin', Hawk? Andre really put it to them, didn't he?"

"Man, you know it! Andre's bad cat, man. Jes' tough, thass all, baby. Tol' it right *to* them."

"He sure did. Hey, Chana," Bill said, "why so quiet? Andre scare you?"

"He was wonderful," she said seriously.

"I hear Bill Chamberlain over there," Andre barked as Leroy guided him toward them. "How are you, Bill?"

"Andre," Bill said, "you were great up there."

Andre chuckled. "This is Gail here. My day is made now. Come here, black woman."

Gail's dark face beamed, and she laughed and leaned forward to buss Andre on the cheek and give him a polite hug.

"Shoot, gal, that's *not it!*" She squealed as he pulled her roughly into his arms. "There," he crowed, holding her close in the folds of his robe.

"Great God," Bill laughed, "I'm going to kill me a blind fool here any minute."

"If you threaten me, I'll put the fuzz right on you, baby. Now, if you say you're sorry, I might let this black gal loose."

"I'm terribly sorry."

"Okay. Let's get out of here and find some coffee, or something. I'm buying."

Sunday morning, Garner shook the sleep out of his eyes and started reading. He raced through the two hundred pages of *Cowboys* in seven hours flat. The book enchanted him, both because it was the first he had ever read entirely by himself, and because when he was through with it, his word list had increased only nineteen words. Beautiful, he mused, just beautiful. And the black saga unfolded as fact and legend by the author of the book was like nothing he had ever heard, or imagined.—*A black man killed seven Apaches during a raid, a young brave, sired of a captured black woman and an Indian chief, led the massacre of eighty-seven whites, two black men riding as hired guns in a range war.*

When he was done, Garner reviewed his entire list of words again.

He chuckled to himself as he read along for five or six pages at a stretch without a mistake. Afterward, he looked over toward the window. It was dark out. He lay back on his bed, imagining himself racing across the western plains—*He straddled a great, black stallion, dressed up in slick, black cowboy clothes, and two enormous revolvers were holstered and strapped down against his legs. The Hawk was the scourge of the Apaches, feared gunfighter, riding into a renegade Indian camp to challenge the fierce chieftain, Long Knife, to a fight to the death for the black woman he had taken from the wagon train at Hawkins Pass*—No. No—*Apache Canyon*—Garner grinned and closed his eyes. His adventure continued—*Long Knife had captured a tall, beautiful woman of honey and orange color, and her hair, her glorious Afro, framed an enchanting, oval face. And her name was Chana—an Indian name—it meant great beauty*—no—*it meant great black beauty*. Why did the Indians name her? *Well—*

"Chana." He spoke the name aloud and opened his eyes, and sat up on the edge of the bed. He lit a cigarette and tried to conjure up her naked body. The effort overwhelmed him. He could only piece her together in parts—*full, orange and honey breasts, a strong, smooth thigh, or a tiny, flat waist*—and as soon as he got one part of her set and started on another, the preceding one blurred and faded. It was worth the struggle, however. Yes, sir, and between those pretty legs—*whee-ee-ee, death to Long Knife, death to the Apaches!*

Where was she today? he asked himself. Home? Where did she live? Maybe he should forget it. Well—okay, he couldn't find her right then, but—he needed a girl bad. Chana's face fixed itself in his mind—*She was smiling. She started to undress, but Garner couldn't see clearly.—But those legs!*—He rubbed his free hand between his legs and fell back on the bed, rolling from side to side, groaning and squeezing his huge erection. The door opened, and he sat up quickly and puffed frantically on his cigarette.

"What'cha doin'?" his mother asked.

"Huh? What'cha mean?"

"What'cha whinin' fa'? Ya sick?"

"Naw."

"Ain'cha gonna eat nothin' ta-day? Ah got supper ready."

"Okay, Ma."

She left the room.

He stood up and crushed out his smoke, still thinking about Chana. Maybe she was out on a date. Sure, she would be. Certainly. With some—guy. And he could be holding her, kissing and fondling her. No, he almost prayed then. No, she couldn't. Could she? Suddenly he felt a little sick. Nauseous fear iced up in his stomach as his mind worked on all kinds of agonizing, terrible scenes—*a man's hands on Chana's naked body, her legs locking around the man's buttocks*—no, his thoughts raged. No, no, *no!* Please, God, no.

He squeezed his eyes shut, shaking his head in angry, helpless frustration. Abruptly, he thought, *selling black women.* Now he knew what Leroy had been talking about. Yes, selling black women, giving their bodies over to be used by—*just anybody!* It was dirty, vile—and low-down. *Would you want your mother to work for Billy Ray?* Oh—*no!* God, no. *Jackie, Carol—Shirley.* And Chana? *Please, God.*

"Garna?"

"Yeah, Ma?"

"Ya supper's gettin' cold, boy."

"Yeah, ah'm comin', Ma."

Monday afternoon, Garner walked into Bill's office. "Janice said ya wanna see me, man."

"Yeah, Hawk. Tom Peterson called me and—look, before I get going here, I want to ask you something."

Garner sat down and lit a cigarette. "What, man?"

"Well—uh, what do you want to do now? I mean, what do you want to do with yourself?"

"What'cha mean?"

"Well, are you going to get a job, or what?"

"Shoot, Bill, ah dunno."

"How would you like to play ball again?"

"Heah, fa' tha Y?"

"No, I mean school ball. You know."

"Ah don' wanna go back ta Tech, man. Sheet, ain' nothin' up

theah. Ya cain' do nothin' wit' shop. Ain' worth nothin' when ya git out."

"Would you be interested if you could go to school somewhere else?"

"Wheah, English? Classical? Shoot, ah dunno, Bill. Ah mean—"

"How about out of town?"

"Huh, wheah at, man?"

"Out in the country."

"Ah dunno. Ah ain' doin' nothin', no how."

"Would you like to play football again?"

"Shit, yeah—ah mean, sho'. Why not?"

"How about school?"

Garner shifted his weight uneasily in the chair and frowned. He thought about the book in his pocket, wondering if he could fight school again. *One more shot at it,* he pondered. Sure, he could read everything then, and play football and basketball, too. Maybe he could run track again. He stood up and walked over to Bill's desk, and put his cigarette out. "Why not? School is books. Right? Ah ain' skeered a' no school," he muttered.

"Well—well, okay. *Good.* Beautiful. See, Hawk, I didn't want to follow up on this call from Peterson until I had some idea—"

"He Shorty's friend, the white guy?"

"Yeah. See, Hawk—"

"Wheah's he frum—ah mean, is him—are him and Shorty tight, or what?"

"Well, yeah, they did their graduate work together at City College."

"What?"

"They were in school together. Tom's an assistant coach up at State—football. He handles the freshmen, I think."

"He want me up at State? Man, ah cain'—"

"No, no—I mean, *yes,* he does, but, see, part of his job is recruiting. State has a massive recruiting program on—they want to go big, see—in everything, especially football."

"Ya think ah kin play up theah?"

"Sure. Listen, you've got it all, size, speed, guts—like to play. State has a schedule coming up that'll put them in against some of the best teams in the country—"

"Ya mean them cats on television."

"Yes—sure. Now, I'd like—"

"Ya mean, *ah* could play? Ah could be on television *wit'em?"*

"Well, yeah, if you get in, if you get back to school, if you stay in, and if you keep the peace, keep your nose clean, and if—"

"Man," Garner laughed as he sat down again. "All them ifs—*if* this, an' *if* that, an'—if *evah'thin'."*

"Listen, Hawk, life is a great *big* if. Nothing is guaranteed. You never know *what's* going to happen. The point is this: if you're interested in this thing, I can start the ball rolling and talk to some people. Peterson's brother—John, or something, I don't know—is connected with a school out in the western part of the state."

"Wheah?"

"Uh—Haviland Academy. The name of the town is Haviland and—. Well, listen, are you interested, or not?"

"Shoot, man, ah ain' worried 'bout no school."

"Well? How about it?"

"Oh—*yeah, man!"*

As Garner walked up the street toward Freedom House, he saw Chana standing at a bus stop. She hugged a stack of school books against her, watching a bus approach from the other direction.

Garner started running. He saw her signal the bus driver with her hand. "Hey," he yelled, picking up speed, "hey Chana, wait up."

She turned and watched him run up to her as the bus slowed down. "Hello, Garner."

The bus glided to a stop, and its doors swung open. An old, black woman struggled her way down the short steps.

"Listen, Chana, kin ah talk ta ya fa' minute?"

"This is my bus," she said.

"Ah gotta talk ta ya," Garner whined. "Ah gotta talk ta ya. It's important."

She turned to face him, hugging her books tightly.

The bus driver grinned, shrugging his shoulders as he shut his doors. Garner held his breath, listening, staring at Chana as the bus whooshed away in a burst of hissing air.

"You made me miss my bus," Chana said, smiling, moving a pebble around with her foot.

Garner watched her intently. *What should he say to her?* "Ah wanted ta know wheah Leroy—wuz."

"What?"

"Chana—look, ah brought tha book back, see?" he tried again, holding the book out to her.

"Are you *serious?"* she said. "Listen, I don't want the foolish book."

He stared at her in the dimming afternoon light. Brown and orange shadows flickered softly about her pretty face. Her hair seemed darker and shinier. She was wearing a white blazer over a black sweater, with a short gray skirt.

Garner's thoughts wavered uncertainly. He felt like a fool, thick-headed, square and uncool. "Kin ah see ya?" he whispered fearfully. "Kin ah meet'cha sometime?"

"Well, I'll be damned." She peered at him incredulously, then threw her head back and laughed. "I'll be double damned and dog-goned! You're bashful, for crying out loud!"

"What'cha mean? Naw, ah ain'. Listen, see, ah gotta—ah wanna take ya out sometime."

"When?"

"Huh?"

"I said, when? When are we going out? I live at three forty-seven Baldwin Street."

"What?"

"Have you got a good memory? My phone number is Garfield six, four three, two five."

"Wheah we goin'?"

"Brother! Garner Hawkins—I don't care. Anyplace."

"Theah's a movie 'bout Vietnam down at—"

"Crazy. Come on, let's go."

"Huh? Wheah? Ah gotta git ta tha Y."

"Come on, I'll walk you down."

"Ya will?"

"That's what I just said. Come on, Garner. It's six o'clock already." She took his arm and smiled at him, shaking her head.

Chana Jackson was on Garner's mind that night. He couldn't concentrate on his reading. It seemed as though he had been struck dumb, as if all the reading and memorizing of words he had worked at over the last several weeks had washed away, been wiped clean—*and there was Chana's radiant beauty, a shining, golden-brown visage under the dark of her buoyant, African hair*—Garner smiled. Her hair pleased him that way, cut even, bending forward with her high forehead, swinging wide in a full, two-inch growth around her head and tapering smoothly, evenly into the ears and the strength of her columnar neck.

Saturday night, he took Chana to see a movie. They didn't enjoy it.

"Can't give a black man credit for anything," Chana said as they left the theater.

Garner scowled. "Shoot, ya see that pit'cha, an' ya think they ain' but one nigga in tha whole—foolish army, fa' crissake—cryin' out loud."

Chana nodded but didn't say anything. She held his arm, and they walked in silence for a while. When they came to the entrance to the subway, Garner stopped and looked around. "Say, baby, les' git us a piece a' chicken a' somethin'. Ah'm hongry."

"Good. You get me on home, and I'll fix you something to eat. Then we can turn on some records, okay? C'mon." She took his hand and led him down the stairs.

The coach was crowded and Garner had to stand, while Chana sat between a middle-aged white woman and a white soldier. Garner stared at her for a while, then she caught his gaze and smiled, her eyes lighting up, gleaming in her burnt-orange face. Garner looked up, through the window, as the dark city flew by outside underneath the elevated structure their train was riding. He remembered how she looked as she had opened the door of her home for him when he arrived to pick her up—*She stood in the doorway and smiled, wearing a simple dress with a white top cinched tight and tiny at the waist over a short, flaring, red skirt. The light behind her set off the orange and honey of her skin and the red and white dress in a rich glow of dazzling colors. She wore black high-heels. Her legs were beautifully, fully turned, and long. He tried to look beyond her at her parents in the hallway, to avoid staring at the swell of her breasts. "Well, c'mon in," she said. "What's the matter?" He couldn't tell her. Her beauty brought a giddy, woozy feeling to his head. His legs felt funny. Real pain attacked his groin, sweet, exquisite, and frightening—.* He peeked down at her again as she smoothed her skirt, pushing it down on her thighs.

Beautiful, he thought. Chana Jackson is what people call beauty, the complete kind—*female.* And she was with *him!* She winked at him, and he grinned nervously and averted his gaze.

Later, on the sofa, he kissed her. Her mouth was moist and cool. A delicious giddiness swelled in him, and for a moment, he felt as though he was going to faint. Then he slid his tongue into her mouth, pushing her down. His mouth began to work hard on hers. He caressed her breasts and felt her shudder. The heady feeling steadied then. The drive of his young manhood took command. It gave him confidence. He understood this. The wooziness no longer made him feel weak, but strong. He was in control. Pushing himself down on her, still controlling her mouth, he slipped a hand under her dress, along her thighs to her panties.

She sobbed against his lips. "Don't, Gar. Please—please don't do that. Gar—oh, Jesus. Oh, *please!*" Her mouth clung in his for a raging instant. Then she tore her lips away, turning her head, and gently covered his mouth with her hand. "Please please don't."

"What'cha mean? What'cha talkin' 'bout?"

"Gar, please—this is our very first date. Be kind—this once. I—"

"What'cha mean?"

"I mean. I never *did* anything before! I never—"

"Sheet! What'choo talkin' 'bout, gal?"

"Gar, please—let's not fight. I want—"

"Bitch, *ah* wants some pussy now, fa' crissake!" His hand fumbled roughly with her crotch. "Sheet, ah'm gonna git it, too!"

"Oh, Jesus—*no,*" her desperate whisper shrieked, and she began to push his hand away. "Oh, God, *Jesus!*"

Garner jumped to his feet then and stood staring at her in disbelief. She wept painfully now, her body shaking with her effort to muffle the sound.

"Ain' this a bitch, now? Ah mean—ain' this a mutha-fucka? Sheet, gal, who you think you *is?* You ain' *shit,* bitch! What'cha—"

"Is something wrong down there?"

With a fright, Garner recognized Mrs. Jackson's voice.

Chana sat up quickly, wiping her eyes and arranging her clothes. "No, Ma!"

"Are you alone, child? Is young Hawkins still there?"

"Yes, he is, Ma."

"Well, child, it's quarter past one, I mean, after all—"

"Okay, Ma."

Garner's face set in a furious grimace. He walked quickly into the hall, heading for the front door.

"Gar," Chana wailed. "Gar, please—listen! Wait a minute, will you?"

But he was gone, already down the front steps, then stomping angrily on his way. Chana stood in the doorway, watching him until he was out of sight, then she slowly closed the door. She was crying again.

The next day, Garner didn't get any reading done at all. He tried to start in again on *Negro Philosophers,* but couldn't concentrate. The memory of Chana's bright, pretty face haunted him. He remembered her tears, her pleading. *Who did she think she was?* If Luther had seen that foolishness, he would have laughed himself sick. And Terry would have rolled around on the floor in hysterics. Garner didn't understand the idea of virginity at all, had never encountered it. *She never did it,* his thoughts screamed. Why? No, that was hard to believe. What was she saving it for? *Never did it before.* He couldn't swallow that. Unbelievable! *Selling black women.* What did that have to do with this? Then he considered telling Leroy about it.

He thought of Janice then, and he felt that it wouldn't be wise to tell Leroy anything. Well, Leroy was—maybe Leroy was nuts. Anyway, Janice was *his* problem. *And Chana?* Well, who needed her? Never did it before, huh? With a body like hers she could take on ten guys, a hundred—. *No—Selling black women.*

He sat up on his bed and tried to review his word list, but as he read over the words, he discovered that nothing registered, nothing. Shaking his head in disgust, he threw the list on the floor and lit a cigarette. *She's crazy!* He puffed his smoke furiously and checked the time. God, he wanted a girl under him, wanted to be in her, just anything female, *anything that would hold still long enough!* Suddenly he found himself wondering if Ellis was at the park.

He hurled himself from the bed and went to the closet and fished around for his sneakers. There was dust all over them. They sagged shapelessly in his hands, as if having once lived and worked, they had become sick from disuse, and the temper of their spirit had atrophied like unused muscle. He put them on. They felt funny, heavy and clumsy. He scowled, then saw Chana's face again—*she was crying, and he could hear her weeping*—now, was that *his* fault? *Was* it? He remembered, then, how he had abused her—*that language!* Well—what did she expect? He was no little kid.

All at once, he had an overwhelming desire to run, or fight, to jump up and down and hit out at everything around him. *The park!* Sure, if he could only get moving—*fast*—he could get her off his mind. He had to run. His head was filled to bursting with her.

He ran all the way to the park. Ellis was there, playing a pick-up game of basketball with a mixed group of high school and college players. Two of the ten boys on the asphalt court were white. As he watched the game, a tall, thin, black boy sauntered over to him.

"Wanna go along?"

"Yeah," growled Garner, anxiously rubbing his hands on the seat of his dungarees. "You got winners?"

"Yeah."

"Crazy. Gotta full team?"

"You make five."

"Crazy."

Ellis's team lost to the team with the two white boys. He came off the court looking peevish. "Shit, man—what's happ'nin', Hawk?"

"Nothin', man," Garner replied quickly, jogging onto the court. The tall, black boy threw him a ball. Garner held it for a moment, turning the orange basketball over in his hands. *All right, now,* he thought. *Going to work.* He dribbled toward the basket then and stopped short; stepping down hard and driving his body high off the court, he fired a long jump shot which banked off the rusty, steel backboard and whipped through the net. He chuckled.

The game started off slowly, but Garner picked it right up. He was running all over the court, stealing passes, rebounding, and driving hard to the basket. He hogged the ball; when he couldn't drive, he shot long jumpers from the top of the key or deep in the corner. His lazy, high-arching shots were ripping the net at a phenomenal rate, too, and his team built up a big lead and finally won the game thirty baskets to twenty-one. Chana was gone from his thoughts.

Ellis led his team back onto the court. One of his players had to leave, and he picked one of the white boys to play for him, a tall, rangy redhead. Garner glanced at the boy's faded, gray T-shirt—CITY COLLEGE: BASKETBALL—Garner was matched against the boy in a man-to-man.

The redhead tried to play him tight, to take away that long jump shot, and Garner whirled by him three times, whipping him badly and scoring, giving his team an early lead. But he had to run hard to get free of his man, and to keep up with him, and soon his wind was burning hot in his chest, legs thick and heavy. The redhead dropped off then and let him have the outside shot again. As soon as he got the ball, Garner stepped down and fired a twenty-footer. He missed. He kept missing, but he went on shooting, much to the obvious chagrin of his teammates.

"Hey, man, c'mon, pass the ball, will ya?" the tall, black boy said.

"Sheet, fuck you, man!"

"What?"

"You heard me!"

"Aw, man, if you don't wanna play, go home, will ya? C'mon, move the ball."

Garner continued to shoot—and miss. His legs were tired, and when he stepped down to go up for a shot, he wasn't getting enough height to keep him in the air long enough to aim the ball properly. Worse yet, the redhead started to hit, driving in to shoot sweeping hook shots with either hand. Then when Garner hung back to prevent the drive, the boy grinned and stepped down and burned the nets with a twenty-five-footer, line-drive style. Garner wanted to dig a hole and bury himself. His team lost thirty baskets to fourteen.

"Man," the tall, black boy began as they walked off the court. "Ya gotta feed more. We shoulda beat those cats."

"Yeah, baby, try ta put it on me, now. Why don'cha stop bull-shittin' an' play some fuckin' ball?"

"Ya gotta pass off more, thass all."

"Aw, go fuck ya'se'f."

"Hey, look, man, we don't need that stuff up here. If you don't wanna play, quit and go home."

"Fuck you, man! *Whyn'choo try sendin' me home?"*

"Fa'git it, man. Jes' fa'git it."

They played until dark. Garner became so tired, he dragged up and down the court, only running when he had the ball. He was almost relieved when his team lost a game and he had to sit one out and wait for winners. Finally he got his second wind. It took a long time because he wasn't in playing condition. His shots still weren't going in, however, and this increased his frustration and anger. He maintained a continuous flow of bitter exchanges with everyone, including Ellis.

When it was too dark to keep playing, they broke it up and straggled off the court.

"Say, Hawk, what's *wrong* with ya tonight?" Ellis asked as he idly dribbled his basketball on the sidewalk. "Man, you're *evil* about somethin'!"

"Sheet, man—nothin'."

"Well, if you're *not* evil now, I don't wanna see you when you are."

"Fuck you, man. Ain' nothin' wrong wit' me."

"Okay, okay! Ya comin' up next week?"

"Ah dunno."

"You down the Y every night?"

"Yeah—'cept Saddaday. Why?"

"Might stop down."

"Yeah? Sheet, well—"

"You goin' anywheres tonight?" Ellis asked, digging his watch out of his pocket and snapping it around his wrist.

"Naw."

"Well, I gotta get home for supper. Gotta hit the books."

"Sheet."

"See ya next week, Hawk?"

"Ah dunno."

"See ya."

Garner stared after Ellis with a vacant expression on his face, not seeing, just standing there dripping with sweat. He was thinking of Chana crying on the sofa. And he remembered the soft fullness of her body. The taste of her mouth was vivid in his mind. He cursed ferociously and started walking home.

By Wednesday, his anger had grown into a state of constant, unbearable fury. Lying on his bed, his temper cooked red-hot—and *Chana—Chana—Chana!* At times, her presence in his thoughts was so strong that he held his head with both hands, eyes pinched shut, his flat, black face contorted with rage. *"Ah'll kill tha fuckin' bitch,"* was a muted scream in his head. "Ah *will!* Ah'll beat'er fuckin' ass! Why she botherin' *me* fa'? What's she *fuckin'* wit' me fa'? Gawddamn bitch."

But nobody was *bothering* him, came the answer. *You* haven't seen Chana. She hasn't asked you for *anything.* So, relax. Go read your book. *"So, fuck you, too!* Ah don' need *her!* Ain' no bitch gonna git on tha Hawk, gawddammit! Terry says—" *Terry?* Isn't he dead? How smart was he? "Sheet." But this argument stopped him and left him smoldering in anger.

"Hey, boy," Harry called and opened the door. "Are you going to come on out of there? You sick or something?"

"Naw."

"You've been shut up in here all day, yesterday, too. You must be reading up a storm."

"Sheet."

"You finish any of these yet?" Harry asked pointing to the books on the night table.

Garner didn't answer.

"Well, do you mind if I take a look at them?"

"Man, take tha fuckin' things, fa' crissake."

"What're you so evil for? Listen, keep your precious books if that's how you feel."

"Sheet, man, am ah botherin' anybody? Whyn'choo go on? What-'cha want, fa' crissake?"

"Now listen, boy—. *Okay!* Okay, fine." Harry left, slamming the door behind him.

Garner could hear him in the living room complaining to his mother. "Boy's evil, I tell you. Just lays there, looking mean and black."

"*Somethin'* wrong wit' that boy."

"He acts like he's sick."

"He readin'?"

"No, just laying there, staring at the ceiling. Acts like a man with a wife who won't give him any."

"Shoot, you makin' a big thing outta nothin'. *Now* wheah ya goin'? Leave'im 'lone."

Harry opened the door and stood watching Garner, with a smile working at the corners of his mouth. Then he chuckled and closed the door.

"What'cha doin'?" Garner heard his mother ask.

"Shoot, woman, that nigger's got himself a gal."

"What? Shoot, Harry, that don' mean nothin'."

"This girl does."

"Naw. Him and Terry wuz alla time foolin' wit' girls."

"Maybe so, but this one's different. Boy's got a girl, that's what's wrong."

Garner couldn't stand any more of this. He stood up and threw on a sweater and a light windbreaker. Who did they think they were? Harry's mouth was too big, anyway. Well, he was leaving. *Chana,* he pondered. *There,* that's what he'd do, find Chana and set her straight. Sure, he'd tell her exactly where she could go. Maybe then she'd get off his back. He looked at his watch: four twenty-five.

When he arrived at Freedom House, he stood outside for a while, rehearsing an appropriate tirade. His concentration was broken by the enthusiastic rush of noisy black children who scampered in and out of the building. He watched them for a bit, then went inside.

"Hello, Hawk," Andre said as Garner walked into the office.

Garner wondered how the blind man knew who he was. "Hi, Andre."

"What brings you up here today? Bring back my books?"

"Uh, naw."

"Oh, are you looking for Chana? She hasn't been in all week. Mother said she's not feeling well."

"Oh."

"How's your history coming?"

"Huh? Okay, ah guess. Well, ah gotta git goin'. Ah see ya, Andre."

As he walked home that night, a light rain was falling. His thoughts were still on Chana. *She didn't feel well, huh?* He puffed a cigarette, feeling the cool rain wash against his face. *She did have a body, though, didn't she? Well, so what? What good is it if you can't use it? She never did it though, she said. Yes, she was saving it. Well, who needs it?* He trudged up his front steps and along the dark hall.

Chana was sitting above him under the light at the top of the stairs. For a moment, he didn't speak. He stared up at her in shock. A dazzling expanse of burnt-orange skin beckoned to him from under her blue, denim skirt. A thickness clogged his throat. Then, when he opened his mouth to hurl his anger and bitterness up at her, all that came out was *"Chana."* His voice shook noticeably. "Chana," he spoke the name again and started slowly up the stairs.

She got to her feet, a weak, frightened smile beginning in her face. She leaned against the wall, dropping her eyes and slowly shaking her head. "I wanted to talk to you," she breathed.

"What fa'?"

"Just—*talk,* that's all, Gar."

"Don' wanna talk," he muttered and swept by her with a flourish.

"Please, Gar—"

"Ah'm hongry. You wastin' ma time, bitch—gal."

"Can't I come up and talk to you? Please?"

He shrugged and went into the apartment, leaving the door open. Then he made a show of busying himself in the refrigerator, peeking up at her when she came to the door.

"What'cha want, gawddammit?"

She began to cry then. Her hands covered her face as she sagged against the door frame. *"I love you,"* she wailed.

"Huh? Well, sheet—gal—aw, gal—if ya come ta cry, g'wan outta heah." He slammed the refrigerator shut and tilted a quart of milk up and drank deeply.

"I love you," she repeated in a soft, sobbing voice.

"Shee-yee-yit—gawddammit, gal—ah don' wanna heah lotta shit."

"Well—what *do* you want, then?"

"Ah ain' asked ya fa' nothin', sheet."

"What do you *want?"*

"Aw, gal—"

"I'll do anything—you want."

"Shee—*what?"*

"I'll do anything—anything you ask me to do."

He peered at her, still holding the milk bottle near his mouth. The fingers of his free hand played idly with the zipper of his jacket. He tried to say something, but he had to wait until he could be sure of his voice. "Anythin'?"

She nodded her head with vigorous determination. "Yes."

"What ah say, huh? Anythin' ah tell ya ta do?"

"I said so, didn't I?"

Garner hesitated, watching her as she stared at the floor. Shivers of dizzying excitement racked his stomach and groin. He put the milk away in the refrigerator. His hands were shaking. "Shut tha do'! Yeah. Now, c'mere."

She rushed into his arms, and he found her mouth with a hard, cruel kiss. He opened her jacket and slid his hand under her sweatshirt. She wasn't wearing a bra. His fingers recoiled momentarily, as if burned. Then, gingerly, at first, he caressed her, cupping her smooth, heavy breasts and kneading the hard nipples. He grunted a rough sigh as she trembled in his arms, and pulled his head back to look at her.

Chana hid her face against his neck. "No panties, either," she moaned.

He investigated immediately. The flesh of her thighs was firm and tight. He worked a hand around her thick, contoured buttocks. Then he found the springy down of her pubic hair. He stepped back and lifted her skirt to look. *"Jesus!"* he groaned, and reached down and bore her up in his arms.

She tightened her arms around his neck as he carried her into the bedroom. "Oh—*Gar!*"

He lowered her onto the bed and tore off his jacket and sweater. She watched him, tears streaming over the gold of her face. His body amazed her. Flawless, black skin spread up from the narrow of his hard, flat waist and muscular stomach to a great width of shoulder. Bunches of long, massive sinew rippled in his chest, arms, and neck.

"You're gorgeous—*beautiful,*" she breathed.

Garner grinned at her and sat on the bed to remove his shoes and socks.

She took off her jacket and sweatshirt. Then he felt her naked breasts mashed against his back as her hands slid around his waist, running tenderly over his chest.

"Jesus, but you're beautiful," she wept.

He turned his head, and her mouth gripped his in a clinging, wet kiss. He jammed his hands against her breasts, and she locked her arms about his neck, driving her tongue back and forth into his mouth. Garner pushed her down and started kissing her breasts, his hands fumbling with the catch to her skirt.

"Here," she moaned, "let me. Oh, God—here, let me. *Quick, let me do it!"*

He stood up and unzipped his pants. Chana flipped the skirt open. Garner froze, heart belting away in his chest, gaping at her naked body. Warm, brown honey glowed in her skin. The light above the bed colored her in shimmering whispers of gold, orange, and brown. The awesome shock of her beauty exploded in his blood. His knees nearly buckled, and his legs trembled.

"Gawd-a-mighty," he choked, staring at her in disbelief, his eyes raking over her globular, orange breasts, the brown nipples, the wide flaring hips, her thighs, rounded, sinewy, and statuesque. When his eyes fastened on the black thickness of her pubic hair, he was overwhelmed. *She never did it before!*

"What's wrong?"

Selling black women! "Git up!"

"What?"

Virgin! "Git up, gal," he screamed suddenly. "Git'cha fuckin' clothes on. Git dressed."

"Why? What's—"

He shouted at her, *"Move,* Chana!"

She reached for her clothes, gratitude shining in her face, loving him now, she knew, forever.

Garner zipped up his pants and stomped out of the room. *I love you, Chana.*

The schools closed for the summer. The days were blazing hot, and at night there was almost no relief. It was hard to sleep, and there was little to do but sit on the stoops or hang out on the streets.

"Christ," Garner said to Chana as they left the Y one night. "If it gits any hotter we gonna burn up fa' sho', man. Jesus!"

"It's not so bad in the pool."

"Yeah, but when ya come out it's a bitch—*it's bad!"*

"What was the fight about?"

"What? Oh. Niggas crazy. Ah'm gittin' sick a' that—stuff, too. Niggas wanna fight alla time, now, man. Evah' day somebuddy gits evil an' gonna hit somebuddy. Tired a' that mess, man. *Niggas is evil!* Jes'—gittin'—*evil,* thass all."

It was after midnight when he got home. The phone was ringing.

It was Leroy. "Hawk, I've been calling all night. Where've you been?"

"Chana's house."

"Listen, is your mother home?"

"Naw, they be—they're workin'. Why, man?"

"Good. Hawk, I got a call from Luther and—"

"What, man? *Lutha?* Is *he* out? He outside, Leroy, no lie?"

"Yes—listen, now, Hawk, keep this to yourself—"

"Aw, man—"

"I mean it, Hawk. Don't even tell your mother—*nobody*. Hear?"

"Ah know what's happ'nin', Leroy."

"I hope so. Luther sounded kind of funny—keep this cool, man."

"Yeah, man. See ya."

Garner put the phone down and went to his room. *Luther.* He tried to remember the last time he had seen him. *Long time ago.* Years. *Buzz*—a feeling of uneasiness flooded over him. Luther was out. How? Parole? He wouldn't break out, would he? He might have. Leroy said he sounded funny. Garner switched the light off. *Was Luther coming home?* No, he decided, he wasn't. If he was on parole, he'd have to stay in New York, wouldn't he? And—if he had broken out, he'd be on the run. Well, anyway, he was out, that was—

There was someone in the kitchen. For a moment, he lay perfectly still. Then there was movement in the living room. Garner sat up quickly in the bed. Light shone beneath his door. He switched his light on and stood up. The door opened, and Luther walked in.

"What's happ'nin', Hawk?"

Garner stared at him, stunned. Luther was bigger than he remembered, but lean, almost gaunt. He had an Afro and a thick, heavy mustache with a small beard. He wore dungarees, sandals, and a sportshirt.

"Lutha," Garner breathed. He gripped his brother's hand. "When ya git out, man? How long ya been outside? How ya been, fa' crissake?"

"Few days. Good behavior, man." Luther threw his head back and roared laughter, loud, raucous, filling the room. "Whitey say ah'm a *good* nigga, baby! Shit yeah." He laughed again. "Sheet, Whitey don' *know* what ah got fa' *him,* gawddammit!" He glanced around the room, then fixed a hard stare on Garner. "Terry dead, huh?"

Garner nodded. "Yeah. Yeah, man." He sat down on the bed. "Lutha, they give ya parole, man?"

Luther erupted into noisy laughter again. "Fuckin' right, nigga! All us good niggas gits parole! Yass-*suh!*" He shook his head. "Yassuh."

Garner looked at him, glad to see him, yet nervous, filled with an anxiety he couldn't explain, almost—frightened. "They let'cha come home, man?"

Luther grinned at him and pulled the straight-back chair over in front of the bed and sat down straddling it, resting his arms on the back, watching Garner, his eyes like burning coals in his black face. "Don' worry 'bout it, baby. Whitey don' know evah'thin' *ah'm* doin', sheet. An' when he find out, gonna be too mutha-fuckin' late!" He hesitated, scowling. "What time Ma be home?"

Garner looked at his watch. " 'Bout an' hour. Gawddamn, man, what'cha doin'? Ya got any money? They git'cha a job, or what?"

"Yeah, nigga, *they got me a job!* Shit yeah, man." Luther laughed and shook his head. "Fuckin' right they got me a job, man." His voice grew louder, his eyes boring into Garner's. "Whitey gits all his good niggas jobs, man—*good* jobs! Workin' in a lumba' yard, man. Shit yeah. Ah git *two* dollas an' fifty cent a hour. Me'n two otha' niggas—we unload tha freight cars. Yeah. Yeah, we *good,* hard-workin' niggas. Sheet, jes' like—fuckin', dumb, black-ass niggas, we works. Sweatin'—all fuckin' day, man, jes' pourin' off us. Jes'—gawddamn—stupid, black-ass—" He started laughing.

"Cain'cha—mebbe ya kin ask'em ta git'cha somethin' betta, man. Mebbe—"

Luther's laughter crashed into the room. "Yeah, baby! Sheet, ah be a good nigga, ain' no tellin', yassuh!" Abruptly, his face was serious, voice hard. "Only job *ah'm* gonna git be 'notha' fuckin' *nigga job!* Whitey don' give a nigga *nothin',* fool—ya simple, black-ass, ig'rant fool! Sheet, Whitey gonna shit on *me,* man—alla—resta ma fuckin'—*life!* Evah' day ah live—jes' gonna shit all *ovah* ma black ass. Well—he done fucked wit' me fa' tha last time. Nobuddy gonna fuck wit'

Lutha no mo'. Nawsuh, gawddammit! *Ma* turn comin' now!" He paused momentarily, lowering his voice almost to a whisper, almost pleading, "Ah mean—ya see, man—*we* ain' *nevah* gonna git a *fuckin'* thing—till we git *rid a' Whitey,* git us some guns—an' go on out an' kill evah' white mutha-fucka we kin—kill evah' one a' them gawd-damn—" He stopped talking and sat staring at Garner, clenching and unclenching his huge hands. He smiled. "How *you* been doin', Hawk? How ya been gittin' 'long, man?"

"Shoot, man—evah'thin's cool," Garner said nervously. "Lutha—are ya gonna see Leroy, man?"

"Sheet. Fuck that shit-colored—fuckin' Uncle Tom nigga, man! That nigga goin' ta school! Gonna git *married* an' shit! Shit yeah. Gonna settle *down*—jes' like tha *white* folks! Fuckin'—black-ass—bitch he fuckin' wit'—*wheah you hang out, nigga?"*

"What? Uh—down tha Y, man. Most evah' night."

A horn sounded. Luther stood up. "Yeah, well, ah see ya in a couple days. Might put'cha onta somethin'—'long's ya don' mind kickin' a few white folks in tha ass. Ah gotta split, man. Don' tell Ma ah wuz heah. Don' tell *nobuddy* ya seen me, nigga! Ya heah? Ah break ya fuckin' ass! Don' tell nobuddy nothin'. Ah see ya in a couple days." He hurried from the room.

Garner sat dumbly on the bed. He wondered if he should call Leroy. Outside, a door slammed, then a car drove off. Garner was bewildered. Luther sounded—*frightened him!* He thought of Terry then—and Buzz. He decided to call Leroy, then he heard Harry and his mother come in. He lay back on the bed and switched off the light. He was crying.

The next day was Saturday. It was hot. Leroy wasn't home when he called. He tried Janice's home, but her mother said she was out with Leroy. Garner was worried, nervous. Where was Luther, he wondered. What was he doing?

Sunday it was still hot. Garner finished buttoning his light blue, short-sleeved shirt and put on a white tie, then reached into the closet and pulled out a white, summer-weight sport coat and checked it against the blue pants and shirt.

Leroy came into his room. "You ready, Hawk?"

"Yeah. Man, les' git outta heah. Got somethin' ta tell ya."

Downstairs, Garner stopped in the hall and faced Leroy. "Man, Lutha wuz heah. He—"

"When?"

"Friday night, man. Talkin' crazy an'—"

"Why didn't you let me *know,* Hawk?"

"Ma came home, an' Saddaday—"

"Yeah, Janice and I went shopping. How's Luther look?"

"Diff'rent, man—bigga an'—gotta beard. Talkin' *crazy,* man! Ah mean, he *seems* tha same, ya know? But he seems—kinda—"

"He's the same," Leroy said, "only—*more* so, that's all. Listen, Hawk, if he shows again, you've *got* to let me know, hear?"

"Yeah. Okay, man. Leroy, he wuz—talkin' 'bout *killin'* somebuddy! Wants me ta go wit'im, ah think. Ah think he's broken parole, too, man."

"I know he has. Listen, if he wants you to go with him anywhere, tell him—*that I want in on it,* whatever it is. I've *got* to see him, Hawk, got to talk to him. Understand?"

Garner nodded. They went down to the Chevvy. Janice was waiting for them in the car, fanning herself with a handkerchief. They stopped to pick up Chana and drove over to Bill Chamberlain's house.

"You know," Chana whispered to Garner as they walked across the street to the house, "Andre's wife is white. You'll meet her today."

"Naw, gal—*c'mon!*"

"She *is,* Gar!"

"He love her?"

"They have eleven children."

Garner chuckled. *"Man!"*

During the meal, Garner guardedly observed Andre's wife. She was a small redhead, with a slight figure that showed the effects of repeated childbirth. She wore no make-up. She was homely, except when she smiled or laughed, and sometimes when she looked at her husband. Her name was Laura.

"Are you going back to school, Garner?" Andre asked as they sat around the table after dinner.

"Gar's going to prep school next year," Chana announced with pride.

"Where to?"

"Haviland," Garner said. "It's out in tha west—tha western part of the state."

"How many black kids do they have at *that* school?"

Bill answered. "Damn few. Something like sixteen or seventeen in three years."

"That's about what I figured. What're *you* going up there for, Hawk?"

"They're giving him a scholarship," Bill explained, glancing quickly at Leroy.

"Yes, I'll *bet* they are. What in the world would a black kid want at a school like that? It's *lily-white,* hidden away—from the nasty old city folks—*especially the blacks—*"

"Andre, it's a great chance for the boy. Haviland's a fine school."

"Yeah. They'll dump him in the brain laundry just like they do their own kids, only their kids'll come out white. Garner, here, will still be black."

"Well," Bill said testily, "do you think he'd be better off at Tech?"

"At least he'd still be in the black community."

"Oh—c'mon, now, Andre—"

Garner watched the two men, listening to them argue. It made him uncomfortable. Leroy scowled and looked around the table as Gail and Laura exchanged glances and fidgeted uneasily.

"Bill," Andre growled, "when they get this boy up there they're going to try their damnedest to make him over into one of their own—*a white boy!* It can't be done."

"Look, now, Garner has a chance here to better himself personally, to play football—and basketball—and get a free education, to go on to college. A better life, see, that's all."

"Sure, he can go to college—a white college where he'll get some more white education."

Leroy tried to mediate. "Uh, look, Andre, *you're* talking about education, and it seems to me as if Bill is talking about—*certification.* It's not at all the same thing. It's—"

"Yeah, *white* certification."

"Okay, *white* certification. In *white America,* what other kind is there? Most of the machinery that grinds out the money—*which we need to live*—is white. So if anyone, white *or* black, wants to get some of the action, he has to get that certification."

Andre shook his head. *"If you want a good job, get certified!"*

"Look, Andre, now, a man does what he has to do in order to improve himself, get the things he wants, do the work he wants. I want to teach. *I* go to a white school, and I *need* that hunk of paper."

Gail Chamberlain cleared her throat. "Listen, if you people are going to fight, the girls and I are going to clear out of here. It's too hot for this foolishness."

"So, go ahead," Bill said.

"Okay, we *will!* C'mon, Laura, Janice. Let's go in the parlor. Chana?"

"Leroy," Andre began as the women left the table, "you're teaching right now—and black kids, too, who—"

"Yeah, *for nothing*—and that's fine, up to a point, man, but I want to get married and raise a family, so I need a job. Besides that, I want to go on to graduate school. I want to *write* history, Andre, textbooks that tell it like it really was. I only reach a handful of black kids up at Freedom House; man, I want to spread the *word!* I need training, see? I have to know *what* I'm teaching and *why,* what I'm *not* teaching and—I have to know *how* to teach."

"Leroy's right, Andre. When I applied for this job with the Y, I had to have the papers. *Had to have them,* the degree *and* YMCA certification. I had to *compete,* Andre. And certification qualified me to enter competition."

"That," Leroy said, "is the crux of the whole deal. This is a competitive society, baby, and without certification—well, they just won't let you play."

Andre grimaced and waved his hands to quiet them down. "As

long as we give in to the pressure of certification on Whitey's terms, *we're licked!* He can continue to exploit us, *kill* us—anything he wants—turn us into little black puppets, Uncle Toms who—"

Garner sat back in his chair and lit a cigarette, his eyes darting from one man to the other. He was confused. Somehow, he agreed with most of what was being said. He wondered whose side *he* was on.

Andre went on, "The only way that we can beat Whitey is Black Power. *That* is freedom, man, and the roots of that power are in the black community."

The table was quiet for a moment. The women, in the other room, were quiet, too, evidently listening to the argument. Garner looked around the table at the three men, then lowered his gaze. Outside, he could hear sounds of the city, children playing in the street, the occasional blare of horns honking. A plane flew over, the noise of its engines waning in the distance. Absentmindedly, his thoughts still on the discussion, he surveyed the food on the table, turnips, greens, chicken, wine, and apple pie. Suddenly the room seemed too stuffy, his stomach too full. He crushed out his cigarette.

Leroy sat forward in his chair and folded his arms on the table, his head down, eyes on the white tablecloth. "Roots," he murmured, "have to be nourished, if the body they support is going to thrive and grow, Andre. The roots of the black community are planted in the soil of this country. The main source of nourishment available to the black community is schools." Leroy raised his head, eyes searching the wall as if for the threads of a stray thought. "In schools, a black man can learn to play Whitey's game—*if nothing else!* To get into the game, as Bill pointed out, you've *got* to have certification. Whitey calls that *education!* Whatever you call it, whoever has it often has access to some of the things which control—*America.* Control is *power!* If a black man can sit at the controls, he has—can have—*black* power. *We* have to have black people sitting at the controls along with white people. The schools, industry, politics, law—even the army and the police—*wherever* we see power, we have to push and get some—*black*-body certified to use it."

Andre scowled, shaking his head. Bill pushed his chair back from the table and stood up. The others got up, then followed him into the parlor.

"Say, kin ah say somethin'," Garner ventured hesitantly.

"Sure," Andre offered quietly, "say something, Garner. Hell, everyone else has."

Garner hesitated, his gaze wandering nervously about the room. Chana sat beside Laura watching him intently. Bill waited with Andre and lit a smoke, and Janice moved over beside Gail to make room for Leroy on the sofa.

"Well, ah think ya shouldn't be fightin' an' arguin', ah mean, we're *all* black heah, so—" Garner winced and peeked at Laura Saint Pierre. He blinked in uncertainty as she nodded slowly, a faint smile lighting up her face under the red hair. *"Yeah,"* Garner continued, steadying his voice, "we're all in this ta-getha. So we hafta do our thing, the *black* thing, *ta-getha!* You *all* are talkin' 'bout Black Power. Sayin' tha same thing in diff'rent ways, thass all. Black Power's no one thing, man. It's no 'Ah got it, an' you don't.' You're *all* right, see? Ah mean, black people hafta do they—their own thing, but they still hafta do tha personal thing, too. If someone's a teacha, an' he's black, he's got *power*—an' if someone else is a Y man, or an—actor, or headin' up a Freedom School, or a policeman, it all comes out ta tha same thing. Ya put it all ta-getha, workin' ta-getha, an' ya git *Black Power.* Bill says ah got a gift, an' *ah'm* gonna git all ah kin outta it, work hard's ah kin to be tha bes' *ah* kin at what *ah* do, see? Anybody who don't—*doesn't*—isn't gonna evah have any kinda power at all." Garner paused, trying to think of something else to say, but he was embarrassed. He strode quickly across the room to stand beside Chana who clasped his hand and squeezed it.

"Well," Andre said as Bill guided him to a chair beside Laura's. "That *sounds* reasonable—but, so far, Whitey hasn't been at all receptive to reason. *I don't know.* You do your thing, Hawk. Go to your school. But you come back to us, hear?"

The next day was Monday, another blazing day. It was the week of the Fourth of July. For days, the temperature in the city raged in the high eighties and nineties night and day. At night, older people sat out on the stoops, perspiring, grumbling irritably. Gangs of young blacks stalked the streets, cursing and sweating. Fist fights occurred frequently, and occasionally a knife blade gleamed wickedly in dim light. The cops walked in pairs, black and white, mentally and physically on edge. They were sweating, too.

There was no word from Luther, and Garner continued to worry. Leroy called him every night—even if he saw Garner during the day. When he got home at night, Garner waited expectantly. But Luther didn't show.

The night before the Fourth, Garner stepped up on the diving board and watched the last of the late swimmers climb out of the pool. A lifeguard turned off the lights in the office, walked along the pool deck, and disappeared into the locker rooms. A siren sounded in the night outside. Garner wiped his hands slowly along the seat of his satin trunks and poised to take a dive. Another siren screamed, then another.

Mr. Lewis came through the big doors to Garner's left and started switching off the lights. "Hey, boy, thought you had to go somewhere."

"Yeah," Garner answered, looking down at the lights under the glassy, green water.

"Well, it's long after nine."

"Huh?" Garner looked up at the clock. He was supposed to be at Chana's house at nine-thirty. He hadn't seen her in three days, since Sunday, when he took her to Bill's house for dinner. He climbed down to the pool deck. The lights dimmed and the pool was dark.

"Helluva fire goin' somewhere," Mr. Lewis said.

"Guess so," Garner answered, walking toward the locker rooms.

"Yeah. There goes another one."

Garner dressed hurriedly and jogged up the stairs to the corridor. A sense of urgency quickened his pace, not because he was late, but because of something else, something scary. He was thinking of Luther as he walked, then ran, down to the lobby. Perspiration had already begun to soak his shirt. Mr. Lewis let him out. Another siren bawled. He stopped outside on the sidewalk and lit a smoke. A pack of boys ran by him, and another siren sounded in the distance. He set out at a brisk pace toward Chana's house.

He had walked just a few blocks, when he came to an intersection that was swarming with black people, children, teenagers, men and women. Some of them were breaking windows, heaving rocks through them, or sticks, cans, or trash barrels, full or empty. Alarms sounded. There was yelling and cursing as people jostled and shoved one another to get to the stores. A police cruiser, siren wailing, tore down the street toward Garner, people scattering frantically to get out of its way. It whirled around the corner, tires screeching, then losing traction, the car out of control, careened off a lamp post, and sent a small boy spinning in the air like a broken, bloody, black mannequin, the impact instantly smashing the life out of him.

Garner's cigarette fell from his mouth as he stood gaping across the intersection. Within seconds, a mob of maddened black people raged around the car, shrieking obscenities, crying, beating on the car with their fists, kicking the doors.

Garner started running toward the cruiser to get a closer look, but stopped halfway across the street, staring in disbelief as the driver, a white policeman, back the car up, slammed a woman to the ground, and backed right over her. A black man, in an insane fury, yanked the driver's door open and was shot in the face by the cop, the bullet smashing up through the man's jaw and teeth, tearing his head to pieces. The cop fired again and again, wounding two boys and killing an old man while the other officer, a black man, was hauled from the vehicle by three men screaming curses and ignoring his flailing nightstick. They wrestled him to the ground, preventing him from drawing his revolver which was finally ripped from its holster by a tall, brown man who then aimed the gun through the opened door at the driver and rapid-fired one shot after the other until it was empty. The flying slugs tore into the cop, blowing away the back of his head in a shower of bone, blood, and brains. One of the bullets hit a black woman between the eyes, killing her instantly.

Garner's eyes were riveted to the spectacle as people swarmed around him, hurling curses, pushing each other, trying to get closer to the car. A bunch of black men and boys overturned the vehicle and set it afire, then joined others in stomping the second officer until he was dead. Two sirens sounded, their wail growing louder and louder as the flames from the burning police cruiser leaped in the night, the flickering, reddish glow lighting up the intersection and the faces of the feverish black throng.

"Les' git some mo' these white mutha-fuckas," someone screamed. *"Les' kill all these honkies!"*

Garner ran back across the street in terror, hearing another frenzied voice replying to the first, *"Yeah, man, c'mon! Les' git Whitey!"*

The crowd surged forward, bunching in a tight pack of shouting, angry people who ran down the dark street. Garner stared after them, the stench of burning rubber catching in his nostrils. Then someone grabbed his arm, and he whirled, frightened, ready to fight, and stared, unbelieving, into Luther's face. *"Lutha,"* he croaked. "Wheah ya been, man?"

"Fuckin' wit' Whitey, baby! C'mon!"

Garner's eyes fastened on his brother's fierce black face glistening with sweat. A dirty piece of cloth was tied around his head. Luther started laughing.

"Huh? *Wheah,* man?"

"Ta git us some white folks, nigga! Look heah!" Luther pulled a long, bolt action rifle from a brown cloth sheath and held it out for Garner to see. A siren cut through the night shrieking harshly close by. "See this, baby? *That's Whitey's mutha-fuckin' ass! We gonna kill evah'thin' white we can find! C'mon!"*

Slowly, hesitantly, Garner shook his head, looking at the burning police cruiser, bodies strewn grotesquely around it, thick, black smoke rising with the flames to mix and disappear in the night. Two black men were busily fleecing the pockets of the dead men, emptying wallets, taking watches. Then the car exploded with a thundering, earsplitting boom, and the man nearest the car was killed, his body ripped into flaming bits. The other man was knocked unconscious. Garner was rooted where he stood, holding his ears, mouth open. Two of the corpses caught fire, and the foul stink of burning flesh, mingled with that of cloth and rubber, reached him, making him retch.

"Gawd," he groaned. *"Gawd-a-mighty Jesus!* Aw, naw—naw, man."

Luther, awestruck by the explosion, regained his composure. *"Whoo-oo-eee!* Man, this whole, stinkin', mutha-fuckin' town gonna go ta-*nite!* Yassuh! Niggas gonna fuck Whitey *all* up, baby! Les' go, Garna! We got ta find us *some* white mutha-fucka *now!* Gonna *teah his ass!* C'mon, man!"

"Naw."

"Huh? What, man?"

The squeal of a siren was approaching, coming fast. The few people left around the intersection started scattering.

"We gotta find Leroy, Lutha," Garner said quietly, listening to the approaching siren.

"What, nigga? What'choo talkin' 'bout?"

"Leroy wanna *see* ya, man—wanna go 'long *wit'*us. C'mon, Lutha, les' git Leroy—an' then we kin go."

"Nigga, *fuck* Leroy, fa' crissake! What's wrong wit'—"

A fire engine rumbled by, siren screaming full out. A red chief's car howled along behind it. Luther swung the rifle up, chambering a round, and took aim.

"Naw," Garner yelled, hitting his brother's arm as the gun roared.

"Ya simple mutha-fucka!" Luther swung the rifle butt around, crashing it against Garner's head, splitting his cheek open and knocking him unconscious.

When he came to, someone was shaking him. A bearded, white face peered down at him. His head was bursting with pain and the clanging of alarm bells.

"I thought you were *dead,* Hawk," Leroy rasped. "You're bleeding like a stuck pig! My God, I thought you were dead! What *happened?"*

Garner lay there, blinking, trying to focus his eyes. The pain in his head muddled his thoughts. When he spoke his voice was shaky, incoherent. "What—wait, man—les' find—Leroy?"

"It's me, Hawk! It's me—I'm right here."

"Leroy—what—what tha fuck's *happ'nin',* Leroy?"

"All hell's breaking loose! What happened to *you?"*

"Leroy—uh, Lutha—he—"

"Luther? Where? Where'd he go?" Leroy yelled.

"Don' know. Had a gun. He—hit me an'—"

"C'mon! We've got to find him! You *okay?"* Leroy began pulling Garner up from the pavement. "C'mon! Got to find him, *got* to, man! You okay? Can you make it?"

Garner stood and wiped some blood on his shirt. "Ah—yeah, ah kin make it. Ah'm okay."

"C'mon, then."

They took off, stumbling by the dead bodies and the smoldering remains of the police car, and on down the street. People passed them, racing in both directions. Most of those coming toward them were lugging television sets, radios, liquor, food, tires, clothes. Rounding the corner, Garner and Leroy came face to face with a steel-helmeted, white policeman aiming a submachine gun at them point-blank.

"Hold it," he cried. *"Don't move, nigger!* Get your fuckin' hands up, you black bastard, and you, too, buddy. That's it. Now, get over there." He herded them, prodding them roughly with the snout of his gun, into a crowd of glowering black people, men, women, and children, who were bunched up against a wall, held there by another white cop leveling a machine gun at their bellies. A pair of shots cracked in the night nearby. The two cops flinched momentarily, then hurriedly looked back to their prisoners.

Garner stood beside Leroy, staring at the guns, then across the street at flames raging around a block of old tenements. Fire trucks and police cars ranged the long, narrow street for blocks in disordered clusters between the cars parked on both sides. Policemen were everywhere, helping firemen push people away from the burning buildings. Sporadic bursts of gunfire cut down looters. Others were shot, too. *Anyone* running from *any* building was slammed to the pavement by a hail of police bullets. Scuffles broke out, and police officers lashed out at everyone around them, man, woman, or child, knocking them to the ground and beating them senseless. Fire hoses ran over and around parked cars like a tangle of thick snakes. The intersection where Garner and Leroy were standing was blocked by a huge trailer truck which lay jackknifed on its side against a pole, its tractor reared up on its back wheels.

Garner held a hand against his face, and blood oozed through his fingers. Leroy was crying, tears washing down his cheeks, his face contorted as if in pain. The machine guns glinted at them in the light of the fires which rose upward higher and higher.

A shot rang out, then another, then a series of them. A white fireman fell near the trailer, doubling up and clutching his stomach. A score of policemen ran for cover, or squatted in the street or behind cars and trucks. Another shot cut through the night as firemen ran for the safety of doorways and alleys or flattened out on the ground, and a policeman, running for cover, pitched forward onto his face, his rifle clattering away from him in the street. Two policemen ran out from behind the trailer and dragged him and the fallen fireman to safety.

"He's on the roof," a police officer yelled, pointing toward a burning building across from Garner and Leroy. Immediately, a deafening storm of gunfire erupted as police raked the whole building, and those adjacent to it, with bullets. The crowd around Garner started to break and run.

One of the cops holding them howled a warning. *"Hold steady, dammit!"*

Leroy knocked Garner down on his back, falling beside him as the two machine guns opened up, spitting death in streams of orange and red flame. Garner lay still, filled with terror while Leroy pinned him down. A woman fell on top of them and rolled away. Almost at once, her entire body was a mass of blood. Her face was gone. Garner squeezed his eyes shut and hung on to Leroy as a spray of warm blood and bits of flesh washed down on them and bullets splattered off the wall above their heads.

The machine guns stopped firing, and the other shooting subsided to short, fitful volleys. Garner opened his eyes as someone yelled, *"They got him!"* He saw one of the cops standing over him aiming his machine gun down into his face. Reddish light from the scorching fires gleamed along the barrel. Garner didn't move, but closed his eyes, certain he was about to die, unaccountably prepared for it, resigned to its coming.

The policeman's voice grated, *"Get up, nigger*—you, too, mister!"

Garner was in a daze. Leroy helped him to his feet. A squat, white man, in a gray suit, a steel helmet on his head, ran over to them. He was carrying a revolver in his hand. "What happened over here?" he shouted and ducked as a flurry of shots cut loose nearby.

"Goddam niggers went crazy, Lieutenant," one cop bawled. "We told them to hold still, and they started running!"

"Yeah," the other officer seconded.

The Lieutenant's eyes swept over the dead and wounded strung out on the sidewalk in a lake of blood which shone in the fiery light. Garner saw them, too. A man lay moaning in agony, a little girl pushed herself onto all fours, fell, and started crawling on her belly. Garner counted them and nine others, including the woman with no face.

"You goddamn fools—well—okay, get the people who aren't hurt the hell out of here. And get a couple of meat wagons down here to clean up this mess before the newshounds—*who's this guy?"*

All three policemen looked at Leroy. Garner looked down at the little girl. She had stopped moving. He looked away, across the street. The firemen were already back in action, despite frequent gunfire, hustling up ladders, climbing through broken windows into burning buildings, and shooting foamy, white geysers of water at the fires.

Leroy didn't speak. His tear-streaked, white face glowed red and hard.

"He was with them."

"Well, move them out. Get them out of here."

They didn't find Luther that night. He was hiding in the dark, smoke-filled cellar of a burning tenement, feverishly reloading his rifle. When he had the weapon loaded, he chambered a cartridge, huddling in a corner behind some wooden crates, his enormous hulk almost totally obscure in the dark. It was hot, and he couldn't see. Oddly enough, it was quiet in the cellar. Then he heard the cops stealing down the stairs. He adjusted one of the crates and rested the rifle on it, holding the gun steady, finger on the trigger, ready to fire. He thought of Garner then, remembered his pleading voice—*"Les' find Leroy"*—. What had happened to everybody, he fretted. Nothing seemed to be the way he remembered it. His city was different, foreign. *Leroy*—was different. Terry was dead—God. And *Garner*—maybe he shouldn't have hit him. The door creaked. He couldn't see anyone, but his finger tightened on the trigger. The *fuzz—how many were there?* He remembered his cell—*it didn't matter how many;* he'd kill them all. Then he thought of his mother, felt an insane urge to see her—*right now,* to touch her, speak to her. *Leroy—Garner*—suddenly, he knew that he couldn't leave that cellar. *He couldn't!* He was glad it was dark. *Why did it feel so cold now?* No, he didn't belong in this city anymore, he was sure. Then he tasted the tears. He hadn't cried since—*since he was eight years old.* Yes, when his father left—*no.* No, the night that *Buzz*—. The cellar door was smashed from its hinges, and the dark was instantly engulfed in a blazing holocaust of machine gun fire. Luther saw an explosion of glaring, fiery light, felt the crates give way in front of him, blasted to splinters, the rifle torn from his hands, felt the red-hot blows of the slugs that knocked him backward into the wall, then felt nothing, was killed, his corpse pinned to the wall, bullets still ripping into it, chewing it to bloody scraps.

The morning after a mad Fourth of July, two days after the city's savage paroxysm of bloody carnage and death, the phone rang in Garner's home. His mother ran to answer it. "Yeah. Ah'm Ella Hawkins." Then terrible pain contorted her face. "Aw—*aw, naw—ma gawd, ma gawd—*" She collapsed on the living room floor.

Garner ran over to her as Harry came running from the kitchen. Ella stared up at her son, her eyes vacant, body shaking. Harry picked up the phone.

Garner lifted his mother's head. "Ma? *What'sa matta, Ma?* Please, Ma, *say* somethin'!" He cradled her in his arms, squatting on one knee, and looked appealingly at Harry.

Harry was yelling into the phone. *"When?* I don't *know!* For God's sake, the woman has fainted! Are you sure it's him? What? *This* afternoon? I don't know. Someone will *be* there! Yes! *I said yes, dammit!"* He slammed the phone down and knelt beside Ella, looking at her, his round, black face scowling. "Luther's dead," he muttered. "Cops shot him." He touched Ella's face. "Baby? Ella, honey—"

Garner started to cry and buried his face against her neck as he rocked her back and forth. His mind conjured up horrible scenes—

Luther's body lay riddled with bullets, but the body didn't look like Luther's. It was Buzz. His stomach was ripped open, guts bloody, spilling over his hands as he tried to hold them in. Then it was Terry, his orange face carved in red, butchered shreds—. Garner's big frame shook convulsively, and he saw his own face in Luther's.

Luther was buried on a Tuesday, Garner remembered, easing back in his seat as Harry's big Oldsmobile rocked forward. This was also a Tuesday. As Chana held his hand, he felt the car surging powerfully beneath them. *Tuesday—there were only four cars in the funeral procession, three black Cadillacs and Leroy's dull, green Chevvy. They wound their way through the city's ravaged streets, by gutted buildings, soldiers and policemen cradling rifles and machine guns, who looked on grimly as the procession passed—.* Yes, Garner thought, there were a lot of funerals that day.

"A penny," Chana murmured, her face beaming a smile.

"Huh?"

"*Quarter?* What are you thinking about?"

"Nothin'."

"Don't look so mean, then."

"Thinkin' 'bout Lutha, an' tha cops—killin'im."

Ella turned in the front seat to look at him. "That's ovah, Garna. It's all ovah, ovah an' done wit'. Ya heah?"

"Yeah."

He stared through the window as Chana snuggled closer to him. He watched the city flying by as Harry, dressed in his dark suit, drove toward the freeway. Garner looked at his mother then. She had cried very little at the cemetery—*A thin trickle of tears inched down her face. Her grip was tight on his arm as Leroy, weeping like a child, knelt by Luther's grave. Janice stood beside him, her hand on his shoulder. Garner touched a hand to the bandage on his cheek and looked down at his mother's soft, dark face. She blurred in his tears—.* Garner grabbed the door handle as Harry swung the car up on a bridge. The traffic was thick. Garner looked down at the water—*was Buzz still there?* No—bones, maybe, but not Buzz. He trembled slightly.

"What's wrong, Gar?" Chana whispered.

"Nothin'."

"Evah'thin' awright, baby?" his mother asked, watching him.

"Yeah, Ma. Evah'thin's okay."

"Ya don' hafta go, if ya don' wanna."

"Yes, ah do, Ma—an'—ah wanna."

"We'll be at least three hours on the road," Harry said.

Garner looked at him and remembered what he said to Andre at the wake—*"I don't think this foolishness accomplishes anything, man," Harry argued. Andre bent forward slightly on his cane. "In the long run," he said, "you'll see that it does. Whitey doesn't listen to us very often, but he heard us this time—he better had, anyway." Leroy looked at the closed coffin. "Andre, all this can't be necessary. There has to be a way—a place for reason. My God, men must be better than this. Somebody, somewhere, has got to go to work before the soldiers and the police bring in the guns. Jesus Christ!" "But they haven't, man," Andre replied calmly. "That," Harry said, "doesn't mean that they won't. Eighty-four people just got killed, for God's sake! And, man, seventy-five of them were black!" "He's right," Leroy said. "If we have to go to the streets, then we may as well pack it all in. I don't believe in this kind of senseless violence, Andre. I can't! People who do—well, they aren't tough enough. Even Luther there—who I loved, man—wasn't tough. He didn't believe in himself, didn't want to be who he was, didn't—love himself." "Whose fault was that?" Andre demanded. Leroy hesitated, glancing at Garner. "Whitey—and Luther," he said, "and us, man. Hell, Whitey's a dog, but we've got to be smarter than any damn dog. We can teach black kids to believe in themselves, Andre. We've got to be tougher, work harder, and—" "There is nothing," Andre replied, "we can do if Whitey won't listen to us. We've got to get him off our backs, shake loose from Whitey, man. Black and white just don't—" "Andre," Leroy barked, "think of Laura and your kids when you talk like that, and remember that you're talking about Whitey collectively, his history, his viciousness, his propaganda and prejudice, not a white person alone, and not the woman who loves you. We've got to live with Whitey, man, and he's got to do the right thing—because he has no choice—and neither do we." "Whitey do the right thing?" Andre scoffed bitterly. "Baby, I'll believe that when I see it. He's got to show me." "He will," Harry said—.* Garner lit a cigarette. A man has to believe in himself, he knew now, or he couldn't be hard, not really hard. Luther was like that. He wasn't *hard. A hard man is as tough as he has to be!* Luther, he decided, wasn't hard, because he wasn't able to learn—really learn—not just what a white man puts down in a book, but about himself, about people, why the book was written, what circumstances in human history made it the kind of book it was, why, and how, he was, or could have been, a man as good as any other, and better than most. Well, Garner swore, *he* could learn, was learning. He was hard. A man *has* to learn, or he was dead, not like Luther, or Terry, or Buzz were dead—that kind of death was only the end product of the other kind. No, what died was what a man *could* be—himself. That was dead. And a long and agonizing death it was, too.

Garner paused in his thoughts. He smiled at Chana. Looking at her made him think of someone else. Who? he wondered. Gail Chamberlain? Janice? No. Who then? His mother? *Pat*—no. One of his teachers, maybe? Yes. When was that? The second—third grade? What was her name? He couldn't remember, and suddenly, he realized that it wasn't her, either. Chana smiled up at him then, her face so pretty, so god-awful pretty. There was that look in her eyes, a longing, a promise, a total commitment. *There*—there it was, it was Chana herself, what she meant to him—love, being loved, loving a woman—*woman.* Yes, the clean smell, the beauty of her face and body—*that she loved him, too!*

The Olds stopped, and Harry paid a toll. Garner put his arm around Chana, holding her tight as the car rocked forward again. They were on the freeway. He threw his cigarette out. *Luther.* He and Luther were so much alike. Why was Luther dead and not him? What had happened? Had their lives been so different? Maybe Luther had to be what he was, and—maybe *he* would not be going away to prep school if Luther had not lived so much suffering before him. *Maybe.*

Garner turned to look back then, and it occurred to him that he was leaving the city for the first time in his life. But he would be back. That was sure. His arm tightened around Chana. Yes. He understood something about the city now. He was—Garner Hawkins.

About The Author

DANIEL SMITH has lived most of his life in and around Boston where he was born. He has worked in a number of different jobs, including construction laborer, truck driver, carpenter, camp counselor, and dispatcher for an automobile club. A football scholarship enabled him to study in Mexico, and since then he has studied and traveled extensively abroad. He is fluent in several languages.

After earning a degree in physical education at Boston University, Mr. Smith was awarded a teaching fellowship at that school to study the foundations of education and earned his master's degree in the area of social foundations and philosophy.

He worked three years as a physical education teacher and coach of athletics and now teaches black studies in a suburb of Boston, where he is the Director of the Metropolitan Council for Educational Opportunity.

Writing has always interested him, and after some discouraging efforts, he finally sold a short story. This is his first novel.